The Dragon's Breath

The Dragon's Breath

by

James Boschert

The Dragon's Breath by James Boschert

Copyright © 2016 James Boschert

ISBN-13: 978-1-942756-52-1(Paperback)
ISBN :-978-1-942756-53-8 (e-book)

BISAC Subject Headings:
FIC014000FICTION / Historical
FIC032000FICTION / War & Military
FIC031020FICTION / Thrillers / Historical

Editing: Chris Wozney
Danielle Boschert
Cover Illustration by Christine Horner

Address all correspondence to:

Penmore Press LLC
920 N Javelina Pl
Tucson AZ 85748

Acknowledgements

My sincere hanks to Chris Wozney and Danielle Boschert for their
tireless efforts and help.

Rubayat of Omar Khayyam; Persian Miniatures	By Liber Press
China The Beautiful Cook Book	Culinary Authorities of Beijing
The Legendary Cuisine of Persia	Margaret Shaida
The Valleys of the Assassins	Freya Stark
A Fool of God [Poems of Baba Tahir	E. Heron Allen
Art In China	Craig Clunas
Wikipedia	
Google	
Confucius	
Arab Seafaring	George Hourani
The Art of War	Sun Tzu

Table of Contents

Names

Name	Title
Talon's Family	
Talon de Gilles	
Rav'an	Wife of Talon
Reza	Friend
Rostam de Gilles	Son
Fariba	Aunt
Dr. Haddad	Physician
Jannat	Princess
Yosef	Soldier
Dar'an	Soldier
Salem	Maid
Omani family	
Sheik Al Mardini	Father of the family Mardini
Allam al Mardini	Family Oman
Boulos al Mardini	Family Oman
Imaran al Mardini	Family Oman
Ismail	Camel Jockey
Tribe Arabs	
Najem al Khulood	Tribal Leader
Sayf -ul -Mulk	Camel thief
Sameer	
Yasser	
Sailors	
Safa al-Dandachi	Captain of the ship

Name	Title
Tarif	Crew
Umayr	Crew
Waqqas	Crew
Abdullah	Crew
Chinese	
Lord Meng Hsü	Clan Leader
Wong Meilin	
Meng Lanfen	Grandmother on Hsü's side
Wong Cheng Kean	Brother of Meilin
Lihua	Concubine
Meng Fuling	Elder son
Meng Lun	Boy, second son
Jiaya	Old man Clerk
Fang	Body Guard (Mental)
Chang Mai Ling	Administrator (Friend)
Kee Wen Hua	Servant Traitor
Low yen Bong	Gardner
Bolin	Servant
Tem Pau	Cook
Tseng Jung	Street vendor
Japanese Dojo	
Saiki	Master of the School
Liu	Student
Qian	Swordsman instructor
Hu Ssu-ch'i	Head of Monastery
Opposition	

Name	Title
Lu Buwei—	Tong leader
Hua Rong	Chief of Police
Lin Chong	Henchman and spy
Officials	
Wu po-ku	Prefect
Li Shou-cheh	Prefect
Yen Wei	Prefect
Meng Hsüg	Lieutenant
Murong	Prefect. Governor
Yang Hsün	General
Hayan Zhou	General
Ximen Quing	Lieutenant
Mongol Names	
Badzar	Leader Thunderbolt
Muunokhoi	Vicious Dog
Khoonbish,	Not A Human Being
Wàiguó rén	Foreigner
Indian Names :	
Sing	Malay Ruler
Amar	Pirate captain
Bijay	Lieutenant
Debdan	Soldier
Gauri	Woman betrayer.
Ajay	Indian servant
Hanji	Pirate prisoner

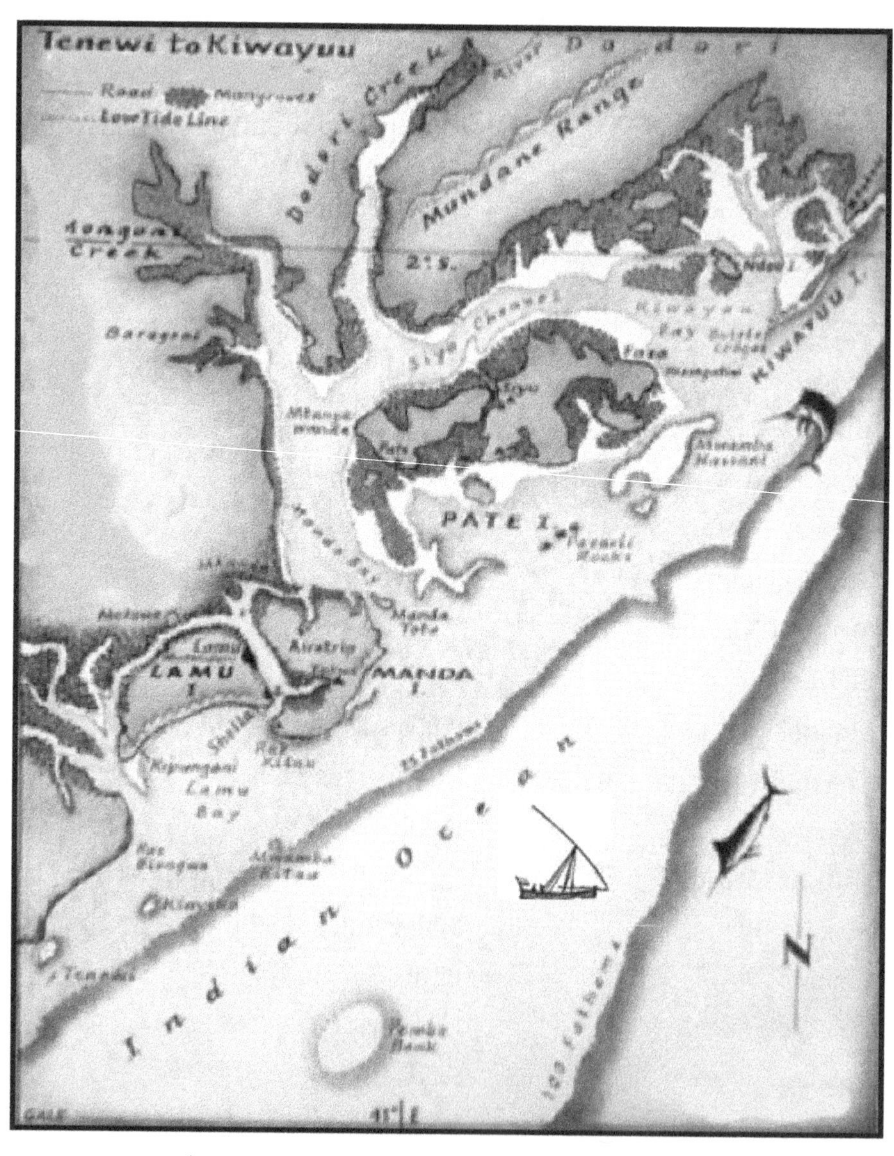

Island of Lamu off Africa

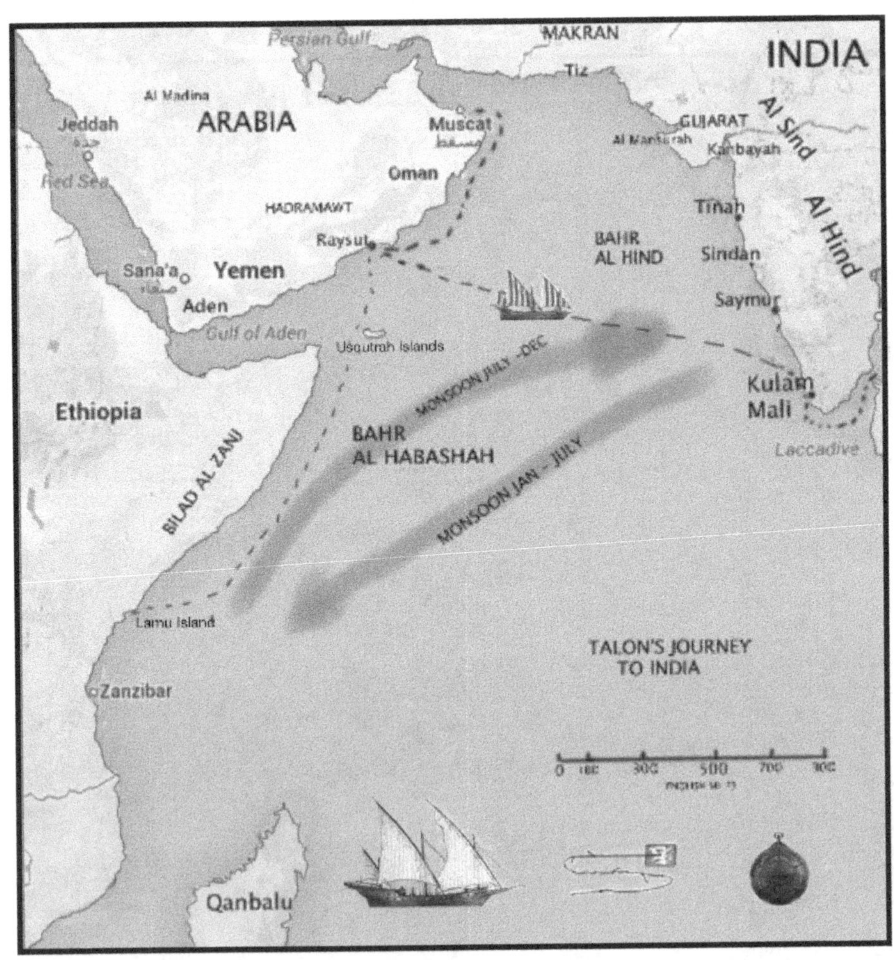

Talon's Journey to India

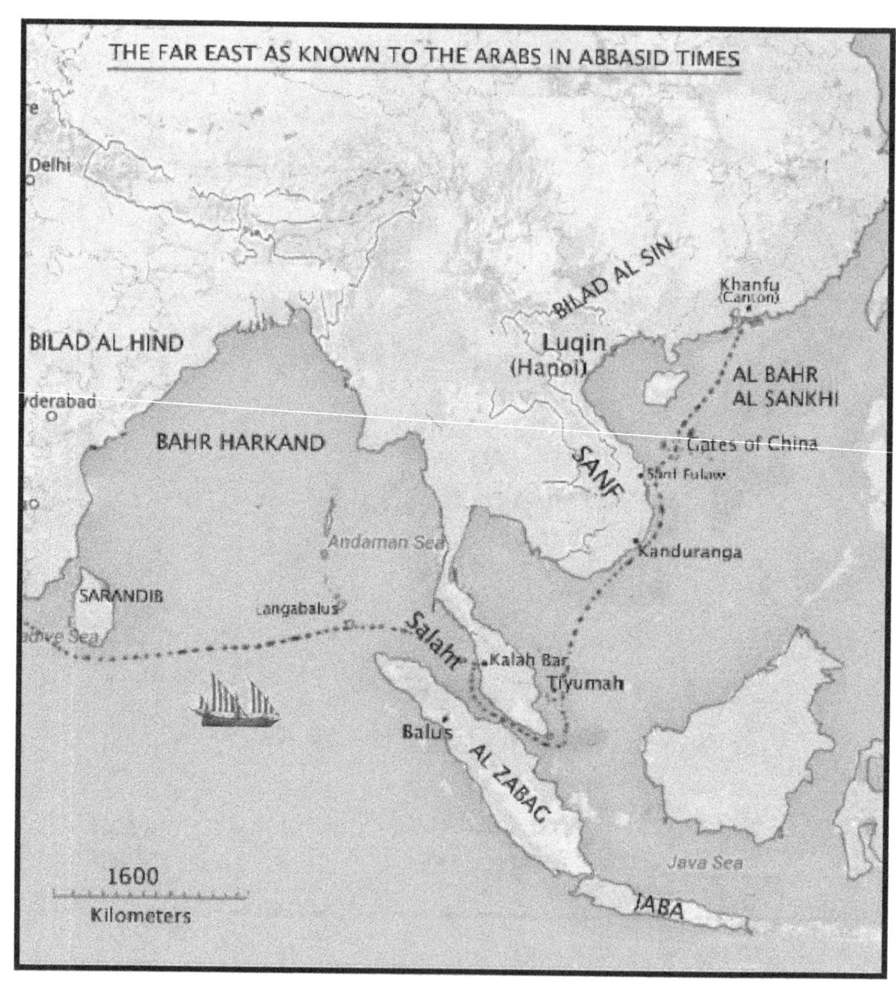

Talon's Journey to China

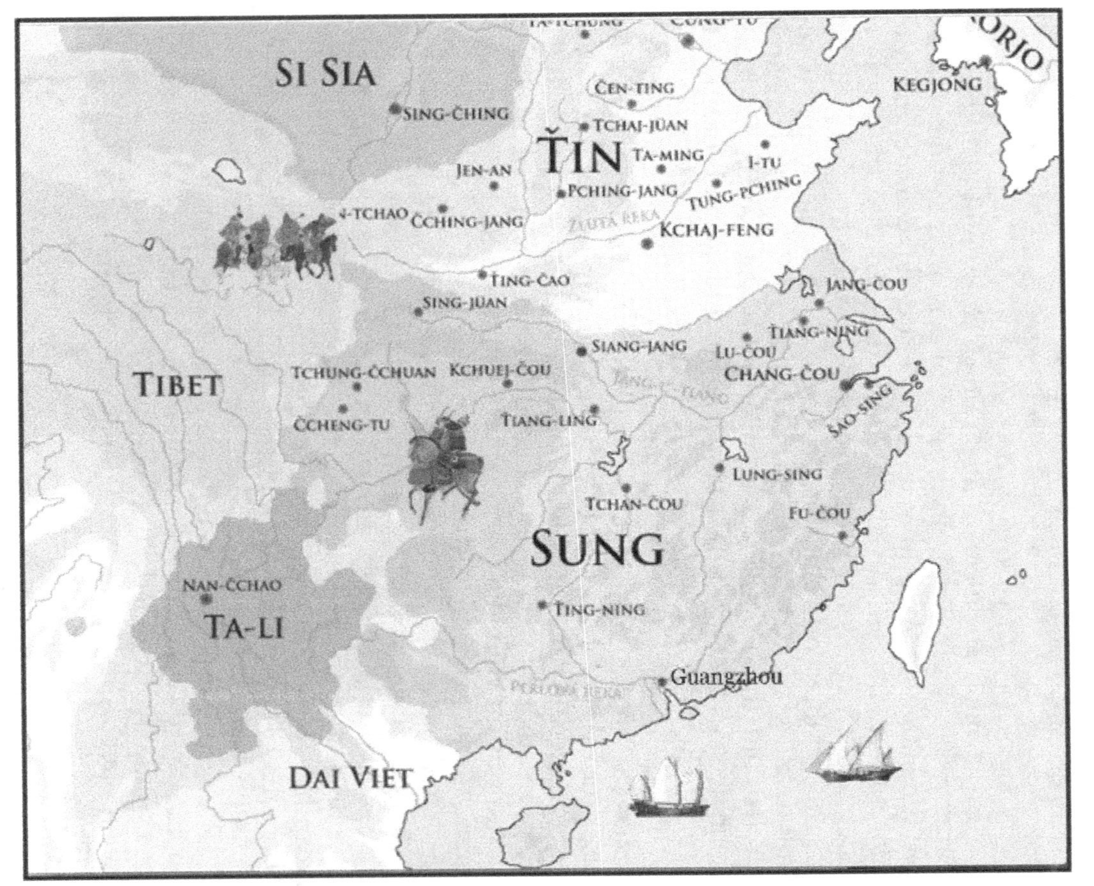

China Sung Dynasty

<h1 style="text-align:center">Prologue</h1>

In the book *A Falcon Flies*, Talon, while fighting the much feared Assassins in Syria, discovers that Rav'an is not dead, as he had imagined for six long years. Before he can act on this information fate steps in and Talon is dragged into the Battle of Montgisard. King Baldwin of Jerusalem and the Knights Templar have a terrible confrontation with the formidable army of the Sultan of Egypt, Salah Ed Din. Talon and his comrades barely survive, but the Templars are hailed as heroes. After the battle Talon decides that it is time to find Rav'an and keep his promise to return to her.

The King of Jerusalem grudgingly gives his permission but demands Talon's word that he will return. Talon survives the vicissitudes of the long and arduous journey across the barren deserts and the prisons of Baghdad to find that all is not well. He discovers that not only does he now have a son but his lover Rav'an was unwillingly 'married' to the sultan of Shiraz and is now imprisoned in a seemingly impregnable fortress.

Talon unexpectedly meets up with Reza, his brother-in-arms from their days in the Assassins' castle of Alamut, who is also going to rescue her. They succeed, but in doing so they are forced not only to flee the sultan's men, who make a determined effort to recapture Rav'an, but the wrath of her brother the Master of the Assassins. They evade the sultan's men but the threat of the assassins is never far away.

Because of this they cannot remain in Persia but flee instead to Oman, where Talon has an acquaintance who shared a prison cell with him in Baghdad and whom Talon helped escape the executioner's sword. There is a debt to be repaid.

PART 1

The camel has a single hump;
The dromedary, two;
Or else its the other way around.
I'm never sure. Are you?

—Ogden Nash

Chapter One
A Camel Race

There was a palpable sense of excitement from the crowd gathered on the flat sandy plain. The Omanis jostled and elbowed one another to get a good view of the race track, while ignoring the persistent flies buzzing around their heads. For the most part they were men, dressed in dusty *thobes*, loose tunics that came down to their ankles; most wore a ragged turban wound loosely around their heads. There were also a few heavily veiled women standing behind their men, craning their necks like everyone else to see what they could of the milling group far down the wide sandy track. A haze of fine dust obscured the starting line and hung over the area where the spectators were gathered waiting for the race to begin.

Young boys rushed about, yelling and getting in the way of the men, who would round on them if they came too close and slap them away. Even the stray dogs that were always skulking around had caught the mood and were barking and dodging the stones that the boys hurled at them. The roars of the camels and the bleating of goats, combined with the chatter of the tribespeople, only added to the festive mood.

A light wind lifted the banners that hung from the top of the large tents where the Caliph of Oman and his retinue were seated. They were in full view of the Muscat citizens and other tribesmen who had come to witness this singular event. In sharp contrast to the milling crowd, these people were dressed in grand clothing. Their *massars* were made of the finest wools and decorated in the traditional Omani patterns. Some were even stitched in gold thread, thus demonstrating the affluence of the wearer. The men were wearing *dishdashas,* the fine, primarily white tunic worn by men of stature. Some also wore a *bisht,* a black woolen over robe.

To a man they sported elaborate belts of the finest silver filigree on leather that held the obligatory ornate knife known as the *Kkhanjar* at their waists: it was usually turned so that it sat on their stomachs for all to see and admire. They were the sheiks and royalty of Oman, accompanied by their watchful bodyguards. Many of these were tall, glowering, black men chosen for their fierce looks and strong physiques. The guards held lances and carried swords through their sashes.

This was the final race of the day, but by now, with the sun low over the distant mountains to the West, the haze of dust thrown up by people and camels made it hard to identify the individual riders from a distance of half a league away. Those who were nearest the edge of the wide track strained their eyes to see the colors which identified the runners. Most had placed a modest bet of a few dinars or lesser coins on their favorite animal, but in the grand tent there were those who had placed huge bets.

These same people were now sweating with anxiety as they fingered their prayer beads and wiped the perspiration off their brows, while at the same time trying to look unconcerned. For the most part they were sheiks, wealthier merchants, and other men of note. If their expensive clothes were not enough to distinguish them from the noisy throng on the other side of the track, the armed guards and the slaves attending to their needs indicated that much power was gathered here on the outskirts of Muscat to watch the final and most prestigious camel race of the year.

There was a hush as all eyes turned to the stone tower opposite the Caliph's stand. A figure appeared on the top, followed by another, smaller one carrying a rolled up banner. Standing high above the crowd where all could see him, the frail old man with a long beard looked over to the stands to where the Caliph of Oman and his attendants were seated. He bowed low, and when the Caliph raised a languid hand he took the rolled up flag from the boy beside him and began to unfurl the silk material. By now the entire crowd was tense with expectation and had quietened considerably. Everyone watched with impatience while the old man, fully aware of his moment of importance, took his time to unfurl the large cloth emblem of the Caliph emblazoned upon the green silk background.

Finally he lifted the banner, which instantly caught the light breeze and spread its wings like a huge undulating bird. It nearly tipped the old man off the tower, but the boy seized his belt and hung on. The old man began to wave the flag slowly from side to side and the crowd roared.

In the distance the milling camels at the starting point began to move. The twenty or so finely bred racing camels had been roughly lined up by attendants who shouted, sweated, and cursed them, and by their riders, who used their whips to prevent them from taking off before the starting flag had been raised.

The choking dust kicked up by the agitated animals made it difficult for the harassed men to account for everyone, so there were no lack of opportunists who tried to get a head start on their competitors. The riders of the camels, mostly young boys, jostled for the best place with savage intensity, using their short whips and cursing each other. They beat their roaring charges into place and even used their whips upon one another when the chance to gain a small edge presented itself.

Then the sharp-eyed attendant in charge noticed the old man's arrival on the tower in the distance and screamed at them all to get ready, waving his arms and pleading with the mounted boys to prepare. They had barely settled down when the banner was raised and the attendants screamed in one voice, "*Allah Akbar, Go!!*"

The mass of camels and riders were off. The boys flapped their legs and thrashed their mounts. The camels snarled, bared their yellow teeth, ambled into a trot, then rapidly moved into an all out gallop that ate up the distance towards the stands. Their necks were stretched forward and their heads lowered on their seemingly ungainly bodies, but their long legs were covering the ground in great, loping strides.

The small riders perched on the light, ornate saddles strapped to the humps of the camels screamed as they urged their mounts forward, even though few of the animals needed much persuasion. However, they ran closely bunched, and it was not long before legs became entangled. One camel went down, bringing three others with it in a dangerous flurry of limbs with boys shrieking abuse at one another as they scrambled about, trying to avoid being crushed by a rolling body or killed by the flailing legs of the downed animals. The remaining racers spread out and concentrated on the distant stands and the ever louder roar of the crowd.

The soft thud of many padded feet could barely be heard as the boys continued to breathlessly urge their mounts forward. The screaming and yelling of the starter line had been replaced with endearments and pleading words addressed to their precious charges. The boy who won this race would be hugely rewarded for his efforts, and his camel would represent a breeder's dream, male or female, and make its owner very rich.

Ismail rode Jasmine with a light hand and called to her over the noise all around them. "Go, my sweet Jasmine. May your legs run faster than ever before. Do what you do best, my sweet Jasmine!" he pleaded, and only occasionally snapped his stick onto her shoulder. She gave a low grunting roar in acknowledgement and affection for her rider, and jostled her way towards the front of the pack. Ismail was watching for any kind of dangerous behavior from the two remaining boys in front of them. Neither would allow Jasmine through if they could prevent it, as they, too, stood to gain great prestige from winning the race; and while they were in the pack almost anything went.

Ismail coaxed Jasmine on with shouts of encouragement, and she gained steadily on the two camels ahead of them. He tapped her on the right shoulder and she veered in that direction just a little; this suddenly gave them a clear view of the tents and the by now hysterical crowd screaming and waving in the distance. They still had three hundred paces to go, but with their two most serious competitors off to the left of them Jasmine was now able to really get into her stride. She began to move past the closer boy, who was momentarily unaware of the threat on his right. He had been concentrating on trying to keep pace with another opponent. Suddenly his mount became aware of Jasmine and tried to bite her. Jasmine grunted as the teeth tore at her neck, but Ismail snapped his whip onto the nose of the offender and edged Jasmine on past. As he drew parallel to the rider, who was a larger boy, Ismail could not resist flashing a wide, cheeky grin. He was small for his age, and when he laughed he presented white teeth in a wide open mouth.

The other boy was not going to let this new threat pass him by without doing something about it. He scowled angrily and swung his whip hard at Ismail's head. All Ismail could do was to lift his arm and take the blow. He retaliated instinctively by poking at the other boy with his whip and inadvertently stabbed him in the eye. He hadn't meant to hurt, but the sting of the blow he had received made him react. The other boy howled and clutched at his eye and almost fell off his camel. Ismail snapped his stick onto Jasmine's long thigh behind him and yelled. "Go, beloved! Go, or I am done!"

They were now only fifty yards from the finish line and there was still one other camel in the lead, ridden by another older boy who was very skinny and therefore light, who knew how to ride, but he was shouting abuse at his camel and beating it hard with his stick. The animal rolled its eyes and bared its teeth with anger and fear, but it fled the whip nonetheless. Ismail was very tempted to use his stick but was reluctant because he loved his mount.

"Jasmine!" He screamed. "For God and for me, run for your life, run, run, run!"

Hearing her name, despite the roar of the crowd who were now on either side of them, his mount put in a last burst of speed and they hurtled across the finish line only a short neck ahead of the other camel. The crowd went mad, screaming and waving their hands in the air. Turbans were unravelling and some men were waving them like banners. Men who had won their bets were dancing and hugging one another, shouting with glee. The losers were shaking their heads in disgust and some were even wondering where they were going to sleep that night, having bet almost all their possessions, including their own camels. The normally impassive visiting tribesmen who had accompanied many of the desert Sheiks to witness this very special event joined in the general atmosphere of celebration.

Ismail allowed Jasmine to run out her race and return to a trot before he turned her. With words of love and affection he talked to her all the way back to the victor's stand, where her master stood with a cluster of family members around him. Ismail leaned forward and stroked the back of her neck, he rubbed the welt from the bite and spoke soothingly to her. "My lovely Jasmine! You won, you won! We are famous!"

She rolled her eyes back at him and groaned. As he murmured her praises she lifted her head to turn it and give him a look of affection, because she loved this little imp who slept in her stall and ministered to her every day. They walked back towards the excited and noisy crowd.

The chief camel *syce* for the master dashed out from the press and ran up to tie a strap onto the headdress of Jasmine. His dark, bearded face was beaming so that his dark eyes had almost disappeared in the creases of his sunburned face.

"God be praised, Ismail," he called up to the proud boy. "I never doubted you, but that was so very close!"

"God be praised indeed, Mehmet. She gave me everything she had!" There were tears in his eyes as Ismail said this. The huge smile of happiness lit up his dust-caked features and he thought his heart would burst. By now they had arrived at the enclosure and it was time to ask Jasmine to go down on her knees so that he could dismount to prostrate himself in front of his master.

Allam al Mardini stood in front of the kneeling camel and the boy; he was trying hard to control his emotions. He was shaking with relief and felt like weeping with joy, but forced himself to present to the world and its people a look of pleased satisfaction instead. He reached down and pulled the boy to his feet, embraced him hard, then turned to the crowd, his arm still around the small boy's thin shoulders, and waved. The crowd of onlookers cheered and shouted praises to the boy.

After a few moments, Allam turned back to Jasmine and put his hands on either side of her long head and stroked her gently with much tenderness. She gazed back at him with her limpid eyes under long eyelashes and grunted with pleasure; the sound rumbled deep inside her, and her upper lip bobbed about, showing her yellowed teeth, but it was clear that she was happy. He slipped a small but very sweet cake under her nose and stood holding her head while she drooled spit in the sand while chewing and then swallowed it with a small shudder of pleasure.

"You have done me a great service, my dearest Jasmine. God is kind. You will bear many young and I shall finally become very rich!" he murmured, and he patted her cheeks once more before turning again to face the crowd.

He noticed the Vizier approaching and promptly gave a very deep bow. Everyone else around him of the lower orders had gone to their knees and were prostrated.

The vizier, one of the most powerful men in the country of Oman, dressed in long flowing robes and the *egal* bound with silver ropes about his head, gave a short inclination of his head and then addressed Allam in a low tone.

"You are to be congratulated on your fine beast, Allam. His Excellency my Lord the Caliph wishes to see you tomorrow, in the morning, no doubt to discuss the race ... among other things."

"God looked down upon us and favored my fine beast today, Your Excellency, I am honored, and I shall be there as commanded," Allam responded.

The vizier nodded, then turned on his heel. The crowd parted to let him and his two guards through.

Allam touched his brow and heart to the departing dignitary with some relief. The vizier was a man to be feared, but his father was a close friend, so he had no real concerns.

He turned back to find another man coming his way, and not one that he particularly wanted to meet. His rival of many a race, Nejem al Khulood, walked forward with his arms outstretched to greet him and a smile stretched across his dark, almost cadaverous features. The man was taller than Allam, with wide shoulders, and he walked like a cat. He bared his teeth in a smile that was utterly insincere.

As they embraced, Nejem said almost into his ear, "I hear that your little creature tried to blind my boy while the race was on. That was not a kind thing to do, my friend, it will be remembered."

"I wonder how much you lost on this race?" Allam could not resist asking.

Nejem stiffened, then drew away, still smiling, but his eyes were cold and dangerous. He said for all to hear, "A good race, my friend, and the best camel did win. It was the will of God today. I congratulate you." He took one step backwards and then turned his back on Allam, leaving him to watch his dark cloaked figure cut a path through the throng of gawping onlookers.

Allam released his breath slowly through pursed lips and fingered his *khanjar*, then he shook his head dismissively and turned back to his chief syce and gave instructions for Jasmine to be taken under guard to his stables, where she was to be pampered and examined for any wounds or scratches. His syce nodded agreement. "It shall be as you instructed, my Lord. Ismail told me that one of the leading camels bit her, but it was not serious, and he will be with her all night."

Cognizant of the remark made by Nejem, Allam planned to ask Ismail about the incident when next he was at the stables. He doubted the boy had done anything without provocation, and he knew the lad would tell the truth.

"I want armed guards to be there all night as well," Allam told his man. "Do not let Ismail go anywhere away from the stables unaccompanied. I do not intend to lose him, nor her, at this delicate stage." His brown eyes roved over his favorite camel with concern and his slightly rounded face broke into another smile, displaying a gold tooth. "My treasure!" he crooned and watched her leave.

One of his retainers sidled up to him and leaned close to tell him something. Although the noise of the crowd had died down and people were leaving to go back to their tents, in the case of the tribesmen, or to the town, he still had to cock an ear to hear what was said.

"There is a man who says his name is Suleiman, my Lord."

Allam jerked upright. "What did you say?" he demanded, surprise written all over his face. He tugged on his short beard as memories of the prison in Baghdad resurfaced. They were not good memories at all. But there were many men called Suleiman, he reasoned.

"A man named Suleiman, who says that you know him well, is here in Muscat, my Lord," the retainer repeated. "He arrived early this morning by ship and awaits to hear from you. He said that you might remember him from Baghdad?"

Allam had begun to recover. So it was that Suleiman. "A ship you say? Well of course, I suppose that makes sense. Send for him at once. No..." he thought about it for a moment.

"Invite him to my house this evening, so that I can prepare for him. It is time for prayers, and I need to refresh myself after this dusty afternoon." It would be dark by then, and Suleiman would not be noticed on the streets, nor would it be remarked should he come late. It wouldn't hurt to be careful.

"As you wish my Lord." The retainer disappeared into the thinning crowd.

A distracted Allam could now go to his relatives who had come to the see the race and receive the congratulations they were eager to bestow upon him.

His elder brother by two years, Imaran, slapped him on the back and laughed. "Now that was a close thing, brother. I was almost sure that your boy would make a mistake, but he had the wits to keep clear of the those two little bastards of Nejem and Hakim. My, but that is the most beautiful camel I have seen anywhere for a very long time!" he teased.

Allam smiled. "She is my prize and my darling. I bet a huge amount of gold on her today, and she delivered. She alone, today, has earned back every dinar I have invested in her breed."

"You ever were the gambling man, brother. I noticed that Nejem came to congratulate you. I wonder that barracuda didn't bite off your ear when he embraced you," his oldest brother Boulos told him with a grin.

"We have to go home and celebrate this great victory our younger brother has brought us. I think he can afford to give us all a feast after this," Imaran said happily.

Allam gave a reluctant shake of his head. He, too, wanted to celebrate, but the news he had just received made him hesitate.

"My brothers, I would like nothing better than to celebrate this victory today, but I have a pressing matter I must deal with this evening that cannot be put off. Let us celebrate tomorrow when I can relax with you."

There were disappointed noises from his brothers and his friends, but they all knew that if Allam said he had to defer the celebrations it was for a good reason. No one liked a party more.

When you and I behind the veil are past,
Oh, but the long, long while the World shall last,
Which of our Coming and Departure heeds
As much as Ocean of a pebble cast?

—Omar Khayyam

Chapter Two
A Meeting and a Marriage

Allam had time to reflect while he went through the routine of his prayers. The memories that the name Suleiman brought to him were fearsome. However he was clear about one thing. Suleiman, or Talon, as he also knew the man, had taken him out of that hell of a Bagdad prison and paid his way home: if in rags, still nevertheless alive. He was looking forward to seeing his erstwhile friend, his anticipation mixed with apprehension. *Insha'Allah,* there would not be a problem.

That evening, he carefully checked the food that had been prepared and the condition of the room where he would receive his guest. He was tense and snapped at the senior servant who was responsible for the reception. Soon enough, the sound of horses could just be heard outside in the small courtyard.

Allam waited near the main entrance. A slave opened the doors, and there was Talon.

The man strode up the stairs with the fluid motion of a panther. Allam remembered that pace well, then he had a chance to see his friend's face. Talon was taller than his host, and he seemed to fill the room with his presence. That, too, Allam remembered as he regarded his friend's scarred features.

He was relieved to see that Talon wore a smile of genuine pleasure at seeing him, and they embraced hard. Then they held one another at arm's length and looked at one another.

"You have not suffered greatly since your return home, I see," remarked Talon. His tone was dry, but his smile indicated that he was clearly pleased to see Allam.

Allam laughed. "God's will. I have been received back within the bosom of my family and I prosper, my friend. You will remember that those torturers of the grand Vizier broke several of my teeth, so I have replaced them!" He touched his lips. "But you, my friend still look like the wolf I left in Basra. What have you been doing since we parted? You are very welcome to my house."

He looked into the green eyes of his friend and remembered the man who killed so swiftly. When it was time, he would ask just what had brought Talon to his home in Oman, but first they were obliged to go through the mandatory ceremonies of welcome.

"I have brought some people with me from Persia, one of whom is my brother, Reza, who is with me now," Talon said, and turned to another figure who had been several paces behind him.

Allam felt a trickle of fear. The slim, hard looking man standing just behind Talon looked very dangerous. His cold eyes were watching him, assessing him with care and missing nothing.

Allam nodded and smiled at Reza. "You are very welcome to my house. I owe the debt of my life to Talon, and all who are his family are my family," he stated. He clapped his hands and servants appeared to escort them to the garden. Evening had set in, and it was cooling down. The scent of flowers wafted in the air and lanterns were lit around the walls.

"We will be both comfortable here and secure from prying eyes," Allam informed Talon as he walked alongside, indicating the way.

He went to the far side of a large carpet spread out on the ground just in front of a small fountain, which lent its tinkle of sound to the general ambience of the garden.

Once his two guests were seated, with Talon to his right hand in the position of honor, Allam clapped his hands again and servants appeared to serve tea in tiny cups poured from long-spouted pots.

Allam glanced at his guest and found Talon watching him. To put him at his ease, he stated, "You will eat with me, and then we will talk about what you have done since I saw you last."

They ate very well that night, of rice and tender pieces of lamb, newly slaughtered. The small cups of tea were refilled whenever they were emptied, and the conversation was polite, but it was not until they had eaten their fill and the servants had left them alone at Allam's command that he finally turned to Talon and addressed him.

"My friend Suleiman, or is it Talon now? It has been barely five months since I last saw you. God be praised, you are still alive; but I have to confess I had my doubts when I left that I would ever see you again. That crew I left you with were as murderous a lot as I have ever come across."

Talon smiled ruefully. "I finally gave them the slip, but it was not easy. They were *Batinis* from Isfahan, linked to the Master in Alamut."

Allam gave small shudder, then shook his head and said with some relief, "God be praised that they went their way and you yours. Did you finally meet up with your uncle in Isfahan?"

Talon glanced at Reza and said, "Yes, indeed I did, and that is partly the reason I am here with my family and Reza. The danger from those very *Batinis* was too close, so we decided to come to Oman, where I hear that an honest merchant can make a good living."

Allam leaned back against the cushions and contemplated the two men, one of whom he had seen strike like a snake, while the other gave every indication that he was fully capable of the same. They did not give him impression that they were merchants at all, but he was indebted to this strange man and would help in whatever way he could. The questions and answers could come later.

"Do you have any accommodation?" he asked.

"No, we are still on the ship that brought us here, and there are other members of my family who are on board; my wife and Reza's wife, my son, and my uncle the doctor and his wife my aunt. There are a few retainers besides." In truth, he and Rav'an were not married, save in their hearts, but it would hardly do to say so.

Allam tried to hide his surprise. There was a great deal more to this than he had originally surmised, but again he remembered his manners and said, "You shall have my house on the outskirts of Muscat; there you will have privacy and every comfort I can provide. I regret that it is only modest accommodation, as I only use it when I wish to be near my animals: my horses and my beloved camels," he said with a smile, "but it is comfortable enough, and there are adequate quarters for the womenfolk."

Talon and Reza both touched their lips and hearts and thanked him. They talked some more, and very slowly the conversation moved around to what they might do while in Oman.

"If I can visit the Jewish people in the bazaar, I should have access to funds and can pay for everything we need for some time to come," Talon stated.

Allam nodded. He had wondered about that. "Yes, they are here, and I will have one of my people take you to them when the time is right for you. However, as long as you are in Muscat you are my guests, and I insist upon that, my friend. I remember only too well the comforts of the cell that we shared."

Talon laughed, and they began to recount to Reza, who had said very little up to this point, their combined experiences.

"Talon and I agreed that we should scream and wail when they began to torture us, so that they would not be inspired to ingenuity in their determination to break us," Allam said with a rueful chuckle.

"I hope it worked," Reza said with a grin. It lit up his face, and Allam relaxed a little more. The man made him uncomfortable, but he reasoned that if he was Talon's brother then Reza would not harm him.

"I am not sure who screamed the loudest, but we competed well with one another. I would rather not contemplate what might have happened had they not finally given up on us both," Talon said with a laugh.

"We were going to be sent to the Maidan of Baghdad to be relieved of our heads. I am thankful that I still have mine and you yours, Talon. Has he told you of how we escaped?" Allam asked Reza, who nodded.

"Talon thinks on his feet, and I have been glad of that myself in the past," Reza answered.

"Yes, that is true,"Allam mused. "If you so wish it then, we can talk more about trading and how you can take part, but that will be a subject for my brothers to discuss with you," he said switching the conversation.

"What do they do, as merchants?" Reza asked with interest.

"Why, they are skilled sailors and they trade far to the East across the sea from this country: in Al Hind, India, down south in Africa, and even further afield in the spice lands where there are strange and wonderful sights to see," Allam stated.

"Have you ever been there?" Talon asked, looking interested.

"Only once, and that was just to Gujarat with a cargo of horses; I do not like the sea and its unpredictable behavior. I prefer to stay close to home, where I spend much time with the desert Sheiks, providing them with the best camels in the world." He sighed with contentment.

"Today you just missed the most important race of the year! This is when the Caliph himself comes from the city to witness the race of the greatest camel breeds in the country. The man who wins this race receives a purse of five thousand dinars; even more importantly, the men of the desert, and even the Caliph, God protect him, bid on the winner's breed. The price they are prepared to pay for the animal and others of the same lineage is huge."

"Who did win this race, Allam?" Talon asked with a knowing grin.

"Why, with God's good grace, *my* camel did, and you will see her and her herd when you go to my house on the outskirts of town," Allam laughed.

"I am very happy for you, sir," Reza spoke respectfully.

"Please call me Allam. We are friends, and you are the 'brother' of Talon here. Yes, Allah be praised, my fortune was made today; I am twice happy because I have won the race and my friend is here with me again."

Reza had a question. "What of the lands across the sea to the east of here? I have heard of Al Hind, but not of the spice lands. Are they then further east again?"

"Oman has traded with the Indian people for many generations, but we also have ships that have sailed even further beyond to the fantastic lands of China," Allam informed them with pride in his voice.

Talon and Reza could not hide their amazement at this statement. Neither of them had any idea that one could reach the fabled country of China by sea, and they had only the vaguest idea of what that country was like. Talon indicated one of the fine porcelain bowls that still remained on the carpet in front of them. "Where did this come from? I have never seen such fine work. Not even in Isfahan, where the best craftsmen in the world ply their trade!"

Reza nodded his head in agreement. "It is incredibly fine work, and the decoration and markings are like nothing I have seen before." He was alluding to the milky white color of a bowl with intricate designs on its surface. The porcelain was so thin it was almost transparent.

"Ah, now you see, this came from China, where they make the most beautiful of porcelain, and much more besides." Allam could not keep the pride out of his tone.

"My brothers can tell you so much more than I, because they have both been to Khanfu, which is a vast city in that land. There has been a great amount of trade between our world and theirs. My brothers are excellent sailors who understand the ways of navigation and the winds of the monsoon that carry them east and then bring them back home months later. The travel is worth it, despite many dangers from the sea and its monsters, not to mention pirates and savage men."

The conversation became animated as Talon and Reza fired questions at Allam, who answered as best he could, but finally he threw his hands in the air with a laugh.

"My friends, I cannot possibly answer all the questions you ask tonight! It is very late, and you must still be tired form your voyage. I am sure that you need to rest after your journey, and your womenfolk need to be taken care of. I shall make arrangements for you to leave the ship tomorrow. Also, I have to report to the Caliph tomorrow to talk about today's win at the races. I shall bring my brothers to the house in a day or so for you to interrogate about their experiences. I am very sure they will be eager to tell you all they know."

They parted with embraces and words of affection; Allam by now had decided he liked both men, and it seemed Talon and Reza felt the same way about him. It was very late by the time Allam went to bed, to find his favorite concubine waiting for him to arrive.

"My Lord is up later than usual. I hope all is well?" she asked sleepily.

"I had a momentous day today, and it was not just about winning the race," Allam said as he drifted off to sleep.

*****

The villa Allam offered them consisted of a spacious group of buildings set just outside of Muscat town itself but still within the protective walls. The main building, a large, flat-roofed structure with thick, mud brick walls, faced the sea, which was a short walk away across some dunes. Behind the walled garden, situated at the back of the villa, were stables. Tall palm trees and some dense shrubs offered shade from the fierce sun, and doves cooed in the pigeon house at the corner of the garden.

It took two full days to move their entourage from the ship to this villa, where Talon and his friends would stay until they found somewhere of their own to live. Fariba remarked, somewhat resignedly, that although the villa could not match Isfahan, it was sufficient for their needs, and they had all the privacy they could desire.

Talon was not concerned about being able to pay for what they needed, but wondered how long he wanted to stay in this curious land of the Omani Arabs. He knew that behind this kingdom was the wasteland of the Empty Quarter, of which he'd had a taste while on his way south from Palestine. He had also heard, however, that it was very green in the south on the escarpment above a place called Raysat, especially when the monsoons arrived to dump a lot of rain on the area.

In keeping with local custom, the women were given separate quarters. Rav'an chaffed at the enforced confinement, but Fariba told her to remember the prison in Isfahan and not to fret. At least, she pointed out, they did not have to wear the suffocating veils, which were commonplace on the streets of the city, here within the premises.

Rav'an loved the sound of the sea and the wind rustling the palms. This place was pleasant; and yet, they were once again fleeing their enemies, and now her own brother. She was reminded of the many mornings she had spent in Isfahan, when the three of them, herself, Talon and Reza, hunted and frightened, used to meet before the day began. Now, at least, they were less alone. Her son, Rostam, was reunited with her; and Doctor Haddad and Fariba, who cared for her son, were there; as well as Jannat, who had been in the Sultan's prison with Rav'an. Their presence filled her with joy, but also terror, for she feared for them more than for herself.

Rav'an observed that Jannat was fitting into the group quite well, although there was tension between her and Reza, which Rav'an guessed was because of attraction. Jannat had asked Rav'an many questions about Reza while they were on the ship. Reza had kept his distance, which was proper, but Rav'an suspected that interest was mutual. Jannat was a very beautiful young woman, with long, flowing black hair, pale olive skin, and large, expressive, light brown eyes.

Then there was Rostam, who was becoming restless. He didn't fully understand why they were there in Oman, why he had had to leave his wonderful, familiar home in Persia. The journey on the ship had been of great interest to him and very exciting, but the times with his father had been tense.

The boy did not know quite what to think of this imposing man whom he was expected to call Father, and often he turned to the more familiar Reza when he spoke, rather than to Talon. During the voyage, Talon had said nothing of this to Rav'an, but she could see that he was struggling.

Fariba had said to her, "You should not expect Talon to become a father to the boy just like that, my dear. Look at him. He has been away for six long years, and God alone knows what he has lived through. He now has to become a father to a small boy whom he does not even know. From what little he has told us, he has lived a very hard life indeed."

"I realize that, Auntie, but I worry all the same. Rostam is a little wild, and like all boys he will need some discipline in a short while. I don't want his father to have to start their relationship with that."

"I think you should talk to Reza about it and ask for his help, Rav'an. The boy dotes on him."

It had been good advice, and subsequently, whenever the boy became too restless and about to break out, Reza had stepped in and restored some calm. Talon, however, found that his advances to the boy were met with a reserve that concerned him. He finally mentioned this to Rav'an, and she counseled patience. "Let it happen, my Talon. He will come round to you in time."

*****

It became customary for the guests to gather in the mornings, before the sun had burned the thin dew off the leaves of the shrubs. Secure in the knowledge that none of the servants could understand them, they could relax and enjoy each other's company. A servant, usually Salem or Dar'an, would provide tea and some small sweet cakes and then leave them to themselves. The sense of being fugitives from both the sultan of Shiraz and, even worse, Rav'an's brother, the Master of the 'Assassins, gradually receded, to be replaced with optimism as to what the future might hold.

Talon and Reza called everyone together to put forward ideas that they had talked about with Allam. Since that first meeting, they had held several conversations with their host, and the two of them had come back from the last one brimming with excitement.

Now they all listened with keen interest as Talon and then Reza told them about the meeting with Allam. Rav'an felt a trickle of apprehension when she realized that these two were on the edge of planning to travel over the sea again. Were she and Jannat to be left behind? That she could not bear.

"His family is one of the most respected in Oman for their navigation skills and their trading," Reza told the group, barely able to contain his enthusiasm. "We plan to meet the brothers and find out more."

"What are you saying, Reza? That you wish to sail to distant places and trade? What do any of us know about trade?" the doctor asked. He popped a sweet cake into his mouth and chewed with evident enjoyment. Fariba pushed the tray a little further out of reach, whereupon Rostam tried for one.

"Rostam!" Rav'an exclaimed. "Where are your manners?"

"May I please have one, Mama?" he asked, looking wistfully at the cakes.

"Very well," she relented. "But make sure you offer them to your uncle and your father first."

Rostam pouted, but one glance at his mother's stern face and he complied. Reza took one with elaborate thanks and a grin, and so did Talon, leaving only one, which Rostam would have taken, had he not heard a deep sigh and turned to see Jannat looking longingly at the cake.

He hesitated, then, with an effort, offered the cake to her; but she laughed and said, "No my Rostam, you shall have it. I do not need it. I was making you suffer!"

He giggled with her and took the cake happily.

*****

One morning, Fariba raised an important issue that had been under discussion between her and Dr. Haddad.

"You must all understand that this is not our home, so rumors will fly, especially among servants, and then out onto the streets," she said. The others settled down to listen carefully, as Fariba did not demand center stage very often.

"You two," she said directly to Talon and Rav'an, "*must* get married. We shall conduct the marriage right here in this garden."

Dr. Haddad beamed at their surprised looks. "She is right, you know, my boy," he said to Talon. "It is an important thing you should do properly, and we will witness it. God be thanked, no one has thought to ask us about you two. We don't want to start off here with lies."

Talon glanced at Rav'an out of the corner of his eye. "Don't we need a mullah or someone like that, Doctor?" he asked carefully. He couldn't fault the garden as a place to get married; it was well tended, and there were many birds coming and going, which attested to the skill of the gardener who had planted shrubs and rows of flowers. It even had a small fountain spluttering in a corner. It was no match for the garden of Fariba's house in Isfahan, but it would certainly do.

"You shall have a Persian marriage. I shall officiate, and we can declare to the world that you are man and wife," Haddad stated with conviction. "I shall even write it down on a paper."

The two girls looked happy, especially Rav'an, who hugged Fariba and asked, "When shall we do this, Auntie?" She had been wishing for this ever since they'd arrived in Oman.

"As soon as possible, I'd say," Dr. Haddad stated.

"Within a couple of days, at this time in the morning, before the heat," Fariba said. "We will need a mirror of some kind, even if it is only a sheet of burnished copper."

Reza grinned. "It's about time, my brother," he said, looking over at Talon.

"Hum, your turn next, *Brother*," Talon threatened. Reza gave him an alarmed look and stole a sideways look at Jannat, who was gazing fixedly at the palm trees above them. Fariba smiled to herself.

*****

Two days later, they all assembled in the garden. Salem and Dar'an were there to witness the occasion. No other servants were invited, and Youssef was charged with making sure none came to spy on them.

Talon and Rav'an sat on cushions, dressed in the best clothes they could find, facing the mirror, but also half-turned towards one another. Dr. Haddad read a passage from the Koran, then gave a mercifully short speech that charged them both to love and honor one another.

While he was doing this, Fariba and Jannat held a prettily decorated silk cloth over the couple's heads. Salem and Reza rubbed two small pastries with sugar over the cloth to represent a rain of much joy and happiness for them.

The Doctor then asked Talon if he wanted to marry Rav'an, to which he replied quickly in the affirmative. However when Haddad asked Rav'an if she wanted to marry Talon, she said nothing, pretending she had not heard. She was looking straight into his eyes, and she smiled, noticing with amusement a flicker of concern in his eyes. Fariba and Jannat laughed and said in unison, "She has gone to pick flowers!"

Haddad smiled and repeated the question; again, Rav'an smiled and said nothing. She could hardly contain her laughter at the expression on Talon's face. The corners of his mouth turned down, giving him a lugubrious expression. "She has gone to find rose water!" Fariba and Jannat said loudly.

Haddad asked a third time, and this time Rav'an smiled right into Talon's eyes and said, "Yes, yes, yes, I do!"

He reached over and embraced her hard, while everyone else laughed and pushed forward to embrace them both. Rostam, who had not fully understood the ceremony until the end, squealed with excitement and rushed into his mother's arms. She hugged him close, smiling across at Talon with tears in her eyes. "Now I am the happiest I have ever been!" she murmured. "I am with my family, all of us together at last."

*****

Reza and Talon were expert bowmen and trained constantly at one end of the garden. Rostam often came to watch; sometimes Rav'an joined in, and even brought Jannat into the play. Jannat had never been allowed to participate in a sport that was essentially for men only. She was awkward and self conscious, and found it painful to her fingers, but with encouragement from the other three she soon shed her embarrassment at her clumsiness.

Talon found some good wood and fashioned a small bow for Rostam, who was delighted and spent as much time as he could practicing. Reed arrows began to fly in all directions as he began to find birds interesting targets.

"He is just like his father, a perfectionist!" Reza laughed, as they watched the boy become more skilled.

"Just so he does not hit anyone in the eye," his mother remarked with a wary look over at the boy, who was stalking some sparrows.

Jannat sighed and said in a tone of woe, "I shall never be any good at this. Even Rostam can hit the target, but not I."

"I can show you how," Reza said impulsively, but then glanced at the others as though he had said something wrong.

"You could not have a better teacher, Jannat," Talon told her solemnly. "Let him show you, and you will become one of the best."

"Talon, I wish to talk to you. Let us leave them to their archery and go somewhere quiet," Rav'an said. Then, with a sharp look at Reza, "Reza, you should help Jannat to become proficient. Remember the time we were with the caravan and the bandits attacked?"

He nodded, wide-eyed, and she and Talon drifted away, barely able to contain their laughter.

"I swear that he looks like a deer confronted with a lion!" Talon laughed, as he put an arm around Rav'an's shoulders.

"It is high time those two did more than just moon over one another," Rav'an said, as she leaned against him, smiling. "I can't wait to tell Fariba!"

"Don't be unkind, my Love. We should not tease him."

"We have done nothing of the sort, but we shall, unless he does more than he has to let her know how he feels." She was holding onto the back of Talon's shirt and pulled it in fun.

He turned to her and looked down, seeing again the face of the woman he loved. She smiled up at him, showing her white teeth and a tiny crinkle on the sides of those gray eyes that had haunted him for all those years. He read in them the love he felt and took a deep breath.

"What are you thinking, my Love?" she asked innocently, looking up at him, her eyes luminous.

"You know perfectly well what I am thinking, and if someone wasn't running towards us I would kiss you very hard," he growled.

"Then kiss me anyway!" she commanded.

He glanced towards Rostam, who was scampering towards them through the bushes, but she poked him sharply with her forefinger in the ribs and said, "Are you not my Husband and his Father? Kiss me!"

He needed no further invitation. He leaned down and kissed her upturned lips, reveling in the taste of her, inhaling her scent. She reached around his neck and pulled him to her hard. His reaction was almost immediate and she laughed wickedly into his cheek as she felt him grow against her belly. "Hmmm, it would seem that you are...." She chuckled deep in her throat.

They parted just as Rostam arrived. He had obviously seen them and looked a little confused. "Mama, Jannat told me to join you, even though I was doing well and having a good time," he said with a tinge of resentment in his voice. "What were you doing with Father just now?" he asked them with wide eyes.

"Your father and I were... er, discussing something, my Little One."

"But I saw—"

"Isn't it time for your lesson with Auntie Fariba, my darling? Off you go. We will be right behind you." Rav'an said firmly, and chased him off with both hands. "Go along now, and we will see you later."

Rav'an took Talon's hand and led him upstairs to the bedroom she had taken for herself. In the adjoining bathroom, they bathed in the tiled bath in hot water prepared by their servants, before moving toward the bed.

As they made love, Talon recalled with acute pleasure the feel of her body entwined with his, then the small sounds that seemed to come from the back of her throat as they moved. These became more intense and urgent, until she arched her back and drew him hard against her as she smothered her cry in the hollow of his shoulder, followed by a nipping bite that made him wince but then grin as he looked down on her. He moved a strand of her hair aside that had plastered itself to her glowing face. It was warm in the room.

"Ah, but you were away so long, my Talon. Where have you been?" she asked wistfully. She knew something of what he had done since they had parted on that fateful day, but still there was much to hear from him. She sighed contentedly as he gathered her up and held her with her head on his chest.

He was sure he would tell her all in due course, but that would take time.

He was not satiated and neither was she, so when he leaned over her and kissed the tight nipple of her breast, she gave a low groan and shifted herself so that she was spread beneath him. He stroked her stomach and let his fingers drift slowly down her belly. Her sigh was all the encouragement he needed, and they moved to her soft junction where they lingered, kneading her gently while he kissed her breast. "I like you with no hair down there," he murmured.

"I can tell, my lover, it has a wondrous effect upon you!" she whispered into his ear with a low laugh.

They made love several times that morning, until neither of them could find the energy to do more. Then she slept with her head on his shoulder, her rich dark hair spread all around them like a veil, while he stared up at the ceiling and marveled at this woman who had recaptured his heart and body so effortlessly. Then he, too, drifted off.

Later, when the sun had dipped behind the mountains to the north and she was still in a deep sleep, he climbed carefully out of the bed and went to stand by the window that overlooked the stables and fields owned by Allam.

He barely heard her get up and come silently up behind him. She wrapped her arms around him; her scent and that of their love making was on them both.

"What are you thinking, my Talon?" she murmured as she kissed his shoulder. Her head barely came to his shoulder now, so he could kiss the top of her head easily.

"I am wondering how long we will stay here, and what we will do while we are here," he responded.

"Is this where you want to make a new life?" she asked him.

"Of that I am not sure. We do know that the Omani are great traders, and that does intrigue me; but as to staying for very long, I am not sure, my Love. I cannot forget the oath I made to the King in Palestine, which I told you about on the ship. I cannot easily forget that responsibility."

"I remember how excited you and Reza were at what Allam told you," she said with a smile and a touch of concern in her voice.

"Well, it was intriguing to hear him talk about trading all over the world, but we are still waiting for his brothers to come and explain that. I think that time here is not the same as we are perhaps used to in Persia," he responded with a small grin. "Meanwhile, I see that they play Chogan here, and I would like to play again. Does Reza still play?" he asked as he sat on the bed and took her hand in his.

"Yes, he did sometimes when he visited us in Isfahan. He enjoyed it a great deal when he had the chance. As you know, there is nothing of the kind in the northern mountains."

He nodded. "I must ask Allam if he has a spare horse or two. He lavishes great care and affection on those smelly camels of his, but I have also seen some splendid horses at his stables too."

"We must also ensure that our boy continues his education while here, so we must find a tutor for him. I am unsure what

Doctor Haddad and Fariba will do once we are settled in. He is a very skilled physician, so I doubt if he will have nothing to do for very long," she put in on a more practical note.

He thought about that for a moment. "Who taught Rostam while you were in Isfahan?"

"We had a tutor for all the usual things, such as calligraphy and his counting, while Fariba taught him some of the history and poetry he should know. But he is now going on seven, so he needs to be taught some of the more manly things of life," Rav'an said with a smile. "He needs you more than ever, Talon. It is time to become his father."

He turned her in his arms and looked at her. "I am not sure how good a father I will be, but I wish to be the best I can, my Rav'an. You must guide me from time to time. I might be too harsh on occasion."

"I do know life has not been particularly kind to you, Talon, but there is kindness in your soul. That I know, and I love you the more for it, and he will find it too, one day."

He couldn't stop watching her mouth as she smiled and spoke; the tiny quirks of amusement and expression enhanced by her eyes rendered him dumb with love.

He put his forehead to hers and said, "Where have you been all this time? For I have missed you."

Chapter Three
Chogan

Talon and Reza were mounted on two small, finely bred ponies that were from Allam's stables. They were hitting a ball back and forth about on the wide maidan behind the house with some of the *syce* who worked with the horses. Talon reveled in the feel of a good animal between his thighs again and could see that Reza was just as happy. They were jostling one another for the ball and chasing it across the dusty field, enjoying the last light of the day a couple of hours before prayers, when Talon glanced up and noticed Allam standing at the stable end of the field with some other men.

Allam waved, beckoning them over. The two of them stopped their play and rode over to the small group. Talon acknowledged Allam with a sweep of his mallet and then dismounted, handing off his reins to a syce, while another took the reins from Reza. Talon and Reza both ducked their heads to the assembly and said in unison, "Salaam Aliekom."

The men were dressed in the traditional Omani white *dishdasha* that came down to their ankles, and were wearing m*Massar,* a kind of loose embroidered woolen turban, on their heads. All three carried the beautifully crafted daggers, or *khanjars* as they were known, attached to their waists with ornate silver belts, which Talon now knew were called *shal.*

The three men replied with, "Wa Aliekom Salaam." They smiled back in a friendly manner.

Allam, waved his arm out towards the field and said, "I did not know you played Chogan in addition to your other accomplishments, my friends." He then his companions introduced his companions as his brothers.

"Both are sea men; they are navigators, Talon. I have brought them to meet you and your friend Reza to answer those many questions you have about their trade and the lands they have seen."

"We were intrigued that you were so interested in Al Hind and the countries beyond," the brother who had been introduced as Boulos said. Even under his loose robes Talon could tell he had a solid physique.

"It is the fault of Allam here," Talon said with a laugh. "He whet our curiosity greatly when he talked of where some of the fine porcelain came from, and much else, but then he said we must wait until we met you."

"Have you ever sailed before you came here?" the other brother, Imaran, asked them. He was tall and lean, with the look of a desert Arab about him. The three brothers were quite unalike, which Talon attributed to the fact that they might well have had different mothers.

Talon glanced at Reza, who r shrugged, so Talon said, "Yes, I have, and I have even been shipwrecked, but I don't want to remember that. I am familiar with the sea, but certainly do not have your experience." A little flattery could not hurt, he supposed. It seemed to please the brothers.

"Our voyages are governed by the monsoon winds," Imaran began. "One wind is called the *Mausim;* it blows at the midpoint of the year, about three months from now. It drives from the West to the East and will carry us to Al Hind. From there we can go as far beyond we wish. This wind lasts for nearly six months and then changes direction. Then the winds come off the land of Al Hind, from the great mountains to the North, and drive Westward; they bring us home, *Insha' Allah*."

"Will you be traveling this year?" Reza asked.

"Yes, but first we have to go to Lamu, an island many leagues to the south of here, close to the coast of Bilad Al-Zanj."

Talon knew this to be Africa. "For what purpose?" he asked politely.

"Why, trade, of course! For slaves, although we the Mardini are also interested in the teeth of the great elephants, and the gold that the people from the country bring to trade with us. Also Ambergris, the spit of the huge fish that washes up on the beaches in the storms; and the horns of the great beasts that live in the savannas, one of them is the *waheed al qarn*." He used Arabic words for the creatures, which confused both Talon and Reza for a brief moment; a puzzled Reza asked them to describe the creature.

"It has a huge horn on its long nose and is covered in armor. It is enormous, short-sighted and dangerous, living a solitary life on the great plains in the interior of the country. The horn is much prized in China." He smirked. "They think it helps the old men to keep it up in the bedchamber."

His brothers chuckled at that. "It has enormous value to the Chinese people, who will trade with us either in Al Hind or still further East, should we chose to go there and meet with them," Imaran finished.

Talon glanced at Reza and noticed that he too was intrigued. "What would we have to do to take part in this adventure?" he asked carefully.

The bothers stared at him in silence for a long moment.

"You would need a ship to begin with, and a large one, not some small boat, one that can deal with the great storms and survive. If you did come along in accompanying ships, we could all be very rich when we returned home. However, it can be very dangerous, and some ships never come home," Boulos told him, as though it were a challenge and a warning.

Talon thought about that. It was not because he feared the adventure; it was more a question of funds. He had discovered with some satisfaction that he had a good amount of credit with the Jewish merchants in Muscat when he visited the bazaar. The man's eyes to whom he had shown the chits had widened after he had examined them closely. He had ascertained that the chits were good, and over several tiny cups of tea they had compared notes. Much to Talon's surprise the man, Joshua, who owned a spice shop, professed to know Levi in Cairo, a man with whom Talon had done business some years ago.

That had broken the ice, and they spent a comfortable hour gossiping about Egypt and the region of Palestine. Joshua was well informed, but still eager for more recent news, which Talon was able to supply. Talon resolved to keep visiting him, as it would do no harm at all to keep a finger on the pulse of events in the Crusader regions.

He knew that Max, his sergeant friend in the Templars, would become aware of his existence from his own contacts in Acre once he, Talon, had drawn on his reserves. The Jews there would eventually inform Max of the withdrawal. Thus, while Max could not hear from Talon directly, he would know for sure that he was alive. Talon was often amazed at how efficient this system seemed to be. He knew it didn't function as well in the European countries, for although there were Jews in Europe, there they were a beleaguered people.

Joshua knew about King Baldwin and his debilitating leprosy. Doubts about his survival for much longer were widespread. Most people, including Joshua, predicted big troubles for the Frankish crusaders, as the Sultan of Egypt, Salah Ed Din, was gaining in power all the time. It gave some cause for concern to Talon, as he had promised to return as soon as possible to report to the King. He wanted to do that before the boy died. The news of the great battle of Montgisard and the defeat of the Sultan of Egypt had also reached Joshua. Talon was careful to look noncommittal at that news.

Talon had taken some gold, enough to help his extended family, leaving the rest with the trader for any future eventuality. Buying a ship was a heavy commitment, which he would have to think through carefully.

"I noticed that you both appear to play *Chogan*," remarked Boulos, changing the subject. "We, too, play that game when we are back here in Oman. Allam is besotted with his darling camels, so we cannot get him interested." He grinned at the discomfiture of his younger brother. "We enjoy a match from time to time."

"I hear a challenge here, Talon. Be careful of my brothers when they invite you to play Chogan. For a pair of sailors, they are ferocious on the field," warned their host.

"My brother is mistaken," Boulos laughed, slapping Allam on the shoulder. "We were watching you both because we have some men missing from our team, so we are inviting you to play with us on our side. There is a game set for two days from now on the Muscat maidan against one of Allam's friends, Sheik Nejem. He has issued a challenge and is determined to defeat us at the game."

Allam looked nervous and fingered his beads. "He is no friend of mine," he muttered. "He is very upset at losing the camel race, Boulos. Are you sure it is a wise thing to have a game with that man? He treats everything as though it is a fight to be won at any cost."

"Well, Chogan in a way is a fight, and its cost is high," Imaran laughed. "You think you are the only gambler here in Muscat, Brother? We have two thousand dinars on this game, but not enough men to play. That is why we have to have men like Talon and Reza here to help us out. They appear to be able to play. *In Sha' Allah* we will win with their help."

Talon had to stop himself gaping. That was a vast amount of money to gamble. These Omani, he had begun to realize, enjoyed gambling.

*****

The addition of Talon and Reza made up the full number of the brothers' team of players, making it six to a side for the match. The man called Nejem, whose camel had been beaten in the races and who had issue the challenge, wanted ten players to a side. The brothers pleaded a shortage and pointed out that the Caliph wanted a game, not a cancellation at the last minute. Talon's respect for the two men had gone up as he watched them negotiate with Nejem, who seemed a cold and dangerous man.

Now they were all mounted on pure Arab breeds that came from Yemen. None of them were stallions; Talon had learned in Egypt that while stallions were wonderful animals to ride, they were too skittish for warfare, and Chogan, after all, was war. He glanced over at the tall, hawk-faced man and wondered if this game was more about avenging his loss at the camel race than about a sporting display in front of the Caliph of Muscat. His instincts were that it was the former. He sidled his horse next to Reza, who sat his horse quietly nearby, and whispered, "This man is out for some kind of revenge today, Brother. Be careful."

Reza flicked a glance at Nejem and nodded. "I agree. He wanted Allam to play in the game very badly, but his brothers were having none of it. Now he will try for one of us, I suspect, as it would shame Allam badly to have harm come to guests under his protection."

The animals were snorting and fidgeting; they sensed the tension of their riders. Then, as often happens, they began to show off to their immediate neighbors by pawing the ground, flaring their nostrils, snarling, and tossing heads.

The game started almost before Talon realized it had. A man ran out in front of the crowd, just to the front of the pavilion where the Caliph was seated, and hurled a round, whitish ball straight at the milling horses.

Someone shouted and the riders began barging into one another. Several horses kicked out, but their riders managed to control them with whip and spur. Then the ball was struck away. There was already so much dust that Talon could barely tell which direction it was headed. He whipped his head about and saw Reza break free of the mob of milling players to gallop rapidly after the ball. Talon turned his very responsive animal on its haunches and followed. There was a roar from the crowd as the game took off.

He sensed that someone was on his right and glanced over to see one of Nejem's players maneuvering his animal to strike Talon's and drive him out of the play. Talon sat deep, and in response his mount sat on its haunches. The other rider had not expected this, and his horse rushed past without touching Talon. The man snapped his head around with a snarl as he wrenched at his animal, trying to turn it.

He was too slow and Talon rode his horse directly into the back of the man's mount. Although it was a heavy shock, Talon's horse's chest was buffered by the fleshy rump of the other animal. The other pony was knocked forward, staggering, and its rider went flying off its back to land hard in the dirt. Then Talon was off to chase after Reza, who had almost disappeared down the field. He didn't even glance back at his victim, who was scrabbling around on hands and knees in the dirt, looking for his mallet.

Talon had a clear stretch before him. Reza knocked the ball towards Imaran, who drew the pursuing riders after himself and then cleverly passed the ball back to Reza just as Talon thundered up the field. Reza spun his horse neatly and tapped the ball towards the goal, keeping it almost under his horse's hooves as they ran. Now the other team members were desperately trying to catch both riders, who were leading the charge for their goal. Imaran yelled with glee and set spurs to his horse, rapidly overtaking some of the slower members of the opposition. There was one rider, however, riding a magnificent gelding who had the legs on almost everyone. Nejem came up behind Talon at such a speed that one moment there was a distant mob chasing him, and the next time he glanced over his shoulder there was Nejem coming up on his left side.

Reza took a reckless swipe at the ball when it was fifty paces from the goal, but his strike sent it high into the air instead. He continued to ride without stopping to avoid an accident, as by now Talon and Nejem were right behind him, and pulling up short would cause a dangerous pile-up. Talon gauged the trajectory. As the ball plummeted towards the ground, he stood up in the stirrups and struck it overhand while it was still above his head, slamming it straight between the posts.

The already noisy crowd roared their approval, and new bets were taken on who would score the next. Talon did not see Nejem hurling up on his left side. Just as he sat down in the saddle, he felt a sickening blow on his horse's side, and both he and the horse went tumbling. He threw himself as far away from the animal as possible as it went down, and then rolled even further away from the flailing hooves. He came to his feet like a cat and whirled to stare back at his animal, which lay trembling on the ground, its left fore leg broken. Nejem was dancing his horse away from the animal on the ground with a sneer on his thin face. Reza galloped his horse up and halted it in a small cloud of dust beside Talon, who was brushing off his clothes and staring at Nejem speculatively. Reza had a very dangerous look in his eyes.

"I saw what happened, Talon," he said in *Farsi*. "The treacherous dog just wanted to kill you."

"He killed my horse, which was cowardly; neither it nor I have ever harmed him. But now, perhaps, that will change," Talon grunted back, also in *Farsi*.

"As God is my witness, I had no idea that we would have such an accident!" Nejem called over as he directed his animal towards them. By this time, the rest of the players had arrived to surround them and the panting animal on the ground. Boulos leapt off his horse and, with a quick glance at Talon to make sure he was all right, knelt by the horse on the ground. He looked at the break in the foreleg; the bone was protruding just below the knee, and he cursed under his breath.

"This horse was worth a *lot* of money, and one of my favorites," he said angrily in an undertone to Talon.

He whirled on Nejem. "Nejem, you did not have to charge into my friend in that manner! What were you thinking? Were you trying to hurt the man or the horse?" he demanded, glaring up at the man who sat nonchalantly on his mount, sneering down at them. Najem shrugged.

"This is Chogan, Boulos. Your friend knows how to play, but the horse was unfortunate."

"I see," Boulos said, his face flushed with anger. "You have no love of horses; to you they are just tools, nothing more." He strode to his animal, snatched the reins from the player holding them, mounted, and rode off towards the center of the field.

A group of *syce* ran onto the field and killed the animal then and there by slashing its jugular. They dragged its carcass off the field towards a subdued crowd, and another mount was handed over to Talon by an older *syce*, who said in an undertone as he did so, "You are a fine player, Master, but be careful; they will try to harm you and your friend just because you are friends of Sheik Allam. Allah protect you."

Talon nodded and mounted up. "Thank you for the good advice."

Nejem slowed his horse to ride alongside Talon and Reza as they walked their horses back to the center of the field.

"That was a good strike, Persian. But do not think this game is over yet!" he snapped. He then galloped the rest of the way to join the other players.

"He is not happy about that goal, Talon. I am impressed. That was a fantastic shot—at full gallop too!" Reza grinned. "Where have you been to play like that?" he queried.

"The *syce* told me that Nejem has a feud going with Allam. Be careful, brother," Talon said, avoiding the question.

It became an unspoken agreement that Boulos's team should look for opportunities to distract the other team and, if possible, inflict as much in the way of injuries upon them as they could by way of retaliation for the slain horse. Boulos was spoiling for a fight with Nejem, but could not catch him out.

The man was a fine rider and could anticipate most of the moves made against him. Talon shook his head with grudging admiration as Nejem evaded two of Boulos's men as they tried to sandwich him and cause his horse to fall and perhaps crush him on the ground. Nejem slipped away from the trap and made a goal, humiliating them for their pains.

The game flowed to and fro over the field, with first one team gaining a goal and then the other. They appeared to be very evenly matched. It was now clearly a grudge match, but that didn't worry Talon, as he had been in this kind of vicious game before.

Each player took every opportunity to ram another's horse out of the way, using elbows and sticks whenever they could. Reza and Talon were no exception and played as a team within a team. Soon Boulos and his brother were taking advantage of this, sending the ball their way as often as possible, while they ran interference with Nejem's men, frustrating them.

Talon and Reza were both aware that this made them targets. The other team responded to the attacks against them with equal ferocity every time there was a melee where blows could fall that did not have to be explained away and could not even be seen by the crowd, nor by the other players in the dust cloud that enveloped them all.

Talon and Reza were on the alert and warned each other whenever other players might catch up and try some foul play. To Talon it was exhilarating to be on a good horse scrambling for the ball, playing a game that he loved. Covered in a fine layer of dust, riding lathered horses that had to be changed frequently for fresh mounts, they were now playing for that last goal which would put one team or the other ahead.

An opportunity presented itself as Imaran lobbed the ball out of a melee and shouted at Talon to get going. Not needing further encouragement, Talon put spurs to his mount, which jumped away with a snort and hurtled after the bouncing ball. Right behind Talon came Reza, shouting that he was there and that Imaran was following.

Talon glanced behind him and almost laughed. Boulos was exchanging blows with Nejem with the butt of his stick, using the pretense that he was blocking him, and by the look of it he had almost knocked Nejem's turban off. It was a good thing they didn't have anything more dangerous in hand than a mallet, he reflected, as he and his mount hurtled down the field.

He concentrated on the ball, confident that he was protected from behind and aware that Reza was racing forward to pick up the ball, should he pass it at any time. Ripples of dust followed the flying hooves of his mount. The thunder of more hooves and shouting men drowned out the excited yelling of the crowd, who sensed that this might be the definitive goal of the game.

He came upon the ball, still bouncing wildly forward on the uneven ground, forcing him to swerve several times in order to keep his pony lined up on the ball. He realized that it would be better to try for a series of taps rather than a big hit. He tapped it forward, then, as it bounced, lifted it into the air to about the height of his horse's shoulder and tapped it forward. As it came back down, he tapped it again and encouraged his horse to gallop even faster. By this time Reza was almost at the other team's goal. With one long, lazy sweep of his mallet, Talon caught the ball as it descended one more time and lifted it to soar high into the air to drop it right in front of Reza, who cheekily tapped the ball through the posts. The crowd went wild, cheering madly at this impressive play. Even the people on the stands seemed to appreciate the finessed goal.

Both Talon and Reza made sure that no one from the following riders came close, for fear of another 'accident.' Boulos and Nejem were still engaged in a running scrap as the trumpet sounded for the goal, but then it sounded again to announce the end of the game. The crowd voiced their approval as the players walked their heaving, sweating, dust-caked horses back to the lines.

Boulos and Imaran were ecstatic. They galloped up to Reza, and both brothers embraced him and kissed him hard on either cheek in their appreciation. Talon laughed as he witness this, but then found himself subjected to the same treatment, and Reza grinned back at him, his teeth white in his dark, dirt covered face.

"You are great players, my friends!" Boulos yelled, his face flushed with glee. "We managed to get our revenge on Nejem, who has now lost to our family twice within a month. He must be ready to chew rocks, he is so angry!"

Talon wondered about that. He watched as Nejem and his team left the field in a disconsolate group. Nejem shot a look at the excited men surrounding Talon and Reza, and it was full of venom.

"You can control that ball better than anyone I have ever seen, Talon," Imaran said, with not a little awe in his voice. "I saw you juggle the ball at a flat out gallop. How did you learn to do that?" he asked.

Reza was enthusiastic. "You will have to teach that to me someday, my Brother," he said shaking his head with a grin.

They were greeted at the side of the field by an equally ecstatic Allam, who ran up and almost tore them off their horses, then embraced them all.

Then, just as Talon dismounted, a small boy ran out from the group of veiled women who were standing at the edge of the field. Rostam ran full tilt into Talon's arms. "You won! You won! We saw how you and uncle Reza did it!" he piped. Talon laughed with delight, caught his son up and swung him in an arc.

"We did, my Rostam, we did! Your uncle scored the winning goal." He tossed the laughing boy into Reza's arms.

"Uncle Reza, Mama says that you and father were the best players on the field! Everyone did!"

"Of course we were, Rostam, and now you have seen it for yourself!" Reza laughed with the boy and then put him down. "You need to go and see if your father is all right. He fell off, you know. You need to tell him that its all right to fall off once in a while, but not for every game."

Rostam craned his neck to look up at Reza. "Uncle, I saw what that nasty man did to father."

Both men laughed, and then he grinned and walked over to Talon and said solemnly, "You are all right, aren't you, Father?"

Talon twisted this way and that, holding his sides and pretended to wince with pain. "I think so, Rostam, but I shall have a talk with your uncle about this game later." He cast a threatening look at Reza, who smirked, pretending not to hear.

They allowed their horses to be led away by the beaming syce and joined their friends, who were now clustered in a group ready to be taken back to their homes.

Boulos, his teeth showing white in his dust-caked face, lifted his arms in greeting. "We will have a celebration tomorrow evening, my friends."

"Allam can now afford to give us all a great party," Imaran joked, and Allam grinned back at them all and waved his hands in the air. "Oh, yes. God be praised, we have inflicted a great defeat on Nejem today, thanks to our friends. I thank you for all you did today. It was magnificent!"

Sadly, Talon realized it would not include the womenfolk, who would be excluded from the all-male celebration. There was one consolation: the five hundred dinars he'd had Yosef place on their team had now become nearly three thousand. He smiled through grit-covered teeth and said, "We will be honored to attend, Boulos. Now I am ready for a drink of cool water and a bath."

They saw the cables loosened, they saw the gangways
   cleared,
They heard the women weeping, they heard the men
   that cheered:
Far off, far off, the tumult faded and died away,
And all alone the sea wind came singing up the bay.

—"Sir Edward Grey"

Chapter Four
A Ship

A celebration feast was thrown by Allam in the gardens of his large villa situated near the sea, within the ancient walls of the city, between two low hills that were covered with palm trees. These added their rustling sound to the low roar of the surf on the beach. It had a peaceful effect which guests commented upon with pleasure as they sat on the expensive carpets, imported from Persia and further afield.

By nightfall the guests had departed, leaving only the three brothers and their father seated around a single carpet close to a small, still pond in which swam large carp. The men paid no attention to their surroundings; they were too engrossed in their discussion.

The old man who had fathered the brothers, Sheik Al Mardini, leaned over a small bowl of precious shelled pistachio nuts, picked up one of the light green kernels and popped it into his mouth to chew with obvious satisfaction, even though he no longer possessed all his teeth.

"Those two *kharagi* you have as guests do not seem to be the typical merchant kind to me," he stated, and looked over at Allam, who was sipping a small porcelain cup of black *khaffee*.

"I agree, Father, they are not; but before God I am indebted, as I have said more than once, to the one called Talon, who took me out of that pestilential prison in Baghdad. He can call himself whatever he likes; I owe him my life."

"He plays Chogan like a demon, as does his companion. Without those two we would have gone down to an ignominious defeat yesterday," Boulos interjected, shaking his head with a wry chuckle.

"Both of them are superb riders, every bit the equal of Nejem," Imaran said. "I have seldom seen such horsemanship."

"They came from Persia, you say? So why are they here?" the old man demanded with an impatient flip of his age-marked hand. The rings on his long, dark fingers glittered in the firelight.

"I do not know for sure, but he did tell me that they were on a journey and that he had wanted to see me again." Allam said, his round face thoughtful. "He brought with him women; two of them are young and very beautiful by the account of my servants, who are keeping me informed. There is also a boy, and a physician and his wife, who is also beautiful. The physician worked in Isfahan's famous Bimaristan. The two younger women are the wives of our two friends, as far as I can judge. I think the boy is the son of Talon. They keep to themselves and speak *Farsi,* which my servants do not understand."

"You told me that he was a trader, Allam," Imaran said, his forehead furrowed.

"When we were in prison he claimed that he was, but he had also been a soldier, which might explain why he is so good at horsemanship and so forth. They accused him of being a spy. But then, they accused me of being a spy too, so I put little faith in that. And he is certainly interested in finding out from you, my brothers, more about the trade routes. However, I have never witnessed a man kill with the speed and efficiency of this man, and his friend seems to me to be a very dangerous man also."

"You say he is interested in trading; so I would simply ask, does he have the money to buy what he needs?" Imaran asked.

"My servants reported that he visited the Jews in the bazaar and came away with money. I do not know how much, but I suspect that there is more where that came from," Allam stated. "And after yesterday's game, I know for a fact he is richer by several thousand dinars."

The brothers chuckled at this. "We are all the richer by a few thousand dinars from that game, I'm glad he had the wits to bet on our team," Imaran said.

"They appear to be interested in joining us in our overseas ventures, Father. We need to have your permission to allow this," Boulos said to their father, who was ruminatively munching on another pistachio.

"Do you trust them?" he asked.

"I trust them implicitly, Father," Allam stated. "Before God I will affirm that this man is true and would stand by his friends to the death. He has demonstrated that to me already."

The old man looked at the other two.

Boulos spoke for them both. "You learn a lot about a man who plays Chogan with you, Father. You know that already, as you were once one of the best. There is the military skill which these two posses in large measure, and that could prove very useful, should they join with us. Furthermore, they play as a team, which even in Chogan is rare." He chuckled. "Most of the time a game here in Muscat is a ball being chased by a cloud of dust." Imaran laughed in agreement at that, and Boulos continued. "They are tacticians, and we have ample proof that Talon can be trusted, because your son, our brother Allam is here and not dead in some hole in the ground in Baghdad. I think we can trust them."

The old man nodded acceptance of this reasoning. "They need to pay their way. Can they do this?"

"That I shall have to find out, Father. Do we have your consent and blessings to go forward with the planning for a journey to Lamu with them? The winds are already taking other ships south."

"Yes, *Insha' Allah* our decision will be the right one. I shall reserve judgement for the moment, but you may begin planning for your journey."

Allam gave a quiet sigh of relief. He liked Talon, Suleiman, whatever he called himself, although he knew well enough that there was much that Suleiman was not telling him. Pointing him towards the potential riches to be had by going with his brothers to trade was the least he could do for his strange guest. The dangers inherent in trading enterprises notwithstanding, he felt that this was the right thing to do.

His father's blessing had been an important step. Had the old man taken a disliking to either man, then it would have been incumbent upon Allam to ask them to leave. Instead his father had watched and listened in silence as the men were praised for their gamesmanship. He had noted with approval that Talon had offered a warning about the man called Nejem.

Now that that issue had been resolved, the talk moved on to the much discussed camel race, along with the rewards and the consequences of that particular event.

"Nejem is not going to let that pass without some kind of retaliation," Imaran stated with a glance at Allam, who was now sipping another cup of *kaffee* just poured by a silent servant, who had materialized out of the dark to replenish it.

"The sultan has confirmed the result of the race, so there is nothing that he can do about that. You did very well, my son. You have brought much needed gold and prestige to our family," his father told Allam, who glowed from the compliment. Their father was not known to lavish praise.

"What do you call that animal of yours?" Imaran asked with a grin.

"Jasmine," replied Allam.

The two brothers snickered at Allam, who said defensively, "She has earned that name several times over!"

The brothers subsided as their father made to speak again.

"We need to keep an eye on our property at the stables and ensure that guards are set all day and night to ensure that no harm come to our prize-winning camel, Jasmine," the old man said. Allam knew that his father had been through more than one feud and was simply being careful, so he nodded agreement.

"I heard that Nejem is talking about an eye for an eye," Imaran said slowly, referring to the accident that had occurred during the race.

"Nejem comes from a family that is not noted for its trustworthiness in any form," the old man remarked. They are of the tribes of the Yemen , and not Omani, as is ours. It would be well to keep watch on them. Nejem lost a great deal of gold in that race."

"Not to mention the humiliation of losing the game in front of the sultan," Boulos gloated.

*****

Talon was informed that his presence was requested down at the Muscat harbor the very next day. He thought he knew the reason. He and Reza hastened down to the main harbor of the city, following the messenger.

The natural harbor of Muscat was well protected by two main islands that stretched across the entrance. On one of the islands was a fort that dominated the waters in the harbor.

As he and Reza arrived at the stone ramp that defined the harbor, they witnessed a boatload of black slaves being brought ashore by their Arab overseers. Amid much wailing from the prisoners and snapping of whips by their overseers, the slaves clambered clumsily out of the boat into the water, which was waist deep, holding the chains that linked them by the neck high to prevent from being entangled by them and drowned. Talon observed the pitiful sight of men and women, all naked and in woeful condition, and wondered where they would be taken to live out their lives.

He shook his head, remembering his friend Panhsj in Egypt and his proud demeanor, which he contrasted to the stricken and abject look of these poor creatures. He decided then and there that the brothers could transport slaves, but no matter how lucrative that might be, he would not. Had he not also been a slave himself, with no right to anything? It remained with him.

Upon their arrival on the beach they were met by a large black slave, who took them towards a hive of activity on the water front. They found Allam and his two brothers standing on the waterfront, looking up at a huge ship that was drawn up in a narrow channel of water cut into the beach. The only part of the ship still in the water was the edge of the keel; the bulk of the vessel was held upright by stout poles wedged into the sand on either side. Its hull was surrounded by stacks of timber, coils of rope, tools, and piles of stones.

All around the vessel were dozens of men, from Omani ship workers to black slaves doing their bidding, engaged in a wide variety of activities, all of which were focused on the ship towering over the small group of visitors.

Talon had by now been on several different kinds of sea-going vessels, but he was awed by what he beheld here. This boat was massive compared to anything he had ever seen before, and that included the ship in which they had escaped from Persia, which had been a *Xebec*.

He glanced out at the harbor and noticed with interest that among the forest of masts and dhows there were several other ships of comparable size. These looked as though they were well weathered. After the formal greetings, Allam gestured at the ship. The noise of hammering, sawing and creaking blocks and tackle, combined with the shouts of men, made talking difficult.

"Our father, whom may God protect for many years to come, has given his blessings for us to prepare for our venture to Lamu this year, Talon. God willing, he will soon give his permission for you to join us. This vessel is known as a *Baghlah* and is one of the largest of the Omani ships that sail the Indian seas."

"Is this one of your ships?" Reza asked, with awe in his tone. He was craning his neck to look up at the hull above them.

"That depends," Imaran said, giving them a keen look.

"In order for you to become a merchant of any note in Oman, you must own a ship," Boulos stated with a twinkle in his eyes as he regarded Talon and Reza.

Talon immediately understood. "Does it have to be a very, very large ship like this?" he asked carefully.

Imaran laughed. "Yes, Talon. Do you see those ships congregating over there on the south side of the harbor? They are our ships, or many of them. See how large they are? Some are *Baghlahs* like this one, as you can see, and others are the slightly smaller *Ganjahs*. Both are ideal for long distances, capable of sailing in the unpredictable seas of India and riding out the storms. They transport horses by the hundreds to Al Hind. You have to have a large ship to sail in these seas. You will see very quickly what I mean if you come with us."

"How much would a ship of this kind cost a person who was interested in buying it?" Reza asked.

"Close to three thousand dinars, I should think." Imaran said looking up at the ship with a critical eye. "It is not the largest ever build here, but certainly large enough. These are without doubt the most seaworthy of all the ships built in this land."

"Come, we will show you around, and then you can decide," Boulos said. Talon glanced at Reza, who grimaced. Their intent to become merchants was already proving to be pricey. He needed to think hard.

They walked around the ship while Boulos and Imaran pointed out the salient features of a good sea-going vessel, explaining the need for a large water-tight hold and spacious passenger room. Allam was as interested in the ship as Talon. He shrugged and laughed depreciatingly. "My brothers are the sea men and navigators of the family, so listen to them, Talon, and learn from the very best."

They climbed a tall ladder and were shown around the top deck by one of the builders, who was clearly delighted to see the brothers. He almost prostrated himself in front of them, but a sharp word from Imaran made him jerk upright and touch his heart and forehead. He then obsequiously lead them around the wide deck. Wherever they went, men who were working stopped what they were doing and bowed low to the men. Clearly the brothers were well known and very well respected.

Talon estimated that the ship was easily eleven paces across on its waist and probably forty paces long from stem to stern. This was a huge ship by any standards. Imaran pointed out that its hold could accommodate at least thirty horses, perhaps more. He glanced at Reza, who was having trouble keeping his jaw from dropping open. Reza gulped and shook his head with amazement.

"This is so big I wonder that it can float!" he exclaimed in a hoarse whisper aside to Talon.

Boulos spoke rapidly with the shipwright who was guiding them around.

"They are putting the finishing touches to this ship as we speak. It will be launched next week, and then it will have to be fitted out for its maiden voyage to Lamu," he told them.

Talon had noticed the large piles of timber on the beach, but when he considered the countryside around them, he could not see any sign of woodlands that could provide this kind of timber.

"Where does this timber come from?" he asked. "Are there great forests in the south? I cannot see any near Muscat."

Imaran smiled. "No, and you are right, we do have forests, but they are not the forests that can provide this kind of wood. The timber that you see on the beach and on some of those ships which have just arrived is from Al Hind and is known as teak. The Indians sell us their wood, we built our ships with it, and then ship horses to them, which we sell for outrageous prices. Everyone is happy!" He chuckled.

"You should know, Suleiman and Reza, that this is no ordinary wood. Most timber for ships would quickly rot and become infested with worms that inhabit the sea. They bore holes right through the hull of a ship and it will sink, but this wood does not attract the worms, neither does it rot in the water. There are some ships out in that harbor which are as old as three generations, and their hulls are still good. One of those over there was built by our grandfather, may his soul be saved," Boulos stated.

They spent several hours looking over the entire ship, which smelled of new cut timber and some other less pleasant odors. Boulos and Imaran asked the shipwright to show their guests how the strakes of the ship were held together, and he proudly showed them how this was achieved.

Talon had spent some time on the Byzantine ships and understood how they were held together with nails and pegs, so he was astonished to see that the strakes of this ship were sewn together. He stared at the rope stitching that held one edge of a strake tight to another, while the shipwright explained that this was a slow but very sure process.

There were thousands of holes drilled painstakingly in the timber; then they were placed together and a rope of coconut fibre was pushed through from one side. They watched while a man would haul on this until it was taut, while another would beat it with a hammer to make sure it was very tightly hammered home. Then they would repeat the process from the other side. The fibre had the advantage that it would swell when in the water and seal the hole tight. They then hammered fiber into the gaps between the planks and sealed the whole with a tar-like substance which Boulos told theme was shark skin oil rendered down. Talon sniffed at it; the smell was not pleasant close up.

Boulos grinned at Talon's astonishment. "We do not have iron foundries in Oman, so nails and bronze are very expensive," he said. "This stitching can be easily repaired and allows movement when in a storm."

Talon did not see a single nail on the entire ship's hull. It was clearly a very long process to build such a ship, but apparently it was also a very solid process, and the ships would last.

They visited the hold, where Imaran informed them that they could construct more than thirty stalls for horses and then easily convert them for other cargo when the horses had been unloaded. Then they visited the spacious passenger area, which Talon was interested in. There was ample room for the entire group, including space for the servants, a separate women's cabin, and several other cabins for passengers. After examining the rest of the ship, they bade the shipwright good bye and descended the ladder.

Talon and Reza stood on the sand and admired the ship. It was sleek, and to Talon's mind built for any sea. Another was being constructed further down the beach; he could see the ribs and strakes being worked upon.

The discussion about the needs of a ship, its performance, and all the endless details were bewildering, but clearly the two brothers knew exactly what they were talking about, so he resolved to listen very carefully and learn all he could.

It was noon by this time, so Allam invited them all back to his house to continue the discussion. Talon had the impression that, had he not shown so much interest, the conversation would not have continued and the brothers would not have taken his wish to become a merchant seriously. While they were on their way to the house, Reza and Talon had a chance to discuss the ship and the price.

"I have never in my whole life seen such a vessel. If I had not seen others in the water, I should not have believed that this monster could sail at all," Reza muttered, with an eye on the striding brothers ahead of them. Talon scuffed his boot in the sand. Neither he nor Reza had adopted the local form of dress, although he thought it might be prudent before long to do so, as it would allow them to blend in and even disappear if they had to, rather than looking like a pair of scruffy Seljuk cavalry men who had lost their way.

"I will allow it is huge, but I have crossed the Middle Sea in a much smaller vessel, and I agree that when the vessel is larger it is probably safer in wild seas. It has three masts! Even with the largest ships I sailed in before, some had two but one mast was more common. It does not have oars, which I am more used to," he said, thinking of the sleek galleys he now possessed.

"What do you think of the cost?" Reza enquired with a sideways look at Talon from under his dark brows. They were speaking *Farsi,* and in undertones.

"I can meet that cost," Talon told him.

Reza stopped and gaped at him. "You can what?" He held onto Talon's sleeve. "You mean this?"

"I made a bet on the game of chogan, which Yosef collected. That alone will pay for most of the ship; and if the Jews here can cover my chits, then I can pay for the ship and the crew," Talon said. "I will tell you later how I came by it all. Some you know already. I am already rich, Brother, but I want to see these places they are always talking about. Close your mouth; it is hanging open." He laughed at Reza's surprise and tapped his friend lightly under his lower jaw with a forefinger.

"It is the other costs that concern me. There has to be a crew and a captain, I know that much, and then provisions, too.

Then I will need more money to pay for merchandise we will purchase in this place called Lamu. Those costs I will have to discuss with them, to make sure I don't make a mistake and run short."

*****

The brothers were surprised at how much Talon already knew about what was needed for a ship to function. While he deferred to their greater knowledge, they were clearly pleased that he was not a total newcomer to the nautical world. They offered much good advice, even though no one actually talked about the final terms of the ship's purchase. That would have been poor manners.

Eventually, however, they came to this point, and as the sun began to set, the *khaffee* was brought out and placed in tiny porcelain cups before each of them. The father was now present, and both Talon and Reza were scrupulously polite towards him, as it was evident the brothers deferred unquestioningly to him.

He had sailed the Indian ocean from one end to the other, and Talon was keen to ask him many questions about this. However, he confined himself to the immediate discussion, which was about where to find a reliable crew for the ship and a good captain who could navigate.

"You see, Suleiman," the old man said, as he leaned over a small bowl in front of him and picked out a fig for himself, "we are Nabatean people, we of the Omani. Do you know what this means?"

It was a small test, and Talon jumped at it. "You are navigators of the deserts, the great wastelands of the empty quarter and the regions north by *Rekem*?" he asked. *Rekem* was the Nabatean name for Petra, the city of carved rock where he had first met the Nabateans.

All of the other men stopped what they were doing and stared at him. After a long silence the old man said softly, "How is it that you know of our people when you have never been here before?"

"Oh, Hadj," said Talon, using the honorary title, "I have never been here before, but I was guided by the people who call themselves the Nabateans from the North near to the desert of Sinai and the place known as *Rekem* deep into the south. They taught me the use of the *Kamal,* with which I became familiar while crossing the sands."

The eyes of Allam, his brothers and even those of the old man were wide with surprise. After a long silence, during which the men sipped at their *khaffee* and watched Talon, the old man once again began to speak. He appeared to have come to a decision.

"Earlier this week my sons asked me if I approved of your joining us in a sailing venture, first to the South and then perhaps to the East. I confess to having had reservations. It gladdens my ears to hear that you are no novice with too much money who just thinks he can have an adventure. Omani merchants are navigators and sailors first, merchants second. The seas that we venture into are unforgiving and require skill and courage to navigate. You appear to be more accomplished than my son Allam knew. That is very good."

Talon demurred. "Hadj, I am but a child compared to you and your sons when it comes to navigation, but I ache to learn from the very best." He knew a little flattery would not hurt, but he also meant it.

The old man began to stand up and Imaran hastened to assist him. He turned to the men still seated. "I am tired now and would go to my rest. I ask God to bless you all, and my sons have my permission to assist you in every way."

Talon bowed deeply to the old man as he was led away.

The brothers were apparently very relieved by the words of the old man. They immediately continued the animated discussion of everything related to the ship and what Talon and Reza needed to consider.

Reza had up to this point remained silent, but he had been listening carefully. He asked, "How long have your people been sailing to Al Hind and... beyond?"

"For many centuries, Reza." Imaran assured him. "The Nabateans have been sailing to Al Hind since before the prophet, and even before the prophet of the Christians. We have plotted the way using the stars, and there are books written telling of every port along the way, all the way to the fabled city of Khanfu in China. The Chinese call it Guangzhou."

"Navigators, some Nabateans and some even of your people, the Persians, have written manuals as guidance. A few became popular, such as *Kitab Ma'din al-asrar fi 'ilm al-bihar* by Shaikh Nasr bin 'Ali al'Haduri: *The Mine of Secrets in the Science of the Seas*. This book contains drawings of the position of the sun above the ship.

"Have you ever been to China?" Reza asked.

By way of response, Imaran reached into his robes and withdrew something. He leaned forward and flicked it over to Reza, who caught it and then turned the object over in his hand. "What is it? Is it precious?" he asked.

Boulos laughed and said, "No it is not precious. It is a good luck talisman for me, but it is coinage, and furthermore it came from China. It is their coin. This one is made of iron and is called '*cash*'. They make them by the millions!"

Reza handed the coin off to Talon, who examined it with keen interest. It was a small, round, flat item, with a square hole in its middle. There were symbols all around the periphery that were very well defined, but they meant nothing to him.

"It is so well made!" he exclaimed, comparing it with the coins that existed in this part of the world and further west in Byzantium, and the even cruder coins of his own country. He tossed the coin back to Imaran.

"Imaran and I have travelled there, just the once when we were young boys. You have never seen a country quite like it. It is... another world."

Boulos seemed to have made up his mind. He came to the point very quickly. "Do you wish to join us, and are you able to do so, Suleiman?" It was a blunt question that raised the eyebrows of his two brothers, but he shrugged off their concerns about good manners and stared hard at Talon. There was an expectant silence from all in the room as they waited for his reply.

"If the Jews of the bazaar are able and willing to honor my chits, then I have the funds to not only purchase the ship but to supply it and more," Talon informed them.

He sensed the tension leave the others.

"Then you will need a good captain and crew. We will help with that," Boulos stated briskly.

Imaran smiled. "I am impressed that you can afford this, Talon. It is a good thing, as there is much in the way of riches that await you in these distant lands. At least you will have a new ship that will not be filled with rats and nasty insects."

Then he laughed. "They will arrive, of course; they can smell a ship with food on it a hundred leagues away. However, for the first voyage you will not have this problem."

"When do you intend to leave for... Lamu? Or is it Zanzibar?" Talon asked them.

"It will be the Lamu archipelago. The island of Pate is where the Sultan's palace is located, but Lamu is where we find the markets. The winds are right for a journey south at present, so any time soon. We intend to sail south with the *Kaws* wind that will blow us all the way southwest to the island of Lamu, which is off the coast of Bilad Al Zanj," Imran informed them.

"We will stay there for a month, buying the ivory and Myrrh, trading for the gold, and picking up some prime slaves, and then we must catch the wet *Azyab* wind that will bring us home. If we intend to go on to Kulam Mali to the southeast of Al Hind, or beyond to Kalah Bar where the spice is to be found, then we cannot pause for long here in Muscat. We will stop at Raysat off the region known as the Dhofar and pick up some olibanum," he continued. Talon knew by now that olibanum was Frankincense.

"At Raysat we will also pick up horses which have come from the Sana and further north in the Arab deserts. These we will take to Al Hind and sell for an outrageous profit," Boulos said with a grin, rubbing his hands.

"The Indians don't breed horses of their own?" Reza asked with surprise.

"For some reason horses sicken and die there, like flies. They cannot feed them the right food, nor grow it, nor can they breed them. In the hot, wet, heat of that land the animals suffer. The natives, however, seem impervious, although there is much disease."

"You will see, Suleiman, that the land there is mostly jungle which is full of fierce and terrible animals; and you feel as though you are drowning in the air, it is so dense," Imaran added.

Chapter 5
An Eye for an Eye

The discussion was interrupted by a clamor at the gates. They could hear shouts and the voices of men calling to one another. Every man in the room stood up immediately, their hands on their weapons. Within moments, one of the black men who stood guard at the gates to the compound came rushing to the entrance of the room where the group of men were standing. He brought with him one of the *syce* from the stables. After one look at the ragged and shaken man, Talon was sure he knew what had happened.

The *syce* went down on his knees. His turban was askew, his clothes torn and bloody. He looked exhausted and very frightened.

"Allah protect us! They have taken Jasmine, my lords!" he babbled. "They have killed the head *syce* who tried to stop them, and they hurt the boy!" He began to weep.

Boulos was the first to react. "What happened to the boy?" he demanded.

"They took out his eye, lord!" the man clutched his hands together, lifted his grimy, tear-stained face up to Allam and wept. The men in the room stared at him, aghast, and then at one another. "God protect us, but why did they do that, to a small boy?" Allam finally asked.

"To send a message," Imaran ground out between his teeth. "An eye for an eye, brother. I warned you."

Boulos stood up; he was in a towering rage. "This has to be Najem's work. It could be no one else! Why else would the boy be made to suffer like this? He meant to have revenge, and now the boy has paid for it." He shook his fist in the air. "Then we, too, will have revenge!" he shouted.

"We must go at once to the stables," Imaran said. "Fetch our horses!" he shouted. Servants and *syce* rushed about to do his bidding. The disturbance had woken their father, who now stood on the balcony overlooking the courtyard. Behind him was a small crowd of frightened women. He demanded to know what had occurred. Imaran explained quickly, and then followed the rest of them out to the main courtyard where the horses were waiting.

"The boy will surely need attention to his eye," Talon said, thinking of Doctor Haddad. Reza anticipated him. "I'll go and fetch him. I know he will come for the boy, no matter what the hour." He galloped off without waiting. The rest of them rode post haste to the stables. When they arrived, Talon glanced across the polo field towards the villa where his family were housed. He noticed lamps were glowing along the wall. They must have heard the disturbance but had been wise enough to remain where they were until they knew what was going on.

All was chaos at the stables, with the numerous *syce* running about aimlessly, tearing their hair and wailing. The horses and the camels what were stabled were roaring and stamping as they too reacted to the panic all around them.

The riders hurriedly dismounted and were drawn to a small group of workers clustered about a mat, upon which lay a small figure that twitched and wailed. Allam was the first to reach the table and he exclaimed in horror at the sight. His boy Ismail was lying limp and very much in pain, a bloody rag over his right eye. Little had been done by the *syce* to help him, other than to lay him on some sacking. Talon noticed there were other figures lying in the dust which did not move. No one had thought to cover them or move them in the chaos.

Boulos shoved the crew aside, bellowing at them, "By God, you worthless fools! Get out of the way and stop this noise. I want to see!" The *syce* tumbled out of the way and fell to their knees. One of them, the oldest, a man with white hair and a greying beard, stammered out an explanation.

"They came in the dark, lord," he wailed, waving his thin, stick-like arms about. "There was no warning, and the guards were quickly overwhelmed." He swallowed nervously, his Adam's apple jerking. "None of us heard anything until we heard the screams of Ismail here, by which time the bandits were gone with Jasmine!" He wrung his hands and hung his head.

"None of you heard anything at all?" Boulos demanded. He sounded incredulous.

"They came on horses out of the night and knew exactly where she was stabled, lord. They were so quick!" one of the other *syce* muttered in a frightened tone.

"They killed all the guards," Imaran said in a matter of fact voice. "Allam, were these real guards," he jerked his thumb at the prone figures, "or were they just some of your servants you told to be here?"

Allam looked embarrassed, but before he could respond, Ismail began to twitch and wail more than ever. Boulos reached over and held him down. "Talon, is that uncle of yours going to come? This boy could die if we don't help him."

Just as he spoke, a group of people hurried out of the darkness from the direction of the villa. It was Reza, and with him was Doctor Haddad, accompanied by Rav'an. They carried torches and some small leather bags. The Doctor, looking tousled and agitated, hurried over to kneel down beside the mat. "Give me light and space!" he ordered. He was so authoritative that both were provided immediately.

Boulos and Allam issued sharp commands, and the loitering *syce* set to work collecting the bodies of the three unfortunate guards and calming down the restless animals. Meanwhile, Haddad beckoned Rav'an over and opened the bag that she handed to him. He took out a vial of liquid and lifted up Ismail's head. "You must drink some of this. It will help with the pain," he told the squirming boy.

Ismail swallowed the few drops that the Doctor gave him and then settled back, his hands fluttering with the pain. "You must not touch the wound under any circumstances," the doctor ordered him. "I shall be treating you, and if God wills it, then you will get better, although..." He left the rest unsaid. Ismail would no longer have a right eye.

Haddad turned to Allam, who was hovering nearby. "I want him to be taken to our villa, where it is much cleaner and where I can supervise his recovery."

Within minutes the boy was being lifted onto a makeshift stretcher and transported towards the distant villa. Rav'an, with a quick look and a nod to Talon and Reza, hastened to join the doctor accompanying the stretcher.

It was a subdued group of men who stood at the stables with the torches burning around them and discussed the event.

"It had to be Najem; this is his handiwork for sure!" Allam said angrily.

"Of that we can be sure, but now we have to find the camel, unless he has chosen to destroy her too," Imaran snarled.

Allam gasped. "He wouldn't do that, would he?" he asked his brother with anguish in his voice.

"Oh yes, he might. He is that kind of person. He would cut off his nose to spite his face, that man," Boulos said.

"Do we not have recourse to the Caliph for something like this? The Caliph wants to breed her!" Allam said. He was almost wringing his hands as he saw a fortune disappearing into the sand.

"Where does Najem live?" Talon asked.

"I can show you in the morning when we go there to confront him," Boulos informed him, "but you can be sure he will not have the camel inside his compound. It will be long gone, either into the desert or dead and abandoned somewhere. His spite knows no bounds."

Talon and Reza glanced at on another. "We could try to track them in the morning, unless the wind covers their tracks," Reza offered.

Imaran shook his head. "Our best chance is to either find out directly from Najem, who might be prepared to give her back for a ransom, or to find out from one of his men where they have taken the camel," he said.

Talon again looked at Reza, who nodded. "May we come with you to the house of Najem tomorrow, Boulos?" Talon asked him.

*****

The next morning after prayers, Talon and Reza joined a small cavalcade of men and the three brothers to ride across the Northwest area of Muscat to the encampment of Najem, which boasted a small fort that could accommodate the sheik and his family and retainers, should danger threaten. Both Talon and Reza became very watchful, taking stock of the number of men around the camp, the horses and the guards on the tall walls of the fort.

The cavalcade halted well before the camp, and waited. It was not long before a group of mounted men with two in the lead came galloping up to them, sending up a small cloud of dust behind them. They were desert Arabs in flowing robes mounted on beautiful horses, which pranced as they neared the visitors.

"*Salaam Aliekom,*" Imaran called out. He assumed the role of leader, as he was the eldest of the brothers.

"*Wa-Alaikum-Salaam,*" one of the men called back. "What may we do for you?"

"We wish to talk to Sheik Najem al Khulood. God willing, he is here and will see us."

The man looked them over for a few seconds and then muttered something to his companion, who turned his horse and rode back towards the fort.

"Please honor me by accompanying me to our poor abode," the first man replied. He swept his hand behind him and led the way back to the tented camp. The other rider had disappeared through the gates of the fort. Talon noticed that there were a many tents all around the building, some even against the walls, giving the camp a cluttered effect. Strings of camels stood or squatted in among the tents; there were also horse lines off to the side.

They were led towards a large tent, where they dismounted. Boulos told the lead *syce* to stay mounted and to hold their horses, then he and the others were invited to be seated on cushions in a circle on a carpet provided by their host, who called himself Sayf-ul-Mulk. Talon looked him over carefully. He had heard that Najem's family was from Yemen, so it might be that this man was too. He carried a fine Khanjar knife tucked into the *wazar* around his waist in the Omani manner.

No one said anything before the tea was poured into small porcelain cups and offered. Each guest took one and sipped the bitter brew, taking small lumps of hard sugar from a bowl in the middle.

There was little small talk. Everyone in the tent knew why they were here and it would not help tempers to pretend. However, the minutes drew out to the point where Boulos let some of his impatience show on his face. Just as it seemed as though Imaran and Boulos were on the edge of leaving, which would have been a horrendous breach of manners, there was a commotion at the gates of the small fort and a group of men walked towards the tent with Najem in the lead. All the guests stood up, and the words and kisses of greeting were performed by men who loathed one another.

When the introductions were completed and they had all reseated themselves, they drew near to the subject in hand. Najem opened the discussion.

"Word has reached me that there was an incident lat night," he said, his fierce eyes darting to Allam, who remained silent.

"There was an incident at our stables, if this is what you have heard," Imaran replied.

"What kind of incident would it have been?"

"People were killed, and one of our people was badly injured," Imaran responded.

Najem glanced at Sayf-ul-Mulk; it was as though there was a message there. Talon felt Reza tense near to him. He glanced out of the tent towards their two horses, where their bows were sheathed. If this became a fight he would feel a lot better with a bow in his hand, but Sayf-ul-Mulk remained where he was seated, looking unconcerned.

"I am horrified to hear this news. Allah protect us all from bandits who come and rob and kill," Najem stated, sounding pious. He sipped his tea as though waiting. "But why have you come to me?"

"It is thought that you might have heard who carried out this heinous crime, so we are here to find out," Boulos replied, his tone just short of an accusation.

Najem tensed, but appeared to discount the insult and said instead, "I shall most certainly put out the word of this crime, and my people will of course inform me, should there be any news. I was visiting relatives and only heard about this today, just before you came to visit me, in fact."

"There is one other thing," Imaran said slowly.

Najem looked up. 'What would that be?" he asked, a look of inquiry on his sharp features.

"The murdering thieves took the camel, the one that won the great race the other day."

Imaran had chosen his words carefully. The insult was a provocation, but still Najem refused to bite, although Talon noticed his eyes flashed and Sayf-ul-Mulk tensed, his hand creeping towards his Khanjar. Talon saw an imperceptible shake of Najem's head, and his lieutenant withdrew his hand. The tension in the tent had gone up several notches.

"I am appalled," Najem said, his tone tight. "Such an act merits punishment, and we shall do our utmost to assist you in finding the animal. Who could have done such a thing? God protect us all," he wore a pious expression that fooled no one.

Imaran gave him a hard stare. "Yes, it does merit punishment, and my father shall see to it that is meted out to those who deserve it. We wish to thank you for your hospitality and we will now leave you," he finished politely.

Najem bowed them out of the tent and then stood watching them as they left in a group.

No one said anything until they were on a low rise that overlooked the encampment, and then Boulos spat out a curse and said, "The snake! The lying snake!"

Imaran nodded his head in agreement and said, "Of course he ordered it, but then he made sure he was nowhere around when it happened."

"We know one thing at least," Talon interjected.

They turned to stare at him. "The camel is not at that encampment, and that is a surety. Not that it was likely to be there, but now we know for sure. However, I know someone who does know exactly where it is."

Boulos stared at him with a scowl on his heavy features. "Who would that be? You don't think Najem knows?"

Allam gave a sardonic chuckle. "It is possible that he doesn't, because then he would not be lying, nor perceived to be when and if the Caliph takes an interest in the crime. Talon, is it the other man, Sayf-ul-Mulk you are thinking of?"

"Yes it is, and I am sure of it."

Reza chimed in. "I was watching him carefully. He does the bidding of Najem in all things. Talon is right; he knows."

"Well, now all we have to do is to go up to him and ask where he has put the camel," Boulos said sarcastically.

"Quite right, we do have to ask him," Talon told him, ignoring the sarcasm.

*****

Back at their own villa, Talon and Reza checked in to see how the patient was doing. Rav'an met them at the head of the stairs. She looked tired. "The boy is resting. The good doctor has given him something for the pain," she told them.

"I am confident that the boy will live because of the doctor. God bless him," Reza said, and smiled at Fariba and Jannat, who had joined Rav'an.

"Reza and I have to leave for a while," Talon told them. He received sharp looks from Fariba and Rav'an. "You are not going to do anything rash?" Fariba demanded of him.

"No, my dear Auntie. We are just going back to the stables to find out as much as we can abut the incident," Reza told them with a grin.

Late that evening, as the sun was setting in a blaze of red behind the mountains, four men rode out of the stables. They made their way eastwards towards the encampment of Najem, but they went by a roundabout route and headed for the foothills to the west of the camp, keeping it in view but far enough away as not to draw attention to themselves. They looked just like any other desert Arabs going somewhere without hurrying.

When they were due south they came to a well-used trail that led off into the range of hills. Behind these hills, one of the *syce* had told Talon, there was a low plateau which was almost surrounded by hills and rough terrain. Here was where many of the tribesmen grazed their flocks and herds of camels, and even horses were allowed to run semi-wild. The old syce had volunteered that this was the most likely place the thieves would have taken Jasmine, because it was here that she would disappear among many other camels.

"There is a village called Al Amarat just on the other side of the hills. You will have to pass this, and then you are in open country," he had told them. "Find Jasmine for us, lord," he had begged.

Reza had put a hand on his thin shoulder. "We will do our best, *Insha'Allah,* old man."

Thanking the old *syce* and swearing him to silence, Talon and his companions, Reza, Youssef and Dar'an, had ridden out of the stables, ostensibly to visit their hosts at their house in Muscat. They were fully armed with their bows and were covered with cloth up to their eyes.

When they came to the trail they were seeking they halted. There was a half moon in the clear night sky, which Talon didn't like the look of, as it would hinder his work; but at least they would be able to see if anyone came out of the camp during the night. Both he and Reza agreed that it was a gamble to come here, as they might have already missed the departure of their man. They hid the horses in a gully well away from the road where their presence wouldn't be detected by anyone coming up the trail. They set to work muffling the hooves of their animals and put cloths over their noses to discourage them from making any sounds if they heard other animals on the trail below.

Then, while Dar'an and Youssef stayed with the horses, Talon and Reza went back to a rise above the trail and lay on the ground so that only their heads were above the rise. They could just make out the fort and the encampment below them. Lamps were being lit and lights glimmered among the tents. It appeared as though the camp of Najem was going about its evening routine innocently enough.

It was a good hour before Reza nudged Talon and whispered. "Something is going on down there."

Talon shook his head to help clear his vision and stared down into the dusk. Sure enough, there was some activity in among the tents. A rider emerged from the fort, although it was too far and too dark to see who it might be.

"They are coming this way," Reza murmured.

"There are five of them, from what I can see. They are going slowly so as not to draw attention to themselves," Talon replied.

They settled deeper into their cover and waited. Before long they heard the click of hooves on stones and peered into the gloom to see five riders wearing dark clothing and dark *massars* on their heads, walking their horses along the trail below. Talon strained his eyes to try to recognize any of them. It was hard, but the moonlight caught the features of one man he knew. It was Sayf-ul-Mulk who led the small party. He nudged Reza, who touched him on the arm. He, too, had seen their man.

They allowed the party to go by and watched them for several hundred paces before moving themselves. They hurried to the boys and their horses and mounted up. Then with great care they left the gully and took up the trail to follow the party ahead of them. Talon was satisfied that his group made very little noise as they followed their quarry, but before long they could hear the others. They slowed down and listened to the low murmur of conversation and the tread of hooves ahead of them. The men seemed confident that they were unobserved, oblivious of anyone following them, but Talon and Reza were very watchful. The pursued could become the ambushers with little warning, and they themselves could become victims.

With great caution they trailed the five men ahead of them over the narrow pass and down the slopes to the low plateau beyond. A cluster of mud huts loomed out of the darkness, but it was easy to ride past. The inhabitants were either asleep or were not inclined to challenge anyone riding through at this late hour.

Then Reza gave a low hiss and held up his hand for them to stop. He pointed ahead towards a small group of low, dark tents set some way off the main trail. Their quarry had left the trail and were now riding at a faster pace toward the tents. Some figures emerged from one tent to stand waiting with lamps held high.

Talon and his group rode their horses into the cover of a clump of scrub and low thorn trees. There was not much to be had on this side of the hills, but this would suffice until they knew what was happening.

Talon dismounted, and so did Reza. They handed their reins to the two boys and told them to wait out of sight of both the trail and the tents.

"We will be back in a while. Just keep the horses from making any noise," Reza told Yosef.

"And be ready to leave in a hurry," Talon added.

Yosef gave a low chuckle, "Go with God," was his response.

Bows in hand, they scurried along the narrower trail towards the tents. Their quarry had dismounted and followed the occupants of the tent inside. The dull glow of lamps shone through the material, and from time to time shadows moved about.

As they approached the tented community, Talon looked about him for any signs of animals other than the horses hitched to a rope line. Just behind the tents he discerned a group of what could only be camels clustered together. He touched Reza on the arm to get his attention and pointed. Reza nodded; he had already seen the camels. They changed course and headed towards the animals, being very careful not to make any sound. There were guards on the periphery of the camp, but they were not very attentive. It was an easy thing to slip past them and make their way towards the camel lines.

"How will I recognize the camel?" Talon had asked the old man.

"She has a scab on the left side of her neck. Another camel bit her and drew blood when she was racing. It will not have healed so quickly. You should take these with you, lord." He had handed Talon a couple of small sweet cakes. "She loves these and will follow you anywhere to have one."

As they crouched in the scrub forty paces away and down wind from the camels, they searched for the guards who would most certainly be there. It didn't take long to spot them. Two men were squatting near the camel lines, one at the end nearest the tents and the other right next to one of the camels. Talon breathed a sigh of relief; that had to be Jasmine. All was quiet. None of the animals seemed to have smelled them.

Reza whispered, "We need a diversion. We can't just walk up and take her."

"Perhaps we can," Talon responded, "Wait, they are coming."

The two of them blended into the darkness and watched. A small group of men had emerged from the tents and was making its way towards the camels. Talon reasoned it had to be Sayf-ul-Mulk coming to check on his master's prize. Holding lanterns high, the group walked up to the camel lines. Words were exchanged, then one man went up to the camel next to the second sentry. The man reached out to pat her, but the animal snapped at him, making him pull his hand back sharply. He cursed and stood back. They could clearly hear him. "You cursed animal!" He shook his head disgustedly and turned to the others. "Our master wants to keep her and breed her, but I think she should disappear and become meat!"

There was laughter at this and the group returned to the tents, leaving the guards with their charges. Talon and Reza crouched in the bushes near to a palm tree and waited until the guards had settled back down into their habitual squat, then gave them time to doze off.

"It looks like our friend is staying the night," Talon whispered to Reza.

"What do you want to do about him?" his friend responded.

"One of us should make sure he does not leave this place while the other takes the camel away," Talon said.

*****

The two sentries never knew what happened. Both were half asleep when their killers came upon them, and then the one nearest the tents was convulsing with a cut throat while the other, Talon's victim, voided his bowels and was still when his neck was broken with a swift and savage jerk.

Reza, having completed his work, made his way to the tent where he knew Sayf-ul-Mulk would be sleeping. Talon, having checked that it was Jasmine by sliding his hand down her neck and finding the scab, drew out a small cake and slipped it between her eager lips. She grunted with pleasure and then began to follow him as he walked off into the desert in the general direction of the horses, tugging gently on the rope while she padded quietly after him. The other camels paid them scant attention, being preoccupied with their feed or sleepily chewing their cud.

Meanwhile, Reza had cut his way into the tent from the back. He saw that it contained three sleeping men. There was no guard, but he intended to create a situation that would bring them running. He stood silent in the darkness and listened to the breathing of the men lying on mats near the center of the tent. His eyes were searching for something else. He found it without difficulty, and then one other item that he considered important for his plan.

He located Sayf-ul-Mulk easily and disposed of that man efficiently and silently. The only sound was the drumming of Sayf's heels for a couple of long seconds before the body went still. Reza went to the back of the tent, located the cooking oil, and began to make his preparations. He was several hundred paces away before any alarms went off. One of the sentries had wandered near to the tent and had become suspicious of the smell of smoke and the dull glow from within.

Looking into the tent he was confronted with a wall of smoke and flame that drove him back. He yelled the alarm and rushed back in to drag at the sleeping men, who woke up groggy from sleep, realized their predicament and piled out of the tent. One person, however, didn't move. Two of them rushed back in to try to rouse their leader. Failing at this, they dragged his limp body out of the tent. Then they saw what had happened and staggered back, aghast. Sayf-ul-Mulk was very dead.

By now the tent was going up in flames and threatening the nearby tents. The majority of the men were fully engaged in saving what they could of their possessions and had no time for anything else. However, one of the guards on the periphery noticed something odd going on just on the edge of the desert.

As Talon was walking Jasmine away, a man ran up to him and called out, "Where are you going with the camel, my friend?"

Talon, who had noticed him coming, called back in a conversational tone. "I am taking her home."

The man had come very close to Talon by now, his spear held at the ready. "You cannot do this, and as God is my witness, I shall stop you!"

Talon casually handed the rope that led Jasmine to the man. "Here, take it. She is a smelly creature. I can't abide camels anyway."

The astonished man forgot himself and took the proffered rope. Reza stepped forward out of the darkness and hammered the pommel of his knife against the man's temple; he didn't want any bloodshed to scare the animal. His victim dropped like a stone, and Talon, having retrieved the rope, tugged at Jasmine gently, then led the way off into the desert. Had anyone chosen to look in the right direction, they might have discerned in the distance, right on the edge of the illuminated area, several riders and a camel making their way north along the track towards the hills.

As it was, there was panic among the camel lines as the frightened animals tried to get away from the scorching heat of the fire. This resulted in chaos, as they shambled to their feet and pulled at their ropes, some of which gave way. The freed camels galloped off into the darkness, while those remaining contributed their roars of fear to the general bedlam going on all around them. The villagers were too preoccupied with the fire to notice much else.

Men shouted and rushed for their water skins to drop into the well near the center of the tented village, but that took time, and before long the tent that Reza had set on fire was burning furiously. Another tent close by was showered with sparks and burning material. It wasn't long before it, too, caught fire. The panicked shouts of the menfolk and the screams of frightened women and children filled the night.

*****

It took several hours of hard riding, and encouragement with sweet cakes to keep Jasmine loping along with them, before they arrived at the gates of the Mardini compound. Allam was awakened by the noise and hastened to investigate the disturbance. The gates were just being opened by the guards when he arrived.

"It is the foreigners, lord. They have brought Jasmine the camel!" they exclaimed excitedly when the doors were opened.

Allam barely recognized Talon and Reza and two of their retainers, as they were muffled up so that only their eyes were visible, but before he could say anything Talon called out to him.

"Take the camel, Allam, and guard her well. We must go!" Without another word he wheeled his horse, and he and his men disappeared into the night, leaving the camel with one of the surprised guards.

Allam, astonished though he was, had the presence of mind to call out, "Close the gates! Quickly now!" The servants hastened to obey, and then he stared hard at the camel. He knew instinctively that it was Jasmine, but he walked up to the restless animal, laboring from the forced march, and ran his hand down her neck to make sure. He nearly choked with emotion as he stroked her warm furry hide, murmuring endearments while trying to get over his amazement.

"Someone go and find some sugar or cakes, and then we must hide her," he ordered. An eager servant rushed off to do his bidding. "You shall have a room in my house all to yourself, my darling," he told the impassive animal. Having recognized him, she began to calm down and gurgle quietly. A servant rushed up and handed Allam some pieces of cake, which he fed to Jasmine. She slobbered over the food contentedly.

"Allah be praised. You are safe now, my lovely. Perfectly safe, you are home," he crooned.

*****

Najem woke at dawn to shouts and loud banging on the gates of the fortress. As he raised his head, he disturbed something on the cushion where his head had been. He started in horror as though it were a snake lying there. With a gasp he threw himself off the bed to stand trembling with shock, staring back at a long slim knife embedded in the cushion, piercing a scrap of paper. After a long moment of fearful inaction he reached for the knife with a trembling hand, pulled it out, then drew the paper off its blade. Lifting it up he read the following short sentence: *An eye for an eye.*

The banging outside stopped, but now men were rushing up the stairs towards his chambers. The sound of running feet and men calling to one another was loud and urgent.

There was a peremptory knock on the door to his chamber, to which he barely had time to call out "Enter," before the doors slammed open and men poured into the room. Forgetting all decorum they began to shout in a wild babble of voices. He finally shouted them all down and beckoned to one who had gone off during the night with Sayf-ul-Mulk. He was covered in dust and sweat and looked badly shaken.

"What is it, Sameer? What is this disturbance all about?" Najem demanded, glaring at Sameer, who fell to his knees.

"Lord, we were visited last night by Djins. They... they took the camel. They set a huge fire and several of our men were killed."

"By God, did you not see who did this?" Najem demanded. His ashen face betrayed his shock. On top of the knife in his pillow and the message, he was almost ready to believe Sameer's ridiculous tale of Djins.

"Where is Sayf-ul-Mulk?" he demanded, thinking that he might at least get some sense out of his faithful retainer.

"Lord, we found Sayf-ul-Mulk dead."

"Dead you say? How!"

"He had a knife buried in his right eye!"

Najem felt faint; this was no coincidence. For the first time in his life he was very frightened. "Get me some water!" he croaked. "And then get the rest of these idiots out of my sight."

He sat down on a low table, paying no attention to the brass tray and cups that he had just dislodged, which tumbled onto the floor with a ringing crash.

Chapter Six

Pate Island

Their ship had been following the coast of Africa for almost a week, standing out to sea with the land just in sight, when the thin outline of the last string of islands abruptly disappeared, leaving a wide gap. Talon, who had become used to their presence, was apprehensive, but the captain looked pleased.

"We have almost arrived," he stated with satisfaction. He glanced up at the sun, and then forward at the two ships ahead of theirs and said, "We should be changing course soon."

When Talon looked puzzled, he waved towards the West. "We will soon change course and sail due west. The wind will allow us to do this for some four hours or more, after which the wind will change direction completely and come from the land. We need to be in port by then."

He shouted to the crew and sent them scurrying along the deck to haul in the sails. The ship heeled slightly as it came round, and before long they were heading directly towards the coast. Soon the land on their right re-emerged over the horizon, but now to their starboard side.

*****

A few weeks before, Captain Dandachi had put the craft through some maneuvers when they first sailed on a test run near Muscat and had pronounced the ship a well-balanced craft. He'd seemed pleased, although he had maintained his habitual frown, made more forbidding by his dense, graying beard. He'd had the crew move some of the ballast stones about to balance the ship and to provide a little more lift to the bows, but there had been no need for significant adjustments.

"We need a name for this ship, Master Talon," he'd said, looking with pride back at the vessel as they landed on shore.

"*El Bakhar El Nasir*," Talon told him. *Sea Eagle.*

The captain nodded his head. "It is not a traditional name, but it is a good one. She flies like an eagle of the sea. I shall have the name carved and placed on the bows."

So the name was given.

Both Talon and the captain had followed a grizzled old crewman called Waqqas around below decks on a slow but concentrated search for leaks. Waqqas had held the lantern high against the sides and alongside the stitched strakes to check for seepage. While they had discovered several, both the crewman and the captain had dismissed them as normal, saying they would seal themselves eventually. They found only one leak that caused concern, and the captain informed Talon that when they were back at the shipyards he would have that remedied.

Talon had been impressed with how maneuverable the ship was both in port and at sea; it needed only a skeleton crew on board.

On the voyage, the captain had used the following wind to full advantage, so that all three triangular sails were taut and full-bellied, pulling them along directly ahead. The new ship seemed to race through the seas as it followed the other two large ships, with the brothers Mardini leading the way south towards the port town of Pate situated off the coast of the great land mass of Africa.

There had been one mysterious item the captain had persuaded Talon to purchase. Just before they sailed, three camels had arrived, laden with round earthenware pots about the size of honey melons. The neck of each small pot was stoppered with wax, and the crew were told to handle each one very carefully as they made a human chain and brought them aboard. The captain paid off the camel drover with coin that Talon had provided, and then came back on board the ship.

Talon was very curious about what the pots might contain. "They are our only real weapon against pirates, Master Talon," the captain told him. He showed one to Talon and Reza, handling it very carefully. "This is oil that burns on the sea when set alight. A single one can burn a ship to the water if it is used properly."

Talon registered surprise. "Greek Fire!" he exclaimed in astonishment.

"You know of this?" the captain asked him. "I believe it came from the people of Roms originally, but now it is used widely by our merchant people. Master Boulos told me to provide you with some. Pirates infest the coasts of Al Zanj and Al Hind."

Talon had spent the next few minutes explaining to Reza the devastating effects of the strange oil. He looked at the pots speculatively. They were for throwing, he surmised, but they needed something to set them alight. He would have to ask the captain how that was done.

*****

Talon noticed that the leading ships had already changed course as they themselves moved towards the West. The change of direction brought the women onto the deck with Reza, who had been below. Talon waved them up onto the rear deck and told them what was happening.

"We have almost arrived at Pate," he informed them. "The captain tells me we have to make good speed to land before tonight or the wind will keep us out at sea, and he doesn't want that."

"Where is Rostam?" Rav'an demanded. She pushed back some strands of hair that had managed to escape her light veil.

"He is up at the front of the ship," Talon told her. "Tarif, bring Rostam back to this deck," he called to one of the seamen below. The man nodded and grinned. They had adopted the boy as one of their own, patiently answering his incessant questions with helpful instructions and amused grins. Rostam's Arabic was improving by the day.

The captain himself had not been immune to the boy's charm and had instructed him on the behavior of the sea with obvious delight. Rostam had solemnly shared with Talon and Reza the wisdom provided by the captain on the subject of navigation. Talon relearned how to use the *Kamal* from the captain and joined with Rostam in calling out the names of the nighttime constellations, treating it as a game, but the boy soaked up the information avidly. He was even better than Reza at remembering their names, and scornful of a mistake made by either his father or uncle.

The crew would point to the birds flying overhead and tell him what they were called, and just as importantly, why they were so far out to sea. They helped him understand the nature and moods of the sea on which they sailed. Most of the crew had sailed this route several times, so they knew the features of the land over to their west and the sea currents through which they sailed.

"See those birds that dive into the water and fly nearby?" the captain said to the three of them on one occasion. "That means we are only about ten or so leagues from dry land, as that is where they live. Few birds live on the sea far from land; they must return to nest, whether on island or mainland."

The captain would indicate the color of the water, both when they were out of sight of land and while they sailed towards the coast.

"It changes color because it is either a current, as we have seen when we were far out from land, or lighter blue because it is shallow. When you see brown in the water it means that there is a river and it has rained far inland, bringing silt and sand out to sea with the water following deep channels. You can even test it and see that it is still sweet, which will again tell you how close you are to a delta."

Rostam would peer over the side of the ship, excitedly pointing to the fish that sometimes accompanied the vessel as it ploughed through the waves. He became enthralled by the small fish that seemed to fly along just above the surface of the water, to plunge and then take off again to fly many times their own length before diving back into the water. He would lean over the transom watching them for hours. Once he shouted in his high voice, "Papa, there is a huge fish over there!"

Talon walked over to the side and saw a monster fish unlike anything he had ever seen before. It was enormous, with an accompanying shoal of smaller fish, languidly moving through the water just below the surface. Talon experienced a shiver of fear when he first saw it; its body seemed to be almost the same length as their ship, but the captain having come over to look reassured him.

"It is harmless and only eats very tiny sea creatures, not even fish. I have never heard of one of these attacking a ship. It is feeding on the currents that come south with the trade winds," he told them. "There are infinitely more dangerous creatures than that in these seas," he added as an afterthought.

Sure enough, they saw other large fish which the crew and the captain warned were very dangerous, able to gulp a man whole if he fell into the sea. On one exciting occasion, a huge glistening shape with a sword-like point on its nose leapt high into the air only a few hundred paces from the ship. Everyone stopped what they were doing and rushed to watch. It disappeared with a splash, only to reappear far ahead of them as it again rose high into the air in a flurry of spray.

"Look! It has a fan on its back!" Rostam yelled, pointing.

"It is beautiful!" Rav'an breathed to Talon, who was standing next to her at the time.

She glanced up at him and then asked playfully, "Why, Talon, you look pensive. Do you not like the sea?"

"I am in awe of the sea and its creatures," he responded seriously. "But I am always a little fearful, because it is so unpredictable."

He'd had ample reason to remember that statement a week later when the captain pointed to the East. "We have run into the 'mad waves,'" "he stated, with real apprehension in his voice. "You must hang on to something and do not let go! Allah protect us now!"

Talon looked towards where he was pointing, but before he could say anything the waves were upon them. Without warning, they found themselves sailing in turbulent waters. The waves seemed to Talon to be small mountains: they sprang up with no foam on top. The valleys were as frightening as the tops, for the ship plunged into them as though they would never come up. Some of the crew began to sing.

Barbar and Jafuna, mad are thy waves,
Juna and Barbara, see their waves.

The men on deck had to hang onto whatever they could while the strange, monster waves rose and fell and then disappeared, leaving the ships in rough water but not the terrifying mountains and valleys they had just experienced.

Fortunately, the others were all below when this phenomenon struck, but it left Talon shaken. More than ever he resolved to respect the sea and its unpredictable behavior.

*****

Now as they approached the islands, the captain asked them all to keep clear of the steersmen while they prepared to sail into the shallows of a wide bay. He posted two reliable men right up in the bows to look out for reefs. Within a short while, they could discern the shape of a low stretch of land ahead of them, which the captain said was Pate Island.

Talon stood next to the captain, who pointed to a line of white surf ahead. "That is the surrounding reef for the entrance to the bay. The brothers Mardini know the way in, and we must follow them closely or we risk having our ship torn apart by the coral on either side, as it is only just below the surface,"

He turned away and bellowed orders at the crew, who dropped the main sail and its boom so that the ship now moved with only the front and the after sails to drive it forward. The captain adjusted their path to point directly at a space between the surf, where the other two ships had just passed without mishap. It quickly became their turn. Their ship was now sailing directly towards what Talon apprehensively saw as an obstacle rather than a pathway. Although the gap was wide, it was still intimidating for the uninitiated. The white surf and roar of the waves crashing onto the reef water on either side of them became louder and the swell increased, lifting the ship noticeably, but Dandachi held the vessel steady and they moved smoothly through the gap in the reef.

Rostam was leaning over the side watching the sharp fangs of the reef go by, as were Rav'an, Reza and Jannat. All were silent as the captain and the crew took them into calmer water ahead. The two women gasped with relief, while Rostam squeaked with excitement. Talon, remembering another time in far off Byzantium, breathed more easily and glanced at the captain, who nodded and gave a small smile of satisfaction.

"God is with us," he said briefly.

The calm on the other side of the reef was a relief for all, but it was also full of human activity. There were many ships and boats, both large and small, plying the bay. Safa al Dandachi pointed to his left towards a cluster of small white buildings nestling amongst the vivid green foliage against a low rise in the land. "That is the port over there," he informed Talon.

The smells and noises of the land became noticeable. The island was almost completely covered in dense jungle, apart from where the hand of man had carved out a space for buildings, and there were cultivated patches where men had made inroads. The shoreline above the pure white sands of the beaches was lined with tall, slim palm trees, their gentle rustling audible even from a distance of several hundred paces.

As they approached the island itself, they could hear the calls of creatures from the dense foliage. Bird calls intermixed with barks from high in the canopy filled the air, while the smell of rotting vegetation wafted across the water. The water itself was clearly the main highway, as dhows and fishing boats moved purposefully in all directions, the color of their sails ranged from dingy white to dark brown.

Men called up from their small fishing boats.

"*Salaam Alaikum.* Where are you from?"

"We come from Muscat!" several of the crew called back to them.

"*Insha'Allah* you had a good journey?"

"God was kind. The sea was not bad."

They sailed on. The water was translucent as a bowl of spring water. It seemed almost as if they were moving on air. The two women and Rostam were enthralled; leaning over the starboard rail, they watched the jungle shoreline go by and stared down into the water. The myriad of colorful fish that swam in shoals, flicking nervously from one coral outcropping to another or simply drifted next to some jumble of coral, held their fascinated attention as their ship, following closely on the wake of the other two vessels, moved steadily towards the anchorage. They pointed at large white birds that stood fishing on the edge of the water with long beaks, and waved at the sea gulls that drifted over their heads on air currents to investigate this new vessel, their beady yellow eyes watching for scraps, quite unafraid of the beings on its deck.

Talon and Reza stood next to the captain and observed his every move, listening carefully to every command. To Talon this was not only an expedition but a process of study. He remembered Henry, one of his captains in the inner sea, who had told him that he should learn all he could about the sea and ships, as it would make the whole experience less nerve-wracking for him. Well, now he was doing so.

They could see a small forest of masts and sails ahead of them, behind which was the crescent of the port itself. It did not strike Talon as a very significant place, but the captain had assured him that this was the port that represented the vast hinterland, and all the goods of Africa came here.

"This port and that of Lamu are like a spring of riches, from which comes gold, ambergris, ivory, skins and slaves," he told Talon.

Talon recalled the keen interest of the Egyptian merchants and their greed for the riches drawn from this dark and mysterious land. This, then, was one of the spigots of the Omani wealth, he reflected.

The houses along the water's edge were of lime washed or bare cut coral blocks, giving the impression of a row of flat teeth, some of which were bad or rotten, while others retained their natural whiteness. The white sands that sloped into the water were dazzling, even in the afternoon sunlight, although long shadows had already begun to stretch across the water from the low hills beyond the harbor. It was evening and would soon be dark.

Talon felt sweat trickling down his back. Although there was still a light sea breeze, within the confines of the lagoon the air was stifling hot and still. Even the deck beneath his sandals was warm. Shouted commands brought his attention back to the ship itself. They were about to drop anchor alongside the other two ships, which had now dropped their fore and after sails and come to a stop.

He noticed Boulos standing on the after deck of his own ship and waving.

"Bring your ship alongside," he called over. Talon nodded and glanced at the captain, who had already issued orders to do so. A line was thrown and then another, and slowly their ships were drawn closer, until finally they bumped gently and the crews tied the two vessels together.

A wide plank was dropped across the remaining space between the ships with a clatter, and then Boulos strode across to join them.

"*As-Salaam-Alaikum!*" he boomed. "I hope you enjoyed your first voyage in your new ship?" he asked, as he embraced Talon and then Reza.

"*Wa-Alaikum-Salaam,*" they responded in unison.

He nodded politely to Rav'an and Jannat and then led the way back up to the stern of the vessel.

He pointed towards the shoreline. "It will be time for evening prayers soon, so there is no point in going ashore today. We will wait until tomorrow."

He began to point out the features of the town, starting with a large building perched on a small rise to the left of the main town. "That is the palace of the sultan. We will have to go and pay our respects tomorrow, and of course pay some bribes to that venal old pirate, the Vizier, before we can go and have a look at the warehouses and the slave barracoons on the island of Lamu," he told Talon and Reza, who had joined them. Talon noticed Imaran striding across the deck of Boulos's ship to join them on theirs.

"That is the mosque." Boulos pointed to single minaret that stood above the rest of the buildings. "It is almost time for prayers, as the sun has set," he reminded them.

Indeed, the sun had gone below the jungle barrier behind the port, leaving only a red glow in the sky. Long, dark shadows from the tall palms and other trees now darkened the once shining beaches and crept across the water from ship to ship, and the light breeze from the sea had completely fallen off. The dense air, which had just been bearable with a light wind to move it, now became stifling. Talon hoped that the captain was right about the change of wind direction later, because he decided that sleep would be impossible in this heat, certainly in the confines of the cabins below.

Then they heard the call to prayers from across the water. *"Allah Akbaar!"* the call began. The men on the ship immediately began the ritual of the prayers. Boulos joined Talon and Reza on the top deck. The womenfolk had disappeared below to perform their devotions in private.

After prayers, the men were invited to go across to Imran's ship to have their evening meal, while the women and Rostam were left to their own devices on Talon's ship. Talon could tell that Rav'an chaffed at the separation, but she seemed resigned to this custom and simply waved them off.

Later that evening, Talon and Reza came back to the ship and found Rav'an standing on the afterdeck staring at the town. Reza left Talon to go below, while he climbed the stairs to stand with Rav'an in silence, watching the dim lights of the ships swaying with the swell of the harbor and glimmering in the ripples of the dark water. There were several clusters of lights to be seen on land where people congregated.

Above them, clouds moved southward, obscuring the crescent moon from time to time and revealing the dense wash of the stars.

"It will rain tomorrow, I suspect," Talon remarked in a low tone as he inhaled her scent. Her hand was on the rail, slim and pale in the moonlight. He placed his on top and squeezed.

"This place is like a paradise," she said. "Can you hear the noises of that forest over there? There must be many animals within."

Just then something hooted from the trees. The sound was followed by some agitated chattering, which died out as quickly as it had started.

"This is a strange place," Talon remarked. "I am very glad that I could bring you."

"I, too, my Talon, but I chaff at the restrictions these Arabs place on us women. I cannot go ashore without you, or even perhaps with you, and then I must be covered from head to foot or someone will complain."

"Let us take care of the business with the sultan tomorrow, and then perhaps we can look around together. We will take Rostam with us. I do not see very much here. I understand that the real country where everything comes from is on the other side of this island," he said, trying to reassure her.

"Can you smell the land?" she asked as she leaned closer to him.

"The smell of the jungle is strong, but there is one scent that I cannot identify," he told her.

"Hah! That must be Nutmeg! Do you know what that is renowned for when taken as a powder?" she quizzed him with a smile as she turned to face him.

He shook his head. "Will you tell me?"

"Only if you come with me below to our private cabin." This last was said in a whisper.

When they had shut the door and were lying in each other's arms, she murmured with a wicked smile on her lips. "It is known as a very strong aphrodisiac, and wives should not take it unless they are with their husbands, nor should the husbands without their wives."

He chuckled as he kissed her. "Why, my Rav'an! You can see I need no aphrodisiac when I am with you. Just look at me!"

Chapter Seven
The Heyda

Talon and Reza joined Boulos and Imaran on their ship just as dawn was lighting up the eastern horizon. The sky was cloudy, promising a hot day with some rain later in the day. All the men were dressed in their best Omani clothes. They wore clean white robes with ornate worked leather belts with expensive silver clasps. Each man carried a sword, as befitted his station, but also the precious *Khanjar* knives so prized by the Omani tribes people, tucked into the front of his belt.

Talon and Reza had been given theirs as presents by Allam on the day of their departure. As he handed them the finely worked knives in curved silver scabbards he had said, "You are Omani now, and you are my family. It is fitting that you should wear these with pride, my brothers, and go with God."

It had been a moving moment for Talon, as he had come to like Allam as a friend, and now they were brothers. The recovery of Jasmine had been a very emotional moment for the entire family. They had not been able to elicit any information from either Talon or his companions, but Nejem had left the vicinity of Muscat the very day the camel had been returned and had disappeared into the desert. Rumors had flown about the city, each one wilder than the last, but no one knew the truth. Allam's brothers had regarded Talon and Reza with a wary respect henceforth. Allam himself had insisted upon financing the cost of hiring a crew as a gift.

Now they approached the lime-washed gates of the sultan's palace, with a servant leading and a small group of armed sailors who came as bodyguards. Talon found himself sweating in the humidity; he wished it would hurry up and rain to clear the air. The flies were everywhere and seemed to be enervated by the increasing humidity and the promise of a storm; they settled on any exposed skin and nipped painfully.

They were on their way to pay their respects to the sultan, and to pay bribes to the vizier. There would be no trading should they overlook either of these essential steps of protocol

The guards let them into a spacious paved courtyard with a gurgling fountain and he noticed a small open air trough of water feeding it, probably from a spring up on the hillside behind the palace, he thought.

The moment they were in the yard waiting for the servant to announce them, Talon became aware that they were being watched. He glanced up to the second story and knew that the womenfolk of the sultan were there behind the ornamental shutters, observing their arrival, able to see out but not be seen. Doubtless they were discussing the newcomers; life being what it was for women in a harem, there was little else to do but gossip and stare out of their gilded cage, he surmised.

The servant arrived and shepherded the four men into the building. They were honored guests, for the Mardini were were successful merchants, so they would see the sultan ahead of the long line of other people awaiting audiences.

"Our family is well known, so we do not have to wait," Boulos explained to Talon ad Reza as they passed rows of supplicants, who glared at them in resentful silence as they went by. The sailors remained in the courtyard to squat in the shade of some frangipani shrubs and wait.

They were announced at the entrance of a chamber, which was airy and light, with a few rich furnishings around the lime-washed walls of its interior. There were huge polished brass lamps hanging off the black beams above their heads. The brass lamps had been perforated to allow light from candles to shine through. Carpets were strewn on the stone paved floor, and the smell of incense pervaded the air. Talon held his breath; he didn't want to sneeze, not in front of the august figure lounging in the large ebony throne at the end of the room. Behind him stood two huge black men dressed in decorated cotton *dishdashas*, wearing turbans and clutching long spears. They glowered at the newcomers.

They were expected to go to their knees like ordinary supplicants, even though Boulos and Imaran were well known and highly respected merchants. They marched up to the step and went down on both knees, then bowed to the very fat man on the chair above them.

The sultan was dressed in a simple white *thawb* that reached from his thick neck to his small sandaled feet, over which there was a very light *bisht,* or overdress of fine material. He wore a huge turban that Talon assumed must have taken an hour to wind onto his head. In the middle of the turban was an enormous silver broach encrusted with precious stones. His fingers were covered in jewelry, and the hem of the simple tunic was sewn with gold thread.

The sultan seemed pleased to see them. He gave a languid wave of a very elaborately made fly switch in acknowledgement of their presence.

"*As-Salaam-Alaikum*, your Highness. Peace be with you. How are you? We pray for your good health," said Boulos.

"*Wa-Alaikum-Salaam*, Allah has been kind. By the grace of God I am in good health. And how are you, Boulos?"

"Thanks be to God, I am well, Your Eminence. All is well."

"God be praised. Welcome to my hearth. How is your father?

"Thanks be to God, our father is older and wiser and well, and sends these miserly gifts to you as a token of his ardent esteem."

Imaran handed up a beautifully worked *Khanjar* knife. With the knife there was a silk wrapped package giving off the unmistakeable aroma of Frankincense.

The sultan smiled and touched the items, which were then passed back to a secretary.

"I am pleased with the gift. Please wish your father good health and happiness. What is the news from Oman?"

"No news, by the grace of God."

Boulos paused. "But..."

"Ah."

"The Seljuk Turks are making great gains in the Franks holdings of Byzantium, which means they'll leave Oman alone. Closer to home, the trade of horses with India is better every year."

"It is a good thing that the Indians cannot breed horses for themselves," the sultan remarked and waved his fly switch. "Boulos, you look well; and Imaran, you look thinner than the last time I saw you." The sultan's voice was a throaty rumble, as though it came from the depths of his huge belly. He smiled and bade them to be seated on the huge cushions that servants ran forward to place on the floor in front of him. They also brought sweetmeats, a sticky sweet jelly, and tea, which was served in tiny cups and poured from long spouted brass pots.

Talon listened to the usual words of flattery spoken by Boulos and his brother as they all sipped tea. The tea made him sweat but also cooled him. Despite the fans being rhythmically waved by some black slaves behind the sultan and on either side of the guests, the air had become stuffy, and even here the flies were plentiful.

The conversation eventually moved on to trade, so he began to pay attention.

"We are here, Your Eminence, to purchase slaves, and the teeth of the elephants, and more. We can, as you know, pay with gold or silver, whichever you desire."

Talon caught the gleam of avarice in the eyes that were almost hidden under the folds of flesh surrounding them.

"Of course. We are happy to see two of our best merchant friends here. Please inform my Vizier that you have my permission to trade."

Talon knew exactly what that meant. They would do nothing before they had parted with several small sacks of gold handed over to the vizier. The sultan derived income in this manner, and every trade as it was sealed meant that a percentage of the profit went to his coffers, and no one dared to forget it.

The sultan shifted on his chair in order to get a better look at Talon and Reza, who had sat quietly while the opening discussions were carried out.

The alert Imaran waved his hand towards Talon and said, "Your Eminence, may I introduce Talon Suleiman and his companion Reza, who are new to these parts and have travelled with us. Suleiman wishes to trade. We humbly beg that you will give your permission for him to do so."

"You do not look like an Omani," the sultan stated. He twitched his fly switch as he spoke, but his tone was friendly enough.

Talon smiled and bowed politely. "We are both from Persia, Your Highness. We are friends of the Mardini family, who have very kindly offered to show us the wonders of your country. Yes, I wish to trade and to learn from them."

More tea was delivered, and the conversation moved on to the question of the slaves who had arrived recently.

"I am informed that most of them are in good condition, but the crossing of the inland sea took more of them than expected." The sultan wheezed as he took a bite out of a sugary morsel of jelly and swallowed, his fleshy jowls wobbling.

"Are there enough, Your Highness?" Boulos asked. There was a tinge of concern in his voice.

"Hmm, there are fewer this time, so the price will be higher. Demand does not change from year to year, as you are very aware, but when the supply goes down...." The sultan left the sentence unfinished and shrugged.

Boulos glanced at Imaran. This was unexpected.

"What of the elephant teeth? The Nutmeg and the ambergris, Your Highness?"

"I cannot say, but you will find the markets full of these things, and more on the island of Lamu."

They discussed the prices of these various commodities, and also the pirates who infested the coastline.

"They come every year to the area and prey upon unarmed ships like yours, causing great disruption of the trade and even in my city," he almost whined. "What is one to do? *Insha'Allah* they will get the pox and die. May their private parts be infested by flesh-boring beetles!"

Boulos chuckled. "May it be so, your Highness. We will keep an eye open for these pirates."

It was time for them to depart. The sultan was sweating copiously on his perch and looked uncomfortable.

"May God protect you, Your Highness, and bring you good health and happiness," Imaran intoned as they walked backwards to the doors. The sultan waved them off with a pudgy hand.

"He looked ill," Imaran stated as they left the palace.

Talon agreed. He had noticed that the entire staff of the palace had seemed sullen and lethargic. He put this down to the fact that the heat of the day and the humidity were contributing to the general lassitude.

Their visit to the vizier in another part of the palace had been brief. After the usual interminable greetings and flattery, each of them had laid a small bag of gold on his table, and while they had waited for the scribes to write up their permits they had exchanged small talk with the vizier. The man was clearly overworked and seemed glad to get them out of his office so that he could deal with the numerous supplicants seated outside his doors. Wealthy and poor alike, they all came to him begging for an audience with the sultan.

*****

When they had picked up their sailors outside the gates and were on their way back down the road towards the beaches, Talon asked a question that had been nagging him.

"What sea was the sultan talking about, Boulos?"

"It is the great inland sea, Talon. Many of the slaves that come here have a long journey. They are captured in wars or raids, and then they must walk to the inland sea from the west of this huge country. When they get to the sea, the sultan's men put them in holds, lying side by side, then more on the decks above, until there is no more room. The journey takes several days, and they are not released nor fed until they arrive on this side. Many die on the way: the weak, the old, and the very young.

The dead are thrown to the crocodiles, which feed very well, and then the survivors must march some three to four hundred leagues to get here. It is a waste of good material. The overseers are greedy, but they calculate that even with losses like that they can still make a huge profit." He sounded disgusted, but Talon was aware that it was not out of any form of humanity for the wretched people undergoing this hellish experience. He was decrying the loss of a useful and profitable commodity.

Talon thought of his proud and courageous friend Panhsj, who lived in Egypt and shook his head.

That afternoon they returned to their ships and made ready to sail for Lamu, which was just south. This was where Boulos and Imaran would visit the slave markets, and where Talon hoped to be able to trade for the elephant teeth and other luxury goods which he would then take to India.

Leaving it to the captain to negotiate the shoals and the reefs, Talon went and stood at the very back of the vessel, deep in thought. He was in a somber mood when Rav'an, Jannat and Reza joined him there, staring back at the harbor as it receded. Rostam was at the front of the ship with some crew members, who were keeping a watch on him and answering his innumerable questions.

"You have been very quiet since you came back from the palace, my Talon. Is something wrong?"

"Boulos told us how the slaves get to the island of Lamu. It is not a pretty story," Reza explained.

Just as they rounded the final hook of the reef and began to sail south, Talon faced his friends. "I have not had time to tell you of a man I met while in Egypt," he said. "His name was Panhsj and we became very good friends. He was a slave who came from this country, although it was much further north. He was a warrior when captured..." Talon went on to tell them of his experiences in Egypt, leaving out parts that he was not ready to tell them about his association with the Templars, but more about his life as a slave himself in that country and his growing friendship with Panhsj, up to their final parting.

"So you see, I cannot trade as Boulos and Imaran do for these people. I see my friend in all of them, and it feels like something of a betrayal," he finished.

"When they get to their destinations they are often well treated, Talon," Reza pointed out, not unreasonably. "There is much money to be made in this trade; but if I had a friend like that I too, might hesitate. What does the Princess say?" He smiled and looked at Rav'an.

"Reza is right about one thing, Talon. It is a lucrative trade; but I for one do not like the smell hanging over Boulos's ship, and it is there because of the slaves. I do not want to see them die on our ship because we are not able to care for them, nor thrown overboard for the sharks, because that is what would happen." Her gray eyes flashed with determination. "Do what you think is best, Talon, but I think we should not do as Boulos and Imaran do."

"I hear you, my friends. I cannot say I am a particularly compassionate man, and slaves have been part of our lives everywhere, but that account of their passage made me think again. No, I shall not betray my friend. Instead we will load up with the other plentiful goods that should be awaiting us in the markets of Lamu."

*****

They anchored at the crowded harbor of Lamu and almost immediately disembarked, this time with Rav'an, Jannat and Rostam, who was held in check by Salem. The women were closely veiled, so as not to incur the wrath of the mullahs who stalked the streets of the grubby township. There was a shabby mosque just off the main street.

Boulos and Imaran wanted to check out the slave barracoons as soon as possible. "The sultan worried me about how many were available and of what quality, Talon," said Boulos "So we go there first, then we can go to the places of the merchants who have the other goods. They are not perishable." He grinned at his own words.

Talon decided to go along, more out of curiosity than anything else. He had no intention, however, of buying any of the slaves. He sent Rav'an and Jannat, with Rostam in tow, to visit the bazaar under the watchful eyes of Dar'an and Yosef, while he and Reza went off with Boulos and Imaran.

They were greeted by the smell of the barracoons a hundred paces before they saw them. The smell of urine, feces, and rotting vegetation made a heady stink that assaulted their nostrils and seemed to cling to their clothing. Talon, who was no stranger to stinking, confined spaces, didn't care to be reminded.

They heard the sound next, a muted mutter that filled the air. Talon could not decide whether it was the buzzing of the millions of flies or the voices of the people themselves. He realized it was both. From the people who were chained in groups behind the fences came the eerie moan of utter despair. It came from several hundred fettered black people who had not bathed nor had their barracoons cleaned out since the day of their internment.

The crude fences were made from branches of thorn trees with rough-cut stakes hammered into the red earth. The fences were too high to clamber over, and there were sentries posted at regular intervals with spears to deal ruthlessly with any that might still be considering escape. Although some shade was provided it was minimal, leaving most of the luckless people to lie out in the open still chained to one another under the burning sun. All over the compounds were large brown puddles of water that had not drained since the last rains. The surface of the water had a marble sheen and reeked of rotting filth.

Talon and the others pulled the corners of their turbans over their noses and mouths in an attempt to reduce the stench and keep the biting flies at bay. Just inside the gates, where guards could access them quickly, were randomly spaced bins of grain, millet and slops, from which the wretched people could feed themselves. The inhabitants gazed back at the passing men without any expression at all in their black eyes.

Talon wanted to hurry by, but Boulos and Imaran would pause from time to time to examine one or other of the potential slaves. They were soon joined by a hatchet-faced man in a dirty and torn striped cotton *dishdasha* that came down to his mud-bespattered sandals. He wore an equally filthy head cloth. He arrived with his own halo of flies and seemed oblivious to the utter squalor around him. In a barely civil voice he enquired what it was they might be looking for. He carried a short leather whip and looked as though he would not hesitate to use it on any one of the prisoners, male or female, all of whom were naked.

When Boulos explained in sharp tones who they were, the man immediately dropped his surly tone and became fawning, almost groveling at their feet. He hastened to lead them to the main market place where the bidding was already under way for the various batches of prisoners, and where later individual slaves with more potential who would garner a higher price would be offered for sale. As they followed the man, Reza muttered under his breath in Farsi, "*Pedar Sag!* That is some kind of rat from a shit pile."

Talon grinned. Reza could be blunt at times.

Bidding was in full swing by the time they arrived at the maidan. A wide platform had been erected in the middle, and upon this stage was a well-dressed man directing the process. It was speedy and efficient. The participants, buyers and seller alike, had done this many times, and he played the merchants with cunning and smooth words. A batch of slaves, sometimes only women or girls, or men only, would be hauled to their feet from among the others squatting all around the edges of the maidan to stumble up onto the stage; they would be hustled into a line by the slave overseers with curses and the snapping of the whips, after which the bidding would begin. The auctioneer would shout out the batch number and then a starting price.

Boulos and Imaran, leaving Talon and Reza on the outskirts, pushed forward and headed for the center for a better view of the merchandise. They were immediately involved in the bidding.

"Come on, Reza, I have seen enough." Talon turned away in disgust and began to head back the way they had come. Reza joined him in silence and they walked past the barracoons. Something caught Reza's eye as they passed a larger group of prisoners in one compound. He put a hand on Talon's arm to stay him and pointed.

The people were trying to pull away from a member of their group who was lying on the dusty red ground. They could only go as far as the chains permitted, but they seemed to be frightened of a woman who was unmistakably pleading with her outstretched hands as she lay in the sun. One of the other prisoners shuffled forward with a small gourd of water and left it next to her, but drew away hurriedly as though afraid to touch her. The woman tried feebly to pick up the gourd and drink from it, but then fell back, twitched, and seemed to go to sleep. The rest of the people tried their best to keep their distance and chattered in their language with much waving and, in some cases, wailing.

"That woman is very sick," Reza observed.

"It looks serious, and the others are terrified," Talon agreed. Just as he was wondering if they could do anything, one of the overseers and two black assistants came hurrying up to the fence nearby.

"Go and get that," The overseer commanded his two men, pointing to the prone woman with his short leather whip. The men hesitated, real fear in their eyes.

"Do it, or you will be flayed alive for disobedience, you dogs!" the man shouted, brandishing his whip, then he gave a gap-toothed grin to Talon and Reza. "They are cowards, every one of them!" he stated.

Talon gave Reza a nudge. They moved off. The two black assistants, doubtless slaves themselves, ran forward, unlocked the chains and dragged the body away by its feet. Talon could not tell if she was alive or not at this point. He was sure that she would not be for long.

*****

They met up with the women just outside the bazaar. It was, by any standards, a poor replica of the ones they had known in Muscat and elsewhere.

"How was it over there?" Rav'an asked pointing with her chin towards the area of the barracoons.

"It is not a place for any of us," Reza stated with disgust in his voice. Talon was relieved that his brother had undergone a change of mind.

"Now we go and buy what *we* want," he said, and led the way towards the other smaller maidans dotted around the dilapidated town.

*****

It took them three days to visit all of them. They had first to assess what was of good quality and what was not. Imaran took some time off from the slave market to assist with introductions to merchants he already knew, and to make it clear that Talon was under his protection to ensure good prices.

Before long, all of them could discern the good ivory from the bad, the rotten from the sound horns, which they were informed were highly prized by the Chinese people. The Ambergris was difficult to gauge, but they had some help from the captain, who knew the better stones from the poor.

They settled down to bargain for what they wanted, and before long there was a chain of slaves carrying tusks, horns and bags of Nutmeg to their ship, now docked alongside the stone pier. Talon went with Yosef and Dar'an to inspect some precious woods, ebony and mahogany. He purchased several tons of both, upon the assurance of Boulos that they sold for three times the price in Oman or Al Hind.

They bought ambergris, 'the sick of the whales' as Reza liked to call it, once he knew where it came from, and exchanged colored glass beads for gold dust with the black traders who hovered on the edges of the trading maidans. They carried the metal dust inside the quills of an animal called a porcupine, sealed with a small blob of wax. Talon was astonished at how cheap this metal was in this part of the world. He thought of his Jewish acquaintances in Muscat and smiled at the thought of bringing them so much to add to their hoards.

By this time they had spent a week on the island; their hold was almost full, and Boulos informed them that it was time to leave.

"The winds will change in less than a week. We have to have these winds take us all the way to Al Hind, which is months away from here. We must be ready to set sail the day the first winds come to us."

"You have not yet loaded your slaves," Reza pointed out.

"We do that today and tomorrow so that they are on board for as little time as possible," Boulos said. "We have loaded our other cargo, just as you have, so it should not take very long. We must not forget to pay our respects to the sultan on Pate before we leave," he added.

Talon could not help wondering about the sick woman. He wondered if that was all it had been, just one sick person.

*****

The next two days were busy as the captain took on fruit and supplies. He had the crew man the small boats and bring casks of spring water from several miles further along the coast, saying that he distrusted the agents in the town. "Who knows where their water has come from? They piss in it and then drink it in that place," he said to Talon, waving his hand towards the town in disgust. Talon had to agree. The island of Lamu was not a happy place, with the misery of the barracoons and the filth of the town itself. The island of Pate had been pristine by comparison.

On the third day, as preparations were under way for their departure, a messenger arrived by a small maneuverable dhow alongside Boulos's ship, which was anchored in the inner harbor. The man said he was from the vizier. He was in a hurry and carried a letter for Imaran and Boulos, which he almost threw up to them before departing without further ceremony to visit other large ships nearby.

Within an hour Boulos arrived on their gangplank and asked for Talon. His face was grim when Talon arrived on deck.

"What is it, Boulos?" he asked.

"I have a letter here from the Vizier. He tells me that the sultan is taken ill and will not be receiving visitors. We are forbidden to come to Pate and must wait here in Lamu until he is better before we can sail over there to pay our respects."

"But that could be days away! Why do you think we cannot go to Pate?" Talon asked.

"God alone must know, but it is not worth future trouble for us to leave without visiting him. The sultan would be offended, and then it would be very difficult to trade here the next time." Boulos sighed. "It is always something, my friend."

Talon had to agree. He looked out to the sea and noticed that there were many more clouds on the southern horizon than the previous day. The wind had picked up during the night and now came in from the South, bringing with it a fresh smell of the sea, driving away the stink of the island.

Boulos noticed his look and hammered a fist into his palm.

"By God, but this is not good. Here comes the vital wind and we are stuck here!" he exclaimed furiously. He stomped off, demanded to be rowed back to his ship, and then climbed his ship's side, shouting at everyone in his way.

Later in the day when the sun was still strong and the air was thick with humidity, Talon and Reza were sweating in the heat looking over at the town. It was too hot to stay below; the shade of the top deck awning was the only place where a light breeze could cool them.

They were waiting for Rav'an and Jannat to come back from visiting a small shop where they had seen some colored fabric. Yosef and Dar'an were with them, so neither Talon nor Reza were particularly concerned. Rostam had also gone along.

The normally busy quayside had gone quiet, almost too quiet. There didn't seem to be a living soul around. There were some of the ubiquitous light brown dogs covered in flies lounging in the shade of some bushes, but no humans at all. It was unnatural.

"That is unusual, even for the sleeping time. It is well past the hour when they should bring the slaves back to work. Someone should be here," Captain Dandachi observed with some irritation.

There was something about the silence and lack of people that Talon found ominous.

"There are still a few bales on the wharf, Captain. There is nobody about, so we should use our own crew and bring them on board," he said distractedly.

Safa nodded and shouted down into the waist of the ship for men to get to work. Before long, the reluctant crewmen were sweating and heaving the last few bales and boxes aboard, but still not a single person could be seen anywhere, not even the normal traffic among the small boats, which was even more strange. The men looked at one another nervously. All sailors are superstitious and attuned to situations that do not seem right. This was one of those occasions.

Then one of the more alert crew members called out and pointed. In the distance where the center of the town lay, a column of smoke was rising slowly into the heavy air. It was dirty gray and billowed up into the sky, growing more dense by the minute.

"There is trouble in the town, Master Talon," the captain said.

Talon felt his stomach lurch. "Reza, bring some men," he called. "We need to go and find out what is going on, and we must find our people. Hurry!"

He led the way at a brisk pace along the deserted quayside towards the town with Reza and three other men the captain had provided. All of them were armed with spears and swords. Talon and Reza carried their bows.

"Be careful, Master Talon," the captain called out to him, pulling on his beard. "There could be danger."

"Where did they go for the cloth?" Talon demanded of Reza.

"Two streets beyond the harbor, Talon. I asked Jannat before they left. I wish now I'd gone with her!"

The heavily armed group came to the end of the quayside and began to move cautiously along a narrow street. One of the men in the lead stopped and pointed ahead of them. "Allah preserve us! Look!"

There was a body lying in the middle of the dirt road, abandoned. It was one of the slave overseers who had been working on Boulos's ship. Talon walked up to the body and was about to crouch down over it when he glanced up and saw another body lying about fifty feet away further on. He stood over the dead man and could see that there was blood and froth at his wide open mouth. The eyes of the man stared sightlessly up at the sky. Talon felt a cold sweat break out on his brow.

"Stay where you are!" he ordered the men.

Reza joined him and stared down at the man. "Allah protect us all! He died of a sickness, Talon." He muttered in *Farsi* so that the other crewmen could not understand. "We have to find the women and Rostam!" He was tight with the urgency. His eyes flicking everywhere in the hope of seeing them.

"Yes, and I would bet that other man went the same way. This could be the *Heyda*," Talon told him with an alarmed expression on his face. Reza nodded agreement, his mouth tightened in a grim line. The good doctor in Isfahan had explained that this kind of thing could strike anywhere, but in his experience it was mainly in crowded places and towns.

They trotted up to the other body, which was also an Arab. The man was very dead, and the foul smell coming from the body indicated that he had voided his bowels as he died. The stink made the two men step back with their hands over their mouths and noses. Reza pointed up the road. Just a little further on was an almost naked slave lying on his back, twitching and moaning. The man vomited and then almost immediately voided himself. Now Talon was convinced. "This is

Heyda! God protect us! We must find the women and leave!" he exclaimed.

At this moment they heard something that made them look up sharply. It was a strange noise, one that sent the hair up on the back of Talon's neck. It was the sound of a crowd of terrified, maddened people, many of them, and they were coming towards the harbor.

At the same time, they made out six figures running towards them just ahead of the mob: three women and two men, with a smaller figure alongside. Hampered by their dresses, the women were unable to run very fast; it looked as though the screaming people would overtake them before Talon and Reza could reach them.

"There they are!" Talon shouted. "Reza, we have to get to them first!"

Both men reflexively took out arrows, knocked their bows, and began to run hard towards the women, who were now only forty paces away. They called out, and Rostam gave a high pitched yell and ran even faster. Yosef and Dar'an were looking over their shoulders at the crowd behind them, ready to sell their lives dearly should they be overtaken.

"Now, Talon, or we are all dead!" Reza said as he drew his bow in one fluid motion and released an arrow, which sped past Rav'an to imbed itself in the chest of one of the scarecrow figures running towards them; a second arrow, this time from Talon' bow, sped past Salem into the mob and another man fell. Two more arrows found their mark and more men fell.

By this time Rostam had reached the corpse. With a surprised yelp he jumped over it. The women swerved past it with terrified exclamations but didn't stop running.

"Don't stop, Rostam! Rav'an, go for the ship!" Reza shouted as he took aim.

The others came abreast of the two archers, who waved them past. All of them were panting, their faces tight with fear. "You two, go with them, see them on board. There is nothing you can do here," Talon shouted at the two unarmed young men.

The two men loosed more arrows at the slowed, milling rabble, but it was clear that they had only halted them for a short time. The mob began to growl like a live animal. It was time to leave.

"Go! Run! Come on!" Talon shouted, as he loosed one last arrow. He slapped Reza on the shoulder, and they turned to run back the way they had come, towards the crewmen who had come with them off the ship, shouting at them to return. Everyone now fled for the dubious safety of the ship half way down the length of the quay. Behind them, the far end of the formerly deserted street was suddenly full of screaming people in hot pursuit.

'We have to get away from the quayside!" Talon panted as the group hurtled along the wharf side. Rostam was already on board; Dar'an, who could run faster than all the others, scampered up the gangplank of the ship and yelled at the captain, pointing back at the town. There was a flurry of activity as the captain realized the danger and immediately began shouting commands at the already nervous crew, who jumped into action. Eager hands helped the women on board, and then men ran to seize long poles used to push the ship out from the side of the quay.

Talon glanced around for Boulos's and Imaran's ships, but then realized that they were a lot safer than his own ship, as they had pulled away from the wharf side earlier that day and anchored in the waterway.

His vessel was one of only two left tied up. He drew his sword as he ran and slashed at the thick rope that held the bows of the ship to a short stone pillar. When the end of the rope parted and dropped into the water, he ran towards the after end of the quay, but Yosef and Reza were already there. They hacked furiously with their swords at the thick hawser tying the after end of the ship to the quay, and when it finally parted the three of them raced for the gangplank as the crew began to pole the ship away from the stone walls. There were many willing hands to help them scramble aboard and pull up the plank, and then it was all hands to pole the ship from the quay.

Everyone shoved on the poles with the desperation of men who knew they would die if they did not succeed. It was hard work to start the ship moving, all the while watching the approaching mob. Talon and Reza took up station on the high afterdeck with their bows while the rest of the crew reached for whatever they could find to ward off unwelcome boarders.

Men armed with swords and spears lined the side of the ship, waiting. Talon glanced behind him to make sure the women and Rostam were safe, and was rewarded with a quick gesture from Rav'an as she herded Jannat and Salem below. Salem was pulling a reluctant Rostam by the hand, but the boy squirmed loose and dashed up to the top deck to be with Talon. "I want to see! Papa, I want to see!" he squeaked.

Talon and Reza could not help themselves. They laughed. The boy was simply too excited to know fear. The rest of the crew was startled to see the two men laughing. In the face of this very present danger it sounded insane; they shook their heads in wonder.

"Stay close to me and uncle Reza, Rostam, or you will be sent below," Talon told the boy in a stern manner, trying not to smile. He waved to Rav'an, who hesitated, then came up to join them.

"It's no safer below if they get aboard than here," she stated. "Give me a weapon," she demanded of Yosef, who ran off to get his own bow and hers from the cabins. She turned to Rostam. "If you move an inch, young man, you will be sent below immediately!" She didn't appear to appreciate the absurdity of the order.

Rostam looked up at her with wide eyes and nodded wordlessly. The captain hesitated and then came over. "Lady

Rav'an, you should go below. It is going to be very nasty soon. That mob over there will try to take the ship from us."

She gave him a withering stare with gray eyes that flashed. "Thank you for your concern, Captain, but this is my ship, too. I do not intend that those people should take it from us."

Talon bit his lip while Reza stared off into space with a wooden expression on his dark features. The captain saluted in silence, then glanced at Talon, who gave an imperceptible nod. He retired to the steering deck of the ship to join the other men waiting for the onslaught to come.

"Hurry with those poles, get us out away from here!" he bellowed. The men put their backs into the work and the ship slowly, very slowly moved away from the stone wall.

In an instant the end of the quay was full of people, screaming and waving weapons as they ran, shouting and demanding for the vessel to stop and take them aboard.

"The *Heyda* is here!" the cry went up as they swarmed along the quay. "Take us away, take us away! In the name of the Prophet, take us with you!"

Many of the crowd ran straight towards the other ship, which was manned by only a skeleton crew who had only just begun to desperately try to pole their vessel away from the quayside. The maddened mob swarmed over the sides of the doomed vessel, brandishing their crude weapons and overcoming the crew, killing the very men who were their only hope of escape. The men on Talon's ship watched in grim silence as the bodies were thrown overboard to splash into the water, and then the mob began to plunder the ship. None of them seemed to know what to do with their newfound opportunity, although a few fumbled with the sails in a pathetic attempt to raise them.

*****

The rest of the rabble arrived opposite the *Sea Eagle*, where they yelled and clawed at each other as they struggled for a place where they might leap across the widening watery gap. Many fell into the dirty water below with screams and howls of frustration, and then tried to swim towards the ship, which was now fully underway, but oh, so slowly. Others tried to leap across the space and fell short, still shouting. One energetic man managed to land on the side near to a stay where he hung on, desperately trying to pull himself up onto the side of the ship, but Umayr, one of the most senior members of the crew, yelled and slammed the end of a pole into him repeatedly until his grip loosened and he fell backwards with a scream of anger into the water below.

On the other ship, the maddened mob had run below decks, but some accident must have occurred. Flames began licking at the sides of the main deck hatchway, then they leapt to the ropes and canvas on the deck, and finally caught hold on the furled sails. The panicked men beat frantically at the flames with anything that came to hand but were powerless to stop the fire from taking hold of the rigging.

Before very long, the entire vessel, a beautiful three masted xebec, was in flames from one end to the other. The heat of the fire and the cloud of sparks rising into the sky made the men on the departing ship look apprehensively up at their own rigging, but by now their boat was well clear. A snapped order from the captain and men formed a bucket line and sloshed water over the sides and up onto the sails just in case. Talon nodded his approval.

The shouts and screams were of rage and hate as the mob brandished sticks and an assortment of weapons, cursing and screaming imprecations at the departing vessel. But the captain had his ship moving smoothly towards the exit of the harbor.

"*Pedar Sag!*" Reza swore. "I don't care if the sultan is sick. I think we should leave this cursed place right now!"

Talon agreed and gave the final order to the captain to sail out of the harbor. They drew alongside the other two ships, which they could smell as they passed. The stink of human waste and filth was already pungent. Talon wondered how the crew could stand it.

Boulos and Imaran were both on their respective decks and shouted across the water. "What is the disturbance all about? Why are you leaving? Why is that ship burning?" he pointed back towards the wharf and the stricken vessel.

Talon glanced at the men around him, then he jumped onto the side, holding onto the ropes leaning out as he called back.

"It is the *Heyda*! We saw men dead on the street. Look back there! But for the grace of God we could be burning too."

"Allah protect us!" Boulos exclaimed as he stared at the burning ship. He turned and shouted at his men to make sail. Imaran did the same. There was no need to encourage their sailors. In very short time both ships were under way and following in the wake of Talon's ship.

On other vessels moored in the harbor, crews who had seen the incident on the quayside began to make hurried preparations for sea. No one wanted to be even close to a town infected with the *Heyda*.

Jannat came rushing back up on deck, alarmed by the shouting and the unexpected motion of the ship. She took one look a the grim faces of the men on deck and hastened to Reza's side. They looked back towards the land and could now clearly see several fires that had taken hold in the town.

"I pray to God that we do not have the *Heyda* on this ship," the captain muttered as he watched the receding harbor and the thick pall of smoke rising over the stricken town.

There was not much time to dwell upon the troubled town of Lamu, however. The clouds that had risen from the southern horizon were now overhead, and they were dense with rain. The wind picked up almost the moment they were clear of the shoals and sharp fangs of the reefs, causing the ship to heel suddenly as a gust struck as though from nowhere. The crew and the captain became very busy hauling in the three large sails and turning the ship in a northeasterly course as more gusts rippled the choppy sea.

"We are in for a blow, Master Talon," the captain called over. "Please take the women below, and young Rostam, too." This time there was no mistaking his command.

"Thank God we are clear of the pestilence," Reza said, as they made their way to their communal cabin.

"Remember where we saw it first, brother?" Talon asked him in a low voice.

"Oh God! What if...?" Reza left the question unsaid, but his appalled expression said it all.

"What do you mean, my Reza?" Jannat demanded. She looked shaken by his agonized expression.

"When we first went to the barracoons we passed a very sick slave woman. The other slaves were terrified of her condition, and it is very likely that we saw her die of something more serious than just a simple fever. It could have been a sign of the *Heyda*," Reza informed her.

"But Boulos and Imaran have bought slaves and have them on their ships!" Rav'an exclaimed, her eyes widening in horror.

"Yes, my Rav'an, they have. May God protect them," Talon whispered.

There was a long silence in the cabin as they each tried to comprehend the dreadful implications.

Roll on, thou deep and dark blue ocean—roll!
Ten thousand fleets sweep over thee in vain;
Man marks the earth with ruin—his control
Stops with the shore; upon the watery plain
The wrecks are all thy deed, nor doth remain
A shadow of man's ravage, save his own,
When for a moment, like a drop of rain,
He sinks into thy depths with bubbling groan,
Without a grave, unknell'd, uncoffin'd, and unknown.

—Lord Byron

Chapter Eight
To Sail an Ocean

They fled North by North-East for two full days and nights with the strong gusting wind driving the vessels hard. The current that moved in a northward direction helped to speed the ships. The full storm caught up with them in the early hours of the second day and harried them with dense rain squalls and gusts of wind that threatened to tear away their tall triangular sails, but the captain was ready for this and took in enough sail to be able to keep going at a good pace without losing any rigging or canvas.

Talon admired the way the man played the squalls, always one step ahead of the elements. He also marveled at how well the ship handled in rough waters. He remembered the rounded, squat boats that the people from Europe sailed, which depended on the right wind to sail anywhere, and he admired this *Sea Eagle* that seemed to love the sea, rising and falling easily with the waves.

There was no possibility of stopping to see how the other two ships were faring, but there was a sense of dread on board.

On the dawn of the fifth day, the captain consulted his manuals and the watery sun, then turned the *Sea Eagle* on a heading that would take them due north. The wind was still brisk, which pleased the captain. Like everyone else, he kept casting apprehensive looks over his shoulder towards the other two vessels, which had maintained their station to their rear all through the storms; now at dawn he eased sail, and they began to catch up. Within two hours they were sailing parallel to the *Sea Eagle*, and before long they were close enough on either side to be within hailing range.

Boulos clambered onto the high sides of his ship and shouted across to them. Even from this distance he looked worried.

"I cannot tell if the sickness is with us or not. There have been some deaths, but that is normal on a voyage like this," he called over. "Are you all well?"

To Talon nothing about this voyage seemed normal, but he could only take Boulos's word for it. He waved and shouted back. "We are well. No sickness. Not yet, *Insha' Allah.*"

Boulos waved back; he seemed relieved. "What of Imaran?" he called over.

Talon strode over to the other side of the deck to where he heard the exchange between the captain and Imaran. It was a very different situation with Imaran's ship.

"We have the sickness! God help us, but we have the sickness." Imaran called back to them.

There were frightened mutters from the men of the *Sea Eagle* who heard his words; even the captain looked fearful. All eyes were on Imaran's ship as the crew dumped a body over the side, even as he called across to them. It landed with barely a splash in the choppy waters and was gone in a moment. Seconds later the water churned behind the ship and a large fin appeared briefly, to disappear again in a froth of reddish water. There was something terrifying and obscene about the spectacle of the fish feeding on the diseased corpse that left everyone who witnessed it silent and shocked. They all knew that but for the grace of God it could be them.

There was nothing they could do for their luckless companions, and there was no question about taking men off the other ship onto their vessel. Imaran understood this only too well.

"It is in the hands of Allah now. Go with God, and tell my father what happened," he called across the water. They could all hear the resignation and despair in his voice.

"The sharks are following him. I wonder how many they have thrown overboard already if those monsters are following him like that?" Reza asked out loud.

Talon had no idea, but he noticed that there were fewer crew on the deck of Imaran's ship than on his own ship or that of Boulos.

"Our ships are carrying the sickness back to Oman with us. Imaran knows this," he said to the captain.

Without waiting for a reply, Talon hurried back to the starboard side of the ship and shouted the information to Boulos.

There was consternation at the news, that was clear, but Boulos shouted back, "If you are sure you do not have the sickness, you should continue to Aden, and then Raysut. There are horses there waiting for us at Raysut to take to Al Hind."

"What will you do?" Talon shouted back. Horses seemed to be irrelevant, considering the peril the brothers and their ships were facing.

"What can I do? I must stay with my brother. We must find a place where we can stop until this sickness passes, God willing. Imaran cannot go to Muscat, or Aden for that matter, nor can I. It is at Aden we were going to sell our slaves, and then go on to Raysut, where there is also some *al-lubān*." Talon knew this was the word for what he knew as Frankincense, the aromatic resin that was found in the foothills and on the escarpment around Raysat.

Because they didn't carry slaves, they would be able to load up with about thirty horses, perhaps more, and then set sail across the wide expanse of the Bahr Al-Habasha—the Indian Ocean—directly to Kulam Mali, which was where they could sell the animals, and hopefully the rest of the cargo, concluding their venture.

"Go with God!" Boulos shouted.

The entire crew of the *Sea Eagle* called back the same. "God protect you. Go with God!"

The ships drew apart; there was nothing more to do. The *Sea Eagle* slowly pulled ahead of the other two, which had furled their sails to drift while the two brothers discussed their plight. Talon thought their options were bleak. With a heavy heart he joined the others, who were standing on the port side looking back at the two stricken ships. No one said anything.

*****

They stopped at Aden to buy some Myrrh, which the captain told Talon was very important to the merchants and the Chinese traders whom they should encounter in India. However, news of the *Heyda* had spread; there was suspicion and distrust, so they were unable to tarry, and within a couple of days they were sailing northwards to Raysat.

As Boulos had foretold, there were horses waiting for them there, brought all the way from the hinterland. Talon gazed up at the high escarpment several leagues inland and wondered how the tribesmen had managed to bring so many good animals down that steep slope.

It took them almost a week for the carpenters to prepare the ship to receive the horses, check their health, and load them. There were some small accidents, as the horses didn't take kindly to the idea of being loaded onto a cramped ship. Fortunately, the crew had some experienced men among them who had done all this before, and with the guidance of the captain they managed to settle thirty horses in the hold for the long run to Kulam Mali. The strong smell of horses now pervaded the ship, but as Rav'an mentioned to Talon one day, "Rather the smell of these animals than the smell of death and the stench of those pitiful creatures from Africa." He had to agree.

He had gone ashore with Reza and the captain to meet with the agent, a nondescript man who worked for the family Mardini. The agent had been shocked at the news of the brothers' fate and had wept for them. He had clearly expected to send at least a hundred horses to Kulam Mali; for, as he had told the brothers, the prices were high because there was such a shortage. He was now stuck with horses he could not sell and was very unhappy about it.

They had found that the agent was not above slipping in some poor quality horses and weeded these out quickly enough, while he shrugged and pretended that it had been an oversight. Summer was well advanced as the year moved into October; although it was less humid here, it was still with some relief that they set sail again. They had discussed the option to go back to Muscat, but the agent informed them they would lose the advantage of the monsoon if they did so.

"The wind will continue for another three months, which will bring you to Kulam Mali and beyond if you so wish it, but if you delay you will find the winds against you, and then the horses will die of thirst because you will not have enough water for them and yourselves on such a long trip. Even with some good rains you will only just get there without some dying of thirst," he informed them. "Come back to Muscat with the *Kaws* monsoon wind, which begins in the early part of next year, and avoid the pirates; they are a menace, and they appear to be everywhere."

On that comforting note and with great reluctance they departed, leaving letters with him to be sent to Muscat to Doctor Haddad and Fariba and the Sheik Allam Mardini, informing them of the scourge that had followed them from

Lamu and the disaster that had befallen his brothers. It was with a heavy heart that Talon instructed the captain to set sail for Kulam Mali, not knowing for sure when they might next see Fariba and the doctor again.

*****

Neither Talon nor Reza wanted the sea voyages to blunt their skills, so they devised a way to keep themselves both fit and alert.

Telling the captain to ensure that the crew was aware of what they were going to do, he and Reza took some sacks and stuffed them tight with hay purloined from the horses' feed, then hung them off the forward mast at about the height of a man. The target could be clearly seen from the extreme after deck just above the steersmen.

Either Talon or Reza would start off at a run. Reaching the main central mast, which was about ten yards from the forward mast, they would have to spin about and loose an arrow at the target, then race up the first flight of stairs to the steering deck, repeat the action, and without pausing, race up the next short flight and fire an arrow from the railing overlooking the steering deck. The whole operation had to be conducted at top speed. They would do this at least ten times until they were almost spent, and then check the fall of their arrows. Neither Reza nor Talon ever missed the target; but to his chagrin, Yosef began to miss after four runs, whereupon Talon told him he would get into trouble with the captain if he continued to damage his ship.

Both Talon and Reza evoked gasps of surprise and admiration from the gathered onlookers as their arrows sped true to the targets in almost all cases. Yosef found himself a long way behind the others but clearly enjoyed the experience. Both he and Dar'an applied themselves to the task of trying to catch up with their more experienced elders.

Rostam clamored to be allowed to practice, but Talon went with him to ensure that he didn't disable any of the crew or the steersmen. His reed arrows fell far short, but his delighted screams of excitement drew smiles from all.

It occurred to Reza that it might be a good thing if the crew learned to use bows, and Talon readily agreed. He turned the training over to Reza, who took the enthusiastic volunteers through their paces. Very few of the crew on board the ship had ever used a bow before, which surprised the two friends; but this kind of dynamic training appealed to the men, and they began to compete with one another.

Before long, they too were able to strike the target most of the time. The captain was not at all pleased when they missed and his precious railings or ship's sides were impaled by a stray arrow, but Talon told him of the time when he had warded off pirates by means of archery and he was somewhat mollified. Still, those who missed the mark were made to repair the damage. This only served to make them focus the more on their accuracy.

Talon observed that the morale of the crew went up a few notches with this kind of exercise. Conscious of the threat of pirates he decided that he would provide more training with swords and knives. The men, unaware of Talon and Reza's background, fancied themselves as masters of the art of knife fighting, but soon changed their minds after Reza gave the first lesson.

It was Tarif who first stepped forward in response to the offer. He towered over the slim Reza, who looked calmly back at the grinning sailor who held a long piece of wood as a substitute for a sword.

Talon was nearby and listened with silent amusement to the other members of the crew as they discussed Reza's forthcoming discomfort. He knew exactly what was going to happen. The crewmen jostled and chuckled to one another as they stood in a wide circle round the two combatants standing in the waist of the ship.

"Tarif will kill him! Good thing it isn't a real blade, or it would be paradise for Reza," they joked with one another.

On a nod from Reza for the bout to begin, Tarif, still with a wide grin on his bearded face, jumped forward and swung his 'blade' up and then down hard and very fast. His intent had been to strike Reza on the head and end it right there. To his surprise, Reza was no longer where he had been, and then he felt an intense pain in his right shin where he had just been rapped.

"Always go for an unguarded place and strike hard," Reza admonished him from behind.

Tarif's grin had vanished, replaced with a grimace of pain and then anger. He staggered back and rubbed his shin vigorously, then came in again, his stick whirling. This time Reza easily blocked it, then stepped sideways like a dancer and rapped him on the elbow with the tip of his 'blade'.

Tarif uttered a yell of pain and almost dropped his weapon. "Always strike immediately after you have blocked a blow, as that is when the opponent is off guard," the remorseless advice continued.

Tarif was undeterred. A veteran of many street fights, he didn't yet recognize just what he was up against, but by this time the rest of the crew were beginning to regard Reza with different eyes. He wasn't even breathing hard, while Tarif was panting and sweating in the bright sunlight. They grew less boisterous and began to pay attention.

"Lucky blows. Tarif will still soon put him on the deck," someone muttered. Still, it was beginning to dawn on them that Reza would be no easy knockover.

Tarif rubbed his elbow with a rueful laugh and then settled down to circle and watch his opponent more carefully. Reza simply stood in the center of the ring and followed him about as he circled. Tarif tried a few feints, which Reza tapped away with contempt.

Finally, thinking he had judged the moment just right, Tarif again attacked with wide slashing strikes meant to drive Reza back against the side of the ship and deprive him of room to maneuver. Reza met him head on. He deflected one of the wild blows with a light tap and then went well inside Tarif's guard, reversed his position so that he was almost crouched facing away from his opponent, and rammed his 'blade' backwards into his opponent's stomach, putting real force into it. Tarif doubled over with an explosion of breath and fell to his knees. His eyes were already crossed when Reza tapped him gently on the top of his head. The man fell over and lay on the deck, admitting defeat with a groan, too breathless to speak.

Reza stood back and said, "Never rush in, because a knowledgeable swordsman will use that against you... and probably kill you."

The rest of the crew roared with laughter and slapped each other on the back with delight, but they were also looking at Reza with real respect. These were men of the sea, toughened by all manner of hardship, so they could appreciate the clean display of weaponry they had just witnessed. There was no difficulty with the training after that.

*****

The appearance of three triangular sails in the Northeast after almost three weeks of travel was an unwelcome surprise. The lookout posted on the main mast by the captain for this express purpose shouted down that the ships were bearing down on them.

The captain looked grim and began to shout orders to tighten sail and altered course a few more points towards the Southeast in an attempt to avoid the ships if at all possible.

Talon and Reza were brought on deck by the drumming sound of running feet, the shouted orders, and the shift in direction, which was unusual, as they had been on a straight course in calm waters for several days now.

"What is the problem, Captain?" Talon asked when he climbed the last step onto the steering deck.

"I think we have company, and it is not the kind that we need. This is a sea full of pirates, but I hoped that God would spare us this."

He pointed to the Northeast, where three well-spaced lateen sails were just visible on the horizon. There was no land in sight, but the captain said, "We are about four or five days sail out from land, and that is why they are looking for victims." He growled unhappily. "God curse them for the parasites they are. We cannot fight three of them at once." He rubbed his face vigorously with a calloused hand. "I must now try and race them to the port."

Talon climbed half way up the stays and stared at the oncoming enemy. He felt a sense of dread. All the warnings of the dangers of these seas came back to him. They had just sailed into an ambush of sorts. The pirates, who had probably been waiting for easy prey to sail into their hands, were in possession of vessels that, while not as large as the *Sea Eagle,* were speedy and very maneuverable from what he could tell even at this distance. He jumped down to join Reza on the deck and urged him towards a corner of the upper deck.

"We cannot outrun those ships, Reza. They will catch us before sundown, that's for sure."

"Can't we lose them in the dark?" Reza asked.

"Look at them, Reza, they are light and faster than we are. There isn't a cloud in the sky and the stars overhead at night would show them exactly what we were doing."

"Then we fight them and make it very difficult to take us," Reza stated, as if this was a matter of fact.

Talon shook his head. "I agree with you that we must fight, Brother. But it has to be during the day. At night they can sneak up on us, and while we are fighting one the others will come in behind us, or on the other side and board us. It has to be during the day!"

He pounded the rail, tense with frustration. His mind was racing: how to deal with these pirates so that they could gain time to get into port? They could not outrun them, no matter what the captain said. A sea battle was the last thing he wanted at this time, but it looked as though they were faced with one.

Reza tried to reassure him. "You and I have bows. Our men are better trained than they were before. There are bows available for at least ten men, so perhaps we can surprise them," he suggested.

Talon slammed one fist into his palm. "That's it! You are right, Reza. You are so right, we have to surprise them! Come with me."

He led a puzzled Reza back to the captain and asked him to join them. He explained his plan to both men and then waited for their reaction. Reza, predictably, was all for the venture. "I think you are mad, Talon. But you are thinking on your feet, as usual, and besides, I don't see any other choices."

The captain, on the other hand, was horrified. He was almost in tears he was so upset.

"This is utter madness, Master Talon! How can you be sure that they will fall for this?" he exclaimed. "If it goes wrong we are all dead, or slaves, or worse. Think of the women we have on board, Master Talon! We should try to outrun them, there is still a chance."

"I *am* thinking of the women, Captain. I don't want to imagine the fate they will suffer if we *do not* do this. It is futile for us to try and outrun those pirates; they will catch us at night, and then our chances are much worse. Our bowmen won't be able to see their targets until they are aboard us, and by then it will be too late. And yes, we shall all surely die or be enslaved." Talon's tone was harsh. He didn't see any alternative to a fight.

Reza nodded agreement. "In daylight I can kill many of them from a great distance, but in poor light it will be much harder to aim true."

"The nights have all been clear. They will have the advantage and be able to sneak up on us while we are engaged with one of them, and we will not be able to react in time, nor with sufficient force to drive them away. Call the crew to the deck. I wish to talk to them," Talon told the captain, his tone brusque now. There was no longer any time to debate the issue.

Looking rebellious, the captain reluctantly did as he was told, and the crew was quickly assembled in the waist of the ship to hear what Talon had to say. It didn't take long, and without doubt he had their attention, because everyone could see that no matter how much sail they now had on, the other ships were noticeably gaining on them.

"We do not have much time. You must hurry and be in position within the hour. Everyone find a spear and a sword," Talon ordered. "Ten of you will use bows. Do not waste the arrows and do not use them until I say so!" Talon set the men to preparing for the engagement.

Once he could see that preparations were well under way, he made his way below deck. Rav'an and Jannat greeted him with nervous expressions. News of the pirate ships was all over the ship by now, and they knew of it. Rostam was wide-eyed with excitement.

Talon started with a careful explanation as to what he needed from them and was reassured when Rav'an nodded her head in reluctant agreement.

"It might work, Talon, but it is very dangerous... for everyone. Rostam must stay below with Salem all the time, but Jannat and I will do as you ask."

"Thank you, my Rav'an," he said. "There will be a guard on the door, and Dar'an will be here with him." He knew as he said it that Dar'an would give his life for the boy, but if the pirates made it this far, it would have been the end for all of them on deck anyway.

"I once told you that you are like a fox. I have faith in you, my husband. God protect us all today," Rav'an murmured as she kissed him.

*****

It was a matter of scant hours before the strange ships were only a few leagues away. The crewmen of the *Sea Eagle* were in their places, but for the captain and a few men who had to work the sails, and Talon, who stood with the steersmen. Talon was nervous; his plan depended upon so many things going the right way.

He told himself that he should concentrate and see it through, but that did little to quiet the churning of his stomach. He glanced up at the top deck to where Rav'an and Jannat crouched out of sight. Rav'an caught his look and gave him a tense smile. He relaxed a little. They had no choice now but to place their trust in God and the element of surprise.

He wanted to give the impression to the pirates that they were just a fat merchant vessel with a small crew that would look like easy pickings. His bow and a full quiver of arrows were close at hand, but out of sight. Most of the crew was crouched beneath the tall sides of the ship with their weapons ready for action.

He shielded his eyes from the sun as he looked up at the main mast. He could see Reza perched at the top with one other man; Reza had his bow with him and gave him a quick hand wave before ducking out of sight into the large round basket that served as the lookout. The only sound on the ship was that of men using stones to sharpen their swords and spear heads. The harsh, drawn out rasping of the stones on steel jarred nerves already tight with anticipation.

The captain, who was himself very nervous and decidedly skeptical of the entire operation to come, continued to give orders as though they were trying to flee the oncoming ships, but in fact they had slowed considerably. Talon also cast an apprehensive eye to the West. The sun was still high enough in the sky for them to see what they were doing, but it appeared to be descending far too rapidly, and they needed daylight to conclude this fight.

It was not long before two of the pursuing ships made lazy turns and began to come up from behind their quarry like a pair of predators converging on their helpless prey. The third ship stayed clear in the rear for the moment. Talon could now make out the figures on the two ships that were speeding towards them. The vessels were crowded with heavily armed men who looked confident and relaxed as they drew nearer.

"Prepare, they are coming!" he called to the men. The sound of stones on steel ceased and men crouched lower behind the ship's sides. The entire ship became silent, except for the rush of water along its sides, the creak of timbers and the snap of a sail above.

He hoped grimly the confidence displayed by the pirates was going to be shaken very soon. Soon the bows of their ships were level with the *Sea Eagle's* after decks. When the speeding vessels were about twenty paces away on either side, a man called across from the boat on their port side for them to stop the ship.

"Drop your sails! We are coming aboard," he shouted in bad Arabic. He, like most of his crew, wore only a sarong with a knife stuck in a sash wrapped around his waist. He was very dark, almost black, and thin to the point of emaciation. His savage grin displayed large gaps in his teeth and a mouth that was bright red. He spat out a stream of red juice and shouted again, this time with more force.

"Stop your ship! Do as I tell you!"

Talon had no intention of doing anything of the sort, but he nodded to the captain, who shouted an order to the skeleton crew headed by Umayr, and they began clumsily to let the after sail down.

In the short space of time that they carried out this work, both the pirate ships, full of these slim, dark men whom Talon took to be from India, had drawn level with their own. He signaled across to Rav'an and Jannat.

Both women climbed to their feet and began to run about the after deck, wailing and waving their hands in the air. Their cries and their unmistakable female forms and attire made them look like a pair of hysterical women, terrified of their impending fate. They shrieked with terror, both of them calling loudly on God to protect them. On Talon's instructions, they didn't remain in one spot for more than a few seconds.

Talon made a mental note to tell them later how convincing they were. They were succeeding wonderfully at distracting the men on the pirate ships from the hurried activity now going on in the waist of the *Sea Eagle*. The pirates began to point and laugh, shouting obscenities and demonstrating with their hips what they were going to do to the two women, who continued to scream and flutter about with feigned fright like winged birds. All the attention of the pirates was centered now on the two women.

On the *Sea Eagle* men were hastily lighting the oily rags that had been stuffed into earthenware jars stacked on the deck. Many of the rags were alight by now, and the men were looking up at Talon expectantly, waiting for him to say the word. He prayed that no one would drop one of those lethal pots onto his own deck.

He stared at the two ships sailing alongside, willing them to come just a little closer and not to notice the smoke now drifting up from the fuses. The pirates were still watching the antics of the women. It was almost time; the ships were only ten long paces away. Then one of the more alert men on the port boat shouted the alarm and pointed to the waist of the *Sea Eagle*. He had seen the smoke.

"Now!" Talon shouted and reached for his bow. At his command the men hidden below the sides jumped up and, with blood curdling yells, hurled the small pots with all their might over the sides of the *Sea Eagle* to shatter against the sides and on the decks of the flanking pirate vessels. More followed, some hurled from the main mast by strong-armed Reza. The sticky, black, oily substance from the pots spread out from the pieces where they fell. In some cases the flaming rags had gone out, but in others the flame caught and an ominous bluish flame spread across the decks like some living thing. Within moments the pirates went from happily contemplating their booty to panic-stricken sailors on board ships that were catching fire.

It was now the task of the archers to kill as many as they could and prevent anyone from being able to put out the fires. A hail of arrows flew at close range into the ranks of the pirates on both ships, taking surprised men down before they could react.

Talon quickly accounted for three men and was pleased to see that Rav'an managed to strike another in the thigh with an arrow. His orders had been strict: she and Jannat were to shoot through the gaps in the high sides and not expose themselves. He marveled at the calm she now displayed, kneeling on one knee and shooting across the water, while Jannat handed arrows to her.

Reza and Yosef, with help from several crew members, were dealing with the ship to their starboard, while Talon focused on the ship to their port side. The men in the waist of the *Sea Eagle* continued to hurl pots, but now at carefully chosen targets. The next thing to flare was the main sail, first turning a dark color, then exploding into flame and going up like a torch. Then the after sail caught fire also, driving the steersmen away from the intense heat. The ship on their port side lost way and began to wallow in the water, while screaming men were burned horribly as they desperately tried to put the fires out with anything to hand.

Water didn't help; all it did was spread the fearsome, viscous liquid wider and make matters worse. Talon concentrated on a tall man near to the steering bar who was shouting frantic orders at the men. He took him down after two tries, while Rav'an fired her arrows into the milling mob of panicked pirates in the ship's waist, inflicting random damage. Some arrows began to come their way, but this retaliation was half-hearted and soon stopped as the greater danger of fire occupied all the pirates' attention. Men began to abandon ship, throwing themselves into the water to escape the inferno. Talon watched dispassionately; theirs was a choice of fates, the fire or the numerous sharks that infested these waters. What the pirates had had in mind for them had been equally unpleasant.

He turned his attention to the other ship, which was also on fire, and helped Reza and Yosef kill as many of the panicked men on that ship as possible. The steersmen were dead, so Talon assumed that the captain of that ship was too. Reza was deadly at this range from his vantage point.

Captain Dandachi, who had stayed with the steersmen, shouted to Umayr to haul up the after sail, and other crewman ran to tighten the main sail. They needed to get as far away from the two stricken ships as possible. The very real danger of sparks landing on their own ship lent urgency to their actions.

Talon waved to Reza up on the masthead. "Do you still have some pots with you?" he called up. "We have that third ship to deal with."

"We have three left. Send some more up," Reza laughed happily. Talon grinned and shook his head, then turned to the captain. "I hope we have more of these pots, Captain. They work well."

Captain Dandachi looked ready to weep with relief. "Yes, yes we have more, Master Talon. Waqqas!" he called. "Go and get more pots from the hold. Hurry!" He then embraced Talon, slapping him painfully hard on the back. "I cannot believe it!

God has been with us today. We have defeated not one, but two of them!"

"Don't thank God too soon. We are not out of trouble yet, Captain," Talon pointed out, indicating the other vessel with a wave of his hand.

"They are cowards, Master Talon. I don't think they will try to fight us. Not after what they have witnessed."

Just as he said this, Reza gave a whoop and shouted down at them from his perch. "They are fleeing! Look, they run!"

The crew stopped what they were doing and stared in amazement as the third ship turned away, leaving them and abandoning its erstwhile allies to their fate. It appeared that its captain had no stomach for a fight with the *Sea Eagle*. The crew roared with excitement and jumped about on the center deck with glee, waving fists, shouting abuse at the departing ship, and hugging one another. The steersmen shouted praises to Allah and chattered excitedly with relief but dared not leave their place with the captain glowering at them.

Talon turned towards the two women, who were standing on the upper deck. He ran up to Rav'an and, ignoring custom, seized her in a bear hug. "You were both magnificent! You distracted them so well they completely overlooked us. We could not have done it without you!" he shouted, and grabbed Jannat to hold her tightly as well. Jannat was shaking with reaction and weeping with relief.

"I have never been so frightened in my life!" she declared through her sniffles.

"Are you not forgetting your escape through the tunnels, Jannat? You are a brave woman, while our Rav'an here has known much worse in her time." Talon grinned affectionately down at Rav'an, who turned a strained white face up to him and sniffed, wiping the tears away with a shaking hand as she smiled at him.

"I have not forgotten, my warrior, my fox. Now Jannat and I must go below and stop making a spectacle of ourselves. I don't know what the crew must think of us!"

Talon grinned and gave her a light kiss in front of everyone. "I am quite sure that they will worship the deck upon which you walk from this moment on, my Lady," he assured her. Indeed, as they descended the stairs to go below, the men shouted and cheered them until they were out of sight.

At last, we have a ship and a crew! Talon thought to himself as he greeted the exuberant Reza, who embraced him and forced him to do a little dance, to his acute embarrassment.

"The captain of the ship on our starboard side was so agile and skinny that I kept missing him!" Reza complained.

Talon choked with laughter. "Did you succeed in the end?" he demanded.

"What do you think, Brother?"

The sun began to sink into the western horizon as a bright red ball of fire, but it was not the only fire on the horizon that evening. As they sailed on a calm sea towards Kulam Mali, the burning pyre of two pirate ships stayed with them for many hours, lighting up the horizon long into the night.

"How did you know what to do, Brother?" Reza asked Talon as they stood together with Rostam and Rav'an, watching the fire that night.

"This is not the first time I have been attacked by pirates, Reza. Surprise and fire are the best weapons against them. How are our horses faring after all the excitement?"

"Well enough. The noise bothered them, but the men have calmed them and given them food and water, so they are fine for the present," Reza said. "I have to go and comfort Jannat. She is still very upset. Are you coming?"

Talon smiled in the darkness and gripped Rostam's shoulder and Rav'an's hand a little harder. "Yes, we will be there in a moment. Goodnight, Brother."

Charcoal black tip of arrowhead
among these ancient, stones—stained red,
Heartbeats feel rhythms of ghostly drums,
Winds carry haunting, chanting hums,
I feel your blood flow here with mine,
outlasting even decaying time,
I've been told the stories, told by you,
I know we're just spirits, passing through.

—Indian Poet

Chapter Nine

Kalam Mali

The clouds came up rapidly from the South and West like tumbled mountains of black, menacing vapor that roiled into the sky to impossible heights. The warmth of the sun was replaced by gusts of hot wind that made the stays of the ship hum. Captain Safa al-Dandachi glanced up at the sails with a concerned expression on his face as they rattled and bellied, forcing the ship to heel.

He cast a worried look behind him at the oncoming storm and shouted at the crew to take down the main sail. The more experienced of the crew comprehended the urgency and shouted at the others to get a move on, as the storm would wait for no man.

Talon, who was on the after deck with the captain, noted his expression and asked, "Is there cause for concern?"

The captain nodded his head and wiped perspiration from his face with the tail end of his turban. The heat of the wind was fierce.

"We will know very soon, Master Talon. If the cold winds follow, they will tell us a great deal about what we see brewing on the horizon. I think we are in for a rough passage. You must inform the womenfolk to stay below, as well as Rostam, and you yourself should take shelter."

"I shall stay right here with you, Safa al-Dandachi. I own the ship, and I have a responsibility to remain with you," Talon said. "We cannot outrun it, I suppose?"

The captain shrugged and gave a dry laugh. "The storms of this sea come and go faster than an army of galloping horses. No, we cannot outrun it; we have to live through it. As you wish, Master Talon, stay, but the women and boy must go below."

Talon nodded and ran down the steps to the main deck, where he found Reza walking towards him along the waist deck, avoiding the sudden activity as the crew hurriedly lowered the main sail, which was billowing and snapping in the gusts of wind.

"Reza, the captain is worried. Rav'an and Jannat must remain below with the servants. Where is Rostam?"

Reza looked back at the busy crew. "I left him near the front of the ship with Jannat. I'll go and tell them to go to the cabin at once. Is the captain concerned about the darkness over there?" He pointed towards the black swirling cloud mass heading towards them.

"Yes, and it is urgent that we hurry," Talon said.

Reza nodded and ran back the way he had come, while Talon took the stairs down to the main aft cabin to talk to Rav'an.

He knocked on the door leading to the women's cabin and was answered by one of the maids, Salem, who opened the door ."I wish to speak to Rav'an," he told her.

"I am here, Talon," Rav'an called from the back of the cabin, where she was seated on some cushions watching the wake of the ship. A book lay nearby that she had been reading.

"My Rav'an, we are in for a storm. I suspect that it will be a bad one, as the captain seems more anxious than usual. He has asked that you and Jannat as well as Rostam and the servants all stay below."

"But the sea is calm, my Love. How can it be?" she asked.

"Look to the South and West and you will see that the Djins are about to loose their wrath upon us, my Love. The sea here is not telling us the truth," he responded, leaning over her to stare out at the heaving water below. There was something ominous about the oily behavior of the sea at that moment.

"I would ask that you shut all the panels and keep the cabin well closed to prevent water from coming in until we are out of this."

She nodded. "Where are Jannat and Rostam?"

"Reza went to get them and—" just at that moment Jannat opened the door and ushered Rostam into the room, with Reza in attendance.

"Uncle Reza says that we are about to have a storm, Mama! I want to see it."

"You must stay with us below, my darling. It is too dangerous to be on deck at present."

"It does not seem to be, Mama. Papa, may I not be with you up there? Please!"

Talon grinned at him and knelt in front of the pleading boy. "I am informed by the captain, who is most wise about these things, that this is a very bad storm and will be too dangerous for you. I want you to stay and protect Mama and Jannat and the maids. Dar'an will be here too." He glanced up at Dar'an, who reluctantly nodded. It was clear that he wanted to be up on deck where all the excitement was going to be.

"I need you here, Dar'an, with my family, just in case," Talon said, to make him feel better.

"But you are going up there, Papa?" Rostam asked him, staring up at him with wide open eyes.

"Yes. Reza and I will be right above you, helping the captain," Talon told him, standing up.

He looked over at Rav'an, who blew him a kiss and mouthed, "Be careful, God protect."

He strode through the open door with Reza right behind him, and then they were out on the waist deck, climbing the stairs to the long afterdeck.

"You have been in storms before, Talon. What do you think?"

"Each time it has been the will of God that we survived. The first time, I was one of only three who lived, Reza, and... I lost Jabbar. Truthfully, storms terrify me, as it is only the skill of the captain that can save us, and then not all the time. Boulos himself told us that many ships have perished in these seas."

"I shall pray to God that we are not among them," Reza said fervently, as they joined the captain and the steersmen. Talon's mind went back to the reason they were here in this part of the ocean at all, so far from any safe haven.

They had made landfall comfortably at Kalam Mali two days after the incident with the pirate ships. Five horses had died for one reason or another along the way, leaving them 25. The captain had been phlegmatic about it. "Everything is at risk on long journeys, and horses are no exception. I think we were lucky; we had enough rainfall on the journey to keep most of them alive."

Kalam Mali was a bustling port, full of shipping when they arrived. They unloaded the horses and had them penned in an area under guard while they negotiated with the Indian merchants. The Indians had been very eager to pay them the asking price. The amount they were prepared to pay for a good horse had astonished Talon and Reza. The horses more than paid for their keep, and Talon was left with a nice profit from that transaction. He was glad, because there was a tithe for trading in the port of 1,000 dirhams, which the captain considered excessive to the point of robbery, but there was nothing they could do about it.

They spent a week at the port. There was a fort on a hill overlooking the harbor, which was busier by far than the languid ports of Oman and Lamu. The crew were allowed ashore, under the watchful eyes of Umayr and Waqqas, whose responsibility it was to prevent them from getting into fights or lost in the labyrinth of narrow streets where the whores were waiting for them.

The region had been just as Imaran described it. The air was so thick that at times it felt suffocating. When it was not raining it was baking hot, and the ground dried out so fast that by the second day the air was heavy with a red dust. The flies were everywhere and the port was crowded. The Indians enjoyed noisy music that seemed to go on all day; reed pipes wheezed, cymbals clashed and drums rattled with music that was alien to the visitors' ears. The Indians loved parades and colorful religious events, when the cacophony of noise increased to the point where a person wanted to place hands over ears as the garlanded processions walked by.

There were temples to a myriad of gods, major and minor, animal and human in form. Most prominent of all was the elephant God. Talon learned that he was named Ganesha and that he was very important. All of them were painted in garish colors, and their often tiny temples were managed by half-naked priests, surrounded by beggars and supplicants.

They had seen their first elephant lumbering slowly down the main street, ridden by a mahout who sat behind the huge animal's ears. They had all stopped and stared in silent awe as it walked slowly past them.

Many of the locals chewed a whitish paste they called Betel nut that caused their mouths to become bright red, and they would spit out in a red stream onto the ground, caring little where it fell. The food was deliciously scented and spicy, but so hot that Reza said it was the fare of the Devil, which seemed to be confirmed when they all spent far too long over the toilet hole in a cupboard-like room off from the main cabin.

Talon had automatically looked for good grass for the horses on the outskirts of the city but had found none. Only a stiff-bladed grass like weed. It did not take a lot of reasoning to understand why horses did so poorly here, he decided.

Word had quickly spread about the successful engagement with the pirates, so the Arabs they met were effusive with their praise. They begged his small entourage to stop and share some tea and tell them for the hundredth time how the battle had gone. They also warned Talon that he needed to stay vigilant, because the pirates might well be in the port watching them at that very moment, waiting for revenge. There was nothing to distinguish them from any other ship that came into port, and in any event, there were no port authorities capable of apprehending them.

One aspect of Kalam Mali had proved a major disappointment. The man to whom they sold the horses told them, "There are fewer and fewer China ships these days."

Talon had asked why. The man had shrugged. "We don't know. The storms can be very bad or not so bad, but there are no ships here that are going to Kalah Bar this month or the next, which means that you might have to sell your other cargo here in India. If you want to do better, I would advise you to go to Kalah Bar yourself, and then you can come home with spices for Oman which alone will pay for your journey."

"How long would it take to get there?" Talon had asked unhappily, his heart sinking.

"About a month, God willing. If all goes well."

He had boarded the ship in a foul mood that day. When asked by Rav'an why he was scowling and fretting so much, he replied, "I am beginning to wonder about this merchant thing. It is fraught with problems at every turn."

"What do you mean, Talon?" she asked, taking his hand as they stared out at the forest of masts all around them. As she gazed around, both Jannat and Reza joined them on the deck.

"What do you see here?" he asked her, waving his free arm wide.

"Why, I see ships of every kind. Is that not a good thing?" she replied.

"Yes, it should be, but one kind of boat is missing, and it has to be this year of all years," he responded, his tone bitter.

Rav'an sighed. "Tell me what it is. I have not seen you as frustrated as this for some time."

"There are no Chinese ships! They have not come. Normally they are here by now, and we could have made deals through their agents and unloaded our cargo to be sailing back to Oman within a week. Now we have to decide what to do."

"Could we not sell our goods here and depart as planned?" she asked him with a frown.

"We could, but the agent I talked to told me that the prices would be very low. The Indians wanted our horses, from which we did make a decent profit, but we still have a cargo of other goods which they don't want so much, as they have most of what we are selling already. I was told to sail on to a place called Kalah Bar, which is across another wide sea."

"How long would that take?" Jannat asked.

"About another month," Reza told her.

There was a collective sigh from the two women. "Did the man who bought the horses assure you that the Chinese ships would be there to trade?" Rav'an asked the two grim-faced men.

"He told me that the ships of the Omani and the Chinese have been meeting here and in Kalah Bar for generations. They did warn me that even there the trade is sometimes not so good. Trade in general has fallen off, and no one is quite sure why. But he said that it is Kalah Bar where we have the best chance of making a great profit for the kind of goods we have on board."

They spent the better part of the evening considering this option, and even brought the captain into the discussion. Much to their surprise, he was willing enough.

"I will sail there for you, Master Talon. Not just because of the possibility of a much greater profit—and of course I have an investment in that—but because you have demonstrated that you know how to fight off pirates. So many ships perish because of that scourge alone."

What about the men?" Reza asked.

"Master Reza, the men admire you and Master Talon." He turned to the women with a smile on his rugged face. "They also admire the Mistresses Rav'an and Jannat, especially after the incident with the pirate ships. They will sail with you."

Talon sighed. He was torn between going back to Oman or trying for more. Being a ship owner and merchant in these seas brought responsibilities and problems he had not anticipated; however, he hated the idea of arriving home at Muscat with his tail between his legs, their journey largely unfulfilled. He finally nodded his head. "Then we sail. Thank you, Captain. I am grateful for your support."

*****

Talon thought back. Kalam Mali was a long way back to the West of their present position. Three weeks previously, they had stopped briefly at the island of Ceylon, known to all as the Isle of Rubies, where they had purchased some of these precious stones, but it was Rav'an who had discovered that it was really the island of Sapphires and had persuaded Talon to let her purchase a few. Then they had continued Eastward towards Kalah Bar. Now they were being stalked by a nasty looking storm that had the captain very worried. He shook his head and gazed out at the evil-looking sky above them, which had turned an ugly shade of yellow.

The warm gusts of wind abated, leaving an ominous calm and little wind to fill the after lateen sail and the foresail. The huge mainsail was down and secured, leaving the great mast bare. The ship was wallowing, but making some headway. The men on deck were uncharacteristically silent, sending apprehensive glances to the Southwest where the monstrous black cloud bank moved relentlessly towards them. Talon suspected that some among them knew what was to come. The captain kept them busy, shouting at them to double lash down everything, including the two boats in the waist of the ship. They complied willingly.

"Make sure the cook has contained the fire brands in the metal pot, lest we perish from fire within!" he called down to Tarif, who was in the waist of the ship. Tarif rushed off to pass the word.

Then the steersman Umayr called out fearfully and pointed at the sky behind them. The huge mass of roiling storm clouds was now almost overhead, and a column of rain had appeared and was now moving at speed directly for them. The captain remained calm, but he ordered a small shift of direction and then shouted to the crew to stand by.

Abruptly a blast of cold air struck the ship. The sails filled like stretched skin and Talon could have sworn the after mast bent a little. The blast of wind almost knocked him and Reza off their feet, causing them to clutch at anything that came to hand just to remain upright.

A high, keening sound rose as the wind howled through the rigging, followed by a wall of rain. It washed over the men on the decks of the ship in torrents, lashing at exposed skin, soaking them to the bone within seconds. A flash of lightning nearby startled them all, and it was followed almost immediately by a clap of thunder that deafened the men on the afterdeck and made them cower.

Turbans were blown off and men were lifted off their feet as the squall hammered at the ship and forced it to heel over to port. The crew struggled to keep their footing, hanging onto anything they could to prevent themselves from being washed overboard. The awning that covered most of the after deck was torn into strips, the remaining rags flapping wildly against the frame that had supported it.

"We need to find rope to lash ourselves to something, or we might go overboard!" Reza shouted in Talon's ear. He nodded agreement; but just as suddenly the squall was gone, and in the ensuing quiet, dripping people looked at one another with wide, fearful eyes. The sea, however, had turned an ominous darker shade of green flecked with black, while the crests of the waves began to foam. The sun disappeared altogether, leaving behind a menacing diffuse light; streaks of lightning and the ripping, tearing sounds of thunder bellowed overhead. The ship righted itself and continued, but now they were being buffeted by waves that marched in serried ranks up from the South. The entire sky became an unhealthy yellow color. Even the air around them smelled of something unpleasant, almost as though it was burned.

"Be warned, that was only the beginning!" the captain called over to them. He glanced behind him apprehensively. "If you have to stay on deck, which is madness, then tie yourselves to something. You cannot steer, so stay where you are."

Talon and Reza hastened to comply. They wrapped ropes around their waists and then tied themselves to fixtures near to the mast. They saw the steersmen do the same, as did the captain.

"We are useless up here on deck!" Reza said, swiping the waster away from his face. "But I would rather be up here seeing what will befall us than down below."

"It will be very unpleasant for the others, but up here it is far too dangerous for them," Talon agreed. Just as he said this, the wind descended upon the boat, and once again Talon was reminded how insignificant man became once he ventured out to sea.

The storm hit with a force which made the entire ship shudder as though struck with a monstrous hammer. It brought with it slashing rain and lightning that hissed into the sea around them, followed almost immediately by numbing crashes of thunder that shook the air and made their bones vibrate. The ship shuddered and yawed, and then began to rise and fall with the waves. The captain had at least been able to alter their course so that they were going with the wind, wherever it took them. The men at the steering point were thrown about as they struggled with the beam and tried to keep the ship from yawing and rolling them over.

The wind screamed and howled as though a thousand demons were at work, their one intent to sink the vessel and claim all the lives on board. The waves had in the shortest space of time gone from a couple of paces high to mountains of foaming water that formed deep valleys and tall hills all around the struggling vessel. Talon could barely breathe, the air around him was so full of water. He hung onto the ropes, knowing full well that had he and Reza not tied themselves off they would have gone overboard a long time back.

The ship would nose into a wall of water that would bury the bowsprit and then pour over the bows and forecastle in a foaming rush, and then very slowly the forward part of the ship would begin to rise. Water poured off the decks in torrents as they climbed out of the valley between breakers, so that they seemed to be pointing at the sky for one moment; and then they would crest the wave to descend sickeningly into yet another deep valley of water, being pushed from behind by the foaming crest of the wave they had just run over.

The spume and spray from the waves added to the torrential rain which washed over the decks, stinging faces with such force that men who still had their turbans took them off and wrapped the soaking material tightly about their faces and heads, leaving only the eyes exposed. Within minutes Talon felt numb with cold and could tell from Reza's expression that he too was suffering. They looked at one another and could read the fear in each other's eyes. Reza's lips were moving as he prayed. They crouched against the thick trunk of the mast, trying to avoid the worst of the weather, watching the captain and the steersmen fight the sea.

As the ship rolled from side to side it would take on the sea, and the men on the waist deck would be up to their waists in water, in danger of being swept away; then the ship would begin to roll in the other direction. Anything that was not lashed down properly was taken overboard, and Talon, watching this happen, was filled with a dread. He remembered only too well his tragic voyage from France on his way back to the Holy Land.

They stayed where they were, fastened to the deck by ropes, while the captain and his steering men fought hour after hour to prevent the ship from foundering. Those of the crew who needed to be at hand on the waist huddled tightly under the overhang of the deck above, miserable, soaked and cold.

The only consoling thought Talon had was that they were well away from land, hence could use the vast space of water without fear of being run ashore. However, the sea and the tearing, grasping wind seemed to have combined in a determined effort to swamp the ship. He stared out at the darkened sea, watching as the waves crested and the wind tore those same crests away, reminiscent of the dunes he had traversed not so many months ago. There really was a comparison to be made between the two, he reasoned. The only difference being that with the one you could die of thirst, while with the other you could drown. Small comfort in either case.

Chapter Ten

The Wreck

During a lull in the rain, darkness descended upon them. When the wind abated somewhat, Talon and Reza untied themselves and made a dash for the lower deck and shelter, leaving the captain and his men to their exhausting task of maintaining the ship on some kind of course. Reliefs were changed over every two hours, but the captain stayed at his post, constantly examining the elements for change and squinting up at the rigging to make sure that there were no weak stays that might snap or a boom that might break and put their lives in jeopardy.

Talon wanted to make sure that the others were holding up, while Reza accompanied him to find some dryer clothing. Peering into the gloom, Talon was shocked by what he found when they entered the main guest room. Everything had been flung about, and anything moveable had careered along the floor to smash against one wall or the other. The hanging lanterns, which were not lit, swung in crazy arcs as the ship wallowed from side to side or rose and fell with the huge waves. There was a distinct smell of oil in the cabin which worried him; some had spilled on the rumpled carpets. There was also an unpleasant odor of vomit.

Rav'an was wedged in a corner holding a frightened Rostam, with Jannat looking as pale as a ghost nearby. Rav'an was trying to console with soft words one of the servant girls who was on the edge of hysterics. The other servants were clustered nearby, seated in a terrified huddle, and some of them were fervently praying.

The men were accompanied into the room by a gust of wind from outside that had followed them down the stairs. They stumbled in, dripping water from head to foot.

All eyes in the cabin turned upon them and Rav'an gave a gasp of relief. "It sounds terrible out there!" she exclaimed. "What is happening?"

Reza gave Rav'an a smile and a wave of encouragement to Rostam, who was clutching at Rav'an, then crouched next to Jannat. "Are you all right, my Jannat?" he asked gently, while he dripped water all over the floor.

"Allah be praised, I am all right, but you are so wet, Reza! You should change out of those clothes or you will catch your death!" she said shakily as she reached out for him. He took her hands and said, "It is bad out there, and although it might not seem so, you are safer in here. Have courage."

Talon knelt by Rav'an and reached out to touch her cold cheek, then ruffled Rostam's hair. "How are you doing down here?" he asked them with a smile.

"You should change too, Talon. Can you not stay with us now?" Rav'an asked him, almost pleading.

"No, my Love, I cannot. The captain is on deck, and as the owner of the ship I cannot do any less. I shall change and then go back up. We will need to find some food in a few hours, as the cold is sapping our strength, and his. I think he is very tired."

"There is nothing to be done about the food until the storm abates. Then I shall see to it, if there is any to be had, but you must be very careful, Talon."

Talon nodded agreement but didn't say anything. It was a formidable tempest and he was very worried, although the ship seemed to be holding its own for the time being. His faith in ships at sea in rough weather was not great. Not for the first time he wondered why he had wanted to make this journey. The closed atmosphere of the cabin was making him feel nauseous. Surprisingly he had not felt sea sick at all while on deck. He marveled that Reza had not been ill either, as his friend had no real experience of the sea.

Talon and Reza went next door to change and put on warmer clothing.

"I am glad we are going back up on deck, Talon. I was very close to being sick in the women's cabin. I didn't feel too bad while on deck." Reza said as he changed clothes and put on an oilcloth cape. Talon grinned; for Reza that was quite an admission.

Talon took extra capes for the captain and the steersmen; then, after a drink of water, they went back onto the heaving deck. It was dark when they put foot on the waist deck, without a glimmer of light anywhere. They had to feel their way to the stairs. For Talon it was a terrifying experience; he could barely see the foaming water as it came aboard, but he could feel it slosh up his legs and tug at him, trying to pull him into the dark sea. He and Reza clung to one another as they fumbled their way up the ladder to the afterdeck, gripping at any solid structure at hand. The sea seemed to be level with his eyes, or even higher, as it slid by, foaming, malevolent and spume-covered. They made it onto the top deck, their change of clothes already soaked, and then they struggled into the full brunt of the wind to get close to the captain.

He acknowledge their return, but he was forced to shout over the keening wind and the crash of water at the bows to be heard. "God preserve us, but we are not out of this yet, and the next hours are going to be very difficult. *Insha'Allah* we will survive the night. Should we do so, the morning will tell us how much longer this storm will last." He donned the cape gratefully and then called to his weary men to pay attention to the rise and fall of the waves behind them, which they could not even see; if they did not pay attention the ship could move sideways to the waves and they would be swamped.

His main concern was how much water the ship was taking on, but in the darkness it was impossible to tell. "We will have to inspect the hull and to find out how much the cargo has moved when it gets light," he bellowed.

"If this gets much worse, we will have the unpleasant task of jettisoning some of our valuable cargo!" Talon shouted back. He didn't like the idea at all. He had invested a lot of money in that cargo. If they had to jettison it, he would be broke with only a ship to show for his hard-acquired investment, and perhaps not even that, if things got worse. He shook his head; being a merchant was not all it was cut out to be.

*****

Below their feet in the master cabin, Rav'an and Jannat huddled in a corner, braced against the crazy tipping and veering of the cabin, which seemed to move about in impossible ways. What low tables there had been were now a pile of sticks in a corner with the brass trays and pots piled on top of them, clinking and rolling about as the deck heaved in this or that direction. Salem had joined them, along with the maid they had hired in Oman; both had been flung into the corner, almost on top of Rav'an and Jannat, by the gyrations of the vessel. It was impossible to stand or even crawl while the ship heaved and twisted in the raging seas.

Rav'an held Rostam close to her. His head was buried in her cloak and his arms were tight around her neck, and she murmured words of encouragement in his ear. It was all the more terrifying because they could not tell what was going on above them. Despite being tightly closed, the shutters at the rear of the cabin were leaking and water was sloshing around the floor, having soaked the carpets and cushions into a soggy mess. They had all been sick at one time or another, which made the air foul and difficult to breath without feeling nauseous all over again.

Her greatest fear however, was for Talon and Reza out on the exposed deck above. Even in the half-darkness they had looked exhausted and hollow-eyed when they had come down to see them. Despite their encouragement she could see that both men were very worried. She had even detected fear in Talon's eyes. She had never seen that before, and it frightened her.

On occasion she could hear the men above shouting, but it was unintelligible, their words blown away by the wind. Somehow she understood that Talon had experienced this kind of storm before, and by his demeanor she guessed that it had not gone well that time.

In a haze of exhaustion her thoughts drifted to what kind of man he had become. In the relatively short time they had been together again, it was clear to her that he had changed from a youth to a man. Not just any man, but a hardened warrior; also, inexplicably, a rich man. She had no idea how he had accumulated enough to buy the ship and hire the crew, and Reza had not been able to enlighten her on that score. He had simply shrugged and told her that the Jews in the bazar had been extremely polite and had given him as much cash as he had needed.

She sensed also hardness to him that she could not remember from before, but she realized that it was not a cruel hardness; more a tempered strength, as though he had seen more than his share of the hardships of life. There was a certain guardedness that was new; secrets buried deep within that one day she resolved she would hear about from his own lips. There was a set to his jaw and mouth which, along with his old scar, made him seem intimidating to his son. But they were getting along well, she reasoned. Talon spent as much time as his duties permitted with his son, and she had seen them together at the front of the ship deep in conversation.

She knew that Rostam had initially been scared of this stranger who had come from nowhere and had been introduced as his father. She had been pleased that gradually the fear had been replaced by a wary respect and the beginnings of warmth, although Talon smiled less these days than she remembered. When he did, in their private moments, it was more with his eyes, and she could remember with a flood of warmth the Talon she had known before. Fariba, the ever wise Auntie Fariba, had told her that she should be patient, as Talon had not had an easy life while away and he was haunted by many ghosts; but under the slightly gruff exterior he was still their beloved Talon. His tenderness towards her, Rostam, and their companions left her in no doubt as to how much he loved them, from which she drew much comfort.

Rav'an sighed. She wished that they were all back with Fariba and Haddad in Muscat, warm and together in the scented garden. While she understood that Talon and Reza had been seduced by the lure of riches and adventure, she hoped that it would not end here, in the middle of the ocean. She pulled Rostam closer still as the ship lurched and twisted.

*****

The storm abated somewhat near midnight, although the men on deck had little respite. A particularly strong gust of wind took away the after sail. Talon and Reza heard a great crack above them, followed by a tearing sound; then without warning streamers of the sail whipped at them. There was another loud snap above them and they could tell that the rest of the sail had blown away, and the sheet and the boom that held the sail fell to the deck. It shattered the wood awning above them into matchwood, its rollers narrowly missing both men, who were cowering against the trunk of the mast, only just protected by the frames around its base.

The tackle struck the deck with an ugly thud, followed by another smaller one, and they found themselves entangled in ropes and pulleys, as well as being under the boom itself. Reza had the presence of mind to seize the small tangle of ropes and pulleys and tie them off to prevent them from being dragged overboard, but there was nothing else they could do in the dark.

Worse was to come. As the ship wallowed, barely making headway now that they only had the jib sail keeping the bow downwind, an enormous wave rose up on the starboard side and swamped the men at the steering bar; Talon felt the water rise up to his knees then rush out behind him, even this high!

There were cries of fear and then pain in the darkness, but Talon could not make out what had occurred until he heard his name shouted by the captain.

"Master Talon! Help! We need help here, God protect us!"

He realized that he had to go and assist the men, but the danger of crossing that wave-swept deck was cause for hesitation. However, he could hear clearly that they were in trouble. "Reza I must go to him!" he yelled, and hurriedly untied himself, then staggered across the six paces to the steering men.

He took his rope with him and immediately secured himself to the rail before he went on both knees to see better the men crouched over another lying on the deck.

One looked up. Talon could barely discern the bearded face of the captain. "A wave came and smashed into us. It took Tarif down so hard he is unconscious and needs to be taken below! I think he has broken something. Thank God he was not washed overboard."

Talon felt a presence alongside him.

"I shall take him below," Reza said loudly over the din of the wind. Talon slapped him on his soaked back.

"I'll take his place here with the captain, Reza. God protect you!"

"And you, be careful!" Reza shouted. They all flinched when a long streak of lightning struck the sea within fifty paces of them on the starboard side. It sizzled and writhed, lighting up the sky in an unholy glare, and the clap of thunder that followed made them all duck again. Reza shook his head as he gave a lopsided grin to Talon, who only saw the faint gleam of his teeth; then he helped the other steersman carry the unconscious Tariq below decks. It was a perilous journey across the deck and down the steps, but they managed it and disappeared from sight, leaving Talon and the captain alone on the top deck. It felt lonelier than ever to be here with no one else but the captain for company; however, he was determined to help fight the storm in any way he could. Just standing a spectator had been its own torment.

"I have sent for replacements," the captain shouted. "I do not wish to be disrespectful, Master Talon, but can you assist me while we wait for them? The steering is hard on one man."

"Of course I shall," Talon shouted back. "You need not ask. Show me what needs to be done."

****

A cold, gray dawn found them still floating over mountainous seas, held on course with only the jib sail to keep them going with the wind. Reza had reappeared, but not the other steersmen, which angered the captain.

The mess on the steering deck now became apparent, a tangle of ropes and sail remnants, along with pulleys, any one of which would have killed a man had it struck him on the head while falling. Other than this, however, the ship did not seem to have sustained major damage, at least not on the decks. They had not lost a mast, which would have been a disaster. Talon was glad to see that they still had their boats. It remained to be seen if there had been major damage below.

While the ship heaved and rolled in the agitated seas, the captain explained to Talon how they needed to read the sea and take advantage of every small opportunity it presented. It was exhausting work, but now at least the visibility was improving with a watery light. Low clouds scudded past the ship, barely as high as the top of the mast. Of the sun there was no sign, other than a faint glow in the East. The wind had eased, so that the ship was not buffeted as it had been most of the night, and to the exhausted, soaked men on the steering deck it was a huge comfort not to be chilled by the crazed wind.

A man showed his face on the waist deck. It was Umayr, calling up to them on the after deck. Talon could not hear what he said, but the captain left him and Reza holding the steering pole and strode over to the rail overlooking the waist deck.

This time Talon could hear him clearly over the wind. "Get all hands on the deck, and I mean *all* hands!" the captain bellowed. "I shall whip all your rotten hides purple if there is one son of a dog left below. Go!" he waved his hand at Umayr, who vanished.

Minutes later, the crew gathered on deck. They huddled in the waist while the captain harangued them from above.

"While you craven lickspittles have been cowering in the holds, I, your captain, and Masters Talon and Reza here, have been keeping the ship on course all night long, and by doing so have probably saved your worthless hides. I want a sail on deck immediately to replace the one we lost last night, and men to bail the ship. Where are the steering crew?" he bellowed.

Two men stepped forward, looking sheepish.

"Where were you last night when I needed you?" he demanded.

"We were afraid, Rais," one of the men whimpered.

"You were afraid!" the captain shouted. "How do you think we felt up here on the top deck all night? Do you think we were not afraid also? It is fearful men who die, as you should, for your cowardly behavior. You will be punished when we are done!" he threatened. "Get your scaly hides up here and take over from the owners of this ship, who should never have had to do this work!"

He waited until they came on the deck, then slapped them around their heads and kicked them, cowering, to their posts. Talon and Reza, barely able to keep from laughing, stood aside as soon as the chastened men arrived and seized the pole from them.

"If you let this ship drift off the wind I shall cut your throats and give you to the monsters of the sea, although they are likely to spit you out once they find out what you are made of," the captain roared at them. They nodded mutely, cringing.

He turned away and began to issue orders to the crew, putting Abdullah, a large muscular man man with a huge mustache, in charge of the bailing party, while Waqqas was given the urgent task of replacing the lost after-sail. He came back to where Talon and Reza now stood, on the port side away from the steering post. They had left the life saving ropes tied to the rail but had untied themselves, as their lives no longer depended on them. The sea was still dangerous and the ship was still being tossed about like a twig in rapids, but the storm was moving away. Nevertheless, they needed the sail, which men under the direction of Waqqas now struggled to bring up from below and drag onto the after deck.

Now there was a problem. The pulleys which were used to haul the sail up to the top of the mast were in a jumbled heap on the deck, and one important pulley was missing at the top of the mast. The only way they could be repositioned was for someone to climb the wildly swaying mast and attach the ropes that would hold the pulleys in place at the top of the mast, which would then allow the sail to be hoisted.

The captain turned to Waqqas and demanded that he send someone up the crude rope ladder attached to the thick stays that held the mast in place. The four men on the deck at the base of the mast refused to meet his eyes. None would volunteer, although he threatened to throw them all overboard. They were afraid and sullen, which bothered Talon; but before anyone else could say anything Reza stepped forward and called out over the wind.

"I shall go up there, but you must show me what to do when I am there."

Everyone stared at him as though he was out of his mind; but the captain, after a long thoughtful pause, shrugged, and with a wry smile at Reza and Talon said, "By God, but you have a lot of courage, Master Reza. Very well, here is what you must do."

He explained what was needed, and Reza shook off his cape and gave it to Talon with a grin, saying, "Someone has to show them how it is done, Brother."

"Indeed they do, my Brother, but take very good care up there. It is going around in crazy circles and you could be thrown off into the sea. I do not know how we could save you if that happens."

"*Insha'Allah* it will not be necessary. I shall tie myself when up there," Reza responded.

Talon knew Reza was lithe and strong, with little fear of heights, but this was very dangerous work and he was apprehensive. "God protect, Reza. Be careful."

Reza leapt onto the railing on the starboard side and then, taking a rope with him, he began to climb. The ship was still rolling and pitching up and down and from side to side. As the men on the deck watched, he seemed to be hanging from the ropes one minute and lying on them the next as the ship lurched to the port side. He was catlike, clearly able to deal with the dizzying changes, and before long he was at the top with his legs wrapped around the main beam of the mast.

He had been instructed by the captain to only make a temporary repair, as to do otherwise would entail much more work. He locked one rope through another, which allowed him to pull up a large pulley from the deck and to secure it to the loops at the top, whereupon the crew at the bottom fed up to him, the main rope which would be used to haul the sail boom back up. It took some time, and all the while Reza was being spun about in a dizzy circle that Talon was sure would have made him feel too sick to work. His friend, however, managed to feed the rope through the pulley.

Reza was thus engaged when he happened to look up and stopped in the midst of fiddling with the repair. He was staring intently off to the East in the direction their ship was heading.

"What is it you see?" Talon shouted up at him.

"I see something, Talon. Yes, by God, it is a ship, but it is in trouble. It does not seem to have any sails, and only the stumps of two masts!" Reza yelled back down to them. Suddenly he slipped and had to grab and hold tight as their own vessel lurched into a trough.

"Do you see anyone on it?" shouted the captain.

"No, I do not. I think it is sinking."

"Come down as soon as you can, Reza; we do not want an accident," Talon called up to him.

Reza nodded, then to everyone's amazement he took the end of the rope in both hands and let himself drop down instead of coming back down the stays.

He let out a yell of exhilaration as he flew through the air, but everyone on the deck held their breath with alarm. The crew who were holding the other end of the rope only just had the presence of mind to grip their end and let him down to the deck gently. Even so, he swayed out over the sea in an arc, then flew back and landed on the deck with the grace of an acrobat with a great smile on his face. Talon seized him in a bear hug. The men cheered, singing his praises.

"You have shown much courage, Master Reza!" The captain shouted over the wind. "We all thank you!"

"Idiot! You could have gone swimming with the sharks. Your courage is already legend, my Brother, without having to demonstrate it to these fools," Talon said in when he put Reza down. Then, "Tell us about this boat. What did you see?" he asked, as they stood aside and watched Waqqas and his men bend the sail to the boom and haul it up to the top. The sail bellied and then went taut, and they could feel the ship surge forward.

For a moment Reza watched the sailors complete the work he had begun. "Now all we have to do is to find out where we are and in which direction we are sailing," he remarked with a grin.

Chapter Eleven

Strange Survivors

The ship became much more manageable with the lateen sail raised on the after mast, although the captain kept casting apprehensive looks up at it whenever there was a stronger than usual gust of wind. With more control of the ship and with a strong breeze behind them, they began to make good progress. Safa even said he might be able to raise the main sail once the storm had moved on. The seas were still high and agitated, making life on the ship uncomfortable, but the men were able to stand unaided and go about the business of cleaning up the wreckage left by the storm. Food was brought up from the galley by the cook for the hungry men at the tiller, flat bread and some cold rice with cold cooked fish. Nothing hot was available, but Talon didn't care; he was ravenous, and so was Reza.

They finally persuaded the captain to go and rest; he had been on heavy duty for the entire time and was shivering with cold and exhaustion. He left the deck reluctantly, first admonishing the two replacement steersmen and threatening them with becoming shark food if they did not keep on course until he came back. He said he needed to get a sighting on the sun when the sky cleared and to call him the moment there was an opening in the clouds.

Talon rushed down the stairs to tell Rav'an that he and Reza would be remaining topside until they knew the fate of the ship that Reza had sighted. The women looked pale and exhausted, but they insisted upon coming up on the deck to get some fresh air. The atmosphere in the cabin was fetid and unpleasant.

Talon had informed them of the sighting, so once on deck they shared the general sense of expectancy as they stared forward, hoping to see the other vessel. The crew, too, were very interested in what they would find. It might contain a cargo that could be salvaged. Rostam was delighted when Rav'an pointed out a huge rainbow that glowed in the distance.

A man who had climbed the stays to the mast-head shouted and pointed ahead. "I see it! It is a ship, just as Master Reza said."

"Is there any sign of life on board?" Talon shouted back.

"No... I don't think so. It is hard to tell, but we are coming closer. I will see better in a short while."

Not long after that, everyone got a glimpse of the vessel and saw that it had indeed been dismasted in the storm. There was a jumble of tackle hanging off the side and drifting alongside. Everyone peered forward, trying to make out the details.

"That does not look like any kind of ship I know," commented one of the steersmen to his mate.

Neither Talon nor Reza had ever seen a ship of this kind before either. It was low in the water, which was level with the waist of the ship; water from the rough sea was washing along that deck so that the only safe place was on the high afterdeck which was where he thought any survivors would take refuge.

"It looks as though they had a fire on board," Reza commented, pointing to the front of the dying vessel.

"I agree, it looks as though they did have a fire, and I see something else. Yes, there is movement. There is someone still on the ship!" Talon exclaimed. "Go and get the captain, and hurry!" he shouted down to the men on the waist deck.

Dandachi came hurrying up from his cabin, rubbing the sleep out of his eyes. Having greeted them, he turned to peer forward.

Talon pointed. "Look, Captain! There are signs of life still on board. We should try to help if we can."

Dandachi looked at him doubtfully. "My responsibility is to this ship, Master Talon, to you and your passengers. It might well endanger us all to do anything for those souls. It is God's will and we should not interfere."

"We must do what we can for them, Captain. It would be wrong in God's eyes to abandon them to this fate," Talon countered. His features were set in such a determined manner that the captain shook his head.

"You and your friend have shown us what real courage means, Master. Very well then, we shall approach the ship and see what can be done."

"It is not an Omani ship," Dandachi informed Talon, "but I have seen something like this before. Yes, I know it now!" he exclaimed. "It is a China ship. It is one of their vessels!"

Talon and Reza looked at one another. This was the very first time they had ever seen a Chinese sea-going vessel, albeit a badly damaged one. They could now make out the blackened and burned forward part of the boat, which was wallowing half submerged. Talon studied the design with interest, as it contrasted sharply with his own ship. It appeared to have a blunt prow and three masts, two of which were now jagged stumps. The after part of the ship was much more elaborately designed. There were no less than three after decks for his own ship's two, but theirs were short, sloping decks. There were many windows below each deck, most of them shuttered, but a couple hung open, broken and splintered.

Captain Dandachi was speaking again. "We are only a week or less by my last estimation from the coast of Sumatra and the long straits between that Spice Island and the land of the Malay people. That must be a merchant ship on its way to the town of Kalah Bar on the coast of Malaya, where we are also heading. It is a grand meeting place for Omani Arab merchants and Chinese merchants. Goods are exchanged and news is discussed."

He got not further. There were suddenly signs of life on the upper deck of the wreck ahead of them. Three figures on the topmost deck who waved energetically at them, one of them holding a cloth like a flag. They looked very ragged. By now, only about five hundred paces separated the two boats.

"Where is their crew?" someone asked out loud. "Are those the only survivors?"

Those who were not working the sails crowded to the starboard side along the railings to stare curiously at the wreck they were approaching.

The captain roared at them to get back to their stations in case the *Sea Eagle* had to wear away from the wreck. They scurried back to their places but still peered over at the other vessel. The captain stayed close to the steersmen to direct operations and carefully brought their ship to within hailing distance.

Talon leaned on the rail and shouted across.

"How many of you?"

The response was hard to hear, but they could just understand some of the words and the number. "... four... sinking... Full of water. Save us!"

The men on the Omani ship looked at one another. "Only four? Where are the rest, I wonder?" Talon said to no one in particular. Turning towards the captain, he asked, "How could we get them off, Captain?"

"We could throw ropes and they could come across on those, perhaps?" Reza suggested.

"If the rope broke that could be dangerous for them, don't you think? They look too worn out to make it along a rope. We need to do something very quickly." The sea was washing higher than before across the mid section of the ship.

"Then we must make a raft and run it across with ropes. Either way, it will be dangerous work," Reza stated.

The captain corrected Reza. "We still have our boats, one of which we can use, although I would want it to be tied off to this ship in case anything happens, so that we can at least haul it back."

He reluctantly gave orders for a boat to be unlashed. It took many men to lift it and heave it, using pulleys to swung it over the side. The space between the two ships was not wide, but in these high seas it did not look like an appealing venture. Already sea water was slopping into the open boat. There were few men interested in taking the perilous trip across the heaving waters, but as soon as Reza and Talon stepped forward, Waqqas shrugged and said, "Allah protect us! I think it is madness, but I will go too."

Then Abdullah stepped forward as well, and Talon clapped him on the shoulder. "Good man," he said. Abdullah shot him a fearful look and answered, "God seems to be on our side, Master Talon. I will go, but I am afraid." Talon's own fears were threatening to surface, but in front of the crew he was determined not to show his apprehension. Reza seemed of a like mind, and just as determined to put a good face on it.

"Let's go and save what we can," he said out loud. "God protect us," he added in an undertone. Talon agreed.

The four piled into the small boat, and they pushed off as men in the waist payed out the rope that could be used to pull them back. They rowed hard against the tossing seas and closed the distance between them and the Chinese ship. Their boat took on some water, but the fearful Abdullah bailed with a furious energy. Their crossing only took a few very long-seeming, perilous minutes, and then they were bumping against the railings of the ship's waist, which was now almost submerged, leaving only the after decks above the water and a small portion of the foredeck.

Three men were there to greet them. As they came closer Talon could see that their manner of dress was quite unlike anything he had hitherto encountered, although it reminded him of the colorful court of Constantinople. The people on the deck wore expensive clothing, but it was in rags.

One was a teenage boy; another was a fit looking man in his prime, while another was much older. Talon did not have much time to observe more. The middle aged man seized the rope they tossed to him and quickly tied it to the rails and leaned over to shout in garbled Arabic, "We have to go bring woman," which startled Talon and the others so that they all stared up at him. "Come aboard now! We cannot stay long!" Talon shouted back.

He nodded and pushed the older person forward and said something to him and to the boy. Then he vanished inside the second deck while the boy and the older man clambered down into the boat with the help of the crew and Reza. Both were shivering and soaked to the skin. They looked too exhausted to do anything but sit in the middle without speaking. Talon and Reza took off their coats and handed them over, which they accepted with grateful nods, and then sat huddled in silence. Talon and the others looked impatiently up at the space where the other man had disappeared. Despite their efforts, the sea surge was driving their boat repeatedly against the railings, threatening to break it apart if the hammering continued. It was imperative that they pull away immediately.

The sinking ship emitted a deep groan from within. They all looked at one another.

"We must leave, now!" Reza rasped.

Suddenly the other man reappeared, leading a young woman of about Jannat's age. He carried a medium sized lacquer box and now wore a sword strapped around his waist. The crew of the boat held it as steady as they could so he could jump in. After he had placed the box on the floor, he reached up and put his hands around the waist of the young woman and lightly lifted her on board.

"Is there anyone else?" Talon asked pointing back at the ship. He repeated the question.

The man was obviously having some trouble understanding Talon, but he cocked his ear and then said, "Only us," shaking his head vigorously.

Again Talon and the others registered surprise. No crew? Just these people, who didn't look like sailors at all? But they needed to get away from the sinking Chinese vessel, which was subsiding into the sea right beneath them. Dandachi was shouting across to them words borne away by the wind, but he was pointing to the West at some more dense clouds on the horizon.

Talon waved back, then gestured to the new arrivals to be seated. As they were settling, he and the crew took up the oars and, as one, pulled hard in direction for their own ship, hauled at the same time by the men on the *Sea Eagle*. They left just in time. The Chinese ship gave a lurch and settled deeper in the water. There was another deep groan as though the ship was giving up its ghost with a long stream of bubbles from the area of the hold. The front section had disappeared, and the wreckage that had once been cordage and sails was floating over the foundering ship.

They negotiated the strip of heaving water between the vessels without mishap, other than to get very wet. The waves were still dangerous and the boat was taking water, but all of them had been soaked to begin with one way or the other, so it didn't really matter. Abdullah frantically bailed while the others rowed and the *Sea Eagle* crew hauled.

At a sharp word from the middle aged man, the boy gave up the covering provided by Talon to the woman who huddled alongside them in the middle of the boat. She took it gratefully, looking not at the boy but at the man. The man himself disdained any covering and spent most of the short trip watching his ship gradually slip under more water.

Finally, their boat bumped alongside their own vessel and they assisted their passengers up the side, passing them on board to outstretched hands. The Chinese man who had the sword in his sash climbed the short ladder by himself, holding firmly onto the long lacquer box.

Talon was the last to come aboard. He glanced up at the after deck and saw that Rav'an and Rostam with Jannat were standing there with Dar'an in attendance, Their eyes were riveted on the new arrivals. Rostam was held close by his mother, and Talon smiled inwardly at his son's intense expression of interest in all the activities. Talon gave them a small wave and then turned his attention back to the people they had rescued.

The strangers stood in a small bedraggled group, shivering around their leader who carried the box. The crew of the *Sea Eagle* stood around the deck gawking and talking volubly about them. The captain bawled at the crew to go about their business and to leave the Chinese to Talon. They straggled back to their posts, still watching the bedraggled group, their eyes feasting on the female amongst them.

Talon realized that the first thing that needed to be done was to get them below and into dry clothing. He glanced up again at Rav'an and beckoned to her. She understood immediately. The girl needed a woman's care. Rav'an handed Rostam off to Jannat and gave him a stern warning to stay with her, then hastened down the ladder to join Talon, Reza, and their mysterious guests.

Talon could not help but admire how elegantly she negotiated the set of stairs despite the ship's wild movements.

Rav'an's eyes widened as she saw the condition of the girl, and at once she stepped in to take her by her arms. She led the young woman off the deck and away from the staring crew below to the women's quarters. That left the three men standing, dripping water onto the deck and looking lost, the oldest of whom appeared to be in a bad way.

Talon called for Dar'an and told him to take the men below and give them some of his dry clothing and blankets.

"Allow them to rest in the spare store room, and then try to persuade the cook to boil some water for tea," Talon told the boy.

Before Dar'an could lead the Chinese men away, one of the crew called out excitedly and pointed over to the other ship. It was just about to slide completely under water. The Chinese turned and hurried to the side of the Omani ship to stare. They spoke together in a fast, singsong language which no one on board could understand, but it was clear that this was an emotional moment. Everyone on deck watched in silence as the large ship slowly settled out of sight with a hiss of escaping air and roiling water. Soon it was gone into the depths, leaving behind only a couple of spars and some sail material along with other flotsam.

With an audible sigh, the Chinese man with the box under his arm put his hand on the boy's shoulder, and all three turned away from the scene. There were tears in the old man's eyes as they turned to follow the beckoning Dar'an.

Talon and Reza had watched with interest. "I wonder what this is all about," Reza said. "Did you see their features, Talon? They look like those people we sometime used to see in the bazars of Isfahan, the merchants from the East. It's their eyes."

"I noticed it too. They all look like that, it would seem. Where is the rest of their crew, I wonder?" Talon remarked, watching the Chinese leader with care. He noticed the well formed torso and the strong shoulders of the man. He affected a thin mustache, which tapered to points that hung down on either side of his mouth; a small goatee grew out of a firm chin. There was a slight balding on the top of his head. Although plainly exhausted, the man was still alert and observant.

"Well, now we have taken care of them for the moment, we should continue on our way," Talon said. He and Reza went up the stairs to the upper deck, where they were confronted by Rostam, who had broken away from Jannat and wanted to know what was going on.

"Who are those people Papa, Uncle Reza? I saw the ship sink! Could that happen to us too?"

Talon leaned over the boy. "I think we are past the worst of the weather, Rostam, but there is still a long way to go, and we have to find out where the storm blew us. When the sun comes out the captain will know better."

Rostam looked solemn. "The men up here said they were Chinese. Who are the Chinese, Papa?"

"They are a people who come from way east of here," Talon said, waving his arm vaguely towards the eastern horizon.

"Are they our prisoners?" Rostam asked seriously.

Reza gave a chuckle. "No, little man, they are our guests. It was our task to save them, and your papa did his duty to God and man."

"May I stay up here, Papa?" the boy asked, his eyes pleading.

Talon remembered the cabin and the accumulated smells. "Yes, you may, but you are to stay close to Uncle Reza, who I am putting in charge of you. If he says it is time to go below, then that is an order; I want no arguments." He gave Reza a grin.

Rostam jumped up and down with pleasure. "Uncle Reza, I can stay!"

Reza laughed aloud. "Very well, you shall stay close to me, and we must not get in the way of the crew when they have much work to do." He took the boy's hand and moved off to join Jannat, who was watching from the front rail of the upper deck with an amused expression.

Talon smiled at her and turned back to the captain, who had been watching the proceedings with a benevolent smile on his bearded face. Rostam had become very popular among the crew since they had left Oman.

"Do you know how far we were blown off course by the storm, Captain?" Talon asked.

Dandachi glanced forward. The crew were hoisting the main sail, which bellied in the fresh wind. The ship immediately began to move forward at a much better pace, sending up the occasional spout of water at the bow, which would in turn send a thin curtain of spray over the fore deck.

"I shall know a little more when the sun finally comes out before too long, *Insha'Allah*. I suspect that we were blown north, which means we might be heading for the northern end of the Andaman Island chain. It is just north of the course I had set before the storm, so when we find them we can sail south and be back on course, *Insha'Allah*."

Talon nodded. Some weeks before, the captain had shown him the chart and the notebook he held as a prized possession, indicating the islands and their route to him.

"Remember, Master Talon, I showed you the islands called Langabalus and Nicobar. These are stopping places where we would have had to pause for fresh water and provisions in any case before the last leg to Kalah Bar."

Talon looked behind them. "Is that cloud behind us going to be a problem?"

The captain squinted back over his shoulder to the West. "I don't think so. I'm glad to say that it looks as though it is dispersing, and you will notice the sea is also becoming much more calm. God willing, we will have a smooth night of it." He rubbed his eyes, which were red. His weathered face showed marked signs of exhaustion.

Talon shivered as a light wind picked up. He was soaked to the skin, and so hungry he could have killed for a hot bowl of soup. He decided that he needed to go below and take care of both issues, and also to check on their strange guests.

"You should get some sleep, Captain. Can you trust these men to stay at their posts while we get some rest? I shall come back on deck in a couple of hours."

"Thank you, Master Talon," the captain said. "Yes, if they value their hides they will do as they are told. If there is any problem, they know to wake me immediately. Abdullah and Waqqas can be relied upon."

*****

Talon clumped down the steps to the small space that led to the various cabins. His cabin was on the port side; he noticed Dar'an squatting on the deck in front of the door to an adjoining cabin. The boy was half asleep, but he jumped to his feet when he heard Talon come to the bottom of the stairs.

"The men are in this room, Master Talon," he said, indicating the closed door.

It was one of the extra rooms which held the spare clothes and baggage for the passengers. He opened the door quietly and looked in.

The three men were sprawled out on quilts laid out on a carpet. He noticed that the cabin was damp, but considering the ferocity of the storm they had weathered, there probably wasn't anywhere on the ship that was not damp or soaking wet.

The middle aged man must have been a very light sleeper despite his exhaustion. He sat up and stared at Talon, who lifted a hand and then closed the door again. All he wanted to do just now was to change out of his wet clothes and get some sleep. Tomorrow would be a day of questions and answers. Just in case, however, he told Dar'an to go and see Waqqas and ask for two men to come down and guard the door. No one was to leave nor enter unless he, Talon, gave permission. He was sure that these men were simply survivors, but the alertness and obvious physical strength of the one man gave him pause. No point in taking risks when there were women aboard.

On that thought he decided to go and check in with Rav'an, two doors along. He could hear the murmur of conversation on the other side of the door, so he knocked and waited. The conversation stopped and Salem opened the door a crack. She smiled and nodded when she saw who it was.

"You may come in, Talon," Rav'an called.

He entered cautiously, stepping over shattered furniture and the soaking carpet and cushions. The back shutters were wide open to allow fresh air into the room, but still there was a sour, lingering smell.

Rav'an's expression was wry. "I am not sure how much we can save. Salem and the maid have done wonders , but we have much more to do before we will be comfortable again." She smiled at Salem and the wisp of a maid at the far end of the room, then she came over to stand close to him. He took her hand in his, wanting to embrace her, but not in front of the others. She smiled in understanding.

"Where is the girl?" he asked, smiling back.

"We changed her clothes and then put her to bed on that ledge over there," Rav'an said quietly, pointing to one of the sleeping alcoves. "She is exhausted. Fortunately, we still had some dry clothing and bedding."

"Did she say anything to you?"

"No, nothing. She just muttered something and then went to sleep almost before we could lay her down. Are these people Chinese, Talon?"

"The captain says so, and some of the crew have seen people like this before. They all agree they are Chinese."

"They look something like the people who come to Isfahan on their shaggy ponies, but these people seem more refined."

"I agree, and there is a mystery here. Why were there no other survivors? Where is the rest of the crew? The leader looks capable of handling himself. He could be a warrior; perhaps a merchant? Keep an eye on the girl, my Love. I don't want to trouble you, but I need to know who they are before I trust them to wander about our ship." He noticed the alarm in her eyes. "Don't worry, I am sure that all will be well. Just ask the maid to tell you when she wakes up, and keep her from leaving the cabin."

Rav'an nodded, then came closer still, so that he caught her scent. Even after a terrifying night in all the horrible conditions, he marveled at how clean she smelled, but it made him very conscious of how filthy he was.

She kissed him on the cheek and whispered, "I am so glad that we lived through that terrible storm. I am glad that you were not washed overboard, my Love. I was so afraid."

"I cannot believe that you were afraid, my Rav'an. You are my rock of courage. Still, I am glad that we are over the worst, and the captain thinks we are not that far off course, so we should come to land within a day or so." He squeezed her hand hard and then said, "I must change out of these wet clothes and get some sleep, for I am bone tired."

"I shall come with you and help," she stated firmly, and pushed him out of the door. With a smile at the guards now standing by the other door with Dar'an, she led him to their own private cabin, where she insisted on helping him take off his soaking rags and dry off before helping him into a comfortable robe. Talon enjoyed the attention, but he was asleep before his head touched the damp pillow she placed for him. She stayed in the room, watching him as he slept for a long while, and calmed him with a hand on his shoulder when his nightmares started up. She had no idea what kind of demons he encountered when he went to sleep, but she had known for some time that they often waited for him. Finally he breathed deeply and fell into a profound slumber free of dreams and demons. She left him then, to go and find Rostam and Jannat.

From tomorrow on,
I will be a happy man;
Grooming, chopping,
and traveling all over the world.
From tomorrow on,
I will cook foodstuff and vegetable,
Living in a house towards the sea,
with spring blossoms.

—*Hai Zi*

Chapter Twelve
Lord Meng Hsü

Lord Meng Hsü woke up to the familiar sounds of a ship at sea: the hiss of the water flowing along the hull, the creaking of the fitments and timbers as the ship rose and fell in a light swell. He could hear voices above his head on the upper deck. They were not Chinese voices!

He sat up with a start. They were not speaking Cantonese. He reached for his sword and found it by his side, then looked around desperately for the box. It was near to hand. At the same instant he recalled the events that had led up to this moment and paused. He sat still as in his mind he relived the ordeal of the night.

The great storm and the fire in the forecastle of the ship; the panicked yells of the crew men as the storm wrested control of the ship from them. The high winds and enormous waves had already taken down not one but two of the ship's masts and swept several of the crew overboard, never to be seen again. Their cries were still with him as he sat on the thin mattress and shook his head to clear it and adjust to his presence on a strange ship.

He remembered the captain of his own ship screaming almost into his ear that they had to abandon ship. The man was terrified of the fire, which raged in the fore part and had taken hold in the waist where the highly flammable fire powder kegs, cordage, spices and precious woods were stored. They were finished if the kegs ignited, but the storm was probably going to sink them anyway. Hsü had not wanted to entrust their lives to the small boats when the waves were so high and the rain so heavy. The two men had been screaming their disagreement at each other in the baffling winds of the tempest.

Then the main sail had caught fire and lit up the night around them, spraying a long trail flame and sparks in line with the wind like some terrifying firework from hell. They all flinched when the fire reached one of the barrels of powder in the hold and it exploded. In retrospect, Hsü thought that might well have saved them, as it blew upwards, blowing a large hole in the forward deck of the ship, which allowed even more water to pour into the front hold, temporarily dowsing the fire in that area. The howling wind had reduced the sound of the explosion to a mere thud.

Reluctantly he had turned to the captain, a man he didn't entirely trust, who came from the north of China, and told him to arrange for the abandonment of the ship. He had left the deck to go below and tell his administrator Jiaya, and Fuling, his son, to prepare themselves to leave. He'd then hurried to his own cabin and found Lihua, his concubine, crouched in a corner.

"Get up! We must leave!" he shouted over the din of the storm and the crashing of breaking timbers all around them. She shook her head frantically and tried even harder to squeeze herself into the corner, where she remained with her eyes shut, shivering with fear.

It took some minutes for him to coax her onto her feet, and then he had to search for the box which held his most precious jewelry and papers, after which he rummaged about desperately searching for his sword. He knew he would need it in an open boat with an untrustworthy crew. Eventually he managed to move Lihua out of the cabin into the anteroom, where he found his son and Jiaya waiting for him.

"What are you doing here? Get out onto the deck. Come on, we must hurry," he called out, and he pushed Fuling ahead of him up the stairs, dragging Lihua by the wrist.

The scene that greeted them when they'd emerged from the lower cabins shocked even him, and he had left the deck less than an hour before. The ship was a desolate wreck, with the spars and tackle moving about the half submerged waist with the rise and fall of the ship. Even in the dark he could see the ominous signs that they were even deeper in the water than before. Waves were bursting over the transom. The spray stung their faces as they stared about in a darkness lit only by the occasional flash of lighting and punctuated by the crash of thunder.

Despite the storm there was a kind of silence, which at first he could not to identify. Then it dawned on him that, other than his group, there wasn't anyone on the decks. His eyes frantically scanned the heaving deck, the waist of the ship with its tangle of ropes, charred sails and broken masts. They saw with horror that not one of the three boats was where they should have been.

He sloshed across the deck to the side, but saw nothing but darkness and the menacing waves. Still clutching his box, he ran up the steps to the steering level and again peered out to sea. Nothing! With a growing sense of despair he ran across the deck, jumping over more fallen tackle, to peer out into the darkness on the starboard side. The shrieking wind which tore at his clothing and the curling waves almost alongside seemed to mock his distress.

He shouted to the others to get under cover from the storm. They moved in a dazed, ragged huddle to the shelter of the overhang of the steering deck, where he joined them. It was time to pray. He wondered if his ancestors had been displeased with him or some God had been offended in India. He went back to his cabin to place the sword and the box on a shelf, as though somehow that might protect them. He knew full well that they were doomed and it was only a matter of time. Lihua unexpectedly joined him, while his son and the old man hovered outside the door with haunted looks on their faces.

He held her as, in a terrible breach of manners, she put her head into his shoulder and wept, shaking with cold and fear. He tried to smile as he beckoned his son and Jiaya into the pitching and rolling cabin and said, "Well, now we have the ship to ourselves. We can sail wherever we please."

There were no return smiles. Lihua gave a low sob of despair, sank to the floor clutching her arms to her chest, and began rocking herself.

Jiaya knelt before him. "We can only make our peace now, Master Meng. Ahmida Buddha will take us if we merit it."

Hsü, who preferred the reliability of reason to the consolation of faith, rummaged through his extensive memory of Confucius quotes but could find nothing of comfort there. Perhaps Confucius had never been in a mighty storm at sea, he reflected.

Hsü glanced at his son, who was watching Lihua crying on the floor. Not for the first time did he catch the boy's expression. They were about to be either fried to death or drowned, and his son was lusting after his concubine!

He sighed to himself with wry amusement. Perhaps the eminent presence of death made his son yearn to copulate with the girl, anything to forget their predicament. It did that to some people, he'd heard. He waved to his boy to come and sit with him as the deck gave a great heave and roll. The boy stumbled, then sat next to him on the floor. A wave had washed along the deck above them and water was now seeping through the seams and dripping onto the floor. He didn't want to be outside. Let the fates take them here in some sparse kind of comfort rather than freezing up there.

He must have slept sitting up in the lotus position because he snapped awake, aware of the arrival of dawn. Looking around, he noticed that the other two men were gone. Getting stiffly to his feet he tried to rub some warmth into his frozen knees and get the circulation going in his legs. Then he left Lihua, who was asleep in a huddle in a corner, and went to see if he could find out what had transpired during the night.

He found his son on the upper after deck, gripping onto the railing and peering westward. Next to him was Jiaya, who waved at him and pointed excitedly in the same direction. Hsü was astonished that the ship was still afloat. The fire was out, leaving blackened railings and planks where it had raged the night before.

"What did you see?" he asked as he arrived on the deck and clutched a railing to prevent himself from falling.

"There is something over there, I think to the west of us. It is hard to see in this light," Jiaya called out.

"The boat is still sound, and we could have saved her if those filthy cowards had not abandoned us last night!" Fuling called out. "Curse them to death!" He swept a hand through his long black hair, which was being blown about his face. Hsü was irrationally pleased to see that his son's normally submissive expression was replaced by raw anger. *Perhaps a little late, under the circumstances*, he mused, *but better than before.*

Hsü nodded. He had been about to say the same thing. If they had a full crew they might have been able to do something. As it was, the three of them could do nothing to save the foundering ship.

"There it is again! Do you see it?" Fuling shouted, pointing.

They peered aft, and sure enough they had seen the pointed sail of another vessel rising and falling many *li* behind them.

Before very long, the other ship had hove to, and they had been transferred and saved just in time to watch their own vessel go under.

*****

Now Hsü listened to the sounds coming from above; the storm was over, he surmised. The ship was not rising and falling as wildly as when they had come aboard. He wondered if they were any safer. The people had been very helpful, and Lihua had been taken below by one of the womenfolk; that at least was reassuring. He heard a soft snore and looked around. His son was still deep in the sleep of the exhausted, and Jiaya had wedged himself into one of the corners of the small cabin where he slept with his head against the wall, his mouth open, dead to the world. The old man looked very frail.

Hsü got to his feet. His stomach rumbled. He could not remember when he had last eaten. He opened the door. Two dark men with beards jumped up and shook their heads and waved their hands at him, indicating that he could not leave. They were armed with spears and daggers.

He nodded politely, lifted his open hands and said, "I am not going to do anything. I am hungry." He spoke in Hindi.

One of them shook his head and spoke back in Arabic. "You cannot leave. You wait and we bring the captain."

Hsü nodded. He could understand these people, although it was not easy.

"I wait. Hungry!" he smiled and pointed with his fingers to his mouth.

"Allah be praised, he speaks our language!" the other said. He smiled, displaying gaps and stumps of yellow teeth. "You wait. I go for Master Talon." He rushed off up the stairs, calling as he went.

Within a minute there were other voices, and two men came back down the stairs following the sailor, who was explaining something in rapid Arabic. The two men nodded.

"Thank you, Waqqas. I will talk to him now," one said.

He turned and faced Hsü, who found himself looking up at the same man who had assisted him on the other ship. He noticed with some surprise that this man had light colored hair and lighter skin than the other Arabs. He could not fail to notice a long scar running down the man's right jawline, even though the beard hid most of it. A quick glance at the other confirmed his thoughts that he, too, had helped to save them.

Hsü bowed and said, "We owe you our lives. I thank you for the great risk you took in coming to our aid."

"You speak Arabic?" Talon said with surprise.

"I learned a little, while in a place called Gujarat. I apologize, it is very bad."

"On the contrary, it is quite sufficient. I had not expected a ... Chinese to know Arabic," the Talon replied with a smile.

Hsü was only mildly offended. "We learn what we can."

"It will help us to understand what happened to you and your friends. Where is the rest of the crew of your ship?"

Hsü was happy to tell him, but first he asked, "We have not eaten for two days. Very hungry. May we have food?"

Reza chuckled. "He is right, we need to feed them first, Talon, and then we can find out what happened."

Talon grinned. "Yes, of course. I apologize. My companion Reza has more sense than I. Please come with me and we will feed you." He turned and led the way across the short space to another more spacious cabin, where some carpets and cushions had been arranged around a low table.

"We will eat and drink, and then you can tell us how you came to be here," Talon said.

*****

There was little conversation while Hsü ate the cold rice and morsels of meat and lentil in the wooden bowl he was given. He lamented the lack of chopsticks but realized that the rice was very loose and would have been difficult to pick up. He remembered just in time to eat with his right hand. Not to have done so would have been a severe loss of face.

The other two sat across from him and spoke yet another language while they observed him. He in turn looked them over and decided that, while they seemed friendly enough, both young men had that hard, appraising look in their eyes that he recalled seeing in the eyes of other killers he had known. In particular, Fang, his own bodyguard, whom he had left at home to guard his family. He felt a chill of fear. Perhaps he had fallen in among some really bad people.

One of them, the one called Talon, who appeared to be the senior, caught him watching them and stared straight into his eyes. Hsü held the look for a long moment, and then looked away, but not before he remarked the intense green eyes, almost those of a cat.

Even if they were not threatening, it would not be a good idea to offend these people, he decided. He finished his meal, sat back on his haunches, and regarded the others before making a short bow and thanking them for the food. It had been all he could do not to wolf it down, he had been so hungry. As it was, it had only alleviated the hunger enough for him to maintain his dignity and not seem crude in front of these barbarians.

He gave a small smile and opened his hands. "Ask me what you wish to know," he invited them.

Talon was the first to speak. "What is your name?"

"My name is Meng Hsü. I am a temporary ambassador for the governor of Guangzhou. I was on a trading mission."

Talon nodded then pointed to himself. "I am Talon de Gilles, and this is my companion, Reza."

Hsü gave a short bow to them, which they reciprocated with a nod of their heads.

"Where were you heading when the storm struck?" Talon asked.

Although Hsü struggled with the language, he was able to understand and responded in kind.

"We were sailing home to my country, China. I live in a city called Guangzhou. It is in the south of the country. It is a great port where many of your own people come to trade."

Both Talon and Reza glanced at one another in surprise.

"Is that the same place our friends in Oman call Khanfu?" Reza quietly asked Talon, who nodded thoughtfully.

"We have heard from merchants of Oman that they have been to your country, but neither of us has ever met your people before, and we certainly didn't know you travelled this far to the west of ... China," Talon said, pronouncing the strange word carefully.

"We Chinese have traded with the people called the Hind and further west to Oman for centuries," Hsü stated with some pride.

There was a pause while the two digested this information.

"What happened to your ship?" Talon asked.

"There was a fire, probably because some careless crew member or the cook failed to place the embers of the oven in a metal container when the storm struck. I don't really know, but it took hold very quickly and was soon impossible to put out."

Hsü went on to explain what had happened and how they had found themselves abandoned by their crew.

Talon and Reza listened in silence, except for the occasional request to clarify something he had said. When he finished, Talon poured the remaining tea into their small cups.

"Allah was kind to you this time. May the captain of your ship perish for abandoning you like that. It was fortunate for you that Reza saw your ship while he was up one of our masts helping repair it. It is unlikely that we would have seen you otherwise."

They then spoke rapidly in their other language, and Reza shrugged.

Talon turned to Hsü and said, "The captain and the crew of this ship are from all over the Arab world. The captain had to be persuaded to bring his ship near yours so that we could rescue you and your wife and those other two."

Hsü bowed low from the sitting position. They were all seated cross-legged on a thick carpet that was comfortably dry.

"It was great Joss that you found us. I cannot thank you enough for what you have done. The young man is my son; his name is Fuling, while the older man is my administrator, Jiaya."

"The woman? Is she your servant?" Reza asked. It had not been lost on him, nor on anyone else, that the woman, despite her soaked and exhausted appearance when she came aboard, was very beautiful.

"Er... she is my concubine," Hsü stated shortly. The question was rude, but he supposed they needed to know who their uninvited guests were.

The other two looked at one another impassively.

"She will have to stay with our women folk for the time being. You understand why?" Talon asked him.

Hsü was familiar with the Moslem customs, so he nodded his head without comment.

"She will be well looked after. The other women are our wives," Talon stated. "We shall find clothes for you, your son and the old man. You may have the cabin next to this one. It is small, but it is all we have."

"Where, may I ask, are you sailing?" Hsü asked.

"We are going to a place our captain calls Kalah Bar in the straights of Salaht."

"I passed through that straight nine months ago; it is where we were going to stop before continuing on to China."

"Would you be able to find a ship to take you home to China from there?" Reza asked him.

"It should be possible, yes. It depends upon the season, of course, and whether there are any Chinese ships going our way at this time of year. I think so."

"Did you have a cargo for trade?" Talon asked.

Hsü had to control his emotions at this point. He leaned forward and nodded in silence. Then he looked up and spoke.

"I went to Hind, the great land to our west, to deliver papers to a king in the South called Balhara, and then on to Gujarat to assure the sultan that the Sung Emperor remembers him and sends greetings. My mission complete, I loaded our ship with goods to bring home to China."

"What goods would you bring to China from Al Hind?" Reza asked with a sharp glance at Talon.

"Sandalwood, which is precious to us. We also had ivory from Africa, gold, spices, and pelts of tiger and other wild animals, which are popular in our country. Much more." He almost choked on the thought of all of that wealth, now at the bottom of the sea. How he would be able to explain the appalling loss to the other investors, he simply didn't know. He would weather the loss, but some of the others of the cartel would be seriously affected.

The other two could see what a harrowing moment this was for him, so they remained respectfully silent.

Eventually Talon spoke. "We will leave you now, Master Sooh. Your family will be allowed to join you in the cabin next door, and our servants will bring clothes. Please rest, and know you have anything to fear. You are under our protection as long as you are with us."

Hsü resolved to teach Talon how to pronounce his name properly, but now was not the time.

They showed him back to his cabin, where he joined Fuling and Jiaya. Both had been fed, and they now wore the same kind of clothes as the people on board the ship. Jiaya went to his knees and placed his head on the floor in obeisance to Hsü.

"You appear to have appeased the barbarians, Master. We are very grateful for your courage."

Hsü refrained from rolling his eyes. This was something he found tedious: the eternal *Ke Tou* of the minions. "For the moment, Jiaya, just for the moment. They may decide to eat us a little later when their meat supplies run out."

It amused him to see Jiaya looking frightened again.

Fuling remarked, "They are barbarians. Who can say what they will do to us? They might be pirates and wish to rob us before throwing us overboard." He scowled at the door.

There was a knock on the door just as he said this, which Hsü opened. It was a female servant, her head and face half covered with a brown cotton chador. She held out a tray of more hot tea in little cups for them. She also presented Hsü with a folded bundle of dry clothing. He smiled with gratitude.

Hsü bowed his thanks as he took the tray and presented it to Fuling. "I doubt if the tea has been poisoned, but you should try it first just in case, my son." He gave them the benefit of his small, wry smile as he watched their expressions. He sighed, more with exasperation at their needless fear than anything else.

"They might be barbarians, or even pirates, but it is unlikely that those kind of people would have bothered to rescue us if they wanted to loot us; and look, they are feeding us and even giving us tea! I think we can trust them. Their leaders have assured me that we are under their protection while on board, so we have nothing to fear... at this point," Hsü told them. He hoped he was right.

*****

Once the Chinese girl had woken up, Rav'an had managed, by dint of much hand waving and many smiles, to persuade her to allow them to dress her in one of the smaller *dishdashas* that they possessed. Rav'an observed that the girl was fine-boned and petite, with jet black hair that came down to her waist, and dark eyes that gazed out of a well-proportioned face, which, Rav'an supposed, might be considered beautiful in her own land. While Jannat brushed the girl's hair, Rav'an ordered some tea; the cook had been able to do that much so far. Then they provided the girl with a wooden bowl of rice and lentils, with some shreds of meat on top. Having slept like the dead, the girl now seemed barely able to restrain herself as she gulped the food. Jannat pointed to her right hand and indicated that it was the only one she should use.

They tried to talk to her, but she shook her head and murmured something in her own language. Then, when she had eaten and handed the bowl back to Rav'an, she asked a question. It sounded like "Meng Hsou? Meng Hsou?"

There was a knock on the door and Talon poked his face inside. "We have been talking to the leader of their little group. His name is Meng Sooh, and she," he pointed to Lihua, "is his concubine."

"I think she has been asking for him, Talon," Rav'an said.

"Ah, well, Salem can take her to the cabin next to ours, where they will be staying. I am going on deck," he said.

Then he nodded to Rostam. "Rostam, do you want to come up with me?" he asked the boy, who was looking less tired. "Rav'an, you will come too?"

She nodded. "I am sure Jannat would like to go up as well."

Talon looked around and was astonished at how quickly Rav'an had managed to have the cabins cleaned up. The smell lingered, but was rapidly being replaced by fresh air from the open shutters. The soaking carpets were hanging out on the after railing to dry, much to the discomfiture of the captain, who felt embarrassed by all this bedroom clutter on his deck. Mattresses, mats and clothes were hung off ropes in such profusion that the after deck looked like a laundry shop, not a respectable ship, he complained to Talon when he came on deck.

"We cannot live below in the damp, Captain. Even your bedding is hanging out there, I noticed," Talon replied with a grin. "Tell the rest of the crew to do the same. Now that the sea is calmer we should open the gratings and allow the lower deck area to dry out, or we will have sickness below decks. I don't want that, as we are short-handed as it is."

The captain had to agree with him, so he barked some orders at Abdullah and Umayr to comply with Talon's request. Talon noticed Tariq standing in the waist with some men. His arm was in a sling.

"He didn't break anything, just wrenched it and banged his head. Tariq has a very hard head," the captain told Talon.

Soon even the waist of the ship was festooned with clothing and bedding brought up from below. The sun had made an appearance, which allowed the captain to take some readings before he went below to rest. The sun began to warm the sodden vessel and the sea settled down to a long swell. Soon the material hanging from every possible hook or line was steaming as it dried.

Two hours later, Yosef appeared on deck at the front of the ship and waved urgently to Talon.

"What is it, Yosef?" he called.

"We have water below deck in the bow area, Talon. There is a leak somewhere."

The captain, who had come back on deck after a brief rest below, looked alarmed. He began to shout orders for the crew to get a line of buckets to bail the water. "I thought the ship looked somewhat down at the bows! We must find the leak and plug it as soon as we get enough of the water out, before it reaches our cargo and spoils it. We must hurry!"

The crew, who had been lounging about, doing nothing and enjoying the warmth of the sun, were soon urgently applying themselves to bailing the sea water out of the forward compartments of the ship.

Tyger! Tyger! burning bright,
In the forests of the night,
What immortal hand or eye
Could frame thy fearful symmetry?

—William Blake

Chapter Thirteen
Tyger! Tyger!

On a hill situated above the port stood a building, more of a fortress really, surrounded by high stone walls. These thick walls enclosed several compounds and smaller houses, within which lived the most powerful man in the region. From this high elevation he could observe the entire port laid out below, and every ship that came and went.

Sing and his personal guards strode along the roof of one of the buildings towards an opening in the floor that was barred with a heavy metal grate. Through the stout iron bars across the hatch, one could see a set of narrow steps leading down to a tunnel beyond.

Not far from this entrance, just above a deep courtyard, there was a winch with a chain attached to the top of a gate, set into the wall beneath their feet. The gate could be raised and lowered from above. This was not what interested Sing at present. He wanted to descend the stair and pay a visit. A guard lifted the grating and let it fall with a clang onto the paved stones. Sing waited until one of the men carrying a torch brought it to illuminate the dank and narrow stairs ahead of them. Because he was taller than the average Malay, he had to duck as he stepped down into the tunnel to follow the torchbearer.

Sing brought a small silk cloth out of a pocket and placed it over his nose to ward off the stench of a wild animal's urine and feces, mingled with corrupting flesh, that wafted up from the depths of the interior. Clouds of flies in the yard below competed with the carrion birds that hopped about, tearing at rotting flesh.

At the base of the steps the men made their way cautiously along a short, dank passage, wary of snakes, and careful of where they put their feet, as there were splintered bones strewn about the slippery, stony floor. Some even had flesh still clinging to them. Rats squealed and scuttled away into the dark recesses of the stone work. On their left, strongly set into the masonry, was the gate leading into the open air compound; but ahead of them stood a strong cage made of thick, iron bars.

Something large moved within the cage, a somber shadow that came to its feet and turned to face the oncoming light and its jailers. In the flickering light of the torch the tiger glared at them, its teeth bared in a silent snarl. The black and dark yellow stripes along its pelt moved as though the stripes themselves were alive, and the light threw huge shadows onto the stone walls of its prison. The iron cage was small for such a huge cat, to the point of being cramped, which was what Sing wanted. The tiger's yellow eyes were wide with hate and fear. It stared unblinking at the three men, its mouth half open, its fangs gleaming.

Sing approached until he was two full paces away from the bars and the beast; he stared back at it with his own black eyes, assessing its mood.

"There you are, my beauty," he crooned. "Tonight you will feast; but first, we must put you in the right frame of mind."

He held out his hand to the guards, and one of the men handed him a long stick. Another went to the other end of the cage with a similar rod and waited his master's command.

The rods were about ten feet long, made of bamboo, and had at their tips a tiny but sharp metal point. Sing aimed it at the predator. The tiger, knowing what was coming, snarled and then gave out a deafening roar, attacking the solid bars of its cage. The noise from the enraged and frightened animal could be heard outside in the enclosed courtyard, causing the carrion birds to flap into the air and settle on the branches of a tree. They might have been frightened but were not yet ready to leave.

Sing smiled. He prodded the tiger, which cringed and tried in vain to seize the end of the rod in its jaws, snapping and clawing; but Sing knew how to avoid its attempts, and every time the animal lashed out at his rod with its bared claws, the guard on the other side would prod it from another angle. The tiger shrank away from the stabbing points, but then, in its mounting rage, it leapt at the bars, causing them to shake as it reached through, trying to tear at its tormentors. Its roars were deafening in the confined space of the tunnel.

By this time blood had been drawn, so Sing stopped and observed the state of the animal through slitted eyes. The animal was almost crazed with rage and pain, snarling furiously and trying in vain reach for him with its claws extended. Nodding with satisfaction, Sing turned and led the way back along the tunnel and up the stairs. His three assistants hastened to follow him. The enraged roars of the tiger were deafening in the confined space and made them eager to get out of that stinking place.

Sing's parting orders were, "Leave the gate below open to the yard pen and do not feed him. We need to have good entertainment tonight."

*****

Later that evening, as dusk approached, a small crowd gathered on the ramparts of the walls overlooking the yard twenty feet below. The dusty compound was only thirty paces wide and somewhat longer, so the spectators, men and women, servants and armed guards, could see easily from one end to the other, even though in the middle grew two tall shady *cengal kampung* trees with smooth trunks. The servants of Sing's palace all had a clear view of the raised gate beneath the pavilion, which was located high above the dusty ground of the compound.

They were silent and apprehensive. An almost tangible atmosphere of dread pervaded the gathering. They all knew what was about to happen.

Sing and ten of his men appeared on the steps of the pavilion overlooking the compound of death. Sing took a seat on the stone chair under the thatched roof, and his well-armed guards ranged themselves on either side of him.

Sing lifted his hand, and from behind him came four more guards, holding two prisoners between them. One was a mere youth clad in only a loincloth who struggled hard against the firm grip of the burly guards; the other, a young woman of some beauty, had almost to be carried, she was so limp.

The guards brought the two before Sing and dropped the woman to the flags in front of him, while the other two held the young man, preventing him from throwing himself at Sing. His handsome face was contorted with anger and fear as he tried desperately to marshal his courage in front of the person he so feared and hated.

Sing languidly took a finger of Durian fruit, handed to him by an obsequious servant, and regarded the prisoner in silence before he turned his attention to the young woman, who had not moved. She lay on her knees in a state of semi-collapse in front of him with her head lowered. He frowned.

"Ah, my beloved Huriyah, how could you betray me! How could you, when I could have given you anything? Riches, servants and more."

She lifted her tear-stained face as though to answer, but he snarled back at her. "Do not dare to say anything, you whore! You were found to be with this, this pig, and so you shall die together today as a warning to others,"

She gave a small wail of pure terror and threw herself forward to clasp his jewel-studded slippers, trying to kiss them and weeping copiously.

"My Lord, I beg of you, have mercy on me. Have mercy! Remember how much I have been to you!" She pointed to the youth behind her. "He meant nothing to me, nothing at all!" her fear was making her babble now. "I am carrying your child!" she screamed.

He looked at her for a brief moment, and then barked a laugh. "Who knows whose child it is? For all I know, you have slept with everyone with a ready spear. Better this way, so I won't have to worry about it." He snickered at his own wit, then waved his hand in dismissal. The guards immediately seized her and dragged her away from his feet, supporting her upright as they stood by the other impassive guards. She was near to passing out with terror, as she knew there was no hope left, her cries of fear becoming more and more faint.

The youth began to struggle again, shouting, "In God's name, have mercy on her! Kill me! I deserve to die, but not her, my Lord. Spare her, I beg you!"

Sing looked at him directly and the boy could see into the pitiless black eyes. "Why would I spoil a good spectacle and send only you to your death?" he asked rhetorically. He smiled thinly. "You two can meet up on the other side and continue with your liaison there!" He laughed again.

The young man was weeping now, but with frustration as well as fear. He was still yelling and looking back over his shoulder as the guards hauled him to the edge of the rampart and then gave him a push. He toppled over, to land in an untidy heap on the ground. There was a gasp from the watching crowd standing on the walls on either side of the pavilion. The girl, by now in a dead faint, was tied with a rope and then lowered to the ground, where she lay on her side. The boy recovered his feet and stared back up at the people on the wall. There was no way back up unless he could scale the sheer walls of the compound.

The murmur of the crowd rose in horrified anticipation. Sing glanced around; he knew that no matter how terrible the spectacle, people still watched. He smiled to himself and settled back. Then he made a chopping motion with his right hand. Two guards began to winch a chain up out of the paved floor behind him. The chain clinked slowly around the wooden barrel of the winch wheel as it hauled up another iron door deep inside the wall, which would release the animal held prisoner in the cage.

In the pit the youth glanced at the girl, but then he spun around and stared at the dark opening of the tunnel. The iron grill was raised and he knew very well what that meant. He shot a glance at the tree in the middle of the yard. It presented the only safety there was. If he could gain enough height he might live a little longer. Hope was all he possessed, but again he looked at his former lover and hesitated.

He ran to her, hastily untied the rope around her waist, then lifted her limp frame up into his arms and staggered towards the tree fifteen long paces away. The murmur of the crowd increased in volume as he ran with his burden, but then someone shouted an alarm and pointed. The youth heard the shout and knew in his stomach that he had run out of time. He hauled the girl onto her feet and pushed her hard towards the tree, now only four paces away. "Go, for your life! Save yourself!" he shouted at her.

Huriyah awoke from her stupor and gave him a fearful look, then stared behind him. She let out a shriek and began to run. She reached the tree and began to try to scale its wide trunk. She slipped and clawed at the grease-slicked bark in a frenzy of terror.

The youth, meanwhile, had turned to face his nemesis. The animal came out of the tunnel in a rush, then paused just outside the tunnel entrance, shaking its head and growling low in its throat. The myriad torches on the walls and the smell of many humans angered and confused it, but not for long. He focused on the two figures in the compound a few dozen paces in front of him. His tail twitched as though it had a life of its own, lashing wildly from side to side as he registered that they were down on the ground with him. He gave a roar that stilled every other sound in the night and then began to stalk the two humans. The girl screamed in sheer horror, but her former lover faced the king of cats, his eyes wide with fear. The animal, wary of humans, scented the stench of fear.

The young man could not help himself; his bladder and bowels loosed and he voided himself, his terror was so great. He could hear his own teeth chattering as he eyed the huge predator moving towards him, its massive head close to the ground, its teeth bared in a half snarl, its tail stroking the ground behind it. The boy backed towards the tree, his arms wide in a futile gesture of defense; the girl was desperately trying to get some purchase on the tree behind him. He came close enough to feel her heat as she scrabbled at the slippery surface to no avail. In one reckless impulse, the boy spun around and lifted her up, then called to her in a hoarse voice.

"Climb, climb!" The girl, by now almost mad with fear, clambered onto his shoulders and reached up for the nearest branch.

It was too late. In three bounds the huge cat covered the ground between them and was onto the youth's back. Its forepaws clawed his face and head while its back claws tore away the flesh of his back and legs.

The youth gave a strangled scream, released his hold on the trunk and fell backwards, turning as he fell to face the animal, which also fell back; but then with another blood-chilling roar, carrying all the rage it felt for the human tormentors, it leapt on the wailing youth. The boy was in agony, his back ripped to shreds. No longer possessing a face, he did not see the fearsome beast as it came again to finish him off. Its back claws eviscerated the boy, tearing out his entrails, then its jaws closed onto his throat, choking off any further sound as it snapped his neck. The body was still twitching when the animal began to tear at its flesh.

The girl was overcome by the gruesome horror just below; her grip loosened, and she began to slip. She slid screaming down the tree trunk to land within feet of the dead boy and the tiger. With another shriek of terror she picked herself up and began to run. Anywhere, it didn't matter, as long as she could get away from the ghastly sight of the dismembered boy.

The tiger looked up from his preoccupation with the corpse and saw her. The sight of an animal fleeing triggered a predator's response. It leaped after the shrieking girl and brought her down in a flurry of dust and limbs. His fangs tore into her shoulder and then into her neck. The huge cat, its jaws and muzzle covered with blood, stood over the corpse and roared out its victory to the huddled humans on the walls above him. The crowd on the walls gave a collective moan of horror as the tiger seized an arm and dragged the body of the girl backwards to dump her next to that of the dead youth. He settled down to eat his fill, growling to himself and glancing up at the humans who lingered on the walls above with his yellow, hate-filled eyes.

*****

Talon stood on the steering deck with Reza and the captain and observed while the captain conned the ship into the harbor. The shipping was sparse; Captain Dandachi informed them that this was surprising for the time of year. The monsoons were due to reverse direction soon. They were slightly out of time because of the delays and their time on the islands of Langabulos, where they had spent a week making minor repairs to the ship's bows and taking on fresh water, fruit and vegetables, along with several woven cages of squawking chickens.

The tall island to the west of their location provided a good natural shelter from any storms that might fall upon them from the West, as this was still the season for the great winds that came to the Indian ocean.

Hsü was up on the steering deck with them, but he gave the captain a wide berth, having noted the look of fierce concentration on his face. Hsü quietly observed how well the captain carried out the complicated maneuvers of moving his ship past some dangerous looking sandbanks into a good anchorage.

Over the last couple of weeks, Talon had come to know Hsü better and had spent as much time as he could with the man. For Talon this was an opportunity to gain an insight to a culture he knew almost nothing about, and he still wondered at how fate had arranged the meeting.

Hsü had been accommodating and helpful, offering much in the way of information to an interested audience. Talon noticed that there was a coolness between Hsü and his son Fuling but didn't give it much thought; he was interested in learning what the young man had to say too, he spoke a smattering of Arabic and seemed eager to talk about his home country. Rav'an and Jannat had joined in the conversations, as the Chinese did not seem to exclude women folk, as did the Arabs, being comfortable around them in a circumspect manner.

The woman who had come with Hsü was initially very shy, but before long she had come to relax in the company of these strange people who had saved their lives. She began to practice her own vocabulary of limited Arabic with Rav'an and Jannat.

The ship finally came to a point where the captain could drop anchor without obstructing any other vessels. The great lateen sails came down and were lashed and secured. The after anchor was dropped, and they came to a stop altogether.

It was then that Talon really became aware of the dense humidity of the air around them. He was sweating freely under his cotton clothing and realized that, while it was fine to have these layers in the dry desert, they were an uncomfortable annoyance here in the tropical coast of Malaya. He heard the unwelcome whine of an insect seeking his blood and sighed. This was reminiscent of his time in Egypt. He hoped he would not succumb to the fever while here.

The town of Kuah on the island of Langkawi consisted of a nondescript collection of white lime-washed houses along a single street, behind which were many thatched buildings on high stilts, with *godowns* or warehouses lining the east side of the large island. The town faced the distant, flat, jungle and the mangrove swamps of the mainland coast only a couple of leagues away. The island formed a natural harbor, providing exits to the North and South along the strait between the island and the swampy mainland. Behind the main town were some larger buildings, which Talon guessed belonged to the sultan and the wealthier merchants who dealt with both the Chinese and the Arab ships that docked here.

Captain Dandachi, who had been here once before, informed Talon and Reza that although there was a sultan, he was a mere figurehead. The town was ruled by a powerful man known as Sing who was half Malay and half Arab. The trading station itself was owned by the sultan, but the rule of law was dictated by Sing. It would not do to get on the wrong side of this man, he informed Talon. It was rumored that he not only owned the island but controlled the piracy in the region and gave his protection to whomsoever paid him the right amount in bribes.

Hsü came over to Talon as they watched from the railing the activity on the shoreline. "I can only see one vessel that is Chinese in the harbor, Talon," he said. "I would like to talk with the captain and find out if he is going back to China and can take us with him."

Talon was concerned. If there was only one Chinese ship, he wondered, who would buy his cargo? Boulos had mentioned that there were merchants who lived on the island who had *godowns* which could hold a large amount of cargo, pending the arrival of ships going in the right direction. He wanted to sell his present cargo and leave for Oman as soon as possible. The winds were going to change direction in the next two months and he didn't want to be stuck, unable to sail into prevailing winds by the time they arrived on the western side of the continent of Al Hind.

"I would like to come with you, Hsü," he said, mopping his forehead with a cotton cloth. "I need to see to my own cargo, as well as to make sure you find a boat. I can't believe how humid it is here!" he protested.

Hsü grinned. "You are not used to this humidity, are you, Talon? These countries are all like this. Even my own city, which is in a large delta, can become very humid in the summer time just before the real monsoons."

Taking Reza and Fuling with them, they clambered down into the boat provided by the captain and had themselves rowed to the Chinese ship. As they approached, Talon had a chance to observe the design. It was built in an entirely different manner from his own, but appeared just as seaworthy. The hull swept upwards at both the bows and the after end, but they were blunt rather than sharp. The sails were made of some material that looked more like oiled cloth and had thin strips of wood set along their length, but because they were folded he couldn't see much more. The decks were high: there were at least three after decks, and a large rudder projected out of the rear of the boat.

They were hailed from the waist by a member of the crew, and Hsü responded in kind; there followed a rapid exchange in Chinese. The man disappeared for a moment, then he reappeared at the ship's side and waved them alongside. As they clambered aboard, they found themselves facing three men dressed in fine silk clothing with very bright colors and designs painted or stitched on their long-sleeved jackets. Behind these three, the main crew were dressed very much like sailors anywhere. They wore rough trousers, or in one case a sarong, many were bare chested, and several wore ragged turbans. The crew were armed and looked ready for trouble. Talon glanced around and saw that preparations for going to sea were in process.

Hsü, meanwhile, had bowed deeply to the merchants and begun a rapid conversation with them. Their bland expressions changed as he spoke, and all three bowed deeply to him. Then one of them called out a sharp command and waved to their group to follow him into the interior.

Even the smell of this vessel was different, Talon decided. There was much more in the way of scented woods, and the smell of old smoke was pervasive. Their new hosts brought them to a spacious cabin that had windows opening out onto the glittering water of the harbor and provided a modicum of air movement.

After following Hsü's example and bowing to their hosts, they all seated themselves on cushions placed on a thick carpet pile. Hsü turned to Talon and Reza and said, "I have explained who I am and what happened to my ship. Now that they know about this they are more friendly, but we shall see."

Talon sipped his tea and listened with half an ear to the sing-song chatter of the Chinese people as they launched into what appeared to be an intense discussion. To judge by Hsü's tightening expression and Fuling's worried looks, things were not going as well as Hsü might have hoped. Finally, after half an hour of this, Hsü held up his hand to the men facing him and turned to Talon.

"They are very regretful, but they are waiting for the winds to change so that they can sail for India. They cannot take us back to China, Talon. I tried to persuade them, even with bribes, to be paid when we arrived in Guangzhou, but they respectfully declined, as they are part of a consortium of merchants from Fu-Čou, a large port further north of Guangzhou. They would not be able to make the decision without the permission of the consortium, which of course cannot be obtained while here. I did my best to persuade them, but to no avail." Even with his seemingly bland Asiatic features Talon could see that Hsü was concerned.

Talon became worried himself. "I am very sorry to hear this, Hsü, for myself as well. If they will not be going to China, do they know of a merchant who would be willing to buy my cargo and keep it here in a godown until a Chinese merchant could come and buy it?"

Hsü turned back to the three men in front of him. They had round, expressionless faces with jet black hair bound at the back, and thin mustaches that drooped to waxed points. Their clothing was of expensive material and their hands were well-manicured, unlike his own hands or those of his companions, who by contrast looked positively ragged. Even Hsü looked unkempt by comparison to these people.

Hsü launched into another discussion with the merchants, who responded volubly and with an emphatic shake of their heads. They talked amongst themselves for a few more moments, and then Hsü said to Talon.

"They told me that while you might find a merchant ready to take your consignment, there are not many Chinese on the island at this time. There have been... difficulties with the local population; several Chinese merchants have been murdered, their *godowns* pillaged and burned. The remainder of them are trying to protect what they have, and many have left."

"Why? Is there a problem?" Reza asked. "Is it pirates?"

"Most likely, Reza." Hsü responded. "They tell me that this man called Sing is probably behind the trouble, but no one can prove anything, and the sultan is weak. Sing has great influence in this region, especially on the island. He is a dangerous and ambitious man who has no respect for the sultan, who lives on the mainland in Kalah Bar. Recently he has begun to behave as though he is the true owner of this island and the port. They advise great caution at this time."

Talon was dismayed; this sounded ominous. Not only was Hsü stranded, but his own merchandise was in jeopardy and there was not much likelihood of selling it for a good price here. He stood to lose much of his precious investment.

Hsü was still talking to the men, but it was clear that the meeting was over. He bowed from the waist and began to stand up. Everyone hastened to follow suit, and then there was even more bowing and high-pitched chatter before they exited onto the main deck.

As they were being rowed away, Fuling and Hsü held an animated conversation with much pointing towards the shore and the ship they had just left.

It was a somber group that boarded the *Sea Eagle* soon afterwards and went their several ways. Reza and Talon walked onto the steering deck, where they were joined Rav'an and Jannat, who were seething with curiosity as to what had transpired on the Chinese ship. Rav'an noticed their glum looks.

"What is the matter, Talon, Reza? Is something wrong?" she asked, as Rostam came running up the steps and stood with his mother.

"Were you on that Chinese ship, Papa?" he piped.

"Yes, we were, Rostam," Talon said to him with a smile. "We didn't understand a word, but Hsü and Fuling told us that the ship is not going to China, so Hsü is stranded here in this steam bath of a place, while we are going to have a hard time selling our cargo. He told me that even in Kalah Bar, which is just across the straits, there are no Chinese traders."

Rav'an and Jannat looked surprised and then worried. "Is there no one on land who could buy the cargo and wait for a boat to come?" Jannat asked.

"That is for us to find out," Talon said with a hard note to his voice.

*****

The next day, with Hsü and Fuling in attendance, as well as the captain, Talon and Reza set out for the wharf, which was a short row away. One of the houses, according to Hsü, was a meeting place for merchants and ship's captains looking for trade. Leaving the rowers to guard the boat, the men, this time armed against any trouble, made their way along the crowded pier towards a row of houses set off the side. Talon took note of the strange looking weapon that Hsü wore in his belt.

Hsü lead the way, and Captain Dandachi agreed that the best place to make a deal was the more imposing building, so they walked up to the main entrance. They were waved by two doormen into the shadow of a vast room with a tall ceiling of palm thatch and rough beams. Large openings for windows allowed for some ventilation; and the whine of insects, which had plagued them since they had landed, was less annoying here. The room was half full of a strange assortment of people dressed in an equally varied assortment of clothes. The loud chatter ceased as the newcomers were observed by men who could have been anything from sailors or pirates to merchant men, it was hard to say.

Talon saw Chinese wearing their mode of dress that he now recognized, and a number of villainous looking Arab sailors along side smaller brown men, whom he took to be Malays; they wore sarongs and were naked from the waist up and they seemed at ease among the Arabs. He noticed some tall, very black-skinned men who had come from southern India, and other, less dark, better dressed men from further north of the continent, along with a smattering of other people of Asian extraction.

Hsü led the way across the room towards a table by the window, where two sharp-eyed men, Chinese by their clothing and looks, were seated. Hsü bowed to them before engaging in a conversation while indicating Talon.

The men returned their nods and waved the visitors to nearby benches. The murmur of the room returned to its former noise as the traders lost interest in the new arrivals.

Tea was served by a Malay servant, to whom the Chinese men spoke in a language Talon had never heard before, and then he left. Talon could smell the odor of rancid coconut oil wafting from the kitchens at the back of the large room; this combined with the smell of unwashed bodies and thick, moisture-laden air, was almost overwhelming. He smiled as he watched Reza's nose wrinkle, and decided that he would not eat here. Tea, however, might be safe enough.

Reza and Talon sipped the hot brew from porcelain cups that were much too fine for an establishment like this, while Hsü spoke at length with the two merchants, describing and negotiating for Talon's merchandise. After much discussion amid their noisy slurping of the tea, Hsü turned to Talon and explained.

"They are interested in your cargo, but they have full *godowns* because they are waiting for ships to take their own freight to China. Rumor has it that there have been bad storms in the seas the other side of this land, and ships have been lost in great numbers, so the traffic has been very slow. They are also afraid to buy more, as this could be a temptation to pirates who now infest these waters." Hsü paused, and then added, "They are afraid of something or someone."

"What kind of price are they willing to pay for our goods?" Reza asked.

Hsü, who already knew the quantity of their load and their quality, went back to speaking with the two merchants. Watching them, Talon could read that they were interested, but they kept shaking their heads.

One of them pulled over a small abacus from his side of the table and began to flick the beads back and forth along the slides. He stopped and said something.

None of them had noticed that their Malay waiter had disappeared from the building.

Hsü leaned back and pursed his lips, looking embarrassed.

"What did he say?" Reza prompted.

"I am not sure I want to tell you. Their price is so low as to be insulting," Hsü told him.

"Try me," Talon said.

Hsü sighed. "He is offering one and a half thousand taels of silver and two tons of cloves. We all know that the cargo you are carrying is worth far more than that."

Talon looked at Reza. "We can let it go for four and a half thousand taels and three tons of cloves. Nothing less," he stated. Hsü nodded, and then translated Talon's reply.

The man muttered something and thoughtfully clicked the balls back and forth for a few seconds, then made a comment to Hsü; he also made a motion with his hand to indicate that this was a far as he would go.

"He said that he could go to three thousand taels and two tons, but no more," Hsü told them.

Talon frowned. 'The man knows perfectly well what the cargo is worth! They are trying to rob me," he said angrily. "The price he is offering is no use to me. It would not even cover my costs, let along provide a profit."

At that moment, several men appeared at the entrance to the inn; one of them was a tall, dark-featured man who wore a well wound turban and was better dressed than everyone around.

Although he wore the usual Arab dress, the cloth was more suitable for the tropical climate. He had a sparse beard that was flecked with gray. His black eyes fastened on the group talking by the window. Talon sensed the look and turned to see who might be watching them. Their eyes locked for an instant, and then the man smiled and walked towards him. Stopping about three paces away, he gave a curt bow and then said in Arabic, "You are invited to the house of Master Sing."

Talon raised his eyebrows, but then got up and stood before the man, who was closely guarded by several alert attendants. Reza, sensing that something was amiss, got up too and stood next to Talon, assessing the newcomers.

"My name is Amar," the man said. "My master understands that you are trying to sell your cargo?"

Before the surprised Talon could wonder how the man knew this, Amar lifted a bejeweled hand, smiled and said, "My master knows everything that goes on in this town." He smiled again and indicated that they should come with him.

Talon looked back at the two Chinese men and was struck by how frightened they looked. Hsü got up to stand with him, but the two merchants with whom they had just been speaking dropped a couple of coins on the table and made haste to leave.

Chapter Fourteen
Master Sing

Amar's attendants held spears and wore swords. They were unmistakably bodyguards, and there was an unspoken threat in their manner which Talon didn't like.

They walked in silence towards a small group of horses held by Malay *syce,* and Amar indicated that they should mount. There were only three spare horses, so Talon told the captain to go back to the boat. Fuling left with the captain, after his father murmured something to him.

They rode for about half a league, and most of it was along a road that brought them well above the harbor and the township. They didn't have much time to admire the view, however, because Amar led them briskly past a high walled compound towards an ornate stone arch of a gate. There were menacing stone figures of men carved on either side of it, brandishing solid stone swords and threatening visitors with glaring eyes and bared teeth.

They were led along a pathway that followed a tall wall, with shrubs and small trees lining either side. Talon just glimpsed a small pagoda perched on the top of the far wall and wondered what might be its purpose. As they walked behind Amar, he became aware of a sickly and unpleasant smell that emanated from the other side of the wall. He glanced at Reza, who had also noticed the smell, as had Hsü, but neither said anything. Amar hurried them through another entrance which was also guarded, but these guards were very much alive and watchful. They passed into the cool of a tall chamber, thankful for the relief from the intense heat and humidity outside. Talon wiped his face with a cloth, as did Reza; even in here the damp heat was stifling.

A tall man walked towards them with a smile on his face. It was clear that he was of mixed blood, with round features and sporting a sparse but well-trimmed, jet-black beard. He looked comfortable in his loose sarong, wide cotton shirt, and over robe.

"Welcome to my house, gentlemen," he said with his arms spread wide. "I had heard that a new ship was in the harbor, and I wanted to see for myself who the new visitors might be. My name is Sing."

Talon felt Reza tense beside him, but he said nothing. Talon gave a half bow and presented his two followers. He introduced himself as Suleiman, thinking it might be better not to give too much away. Was there a flicker of enmity in those dark eyes when he introduced Hsü? Talon wasn't sure, but realized that it would behoove him to tread carefully with this man who gave off the smell of ruthless power.

Amar had vanished.

"I am given to understand that you have a cargo to sell, Master Suleiman."

"Your information is correct, Master Sing. We were in the middle of some negotiations just as your man Amar arrived with your invitation."

Sing smiled in an avuncular manner. "Yes, I understand that it was not going as well as you expected?"

"We had not quite reached a point of negotiation where I would have liked it to be," Talon responded. His two companions remained silent.

Sing clapped his hands and servants appeared. "Bring refreshments to the pagoda. I wish to show my guests around," he ordered. They vanished, and he led the way up stone stairs to another level. Amar was already waiting for them at the small pagoda that Talon had glimpsed earlier. The servants hastened to provide cushions for the guests. There were fruits of many kinds arranged on rattan platters, including several fuzzy looking ones that Talon had never seen before. Drinks of fruit juice and sherbet were waiting for them.

As they had they emerged onto the second level, Talon found that he could now see down into the other courtyard. It was less well maintained than the other, and there were several dogs growling and fighting over some bones. A man ran out onto the ground and waved a stick at them, shouting. He chased them out through a large, iron-barred gate at the far end. Talon noticed that there were some vultures perched in one of the trees. Why would they be there if it wasn't for the bones on the ground?

Sing didn't seem to notice the carrion eaters and invited his guests to be seated. "Do you not think the view is magnificent from here?" he asked with a smile, displaying good teeth, waving towards the town and the sea below. Talon could even see his own ship at anchor in the harbor.

"Try the fruit; it is from our own plantations, and most of them transport well on ships. I can provide you with all you might for your journey home. You are eager, are you not, to be going home?" Sing asked in a concerned manner.

Talon stared out over the light jungle between their location and that of the town before replying.

"Yes, we are very eager to go home, once I have unloaded our cargo," he said. "You have a magnificent view from here, Master Sing."

"Yes, there is little that goes on that I don't see one way or the other," he responded; his tone implied more. Talon looked back at him. Was this some kind of threat?

"I enjoy watching the ships come and go. Over time the merchants from both your country to the West and the Chinese have made me... comfortably well-off, shall we say," Sing added.

Considering the opulence of the main building interior, the rich hangings and the beautiful glazed pottery, the marble floor tiles strewn with fine rugs, and the numerous servants, Talon could not disagree. There did not appear to be any other buildings of stone on the island; this must have once been a fortress, he thought to himself. He could tell that, even now, it could be easily defended.

They discussed the recent events of the voyage. Sing expressed sadness and commiserations that Hsü's ship had gone down, and then he sighed. "Word has reached me that several ships I sent to China have either gone down or been badly damaged in the typhoons. This means that their cargos are also lost or damaged. It has been a very bad year for trade everywhere."

"We heard that there had been a huge storm in the Chinese sea. Is this the season for storms? The one we encountered West of here was like the wrath of God!" Reza said.

"You could say that, but it is especially bad this year. But you have not taken any refreshments! You must have some of that fruit over there. We call it Durian." Sing pointed to a large, round, greenish object that had shallow spikes all over its skin. He then produced a small knife from his robes, with which he proceeded to start cutting the green fruit. The moment he opened it, the fruit produced a most offensive smell. Talon forced himself not to hold his nose or to sneeze. Hsü, meanwhile, had an enigmatic smile on his face. Reza looked pained.

Having eased the fruit open, Sing exposed soft, yellowish, silky globules within. "These," he said, "are the nectar of the jungle gods. You will enjoy them." He smiled.

Talon wanted to get as far away from the fruit as he possibly could, but knew he was being tested. He felt Reza cringe next to him, but his friend also knew that manners came before all else and subsided. It would be a great loss of face to refuse.

Sing reached for a finely carved ivory spoon, then dug out one of the globules from the inside and offered it to Talon, watching him intently from under the heavy lids hooding his black eyes. Talon gave the rictus of a smile, thought of declining as the smell assaulted him, but knew better and took a mouthful. It took all his self control not to spit it out and to restrain his stomach from heaving. He chewed carefully and forced himself to swallow. He nearly choked as the substance slid down his throat, but tried to look thoughtful. He knew that he was failing dismally.

"My goodness, that is incredible! Reza, you must taste some of this!" he gasped when he could get his breath back.

Reza gave a shudder and very low moan. "Pedar Sag!" he muttered under his breath, but then he, too, trying to smile, received a mouthful. Talon saw that he held his breath while he consumed the awful stuff.

Hsü seemed to be about to have a heart attack; his normally pale face was puce and he was gripping his knees with great force. Sing seemed quite unaware of the misery he was causing and offered Talon another spoonful. This time Talon could refuse without offense. He waved it off with a weak smile. "I am overwhelmed by the extraordinary taste, but I am not a big eater of fruit," he murmured. Even he could hear the desperation in his voice.

Then Hsü casually took a spoonful.

"I had forgotten how good it tastes," he murmured with a glint in his eyes. Talon wanted to stuff the spoon sideways down his throat.

Sing put his spoon down with a half-smile and turned again to Talon. "Please tell me of the cargo you possess, and we can then decide if I want to buy," he asked politely.

Talon was aware that Sing probably already knew to the bale, but he elaborated on the ivory and Nutmeg in particular, and the Myrrh which he had purchased in Yemen, as well as the Frankincense; Hsü had assured him these were sought after for medicines in China and brought good prices. Then he described the ivory, the rhino horns, the pelts and the precious stones he had brought from Lamu, Muscat, and Kulam Mali.

When he had finished, Sing sat back and casually spooned some of the revolting fruit into his mouth and chewed reflectively.

"By weight alone you have a large cargo, Master Suleiman," he said glancing at Talon. "However, most of us already have our *godowns* full to their roofs, and so there is not much need for more unless some ships come by and take our goods."

Talon sighed. This was similar to what he had heard in the town.

"What price are you offering?" he asked directly.

"Sight unseen, I would offer you four and a half thousand taels of silver, some two hundred taels of gold, and three tons of cloves and peppers from the land across to the west."

Talon sat back. This was exactly what he had wanted from the merchants in the town, but now he wasn't so sure. He glanced at Hsü, who imperceptibly shook his head.

"I appreciate your offer, Master Sing, but I would need more than that to cover my costs."

"I can go as far as five taels, but the tonnage stays the same for the cloves and peppers," Sing stated, and his eyes had lost their former friendliness. Talon sensed that the man was not used to bargaining and had been irritated by his response.

"That is a very generous offer, Master Sing. I hope you will allow me time to consider this. I must consult with my friends on the ship."

Sing waved his hand in dismissal. "You should know that no one in the town can make a better offer, Master Suleiman. But... there is no need for haste, and of course I must inspect the cargo before we can conclude, so perhaps we can come to an agreement tomorrow. I shall have Amar take you back to the harbor." It was the signal for them to leave.

They all stood up and said their farewells. Amar led the way back along the patio towards the stairs. Talon glanced again at the now deserted courtyard below. He wondered if the smell he had noticed on their way here had anything to do with the Durian. Something told him that perhaps it did not.

As they were leaving they heard a roar. The horses were startled and would have galloped off if their riders had not held them in check. Amar pretended not to have heard and continued riding down the pathway, but the others looked back over their shoulders. Talon was sure the roar had been that of a lion, and it had come from the compound of the palace.

They dismounted on the main street where Amar bade them an elaborate farewell and promised to meet them with horses the next day. He led the horses off with the help of his bodyguards.

The three of them made for the shade of one of the large trees alongside the street. It was sweltering, even in the shade. Talon watched the Arab ride off; he had already decided that he didn't trust Amar.

"You should learn patience, my friend." Hsü admonished Talon. "This is bargaining, and it requires restraint and patience."

"Do you think Sing is really interested in paying what the cargo is worth?" Talon challenged him. "The price he offered was only just enough to cover my costs, but there is no profit in it. Why did I sail all this way if that is the best we can do?"

"No, and there might be others who could offer more. I think a lot is going to depend upon how much space they have left in their *godowns*. They are all very worried about pirates."

Talon nodded. "Sing has made the biggest offer so far. Arrgh, but that ... fruit as he called it, Durian, is disgusting! I still have the smell in my nose!"

Reza laughed. "Pedar Sag! I am surprised that I didn't vomit all over Hsü here, it was so foul. It is like having to stand in a huge urn of horse snot surrounded by shit! I need a hot bowl of tea to wash that foul taste out of my mouth!" he exclaimed, pretending to gag.

"Neither of you barbarians has any refinement of taste!" Hsü chided them. "This is one of the most popular fruits in the region, and furthermore, we Chinese enjoy it too. The people here love it, and by the way, so do the elephants, I am told."

"You Chinese have just fallen off whatever pedestal I might have placed you on, Hsü. I am not of these people, and neither am I an elephant, so I will decline to have any more of that stuff... ever," Talon stated firmly, with a grimace. "I saw him, Reza, he was enjoying every minute of our pain." He pointed an accusing finger at Hsü.

They all laughed, but Reza wagged his finger at Hsü. "That is one item that does not come aboard our ship!"

Hsü inclined his head slightly and smiled his half-smile.

"Did you notice the smell of that compound?" Reza remarked on a more sober note.

"I did indeed, Reza," Hsü nodded his head. "That is the smell of carrion, and not, as you might have been deceived into thinking, the smell of Durian, your new favorite food."

"Those bones, they didn't look like those of any animal I know of," Talon said slowly. In fact, the last time he had seen bones of that kind they had been of dead people who had lain for some time in the open and been picked clean by vultures. He remembered the vultures at the compound.

"That roar was the roar of a tiger," Hsü informed them quietly.

"What is a tiger?" Reza asked.

"It is a very big cat, and from what I saw, I judge this one is in captivity."

"Big? How big?" asked Talon, images of the lion he had fought surfacing.

"Very big. It has yellow and black stripes all over and is terribly dangerous when angry, I am told. We have them in China, too."

*****

They spent the rest of the day going from *godown* to *godown* and from one trading-house to another, drinking copious amounts of tea and sweating it out on the short walks in between. The humidity climbed at the same rate as the accumulating cloud-banks above them. Talon glanced up at the dense black clouds as the mutter of thunder came to them from the mainland. Flickers of lightning danced accompaniment to the thunder and gusts of warm wind began to ripple the darkening waters of the harbor.

In every trading house they visited, the merchants, be they Arab or Chinese, were cagey and offered minimum prices, which exasperated Talon. He was contemplating ruin if he accepted these prices, even Sing's offer was not a fair one, so he refused each time, hoping that the next house of trade would be better, but it never was.

A very disconsolate group finally turned and trudged back towards their ship. At one point they passed a temple of some sort, and Talon pointed to an image of a creature that looked like a giant serpent with clawed feet painted in garish colors of red and gold; it stood guarding the entrance way to this sacred place.

"What is that creature?" he asked.

"It is a dragon," Hsü responded. "They also can be found in China."

Talon looked suddenly very interested and yet pensive. "So that is where they have gone! The dragon is a creature that we used to have in our country long ago. I have heard about them. I would like to see a real one, very much," he said.

"It will rain very soon," Hsü stated, changing the subject.

Chapter Fifteen

Precious Stones

Within minutes of boarding the *Sea Eagle*, the first warm gusts of wind from the jungle-covered mainland buffeted the town, and Talon could see dust swirling into the air above the distant quayside. On the harbor front buildings, the clothes hanging on lines outside windows were tossed into the air to flap loosely and then wrap themselves, like predatory flying mantas, about unsuspecting people fleeing the storm. The rigging of the ship began to sing with a low, taut hum, and the sea became choppy as the wind stirred up the waters of the harbor.

Talon bid Hsü goodbye and went below, followed by Reza, to join the womenfolk. The windows were wide open to let the sea breeze come into the stuffy cabin, but as the shutters began to slam Salem moved to fasten them, and then the air in the cabin became even more stifling.

Talon and Reza told the women of their unsuccessful efforts and now their concerns. Talon was very worried by this time.

"I didn't expect it to be so difficult to sell this kind of cargo. Boulos and Imaran were adamant that these goods would sell straight off the ship! Now look at us. We have nowhere to sell, except to that Sing man. The merchants all say their *godowns* are full, and there are no ships in sight. Furthermore, Hsü can't get home. He could be stuck here for months!"

"I feel sorry for him and his son. I am sure Lihua also misses her home in China," Jannat commented.

"By the way, what is that horrible smell you have brought with you from the island?" Jannat asked, wrinkling her nose.

Both men covered their mouths with their hands. "Is it really that bad?" Reza asked her, looking guilty.

"Terrible! You both smell as though you have rolled in something disgusting. What was it?" Rav'an demanded. "Unless you clean your mouths out with some cardamom and herbs, I for one, am not going to kiss you, husband of mine."

"We had to eat a thing called Durian. It is a local delicacy," Talon muttered. "You two might even like it. Women like odd tasting things," he said with a weak grin at Reza, who made a comical face. Jannat glared at them. Her scathing look should have turned both of them into blocks of salt.

Rav'an looked equally offended. "I doubt it, my Talon," she said sweetly. "I hope you didn't bring any of it on board?" she enquired with a raised eyebrow. He could almost see her tapping her foot. "If so, then you and Reza will be sleeping on deck."

"Reza strictly forbade Hsü from even thinking about it," Talon assured her.

The first fat drops of warm tropical rain began to patter on deck, followed by more, and then lightning flashed, accompanied almost immediately by a loud roll of thunder. They all flinched as another flash lit up the cabin and the heavens above split with a tearing crash. A downpour drummed onto the deck above. They glanced apprehensively upwards, memories of the storm still fresh in their minds, but there were no leaks, and when Rostam peered out through the partially opened shutters he exclaimed, "Papa, Mama! I can't see the other ships anymore!" they could still hear him over the noise from above.

They laughed, partly at his excitement, partly with relief, and settled in for a long evening in the dry comfort of their living room.

"Well, at least we have some hot tea and our own company," Jannat stated, and settled closer to Reza despite his awful breath—a move not lost on either Rav'an or Talon. Salem lit one of the lamps and hung it from the ceiling, creating a warm glow within the cabin. Talon closed the shutters completely, as the driving rain was now coming through the opening. He was just about to sit down next to Rav'an with a sigh of contentment when a knock on the door was heard. Salem opened it to reveal Hsü standing there. He had to raise his voice over the din of the pounding rain to be heard. "May I come in?"

Talon came to his feet. "Of course, Hsü, come in. You are welcome. Please join us."

Talon guessed that Hsü wanted to talk about having found some accommodation on shore, probably thankful that he no longer would have to endure the cramped conditions of the ship. Instead, Hsü thanked them, bowed to the ladies, who by now didn't bother to cover their heads in his presence, and then he sat down between Talon and Reza.

"I have been thinking," he said by way of a start.

He looked around and saw that everyone was attentive.

"I have been thinking," he said again, "that there might be another way forward."

"What do you have in mind, Hsü?" Reza asked him.

"There is a way for me to go home tomorrow, and for you to sell your cargo," Hsü stated carefully in Arabic.

Rav'an was there first. "You mean... go to China? Take you to China?" she asked with a surprised look.

Reza and Talon were still dealing with their own surprise when Hsü spoke again.

"Yes, yes I do. It is unusual for there to be no Chinese ships here going home, but it is entirely possible that they have all left for the year, or that the storms have delayed them coming here.

I am willing to pay you handsomely if you would consider it. Also, I can guarantee that you will sell your cargo for a very good price. I have some influence in Guangzhou and that will make a difference, I can assure you."

Reza looked at Talon and Rav'an. "We have a cargo already loaded. If we leave soon we will be among the first to China with goods from Africa," he said slowly.

Talon nodded, but he was reluctant to make a hurried decision. "We didn't anticipate that we would be traveling to such a far country. We are already half way around the world," he said to Hsü.

"If you leave soon, you will be able to sell your goods for a premium. It is an uncertain business, predicting who will be ahead of you; but you are having trouble selling here, so why not try for China itself?" Hsü pressed. Reza nodded agreement.

"How much further do we have to travel to reach this Guangzhou of yours, Hsü?" Talon asked.

"About two more months, perhaps less, if the weather stays good and we have a fair wind. The winds are still going Eastward, in our direction Talon," Hsü reminded him. "Also, the time of the Typhoon is over now, so we should not experience very bad weather."

Talon glanced around the group. He looked directly at Rav'an and asked her, "It is a long way, my Rav'an. Are you prepared for more time in these cramped conditions?"

She gave him a meaningful look and replied in *Farsi*. "I am not eager to spend another day on this ship, even though it is ours, but the thought of losing our investment to these wretched people is galling. I can put up with this as long as I know we will do well at the other end. There is also the allure of seeing the fabled country of China. I hope Hsü owns a palace; I want a large room for us alone," she added with a tight smile.

Almost as though he had anticipated this reaction and understood what Rav'an had said, Hsü hurriedly yet respectfully added, "You will be my guests when we get to

China, my honored guests, Talon. Please bear that in mind. I wish to show you my land, and as for your merchandise, you can look forward to at least double what the pirate here is offering," he finished with great sincerity.

"Now I must go and leave you to think about it," he said, as he stood up and bowed to everyone.

When Salem had closed the door on his departure, the rest of them discussed the extraordinary proposal.

"We are in a tight place with this cargo. We simply must sell it, and it was on its way to China one way or the other, no matter what," Reza pointed out.

"I would like to see this country Hsü and Lihua talk about," Jannat interjected with a nervous laugh. "But it is two more months away!" she groaned theatrically.

"This isn't a journey for pleasure, my friends, but it does seem that he has provided us with a way forward. It is our decision whether we take him up on it, and I am not sure yet," Talon told them. "Another two months, and all we have is his guarantee!"

"Do you trust this man?" Jannat asked.

"It is a good question, Jannat," Talon responded. "What do you think, Reza?"

"I am not sure if I trust him, Talon. However he is offering us a solution to our dilemma," Reza said thoughtfully. "There is one area where I do not trust him at all."

They all looked apprehensive. "What do you mean, Brother?" Talon asked the question for all of them.

"We should watch his every move while we are in this harbor. He liked the Durian too much and will try to smuggle some aboard, I just know it!" Reza scowled.

Jannat slapped his arm and Talon grinned ruefully. "I have to agree with you there, Reza," he laughed. "He also said there were dragons in China. I would like to see one of those."

Rav'an spoke up."Well, you yourself have said that there is no trade here, whereas if we are among the first to arrive for this trading season, we will have the market to ourselves. Besides, Hsü told us that he will reward us well for bringing him home. I believe he will, too. He certainly owes us. I hope he is a lord or prince or something like that."

He grinned reluctantly. "I can see that I am outvoted, but yes, I agree. We will sail for China, and God protect us along the way! Now I have to tell the captain. I am unsure what he will say, but I shall remind him that he too, has shares in this cargo."

"What is Durian, Papa?" Rostam asked.

*****

In the cabin that had been allocated to the Chinese men, Hsü and Lihua were alone. He had banished his son and Jiavi, while he spent some time with Lihua. If she objected to his breath she didn't show it, and after they made love she stayed locked in his arms. He wanted to talk, so she listened and offered encouragement as he spoke his thoughts.

"Do they treat you well?" he asked.

"They provide me with everything I need and are very kind. I think Rav'an and Jannat are the wives of the two leaders, Talon and Reza. They might be considered pretty in their country, but not in ours."

"Why not?"

"Their noses are too big, and their breasts are, too. The color of their eyes is strange and they stare at you when they talk to you. They do not seem to respect their men because they talk directly to them."

He smiled in the darkness and placed his hand over one of her petite but well-formed breasts. "Hmm, I see what you mean." He stroked her absently, eliciting a tiny sigh of pleasure. "Everything has its beauty, but not everyone sees it," he said softly.

His mind shifted to Talon and Reza. "We must not underestimate either of those two. They are warriors, and …." He paused.

She lifted her head. "And what, my Lord?"

"I cannot put my finger on it, but Talon and Reza are dangerous men." Hsü was a perceptive man, and since his very first meeting with Reza and Talon he had sensed that they were hiding something about themselves. They had been the perfect hosts; he could find no fault with their hospitality under the circumstances; perhaps it was their watchfulness, the way they seemed to be assessing everyone and everything they encountered. They were certainly more than mere merchants.

They reminded him of cats, big cats. However, in the short time they had been on the boat he had come to like them and the banter that flowed back and forth between the two, and the rapport they appeared to have with their women. He hoped against hope that they would agree to take him back to China. If they did, he would make sure they were very well rewarded.

As though she was reading his mind, Lihua asked him nervously, "My Lord, are we going to be staying here for a long time?" She didn't want to stay on this steam pot of an island any longer. The rain storm earlier had frightened her; memories of the desperate time on their sinking ship were still vivid in her mind. She had clutched at him, on the edge of tears as lightning and thunder played manic tunes over the island.

"I left them with the seed of an idea," he murmured into her hair.

"What was that?" she asked big eyed. She dared not hope, but her faith in Hsü was absolute. He always seemed to be a step ahead. "I invited them to take us to China," he informed her.

She said nothing. She just clenched her fingers even tighter around his arm. *Ahmida Buddha*, she thought, *please make it so.*

"How did you persuade him?" she asked him.

"He has not said yes, as yet, but ...."

"But what, my Lord?"

"I think he believes in dragons and wants to see one."

Lihua snorted softly. "Do we have real dragons in China, my Lord?"

"China is a very big place. There is always the possibility."

She giggled, but then gripped his arm again. "I am so sad you lost your ship," she whispered.

"Remember, we have not lost everything. I still have the stones," he said, and she nodded. The blue sapphires alone were worth a fortune; along with the rubies from Ceylon, even the Emperor would be envious. She knew this, and would guard that long box with her life.

"Talon and Reza had a taste of Durian today," he told her.

"Did they enjoy it?" she asked.

"What do you think?"

She laughed for the first time since their ship had foundered, and went to sleep smiling.

*****

Talon and Rav'an were alone in his cramped cabin, lying on his sleeping mat, making small talk as they listened to the patter of the rain on the deck above. The earlier thunder had moved on and the gurgle of water in the scuppers was soporific.

Rostam was safely asleep with Salem in the women's cabin. Reza and Jannat were tucked away in Reza's cubbyhole. Under the tightlipped supervision of their women, both men had scrubbed their mouths and teeth vigorously with herbs before retiring for the night.

"I am beginning to wonder what I have become," Talon told Rav'an. There was a note of frustration in his voice. "I have always been a warrior. I understand that; but here I am haggling over some goods that a few years ago I would not have even glanced at! I am doing what caravan people, owners of camels do, and what the Jewish people do with more sophistication!"

She sat up on the mat beside him. "You are still a warrior, my Talon. However, you are becoming something else, too. You are right about the Jewish people, they understand trade... and that is why they become rich."

"How is that, my Love?" he asked as he turned his head to look at her.

"They take risks, but they use their heads. Men can become rich by plunder or by trade. You might not be a great sultan, but you are a great warrior, and not a man who plunders. You are learning to be a merchant, which means that you too will be rich, someday. How do you think my brother obtained all his wealth?" she demanded.

"Hmmm," he said by way of acknowledgement, and then smiled up at her. "His cunning is legend. I also had a taste of merchant work in Constantinople, but you are saying that I need to learn to haggle and trade, to become rich?"

"Perhaps, but remember, with wealth comes power. More importantly, my noble Warrior, it brings security to those whom you wish to protect. Add that to your accomplishments, and you will soon become a Merchant Prince!" She laughed.

"You are not so bad at it, you know," she added. "Look what you have already."

"You are very persuasive, my Rav'an. Then which one would you want me to be tonight, my Princess? Warrior or Merchant?" He leered up at her.

"Well now, that depends upon how you wish to negotiate, my Talon," she purred with an impish grin as she came back into his arms. "I prefer the warrior's spear at a time like this."

Head poking from a vermilion tower, all eight
  directions cramped;
one dip of green wine and I go on for a hundred cups,
washing away the humps and hills, cliffs and crags of
  my heart,
cleansing myself so I can shape verses windy and free.

—Lu Yu

Chapter Sixteen
Lun

The wide city avenue was bordered with multistoried houses, their steeply curved and pointed tile roofs giving the impression of waves in a choppy orange and red sea. People were leaning out of second story windows or standing on balconies, gazing at the crowded, tree-lined boulevard below. Some houses had their shutters closed against the heat of the sun reflected off the paved road below. The ground floors were sometimes lined with cool passageways, which opened onto the street side with arches.

Almost end to end along the avenue, on either side were stalls displaying merchandise of every kind. There were hanging glazed dried ducks, brightly colored song birds in tiny cages, fruit stalls with bunches of hairy red rambutans and lychee, cheek by jowl with fish stalls, cloth stalls with rolls of bright silk on display, even fine pottery and polished copper pots.

Adding to the cacophony of other sounds, the vendors shouted to passersby, trying to get their attention. It was in the middle of the hour of the Goat; the sun had lost some of the fierce glare of the hour of the Horse, but the humidity and the roiling black clouds in the distance warned of a storm. Despite the threat of rain, people were coming out to eat a late mid day meal.

Making his way slowly along the crowded avenue towards the river, a small boy carrying a large canvas satchel paused from time to time to gaze at something or other that caught his attention, like a particularly bright robe that was hung out for viewing, or a puppet show that was taking place right in the middle of the street. He didn't stop there for long, as he had watched the show a dozen times before; he made his way steadily towards a small book stall. It was one of his favorite places.

The vendor of the booth, an old man with white hair bound back in a knot, and sporting a long, white, wispy beard and mustache, greeted him politely; not because the boy was anyone in particular, but because he had in the past asked for old poetry, which he would read avidly even if he rarely purchased anything, and a rapport had developed between them over the weeks. The boy asked questions to which the old man was glad to respond.

Lun also liked the two colorful birds that lived in bamboo cages hanging off the rafter under the oiled cloth that warded off the weather. They were *Hwamei* or 'Painted eyebrows' because of the distinctive markings over and around their shiny round beady eyes. They were not singing just now, as the heat of the day subdued all creatures, but he had heard them in the mornings and their songs rivaled the birds which he kept at his father's house.

"Hello, Lun," the old man said as the boy approached. "How was school today? What did you learn about?"

Lun looked down, shuffled his feet and pretended to look over the books and some silk paintings that were on display. "Hello, Tseng Jung," Lun finally greeted the old man respectfully by his courtesy name. "Today they told us to memorize phrases from Confucius which I didn't understand, so I could not remember them very well. I was punished and my hand hurts." He held out his right hand, displaying a red welt along his palm.

"Ah. I see, but you know we are here to learn, and when I was a boy we were beaten regularly. It taught us to apply ourselves," Tseng Jung told him kindly enough. He raised his hands as though to show his own scars, displaying thin, almost emaciated wrists and forearms emerging from the deep wide sleeves of his not so clean green silk overcoat. His under tunic, held together with a grubby silk sash, was of light cotton and frayed at the hem, which came down to his clogs just an inch off the ground.

"I have just the right ointment for that pain. If it continues to hurt, you will have to go to the medicine doctor over there, across the street, for something stronger."

Lun glanced over at the medicine shop and grimaced. He didn't like going into that dark, sinister cave, where just about every living creature that crawled or walked was on display in some form or another. An authoritative placard next to the low door extolled its owner's medical powers. His mother sent her maids there for powders and creams, and he had accompanied one of the servants from time to time.

The old man took a small ceramic jar from behind the counter and opened the lid. Despite the almost overwhelming odors from all around of cooking meat, fish, vegetables and hot oil, as well as more noisome stinks coming from the large drains nearby, Lun wrinkled his nose at the smell emanating from the thick ointment inside the little pot that was being held under his nose.

"It will sooth the pain," Tseng Jung assured him, and put a forefinger of ointment on Lun's hand.

It did soothe the pain, and Lun brightened up.

"I had another dream, Tseng Jung," he stated.

Tseng Jung looked interested. "Your last one was not a good one, as I recall."

"No, but this time I saw Father on another ship. It did not look like his ship, more like one of those Arab ships we see anchored in the straights down by the Arab settlements." He paused and waved his arm in the general direction of a mass of masts and spars down river in the distance.

"I could almost point to one of them and say that was the one, but I know he is not here but far, far away."

Tears formed in his dark eyes when he gazed up at the old man, whose own aged but kindly brown eyes were almost lost in the wrinkles on either side.

"*Ai yah*! I am sure that is a good omen!" Tseng Jung exclaimed, his white eyebrows shooting up. "First you see a horrible storm, and then you see your father on a ship. Even if it was not his own, it must mean that he is alive. That is very good Joss indeed!"

"Do you think so?" asked Lun.

"Oh yes! It is excellent, although I cannot fathom how you dream so. Perhaps you have the gift. Some people do," Tseng Jung told him with assurance.

"Mother thinks I am imagining things, but they are so real when I dream them."

"Never mind. I believe you, and that is what matters," Tseng Jung told him in a kindly manner. "You had better head home now, or she will find another reason to be displeased with you. I look forward to seeing you tomorrow."

Lun smiled and hitched his large school bag more comfortably onto his shoulder. "I will see you tomorrow, Tseng Jung. Stay well."

Tseng Jung smiled and placed both hands together. "May you be at peace! Remember that everything arises from the mind. Study hard and you will win through."

*****

Lun looked up at the clouds boiling into great pillars in the sky to the north of the city. It was going to rain soon, he decided, and hastened his pace. He continued his way along the busy avenue to the water's edge to where the ferry boats waited. He had only two coins on him. One, the larger, would pay for the boatman to take him across the river to his family compound, and the other had been saved from his small savings to buy some of the mouthwatering meat and noodles from a stall close to the landing. His stomach rumbled as he joined the short line waiting to be served.

He was forbidden to linger after school, and he was expected to make his way home on his own in the middle of the afternoon when everything interesting was on display. He would do his best to be home promptly, but whenever he had put aside a little money, he would treat himself to a little food to get him through the rest of the day: supper was a long time away at the hour of the Dog, when it was dark.

The avenue if anything became livelier as the day passed; well dressed clerks rubbed shoulders with stevedores and laborers who were clad in rough, grimy clothes; they all stood in lines just like this one. They ordered their food from the person who owned the stall, behind whom were one, two or even three sweating cooks surrounded by steaming copper and bronze pots, laboring over charcoal fires and wielding wide, beaten iron woks full of smoking oil into which they flash fried fresh chopped vegetables and meat. The oil would hiss and splutter as it cooked the food. The cooks shook the contents vigorously over the glowing fires or briskly stirred them for a few minutes before scooping the food out and dumping it into rows of wooden bowls with the help of a ladle made out of woven bamboo, calling out the orders as they turned away to attend to the next order.

A coin would be passed to the owner, and a laden bowl with crudely carved wooden chop sticks placed inside was shoved into the customer's hands. Then it was a matter of looking for a place to sit and eat among the other people hunched over their food. Most of them were holding their bowls close to their lips and shoveling the food straight into their mouths, talking loudly to one another at the same time. The customers were expected to return the chop-sticks and bowls when finished, and there were attendants there to see that they did.

Lun listened with half an ear to the loud chatter going on all around him. People gossiped about the latest palace scandals, news of which had reached Guangzhou from the capital: this or that eunuch had been caught with one of the numerous princesses in a compromising situation, an execution would result for sure. Smirks and raucous laughter followed, accompanied by obscene gestures. This or that faction in the city of Guangzhou itself was suspected of being involved in a suspicious murder of an opponent from another administrative faction at the college of trade and taxes; the body had turned up in the usual watery grave, the river. The governor was sick. The Mongols had invaded. The gossip continued unabated as rumors were savored and enlarged upon.

Lun was not a part of this community; as a boy of nine, even if better clothed than most, he went virtually unnoticed among the myriad of other children running errands. There were others like him going home after an arduous day under harsh tutelage studying the Rules of Confucius.

He finished his snack of fried noodles and small fish cubes in a brown sauce of soy and gravy with hot chili sauce. It made him sweat in the humid heat, causing his shirt to stick to his back, but it tasted delicious. He handed his empty bowl off to an impatient attendant, then hurried along the busy riverbank. The meal had made him feel cooler.

He sometimes had to elbow his way through the packed crowd towards the boat landing. It was almost impossible to see over the top of them. A sea of wide, coned straw hats, many as wide as the shoulders of the wearer, and of the tall, elaborately shaped silk hats officials wore obscured any view for a small boy. He emerged at last from a cluster of people gathered around someone who was reading an impressive looking document to the crowd in a loud voice. Something about reporting robberies to the authorities. He paid it no notice and looked for a boat. A sharp-eyed boatman spotted him and skulled his light vessel speedily towards him. Waving off others who wanted to board, he called to Lun to get in the sampan. He knew Lun lived on the island of Haizu, which was just across the neck of water to the south of the main city.

Lun tossed the man his remaining coin and jumped aboard. The boatman, who was standing at the very rear of the sampan, clutching his one oar, snatched the coin out of the air, and then waited for Lun to step onto the rocking boat. Lun took care with his step; he certainly didn't want to fall into the stinking mess that rose and fell on the edge of the river. Some of it looked as though it had died a week ago, and the stench was strong in the hot, humid air. The oarsman grinned a gummy smile of welcome and pushed away from the steps before anyone else could get on board. The boy paid just over the odds for a short ride across the river, and the boatman knew him by name.

"How have you been, Master Meng Lun?" the man, clad only in a coarse cotton shirt, much patched, ragged trousers, and a wide rimmed grass woven hat, asked him politely as they negotiated the crowded river. Lun nodded but said nothing. It was cooler under the round mat covering the middle of the sampan.

Lun was concentrating on the ships in the distance further upriver. The boatman knew when to stay quiet, leaving Lun to his thoughts, while he skulled their fragile sampan adroitly around fast moving river traffic, any one of which could have capsized their own should they collide. As it was, their tiny boat bobbed up and down in the wakes, forcing Lun to hang onto the sides. The standing boatman, well used to the river, balanced himself easily against the rise and fall of the vessel.

On the bank where he had just embarked, a man who had been following the boy from his school stood watching for a while as the boat pulled into the center of the river on its way to the other side. He then turned and disappeared into the crowd.

The boy could see several of the Arab vessels in the distance of the type that he had dreamed about. Why, he wondered, would he have such a vivid picture in his mind? Was it simply that he remembered these oceangoing ships because he saw them every day? They were very large, and quite different from the Chinese boats that plied the waters off the coast, bringing fish to the port. Most of the Chinese coastal vessels he knew had blunt bows and a shallow draught for sailing in the relatively shallow waters of the delta. He noticed a flotilla of this kind tied up side by side, their crews idle, sleeping, or having betting games in the shade of temporary stretched rattan overhangs. They waited for the early hours of the night when they would catch the off shore breezes and all sail into the large delta to fish for shrimp and freshwater fish. The people of Guangzhou preferred freshwater fish to the salty ocean kind found further out to sea.

By glancing over his shoulder he could see a cluster of other Chinese ships which were every bit as large as the Arab vessels; they had three masts—in some cases even four—and they were designed for long voyages out into the open ocean. They ventured to places where the Arab ships came from. His father and elder brother had left in one. Why, then, would he dream of one of the Arab vessels, and not a Chinese ship with his father on board?

His first dream had been more of a nightmare. In it he had seen his father and his brother on a distinctly Chinese vessel that was being battered by the fury of a storm. He had woken up crying, which woke his amah, who had rushed in to find him so agitated that she could barely restrain him. After finally calming him down, she had brought him to his mother, who was sitting up in her bed. She had not, however, been very sympathetic and had slapped him, inducing more tears, and told him to stop crying and go back to sleep. Everyone had nightmares, she had told him, and he would soon grow out of it. His amah had guided him back to his own bed and had given him a small cup of fragrant tea to drink. He had eventually fallen into a dreamless slumber, but the memory persisted, and now he'd had another dream. The images were so clear they were frightening.

The boat man brought the sampan alongside the pier and bade him goodbye. Mumbling his thanks, Lun jumped off and walked up the worn stone steps to the paved road, which ran parallel to the river. This was the part of the journey home that he dreaded most.

Between this place and the sanctuary of his home there were small gangs of boys who were from the poorer section of the town, but also other boys who were in his same social class who liked to hang out with the tougher crowd. It was these boys that he feared most, as they were the most vicious, and he had had more than one unpleasant encounter with them.

His eyes flicked nervously from side to side as he looked for any evidence of them among the porters and laborers and the dense cluster of houses facing the river. He wished he had some form of protection, or even a protector. Several of his friends at school had bodyguards; not because they themselves were special, but because their fathers were important people in the administration, which therefore made their sons vulnerable to being kidnapped for ransom, or so they supposed. Lawlessness and banditry had been on the rise recently, or so his Grandmother said.

He, Lun, had a father who was now far removed from the intrigues and infighting of the academics and administrators. Hence he was now unimportant, at least for the time being.

The people on the docks ignored him, engrossed in their work, shouting instructions and ribald jokes at one another. They were a rough crowd, spitting everywhere as they went, and they smelled bad. He shrugged his book bag onto his shoulder and stepped out at a lively pace for home but kept an eye about him as he went. As he came closer to where he lived he began to hope that he might make it home without trouble.

The street was reasonably well paved and cleaner than on the other side of the river on the mainland. Even so, the ubiquitous food stalls were there, although in fewer numbers, with their clients seated on small wooden stools, stuffing their faces with rice and morsels of fish or pork. He was no longer hungry, so looked instead towards the numerous large walled compounds in the distance, one of which was home and a haven from this noisy, bustling world he passed through almost every day.

To his left, large multistoried houses lined the riverbank on the side of the paved road, in some cases joined wall to wall. These houses were owned by wealthy merchants who needed to be close to their point of business. These had well made doorways, correctly positioned per the *Feng shui* directions. Harmony for the inhabitants was of prime importance.

They had ornate shutters and decorations on their roofs. His uncle on his mother's side of the family owned one of them. Their steep, red tiled roofs curved slightly. Some had, at the end of the corners or on their crests, a stone decoration, such as a glaring dragon's head with protruding eyes and bared teeth, to keep away the bad spirits and the hairy-faced, bad-tempered djins. Lun had to keep a wary eye open for carts laden with bales of silk and other goods which ground by, their iron rimmed wheels grating on the stone of the street. Their drovers shouted for passage, and he scurried around the small, dark, sweating porters carrying impossibly heavy loads on their backs.

Although one of many islands in the delta, this particular island was an important trading area where there were several sea going ships tied up alongside the wharf. The warehouses, or godowns, were either behind the houses or were some way along the road. The laborers used flat bamboo rods, which flexed up and down on their shoulders as they loped on bare feet from ship to godown and back carrying merchandise. These ships were of Chinese build; their sails were made of dark painted oil-cloth, ribbed with wooden slats, quite unlike the sails of the Arab ships further down river. The creak of timber and the slap of water between the hulls, along with the low murmur of the crews taking their ease or squatting on the decks eating, lulled him into thinking he was safe.

He heard them before he saw them as they ran down the street in a small mob. They had been teasing an old woman who had a pitifully small vegetable stall on the river's edge. Their loud insults and playful shoving, combined with the agitated, high-pitched voice of the woman as she tried to protect her property, woke him up to reality.

It was Hang who was leading the persecution of the old woman, poking her and calling her names. Lun crossed over the road to be nearer the houses in the feeble hope that he could get by without being noticed, but one of Hang's accomplices noticed him and shouted to the others, pointing.

Lun began to run. The satchel was heavy and impeded his legs as he scurried up the slope towards the safety of his family compound, his heart pounding. The gang of four left off the old woman and began to chase after him, laughing and threatening him with what they were going to do to him.

"Hey, little boy! Run run, run! We are going to throw you in the river and watch you drown!" they shouted as they chased him. Lun didn't look back but raced as fast as his legs could carry him. The gates were in sight and safety was just within reach when he felt a blow to his back that sent him sprawling in the dust.

He rolled onto his back and looked up fearfully to see Hang standing over him, reaching down to grab him by the throat. Suddenly Lun heard a shout, then a thumping sound, and Hang fell, sprawling across him. Lun lifted his head in surprise and pushed the inert body away from him, trying to get out from under. He heard another shout another cracking sound, and a cry of pain, then another and another. He swiveled his head around and found that all four of his would-be assailants were lying unconscious on the ground.

A hard hand attached to an arm made of corded sinew and roped muscle reached down, seized him by the front of his coat, and heaved him back onto his feet.

"You all right?" a gruff voice asked him.

Lun stared around at the devastation in mute astonishment and nodded. "Y-yes," he stammered. He gazed up at his rescuer. Fang, his father's household bodyguard, paid him scant attention. He carried in his right hand a long carved wooden sword that resembled in shape the other one he had in the sash around his waist. He pushed Lun towards the gates of the property and said, "Leave them to me."

Lun retrieved his bag of books and backed away towards entrance of his home, watching, fascinated, as Fang sheathed his wooden sword and drew his real blade. It slipped out of the lacquered sheath with an ominous sigh. He strode over to one of the boys, who was beginning to regain his senses. The boy sat up and groaned, holding his head, which was bleeding at the back. He got no further as Fang stepped up to him, placed a sandaled foot on his chest and pushed him back down again. The steel sword pricked his throat.

Fang leaned his weight on the foot that was holding the boy down, gently probing with the sword; the blade glinted in the afternoon sunlight. To the horrified Lun it seemed as though Fang was going to kill the boy right there and then.

Fang's voice was low but it hissed with menace. "If I receive news that you are pestering Master Meng Lun ever again, I shall cut off your little balls while you are still alive and stuff them into your mouth. I shall then cut off your head and stick it on a pole so that your ancestors will be shamed for all eternity. The rest of your worthless carcass will go into the river for the fish and the crabs to feed upon. Do you understand me?"

The boy gasped out his agreement to these terms. He began to reach for the blade but Fang twitched it and a trickle of blood began to flow down his neck. "I am not finished yet," he rasped. "You will stay away from this place, and you will tell your friends that I shall do the same with them as I shall do to you." He glowered at the boy. From the boy's perspective the sight of Fang must have been terrifying, because he wet his pants and began to whimper.

"Go away! Oh, and do not bother the old woman again, because that would also upset me!" Fang snapped and left, turning his back contemptuously on the boy, who scrambled to his feet and began to shake his companions awake, casting terrified looks at Fang's receding back. The sorry little group shambled hurriedly down the road towards the wharf.

Fang strode back to the gateway on his short but very muscular legs, dusting off his thin black cotton overcoat and sheathing the steel sword as he went in one fluid motion. The wooden sword was in his hand again as he strode between solid wooden doors past the grinning guards who had witnessed the episode. He shot them a glare and their expressions froze.

Lun was scared of Fang. Although he was Chinese too, Fang came from the North, and he had spent time on the Nippon islands, which were even further to the north and across the sea. He used weapons of unusual design, and once in a while Lun had seen him practicing in the back yard of the servant's quarters where he could do incredible things with his sword. Lun had never seen him smile. He always walked in a rolling fashion on the balls of his feet, his black, watchful eyes almost never still in a face that was stern with a forbidding scowl.

"Thank you for saving me, Fang," Lun called out to him.

"It is time you learned how to defend yourself, Master Meng Lun. I am here when you decide to do so," Fang called after the boy. Lun continued apace along the avenue of trees and well kept gardens towards the private quarters of the family. He barely noticed the profusion of litchi, Carambola and Longan fruit trees and the well kept shrubs in between. If anyone could teach him to protect himself it would be Fang, he was sure, but he was not a boy who liked hard physical work or sports, so he dreaded that aspect of training.

"I shall be rich and have a bodyguard like Fang instead," he thought to himself as he walked past the small but intricately shaped Carambola tree from which hung the cage containing his own song birds; they were silent at this time of day.

His grandmother greeted him in the inner courtyard of the main house. She was sitting on a chair, enjoying the late afternoon sun that still shone through the fruit trees, dappling the grass and flat stones arrayed around the pond with shards of light.

"I heard a disturbance outside, Lun. What was it all about?" her voice was pitched in a low tone, but it carried. He bowed politely from a few feet away.

"Nothing, Grandmother. Fang broke up a group of thugs who were making a noise outside."

She gave him a shrewd look. "I trust it was not those boys again," she said. Lun took a seat on the edge of the pond and shook his head. He didn't want to sound like a crybaby, but she probably knew in any case. Little escaped this rather intimidating lady. Although she was quite small, perched on the large, carved, red lacquered arm chair which made her seem even smaller, she still commanded respect, especially from a nine year old boy who worshipped her. He trailed a hand in the cool water of the pond, watching the large carp and the prized goldfish swimming idly among the lilies.

"I heard that you had another dream," she said in her direct manner.

He nodded and thought she must have heard this from his amah, who could never resist gossiping. "This time Father was on one of those large Arab ships," he said, still looking at the water.

"How strange! Anything else in the dream?"

"No, Grandmother, I don't remember all of it." He looked towards her and glanced down at her tiny feet, which just protruded from under her intricately patterned green silk robe. Not for the first time he wondered how she could endure it. Both she and his mother were virtually immobilized by their bound feet and could not walk anywhere without assistance.

The old lady noticed the direction of his gaze. "Don't stare; it is rude, Lun," she admonished him. He blushed with shame and apologized. He wanted to ask about the practice but had never found the courage to do so. Besides, his mother discouraged questions of this nature. He didn't want to add to his collection of wounds.

"Tell me all about what you learned at school today," his grandmother said, kindly enough.

He sighed. "It was Confucius again today, Grandmother," he told her. "I don't understand it very well."

"Tell me about one of them."

"The Teacher told us to remember this one: When the Archer misses his target, he should look within himself for the error."

"That sounds simple enough," she remarked.

"I am not an archer, so I don't understand what he meant," Lun complained.

"It isn't necessarily about Archers, Lun. Just remember it, and one day it will come to you. If you are going to pass your exams you had better understand Confucius, my boy," she told him.

Lun nodded politely. He would eventually have to study for exams, just like his brother and his father had before him, but that was several years away yet, and he wanted to learn more about poetry and art.

"I want to know more about Lu Yu, the poet, and what he was thinking, Grandmother."

"Lu Yu? He talks far too much about wine. Poets are only good at doing two things. They think up nice poems, some of which are successful, but only a few, and most of them drink themselves to death at an early age. Is that what you want to do?"

"No, Grandmother, I really want to be a painter."

It was her turn to sigh. "Painters sometimes do better than poets. At least they don't drink so much, or they couldn't wield a brush, but if you can become qualified as an Administrator you can do what you like after that. You should think about it." She peered up at the sky where dark clouds were now a dense mass overhead. The sun had disappeared and the air around them was clammy and dense with moisture.

"It is time for me to go in, and you too, unless you want to get very wet. It is going to rain any moment. Besides, you need to clean up. You look as though you have been rolling in the dirt."

"Ah Cheng!" she called, and a young servant girl hastened to her side. "Yes, my Lady?"

"Have them bring me inside. I don't want to get wet," the old lady commanded.

The servants hurried out and managed to carry Meng Lanfen, still seated on her heavy chair, onto the verandah that went all around the building just before the first large drops began to fall. Before long the skies opened in a torrential downpour, water spewing off the concave tiled roof. There was a brilliant flash of forked lightning; the cracking boom of thunder that followed made Lun flinch.

Lun ran out to retrieve his birds, getting drenched in the process. He went to his room, took off his wet clothes, and then padded off to the bath house with a large cotton towel wrapped around his waist.

Later, over supper at the family table, he picked at his food. It was dark earlier than normal because of the overcast sky, so the servants had lit candles and placed them inside paper lanterns. They glowed like bright moons, displaying colorful images of cranes and birds on their sides. His mother and grandmother sat at the other end of the long polished oval table, talking quietly to one another, largely ignoring him.

His amah gave him a dish of roasted marinated duck, finely sliced. The incident with the boys had taken some of his appetite away, but she knew that he enjoyed eating this dish. He picked up a morsel to sample; it tasted delicious. The edges were crisp fried, the meat was juicy and flavorful with spices. The flowered cabbage that came with it in another dish was also very tasty, having been cooked with some meat gravy and flavored with lemon juice and hot chili sauce.

His mother evidently found the food to her liking, because she smacked her lips and commented, "Very good! Tem Pau is one of the best cooks in this city. I am so glad that my brother sent him to us."

Her ivory chop sticks clicked rapidly as they took hold of the finely sliced duck meat, conveyed it to her painted lips, and then snapped up morsels of vegetable, fried noodles, and tiny hard-boiled quail eggs in small dishes placed nearby. To the watching Lun, she resembled a fussy crane as she pecked at the food with the sticks.

"Has your brother had any news of my son? It has been a while now since we heard anything at all. " His grandmother paused in her eating, placed her own carved ivory chop sticks, yellowed with age, on a jade rest, and took a sip of warm wine from a small, finely worked porcelain bowl.

Lun pricked up his ears. He had finished his duck but wanted to listen to them talking. They sometimes overlooked the fact that he was still there. They always gossiped at supper time when the men were not at the house. Although he knew his grandmother was not fond of his mother, they still kept up the appearance of civility, and this was one of the few times they met during the day. His mother kept to her large apartments for the most part, while his grandmother liked to spend time in the gardens on fine days. Neither left the compound very often.

"My brother and his two associates are very concerned by the lack of news, but he does not confide in me all that much. Still, I think he would inform me if there was anything worthwhile," his mother replied. She, too, took a long sip of rice wine. Both of them tended to relax more when they drank wine. Kee Wen, one of the discretely hovering servants, replenished the empty bowls with more hot wine from a small ceramic pot with a spout and a bamboo woven handle.

"Well, let's hope that they return with a full cargo. It would take nine months as a round trip if they manage to get to India. Even with your brother's share deducted, my son should do very well, and we can worry a little less about finances," his grandmother stated. She sent a glance down the table towards Lun, as though to warn him not to say anything about his dreams.

His mother nodded agreement, then turned her attention towards him. He shrank within himself, as he knew the daily interrogation about school would begin.

*****

Fang listened to the rain as it rattled on the tiles above his head. He was in his room in the area of the male servant's quarters. He was half drunk, having consumed a good two thirds of a small jug of rice wine, which had been given to him in the kitchens. The cook's maid had handed the bottle to him with a saucy glance at his massive calves. Once he had told her that they were like that because he had been a beast of burden, pulling a plow in the rice fields instead of the buffalo, as punishment for his temper tantrums. This had been while he lived in the monastery up in the North. She was obviously enamored with him, but he had ignored her this evening. Another time he would have encouraged her. The cook and his assistants knew better than to tell him not to take the wine. One look at his grim features was enough to silence them. For sure he would get drunk, and they prayed he would not make a lot of noise while doing so.

The rain calmed him and the alcohol helped to numb his brain, which in turn helped him to forget, for a short while at least, where he was and how close he had come that afternoon to killing all four of the boys.

The memory of the trickle of blood on the throat of the one boy, where his sword had pricked him, set him trembling again as he recalled resisting with all his might the urge to just lean on the blade and run it through the boy's neck and into the ground. He wiped his face with a calloused hand, as though to clear the cobwebs of his mind.

The impulse to kill was now so ingrained that he knew it to be an addiction. However, it clashed with his concerns about the afterlife and the reincarnation that followed. Ahmida Buddha, but he had to control his impulses! He beat his forehead with the palm of his hand over and over. He would be reborn, he knew, in many forms, most of them as a lesser being for all the acts of violence he had perpetrated on others. He had gone straight to his room and lit four candles and apologized for his thoughts. He did this after every fight and every time he destroyed an inn where he had drunk himself brainless, leaving death and destruction behind him, fighting with a drunken fury that left him with little knowledge of what had transpired, and a ferocious hangover the next day.

He muttered over and over the mantra:

Our problems are not solved
By physical force,
By hatred,
By war.
Our problems are solved
By loving kindness.

He took another swig of the bottle and snorted. Not killing the boys *had* been kind!

This time he had been very restrained, but he still berated himself for the deadly urges that threatened to overwhelm him on occasions like this. He prayed to Buddha and promised to do better still. He concentrated on listening to the drip of water from the eaves onto the grass and the distant plop of rain drops on the pond. It helped to calm him as he sat cross-legged near to the window, sipping his wine. He had done his duty, and rescued the boy Lun without killing anyone. It was his duty; he would just have to learn not to succumb to his urge to kill every time.

If you are equal, then fight if you are able.
If you are fewer, then keep away if you are able.
If you are not as good, then flee if you are able.

Master Sun Tzu

Chapter Seventeen

The China Seas

Talon spent some time the next day with the captain discussing their options.

"I know that you only agreed to come this far, Captain, but you also know that we cannot sell our cargo here."

"That has become clear to me, Master Talon,"the captain responded. He sounded deeply unhappy with the situation. "By God, I am sure I know why, too. That Sing is responsible. I've heard from the other captains that he controls everything that comes in and out of this island. Everyone is frightened of him."

"I agree, but we have no leverage with him, and I cannot afford to take his offer, let alone those of the other thieves who are under pressure to bid very low. I don't believe that it is solely because of the full godowns, either. Hsü says that there should be more Chinese ships here."

They were standing by the after railing, staring at the island and another rain storm that was coming their way.

"What about on the mainland over there?" Dandachi waved his hand in the general direction of Kulam Bar.

"Master Hsü talked to the Chinese about that, and they informed him their godowns are full also, with no ships to carry their cargos," Talon told him.

The captain looked morosely at the island and muttered a curse.

"I hope one of the big storms strikes them and washes their warehouses away," he said.

"There is an alternative, Safa," Talon murmured.

Captain Dandachi turned to face him.

"Our friend Hsü came to see me yesterday, during the storm, and suggested that we take our cargo to China. He offered to pay his way to come with us, too."

Captain Dandachi glowered at Talon. "You know that would be yet another month, perhaps two, at sea? I am not sure the men would like that. I certainly don't," he growled.

Talon turned back to stare over the railing at the dense green canopy of the island jungle that came almost to the water's edge.

Dandachi shifted his broad shoulders. "But if we cannot make a profit here, then where can we go, other than to China itself? Will you sweeten the taste of this for the men if they agree to crew us?" he asked.

Talon nodded his head vigorously. "I think I can trust Hsü. He does not give much away, but I know he does not want to remain here, and he has guaranteed that he will help us sell our cargo and pay for his passage handsomely," he replied. "I, in turn, will pay you and the men an extra bonus to take us there."

"I will assemble the crew," said the captain.

Within a few minutes, all the hands were gathered in the waist of the ship and stood staring up at Talon, the captain and Reza. Yosef and Dar'an were there alongside. The women were below. Rav'an didn't want their presence to influence the men's decision.

Hsü, sensing that there was to be an important meeting, had come topside but stood well back on the steering deck out of the way, simply to listen and get a feeling for the mood of the men.

Captain Dandachi opened by saying, "Men... Master Talon, Master Reza and I have spent a considerable amount of time discussing our choices. They are very few, but our new friend, Master Hsü, has offered an alternative, and Master Talon has suggested that we sail for China." He stopped at this point and motioned to Talon to continue. Talon had to wait while the crewmen chattered amongst themselves. Some were agitated and obviously against the idea, while others were more amenable.

Talon noted the men who appeared unhappy upon receiving the news and he addressed his comments to them.

"Men, we have a good cargo, a ship full of luxury goods. However, there are people on the island who are trying to rob us and send us home without a reasonable profit, not because the goods are damaged or bad, but because there are bad men on the island who control prices. Yes, we could sell to them, but we will lose badly, and no one will take home anything like what we should." He paused. They had stopped chattering and were listening intently now.

"Master Hsü, the very man we rescued, has offered to pay a handsome fee for us to take him to his home, Guangzhou, which he tells me is in the south of China. Any of you men know of it?" He paused and couple of the older men raised their hands.

"Then you can reassure the others that this is no wild scheme but a determined effort to realize a good profit on our goods," Talon called out. "I will pay an extra bonus to each one of you who comes with us. Anyone else who wants to leave will be put ashore here on the island to wait for a ship to take them home. They will, of course, be paid what they are due, but will not receive any profit we make from the cargo."

There was complete silence when he had finished. He watched the men carefully for any sign of rebellion. Both he and Reza had taken precautions. They even had their bows stacked behind them against the mast, just in case.

Umayr raised his hand and Talon motioned him to step forward.

"Master Talon, we understand what you are saying, but no one here has navigated to China before. It is a journey full of dangers, such as the terrible Typhoons we have heard so much about. How will we get there without being wrecked?"

Talon waved towards the captain. "Your captain has been to China once before."

The captain nodded.

"We also have a man with us from China who knows the waters well," Talon lied, pointing towards Hsü. "More importantly, we have a cargo that Master Hsü told me would be very much in demand, because it will be the first shipload for many months to arrive at the port from these waters. The Chinese ship in this port is waiting for the Monsoon to change so that they can sail westward to India. That means that when we arrive in China we can ask for top prices, and Master Hsü tells me he has many contacts. He will help all he can to realize a good profit. This means you will go home a rich man, Umayr."

Umayr nodded and stepped back into the group, where a lively discussion was taking place. Waqqas now stepped forward. "We are one ship, Master Talon. You know as well as we that there are pirates all around, and maybe more in the seas beyond. How will we fare if we are attacked? We are a merchant ship, not a war ship!"

Reza laughed at him. "Have you forgotten so soon how we saw off those pirates near to Kulam Mali, Waqqas!" he chided the man. "Why, they ran away with their tails between their legs like beaten dogs! I am sure it was because they saw your lovely face smiling at them."

The men laughed at this and Waqqas looked embarrassed, then grinned and shuffled his feet uncomfortably.

"Allah shall protect us, Waqqas. But it will be up to us to show anyone with ideas that we have a sting," Reza assured him.

Talon let the men talk it over for a while.

"I think we can say that they will come along, Master Talon," the captain muttered in a low voice as he watched the men with a keen eye.

"I see no serious dissenters among them," Reza agreed. "Reluctance, yes, because this way will add another six months to our journey all together, but their greed will move them in the right direction."

In the end there was a vote of hands from the men, and it was unanimous. Talon was very relieved and promised again to ensure that they would not be short on the profits. As he turned away, Hsü, who had been hovering in the background with his son Fuling, stepped forward and smiled.

"I see that you are a very persuasive man, Master Talon. I am impressed. I had supposed that some at least would have decided to leave and take their chances on the island. Many of the pirates hereabouts are men who came from your lands."

"Our men are Omani, Master Hsü," the captain said stiffly from nearby. "We are sailors and navigators, and we seldom become pirates, and these men know each other's families. Besides, who would want to stay in this swamp land where the insects feast better than men?"

Hsü nodded agreement, and went below, looking happy.

"I just don't trust that man: we do not know anything about him," Reza remarked. " I really hope we are making the right decision, Talon."

"I too, Reza. *Insha'Allah* we will not perish on our way there, and when we get there I pray to God he is a man of his word."

He resolved to pay a quiet visit to the cabin of the Chinese to find out what was in the mysterious box. He could do it himself, or ask Reza to do so while he distracted Hsü and his people up on deck. He wanted to know all he could about these people.

The next day was spent under the direction of the captain, who, once their collective minds were made up, insisted they obtain as much fresh water as they could carry. He sent off men with casks in the two boats to find fresh water springs. Having learned the lesson off the coast of Africa, he did not trust the water sold by the merchants in the town.

Natives in canoes or boats approached the ship to sell fruit and vegetables, which were purchased after the usual bargaining. Fresh meat came in the form of noisy chickens and goats, which the captain said they should buy, as he didn't remember a good port on the other side of the peninsular where they could do as well. He drew a crude map of the peninsular, scratching a rough cross where they were at present and indicating where they were going. It gave Talon pause to think about the length of this particular leg of the journey. He thanked God that his goods were not perishable.

He cast many a glance over at the shoreline the next morning, wondering what the reaction of Sing might be to the lack of communication from him regarding the sale of his goods. He knew it would be pointless, perhaps even dangerous, to go ashore and explain the situation and the decision.

"I am sure that he expected us to just hand over the goods and take whatever price he felt like giving us," he said to Rav'an and Reza when they came up to join him on the deck, accompanied by Jannat.

"I wouldn't trust that man as far as I could throw a spear," Reza told him. "There's something very bad about him, and the sooner we are out of here the better."

"Now that we are resolved to go to China, I find I am able to deal with it. The uncertainty was worrying," Rav'an told them. "Did the captain say another month at sea?"

"Give or take a month or so," Reza laughed, and danced out of the way of her raised hand.

"We should place a guard on the ship tonight," Talon told them. They sobered up at that. "Do you think that man would do us mischief, Talon?" Jannat asked

"I don't know, but it would not be sensible to tempt fate," Talon responded.

Talon told himself that Sing would have drawn his own conclusions as to why he had not been at the rendezvous to discuss the offer he had made. Given the kind of man he thought Sing might be, it would not surprise him if the Sing would want to damage their ship in retaliation.

The night, however, passed without incident, and they set sail just as the first streaks of dawn were showing above the thick, dark line of the jungle on the mainland. The fetid, dank smell of the mangrove swamps came with the light wind from the East that pushed them slowly out of the harbor.

From the pagoda on the top of the walls of his palace, Sing stood and watched the ship leaving. Amar was with him, as were the inevitable bodyguards.

"They have to come back this way someday, Amar. We will be waiting. You may have first blood of them," Sing said to his lieutenant, as he sent a baleful glare after the departing vessel. "I hear there are beautiful women on that ship. Make sure you bring them to me first."

He stared dispassionately down into the tiger's yard at the dismembered remains of the two most recent victims. "I want Master Suleiman and whomever else you capture to provide a feast for my pet."

*****

For the people on the ship it was a relief to be moving again, and to get away from the whining insects that had plagued them incessantly while in the harbor. Few of them did not display welts on their faces and any other part of their skin that was not covered.

"I shall be glad to see the back of that island and the man Sing," Reza said to Talon as they watched the island recede. "He made us eat that dreadful fruit... what was it called?"

"Durian," Talon said with a grimace, followed by a grin.

"Ah, yes. He is now an enemy for life for that alone!" Reza snarled theatrically, and then he glanced over his shoulder. "If that Hsü has managed to bring one on board, I shall just have to kill him."

Talon laughed. "I would not put it past him, either. That man is devious!"

*****

The captain admitted that it had been a number of years since he had made this journey, but as both he and Talon pored over the journals of Al-Mas'udi and the Persian named Suleiman, who wrote of the China ships and their voyages, they were reassured by the details provided. Hsü, who now took a greater part in their calculations, regarded the route they would follow and said that if all else failed they could stay close to the coastline of the peninsular.

"Sìyuè, which is the name of this month, is a benign season, so we can expect a calm sea for most of this trip, if not all of the way to Guangzhou. In the winter it can be very bad, and that might be why ships were wrecked or simply did not sail from Guangzhou," he told them.

Talon, who had been counting days and now months, estimated that Hsü was talking about April. They had been at sea for nearly four months already since they had left Muscat.

The sailing was not difficult here, as they were moving down the straits of Malacca and could see at a distance both the coast of the peninsular and that of Sumatra. Both coastlines were composed of dense jungle that came to the water's edge, mostly in the form of mangrove swamps. There were only a few inlets and not very much evidence of human habitation.

After almost a week of sailing with a brisk wind, the coastline on the starboard side dwindled into the white haze of the humid days, and the captain ordered the ship to bear to the port side to keep the land in sight.

"We will round a swampy island at the end of the peninsular, where no one except a few natives live, along with tigers and poisonous snakes," Hsü told them. "Then we will head north until we come to some islands called the Tiyuma, where we can replenish with fresh water, after which we have a stretch of water to cross to the land of the Sanf, and we will dock at a town called Kanduranga, which is a miserable place surrounded by jungle."

They took on more water and provisions at the islands, and sailed on across a relatively calm sea. Hsü informed them that this large expanse of water was bordered on three sides by land, with the Southern end of the sea exposed to the storms of the open ocean. They would be crossing its mouth as it were, with the open ocean to their starboard side and the bay to their port side. It would be here and the sea further north that they would encounter more storms if they were unlucky.

Perhaps due to the time of year and the fact that the Typhoon season was over, they had an uneventful journey across this sea and the next open expanse. Now that they were clear of the brooding, jungle-clad lands and out in the open sea, everyone could enjoy the balmy days and the long starlit nights free of biting insects.

The crew relaxed, as the ship was on a long straight run which did not require constant attention to the sails, and the captain allowed them the freedom of the deck to take care of their personal affairs.

Musical instruments appeared, much to the surprise of the passengers, who despite the difference in status were on first name basis with the crew. Rav'an endeared herself to the men when she assumed the role of ship's nurse, and Jannat and Lihua, who was now accepted as just another passenger, joined her in this occupation.

In a quiet corner of the deck, Hsü and his son Fuling, with Jiaya's help, spent long hours tutoring Talon and Reza and describing their land. There was much to learn, and the language was a formidable obstacle, but they persisted. Before long, they had a smattering of Chinese.

It did not escape Talon that Fuling was wary of his father, and that the boy had difficulty taking his eyes away from the Chinese girl name Lihua. The father didn't seem to notice, but Talon had already decided that very little escaped the attention of this man, so he was sure Hsü had. However, he didn't seem to pay much attention to the issue, other than to appear brusque when he did talk to the young man, and the girl was never left alone in the boy's company.

Rostam was free to play with his friends the sailors, who adored the small boy and his endless enthusiasm for the life at sea. Talon, and to a certain extent Rav'an, had no problem with leaving Rostam in the capable hands of Tarif or Umayr, who would have died rather than let harm befall him. In this way they could turn their attention to their guests, and they attempted to learn from them what to expect when they arrived in Guangzhou.

Talon and Reza also continued to practice with the crew, honing their skills as fighters. As bowmen neither Reza nor Talon could be bested, although by now Yosef and Dar'an were trying hard to catch up. To the astonishment of the crew and the disapproval of the captain, Rav'an and Jannat were allowed to practice with a bow down in the waist of the ship. Neither disgraced themselves, to the satisfaction of their menfolk and the surprise of the crew.

There was one other weapon with which they practiced, which had stood them in good stead: the small, round pots with the Greek Fire in them that could burn on water. Talon wanted to make sure the men could handle these when there was a fight going on. The men practiced with stones collected from beaches, where on occasion they stopped for a night when the weather was balmy and there were no squalls to be seen, throwing them as far as possible out over the water from the sides of their own ship.

"We have no means of launching these," a frustrated Talon told the watching Hsü on the day they were practicing. "I wish there was a way. It would be devastating to be able to hurl these from a ship a great distance away from the enemy."

Hsü looked at him curiously and said, "You think like a military man, Talon. We have ways in China to do this, and I shall assist you to learn how to use them when we get there."

When Talon and Reza gave him puzzled looks, he told them of an invention in the Sung empire called "Exploding Fire". He used the Chinese name, *Zha yao.* "This powder, when enclosed and set on fire, will make a very big noise!" He clapped his hands in an explosive manner sharply. "We use it in many ways nowadays, but it is also a weapon, and we use it to hurl missiles long distances from our own ships, and on land too."

He promised to show them when they came to China. Talon could barely contain his impatience and plied him with all sorts of questions about how it was made. Hsü was amused, but confessed that he didn't know how. However, there were people he knew who did, although it was a well-kept secret.

Talon and Reza now knew what was in the box that Hsü was so possessive about. It had not been easy, but Reza had seized his chance and slipped below on some pretext one day when Talon had them all on deck one balmy morning to watch some dolphins playing. The excited laughter of Rostam as he pointed and called at them had done the trick. Reza had reappeared not long after, his eyes wide, and murmured to Talon in *Farsi.* "He has a fortune in gems in that box, Talon. I have never seen the like of it before."

In some ways Talon was relieved for Hsü; it had seemed that everything he possessed had gone down with his ship. Now that Talon knew about the jewels, he was intrigued. It might also provide him with some leverage, should his trust in the man be violated. It was clear that Reza harbored a deep-seated distrust of the man. Talon preferred to keep his options open, for the time being at least. They had after all saved these people from a sure death by drowning or worse. Surely they would be grateful.

"May I ask you about the nature of your mission to Al Hind?" he asked Hsü later in the day, when they were taking their ease on the steering deck.

"It is a long story, but I will tell you the important part. Have you heard of the Silk Road?" he enquired.

Talon said he had. He remembered that in Constantinople he had seen huge caravans that appeared at regular intervals throughout the year outside the great western gates.

"Good, then you might understand more about what I tell you now. Over the last few hundred years, China, that is to say, the real people of China, have been beset by barbarians who are fierce and ignorant, but very powerful and dangerous. Over a long time we have lost much of our original country and suffered the most devastating defeats at the hands of our enemies. Our advisors were poorly informed and we have made several disastrous alliances: in most instances, the very people we have allied with have turned on us and defeated us.

"This has caused the loss of huge tracts of our former empire. The most recent disastrous event was about fifty years ago when we, the people of the Sung, lost the whole top part of our empire to the Jin tribes. This has meant that the roads that lead to the western countries, cities like Samarkand, and even further west to a fabulous city called Constan..." he hesitated over the name.

"Constantinople," Talon finished for him.

"Yes, that's right, these cities have been denied to Chinese traders. In the recent past, these people to the north, whom we call the Mongols, have destroyed whole cities, and certainly the caravans were easy pickings for them." Hsü paused. It was clearly painful for him to discuss this with someone outside his own people. Talon remained silent.

Hsü shook his head and stared overboard, gripping the rail, then continued. "You are, I think, more of a warrior than a merchant, so you perhaps do not understand that our civilization does not attach much importance to military adventures. We are traders; but the long and dangerous Silk Road is now but a shadow of what it used to be, and is definitely not a road along which I would send my goods."

"So you are looking at the sea for another way?" Talon asked.

"That is correct. In recent times the sea traffic has also dwindled, for your people, the Persians and the Arabs, have come to China less and less. I do not know the reason why."

"Perhaps it is because we, too, have an invader who is more interested in plunder than in trade," Talon said.

"Ah, then it explains a lot. True, our two peoples do meet at Kalah Bar, which is convenient for both of us; but as you have seen, even that is dangerous. The Emperor's advisors approached me to see if there were alternative routes to India, and in particular Gujarat, as from there a caravan can leave and arrive in Persia within two months instead of a year; or ships can sail from there to the city you call Baghdad."

"I know exactly what you mean!" Talon exclaimed. "I have been to Constantinople and seen the caravans there. They brought silk and much more, but there are more dangers these days, for the people called the Seljuk are like the Mongols you talk about. They care nothing for cities and trade. Instead they are herdsmen who prefer to steal and rob to gain their riches."

Hsü nodded and gave him a rueful smile. "That is the problem. Merchants such as we must trade, but the dangers are many and often unpredictable, so we have to learn to defend ourselves. My country is not as skilled as we should be in dealing with barbarians. However, in many ways my mission was successful, and one cannot blame the fates for every setback." Hsü was silent for a while before continuing.

"The sultan at Gujarat was very welcoming, and he is interested in having Chinese ships come to his port, which is up in the North-western corner of India. It is mostly Moslem there now, which is no bad thing for us Chinese, as we have many Arab and Persians who come to Guangzhou and there is an understanding of sorts between us. I was even invited to play a game of polo there; but, alas, that is not one of my skills."

Talon and Reza laughed.

"We play polo, Hsü," Reza told him when he looked askance at their amusement.

He looked at them thoughtfully. "Do you know of the famous, or is it infamous, trophy?"

They shook their heads.

"The sultan of Gujarat told me of it on one of those long, hot evenings at the palace. Long, long ago, there was a game of polo held at a city called... Isfahan, I think. In any case, it was in Persia. A group of Chinese players went to Persia to play, in the name of diplomatic relations or something like that. The Shah had this fabulous trophy made, or so they say, because no one has seen it for hundreds of years. The story goes that against all expectations the Chinese won and took this trophy home. The road is very long and dangerous, especially in those high mountains.

"They say that none of the Chinese ever arrived back in China, nor did the trophy, although it was famous by now and a search was made. It was very valuable, and many men would covet it. The legend also has it that the trophy had strange properties, but again there is little substance to this. It was reported to have reappeared and to be somewhere in India, but no one seems to have seen it. Some say that some Chinese merchants did find a it in India, and were bringing it back to China to present it to the Emperor, but that too is only rumor. The trophy vanished. I know nothing more than that," he sighed. "At the very least I can go back to my Emperor and tell him of a small success. As for the rest...." He shrugged. "It was just bad Joss, but then you came along, and I am still alive, and so is my son, so who am I to complain?" he smiled at the two enthralled men.

"I have never heard of this legend before," Talon said in some wonder. His scalp prickled at the thought of the trophy and the legend.

*****

As they sailed, Talon worked very hard to understand the mysteries of navigation, and here he was unexpectedly pleased to find that Rostam was also keen to understand and learn more. Talon could bring some experience to the regular discussions that were held on the deck of the ship as she ploughed a path across the sea towards their destination. He had studied under the tuition of Henry and his friends Nigel and Guy, the captains of his ships in the Middle Sea.

Captain Al Dandachi, however, had sailed in waters that had few borders, as it were, and crossed vast expanses of ocean that made the Middle Sea look like a large lake. Dandachi invited him to peruse the precious copies of old manuals. Ahbar and al-Maqdisi wrote about the China routes, and *Kitab Ma'din al-asrar fi 'ilm al-bihar* (*The Mine of Secrets in the Science of the Seas*) by Shaikh Nasr bin 'Ali al'Haduri contained drawings of the position of the sun above the ship. Many were the days when they would pore over the pages and try to understand what the words meant to someone following the same path as the early navigators.

Then there were the two other navigational instruments that the captain shared with him. One was the Kamal, which Talon already knew how to use. The captain showed Talon and Rostam an alternative way of using the Kamal, which was to move the knots through the teeth until the piece of horn or wood covered the required star altitude. The captain had added extra knots marking the latitudes of particular ports of call, but he had nothing for the ports of China, having been a very young sailor when he made that journey.

Finally, he rehearsed them in the use of the astrolabe, which assisted the user to find the rising and setting of fifteen stars. The captain had a list of the latitude of every port and headland that had been recorded in his manuals.

Another very simple navigational guide that was used by the captains was the position of the sun or North Star above the boat. By standing on various locations on the boat, they could place the sun during daylight or the North Star at night, above right, left or behind the ship. As long as they kept the star or the sun at a correct position above the rigging, the captain assured them, they could know that they would arrive at their destination. Rostam quickly grasped these methods of calculation and could take the measurements even more accurately than Talon.

Hsü mentioned a strange instrument they used to aid in finding directions and that they called a compass. He promised to show Talon one when they arrived at his country. "This instrument can point with unerring accuracy towards the South, no matter which way the ship itself is heading," he assured Talon. Captain Dandachi confirmed this. "I have never actually seen one of these instruments, Master Talon, but others have described it. They told me that this is a very useful instrument, especially when you cannot see the sun or the stars." Talon went away to digest this piece of interesting news.

They came to the Sea of China which was, according to the captain, the last leg of their journey. Everyone was relieved to hear this, and the fact that they had escaped any rough weather made for a contented ship. Now other vessels were to be seen in the distance, but none came close enough to find out who they might be, or from where. Each time a ship approached, the captain would alert everyone to prepare for pirates, just in case.

Before a week had passed they sighted land, which Hsü informed them might be the islands called the Gates of China. This was shoal water, dotted with many small islands, so the captain posted lookouts who were very alert to the dangers of grounding the ship. At one point a sailor posted on the top mast shouted down that he could see a shipwreck ahead, which denoted a sandbank.

"That could be one of the ships that was driven here by the typhoon," Talon surmised.

The captain made sure that they gave the stricken vessel a wide berth.

They passed through the sandbanks and small islands without mishap and sailed out into the open sea once more to head due north. Before long they encountered a growing number of ships, and within a week they were again within sight of land.

"This is the great delta of the Zhujiam River. We are in the province of Guangdong," Hsü announced to them with happy anticipation in his voice. From here on, he assumed the role of ship's pilot and guided the captain through the maze of large and small islands that dotted the delta. The new obstacles were not only the islands and the numerous sand banks, but the growing number of ships and boats of every shape and size. They passed a large peaked island on their starboard side, which Hsü called Hong Kong. "That used to be where we could find pearls, but no longer. We have to go to your countries for them now," he remarked. Talon was glad to hear that piece of information; he had a few boxes filled with pearls from the area around Muscat.

Hsü appeared satisfied that they were on the right course to the port city of Guangzhou. There was a palpable sense of relief on board as everyone realized that they were finally arriving at their destination. The winds became difficult at times, causing the crew to haul in sail and to tack up the delta, but they had no incidents of collisions with other ships, although there were numerous near misses, and on these occasions the passengers heard high-pitched shouting from Chinese sailors as they went bobbing by, which they assumed to be swearing. Gradually the delta narrowed until it became clear that they were sailing up a very wide river. Signs of human habitation became increasingly evident until, after their third day on the river, the banks on either side were lined with villages.

Talon remarked to Hsü that he could see no walls or defensive areas for a city. At first Hsü looked at him in surprise, and then he shook his head and said, "No, we do not have to have many fortified cities here in the Sung Empire; but in fact, Guangzhou is fortified in the administrative and the temple areas. The major forts are to be found much further north, along the border with our unpleasant neighbors."

Talon and Reza were astonished. They had never before come across a culture that did not need to protect itself with high walls, or at least fortresses.

Hsü guided them unerringly up the river, avoiding the numerous byways and tributaries. The water traffic by now was heavy; Talon had never seen so much shipping before. Not even Byzantium could boast this number of boats, large and small, sailing alongside or floating down river at a fast pace. The captain and the crew were busy all the while making sure there were no collisions.

"How are there so many people?" Rav'an demanded of Hsü as they sailed on up stream. She was standing with Talon and the others, mesmerized by the huge number of ships on the water and the density of the habitation on land.

Hsü smiled and said, "It is because of rice."

"Rice?" she asked, looking puzzled.

"Indeed, Lady Rav'an." Hsü smiled. "We have had our share of famine and starvation in this country, but you see how green it is here? Because of the rice grown here, our children do not starve, and our population has grown."

She nodded. It was not only green but humid. Where there were not houses and villages, there was a thick mantle of green trees and dense bamboo thickets on either side of the river, though not as ominously dense as Malaya, while beyond this barrier one could see endless patterns of dykes and fields full of water. They could see large, black, mud-covered buffalo pulling ploughs in the water-filled fields.

"Is that where they grow the rice?" she asked.

"Yes. Here in Guangdong province we have some of the richest land in China. We have found ways to obtain two crops a year, sometimes three, and we know how best to plant and harvest. We grow enough rice to feed the rest of the empire," Hsü told her proudly. "It is grown everywhere now. Hence we have a growing population. There are many millions of us in the

Sung Empire alone." Hsü smiled at them. It was clear that none of them could grasp this number adequately.

The city itself gradually appeared in the distance, signaling its presence by a haze of smoke-filled air. The buildings alongside the river became larger, taller, and more numerous. Before long they could see a forest of masts of anchored ships in the roads of the river, and long rows of vessels alongside one another near to the quays of the port. Even from this distance they could see that the houses of the city were ornate with red, green, and blue tiled roofs, which gave a very pleasant effect of a mottled sea that rose and fell with the streets, some of which were broad avenues, others narrow alleyways.

"The number of people!" Rav'an exclaimed. "It is teeming, like an ants' nest. I have never seen such a place before! Listen to them, they make a noise like bees!"

The others of their little group were equally impressed. They stood on the starboard side above the steering deck in awed silence as they looked over at the largest city any of them had ever seen. Talon, who had seen large cities before, was struck by several things. The first was the total lack of any form of protection around the port of the city: no towers or walls or any other construction with which to mount a defense. However, he could see, set well back from the busy riverbank, high walls that seemed imposing enough. He observed that Guangzhou didn't compare well to the incredibly beautiful city of Constantinople. That golden city was perched on its hills overlooking the sea, upon which temples, arenas, and palaces of white stone with golden rooftops were prominent. Even so, this Chinese city's sheer size was overwhelming; it was laid out on a series of low hills, upon which were very large multiple-storied houses and temples, each with an imposing tiled roof with its edges depicting strange creatures or ornate carved shapes. It was an impressive sight to the newcomers.

People seemed to be everywhere, both on land and on the river, which Hsü informed them was known as the Pearl River.

The huge number of small boats, filled either with the day's catch of fish or passengers, plying back and forth across the river, presented a real hazard to larger boats trying to sail upstream or down. The wharfs and warehouses swarmed with laborers, porters, builders, and craftsmen as well as sailors.

"It appears that they have many thousands of slaves to do all the menial work," Reza remarked.

Fuling, who was standing nearby overheard him and said, "We do have some slaves, but what you are seeing are the people of the city, not slaves. Father told me that in your country when you have battles and win, you take many slaves and make them build your cities?"

Talon nodded, he remembered only too well the galley slaves in Egypt and the Saracen slaves in Palestine, and, indeed, in Byzantium. "You don't appear to have a lack of people to do the work of many," he responded.

They stayed out of the captain's way as he shouted orders to the crew, who ran to shorten sail and take down the mainsail. He was guided by Hsü towards a spot where there were several other ships similar to theirs, anchored in the river.

*****

The anchors were down and the ship secured fore and aft. It was time for their guests to leave. As they came on deck with their meagre belongings, Hsü caught the look that Talon directed at the box under his arm. They looked into one another's eyes for a brief moment of complete understanding, and then, as though it had not happened, Hsü walked up to him and pressed a small cloth-wrapped package into his hand.

"This is for the transport fee. I think you will find it adequate. Do not worry, Talon. I will not desert you," he said in a low voice only for Talon to hear.

"You will have to wait here for perhaps a day or so before an official will come and discuss the reason for you being here. This is quite normal. I have to get ashore as soon as possible and tell my family that we have returned. After that I shall make sure you are taken care of."

"In the meantime," he continued, "please do not leave the ship and do not go ashore, as the customs officers don't like it and might arrest you. Jiaya here will come back as soon as I can arrange it and tell you what needs to be done."

He borrowed two men from the captain as an escort, promising to ensure they came back safely.

After bidding them all goodbye, he departed with Fuling, Jiaya and Lihua in the boat that the captain had lowered into he water. Hsü was carrying his precious box. They were rowed over to the busy docks and disappeared into the crowd on the quayside, leaving the others on the ship wondering what would happen to them next.

"Well, we have finally come to the fabled country of China!" Talon remarked at large. Rostam was hanging over the side staring at the passing sampans, while the others were gazing in a bemused fashion at the shore. Even out here the din of activity came clearly across the dirty brown water of the river.

"I want to know when we can get off this boat and have a real bath!" Rav'an said wistfully.

Jannat gave a nervous laugh. "Yes, I would like that too. I hope he has not abandoned us to the fates."

"I, as well," Reza said, without much confidence.

"If I remember the last time we came here, the customs men were not pleasant people, Master Reza. We are indeed at the mercy or our former guest now," the captain said. "*Insha'Allah* we will come under Master Hsü's protection and do well. We will certainly need his help," he sounded unhappy.

Talon felt the small package in his sash. He had a shrewd idea what it might contain.

PART II

宋

On my clothes the dust of travel mingles with wine stains
a distant journey—no place that doesn't jar the soul!
And I—am I really meant to be a poet?
In fine rain straddling a donkey I enter the Great
*   Sword Gate.*

—Lu Yu

Chapter Eighteen
Guangzhou

Hua Rong, Chief of the Police for the city of Guangzhou, stood at the open window of his office within a tall building overlooking the wider part of the river, the docks and the Arab quarter. The shutters, which were there to cut the bright sunlight, were today wide open. It gave him a good view of the cluster of Arab ships anchored near to the wharfs that were reserved for their ships. Further upstream he could see the sea-going Chinese ships anchored in the river or tied alongside the numerous wharfs of the main city dockside.

Rong was dressed in the sober, voluminous robes of an administrator, but his clothing carried the sheen of the finest silk. His round, smooth face and small, hooded, black eyes gave almost nothing away of what he was thinking. He stared out over a city that held few secrets from him; he knew that he was feared in this tumultuous city, and that suited him well.

The Governor might think he controlled the city, and indeed probably did have his finger on the political pulse, but he, Hua Rong, Chief of Police, had his finger on the pulse of the city itself, and that was an entirely different matter. There was little that went on, from the depths of the squalid canal area and the Arab quarter to the intrigues and gossip in the governor's palace, about which his spies did not inform him; and if they were tardy about providing him with information, they were severely punished.

The noise of the busy streets below was muted at this height. He turned slightly to look over a wide expanse of the city, including the governor's palace with its ornate tiled roofs. He glanced behind him at the spacious room that was his office. He liked to imagine that he was the spider and this was the center of his web. The ornate layout of the room, the gilded beams and intricate carvings at the top of the roof supports, as well as the polished rosewood tables and the *zitan* furniture, gave the impression of opulence and wealth, as well as power.

A gust of wind brought the stink of the river to his window and rustled the papers on his desk. It even disturbed the heavy silk hangings on the opposite wall. One depicted an image of Early Spring, painted by none other than Guao Xi, which had been presented to him by the ambassador to the Emperor on his last visit to Guangzhou.

They were comforting to the educated eye, as were the expensive and delicate porcelain vases from the time of the early Tang dynasty that held pride of place on the cabinet behind his enormous desk. The exquisite rugs on the polished floor were from the distant land of the Persians and would have cost a fortune, but he had received them in exchange for the right to trade from a grateful Persian merchant.

From this vantage point he could see some two *li* distance to the gates of the Arab quarter and the coming and goings of the Arab merchants and their servants. On this particular day he had noticed a new arrival.

A large Arab boat had sailed into view from down river, then dropped anchor. It was typical of the other seagoing *Baghlah* that lined the wharfs in the Arab quarter, so he didn't remark it, other than to expect some kind of report from his people. He noticed a boat leave the ship, heading for the wharfs, before he turned away from the window to deal with the pile of paperwork on his desk.

There was a discreet knock on the door and his secretary entered, carrying even more papers. Rong watched as the man shuffled quietly into the room, bowed deeply, and then moved to lay the papers on the pile already there.

Rong sighed. The paperwork. Despite his small army of secretaries, most of them eunuchs, he still had to check everything. Mistakes cost money and caused problems. Rong was a meticulous man. It was a matter of survival; as Chief of Police he had many enemies, and not just among the villains of the city.

"The signatures for the executions are on top, my Lord," the secretary said in a low tone. He then backed away and left the Chief to contemplate the papers in front of him with distaste. Executions were messy, but his signature was needed before the governor would sign off on them. The criminals were the usual collection of rapists, traitors, thieves and brigands from the country who had been apprehended, tried by the magistrates and found guilty. The sentence was almost always death; it saved on prison expenses. Beheadings took place outside the prison walls down on the mud flats by the river. The luckless prisoners would be executed in front of the appropriate officials, *not* to include himself if at all possible, or the governor.

He glanced over the pile. He noticed that the complaints from the Arab Merchant Committee about harassment from the guards at the gates of the enclosure had increased. They mentioned that their freedom to move about the city was constrained by unwarranted paperwork, obstruction from the officials at the gates, and even on the streets of the city. How could they do business with the Chinese merchants if they could not move about the city freely? Hua Rong sighed with exasperation.

The *Dashi*, as the Arabs and Persians were known without distinction, whined incessantly about the bonds placed upon their own warehouses and the taxes they had to pay on arrival and departure. Fires broke out frequently, which exacerbated the situation. The Arabs blamed the Chinese, and the Chinese shrugged and asked why would they set fire to goods they needed? Rong found it irritating to sit drinking tea with the *Dashi* leaders, using a translator while pretending he didn't understand them as they negotiated for the release of one or other of the warehouses to the market. However, he had become rich because of them, so he could not complain too much.

He decided that the latest round of obstructions should be lifted... for a limited time. The Arabs knew the power of bribes, just like anyone else, so why didn't they just apply that logic and be done? Still, they might have learned the lesson of humility sufficiently for the time being. The arrogance of the foreigners was irksome to many in the city, including himself. Despite the fact that these intrepid sailors brought to the city much in the way of exotic goods, which could not be found anywhere in China, they were unloved.

Their religion was a singular part of the problem. Their often fanatical insistence upon there being only this 'Allah' and no other gods was absurd and irritating to the majority of the Chinese people, who believed in a multitude of deities, starting with their ancestors and ending with Confucius or Buddha, take your pick. Proselytizing was prohibited, especially after some unpleasant incidents in the not so distant past. In spite of that edict, some of the Arabs, the ones called Mullahs, persisted, which was why they were for the most part confined to a restricted area where they could worship their God as much as they pleased without disturbing the civilized people of Guangzhou.

An hour later he was interrupted in his reflections and labors by another knock on the door. "Come!" he called.

Lin Chong slipped into the room as noiselessly as a cat. He bowed deeply and then, when Rong nodded, advanced to stand before the desk with his head lowered, waiting.

"Well, what is it?" Rong snapped. He had a lot of work to do and meetings to attend later in the day.

"An Arab ship arrived today, My Lord."

"Tell me something I do not know!" Rong leaned back and looked at Lin, a broad-shouldered, tough-looking man from the west, with hard eyes and a thin scar across his right ear that continued down the back of his cheek. In spite of it, Lin could be invisible anywhere, which was just why Rong employed him.

"It had passengers on board, Chinese passengers, my Lord."

Rong sat up and stared at his lieutenant. Lin was his absolute man who did his bidding in all things without question and would not be lying now.

"Chinese you say?" That was highly unusual, although on occasion Chinese merchants had been rash enough to travel with the Arabs. Few repeated the exercise, citing primitive conditions and lack of pork and alcohol. The Chinese liked their drink at meals and found the *Dashi* habit of not drinking deplorable and uncivilized.

"I have learned that the passengers are Lord Meng Hsü and his son, my Lord."

Rong nearly dropped his ink pen. Instead he controlled his breathing and placed both hands carefully on the dark lacquered table-top. His eyes were not focused on the multitude of rings on his fingers, however.

After a long pause, he said, "You are sure of this?"

"Yes, my Lord. He had to explain himself at the gates. He was dressed just like the Arab people, but he used the name of the governor and they let him pass. He is on his way to his home."

For one insane moment Rong wondered if it would be a stroke of luck to have Hsü intercepted and killed before he could get to the safety of his house, but then common sense prevailed. There were too many people in high places who would know immediately who had arranged the assassination.

"Keep a watch on the villa and make sure I know his movements. Is there anything else? Do you know the reason for this? He left in one of his own ships almost a year ago."

"No, my Lord."

"Then find out!" Rong barked.

*****

Hsü and his small traveling entourage, consisting of his son, Jiaya and Lihua, along with two crew men Talon had assigned to him, arrived at the gates of his villa late in the hour of the Horse, which he felt was appropriate to his arrival.

Unfortunately, the guards at the gates were newly recruited and refused him entry. While Fuling began to shout and Jiaya to plead, Hsü stayed calm, although it took an effort.

"Go and get Fang, *my* bodyguard, at once!" he finally ordered the confused youths.

They looked uncertain. They were only young men, almost boys, with not a single jot of sense between them. "Do it!" he roared, and then laid a restraining hand on Fuling's arm. "They do not know us, but Fang will sort this out. Calm yourself, my son."

One of them ran off, while the other assumed an uncertain but aggressive stance to keep them where they were until help arrived.

Fang came striding out of the building complex with a scowl on his stern face. The moment he rested his eyes on Hsü, he marched up to within three paces of his master, snapped to attention and bowed very low indeed from the waist, then bellowed at the two guards to get out of the way. "Pay your respect to your master!" he shouted, his face contorted with rage.

The two young men fell to their knees and banged their heads on the dust of the pathway before another curt order from Hsü made them stop.

"Welcome back, My Lord Meng! We... we had not expected you, er, quite like this," Fang stammered. "I am humiliated that these scum did not recognize you and have not paid you the appropriate respect. Do you wish that I cut of their heads immediately?"

Hsü winced. He knew that the very next thing Fang would request would be his own horrible suicide for allowing such a loss of face to occur.

"I will think on it, Fang. In the meantime, I want you to educate them as to who I am, and that includes my son. They can be forgiven for not knowing... but you are to supervise their reeducation personally. I want you to find some men who actually look like soldiers to augment this sorry lot while you are at it."

"Yes, my Lord."

"And NO, you do not have my permission to commit suicide. It is disgusting. Do I make myself clear?" Hsü demanded.

Fang scowled into the distance and would not look at him. "Yes, my Lord," he replied woodenly.

"I am very pleased to see you again, Fang," Hsü said as he walked away.

He knew what the punishment would be, of course. Fang would sentence the two luckless youths to the cleaning of the night waste from the bowls with their bare hands for a month at least. He shrugged mentally. The process went like that, and there was little he could do to change that aspect of life in the ranks without causing loss of face all round.

Fang couldn't wait to cut open his belly at any excuse, just like those mad people who lived in the islands to the northeast of China who always wanted to die with the scent of cherry blossoms in their nostrils. Why they couldn't just get along with one another was a mystery to him. It also bothered him that the guards had been such inexperienced youths. He would have to have a private word with Fang about that. He suspected that his brother-in-law, a tight-fisted man, had hired them. Fang would have had more sense.

"I want you and one of the other guards to escort these two men back to the Arab quarter, Fang," he called over his shoulder. "Please make sure that they arrive safely. Use my name if anyone tries to stop you."

He knew perfectly well that unless the police themselves intercepted them, Fang would chop anyone who threatened them into little bits, as it would be he and no one else who would escort the men back to their ship. Fang bowed in silence and stayed frozen in that position as Hsü walked away.

Hsü gave Lihua and Jiaya permission to leave and watched them scurry off to their quarters, then he walked alone into his own property with a huge sigh of relief. His son also hastened away to pay his respects to his mother and grandmother, who were ensconced on their thrones deep within the interior of the villa. Hsü smelled the delicate scent of fruit blossoms and his ears registered the sound of water flowing; it relaxed him at once. He looked around him at the dense and complex symmetry of the gardens, the orchards, ponds and tiled roofs of the many buildings of his home, and it felt good.

He barely heard Fang snarling at the guards, whom he had lined up and was 'educating' as to who he, Lord Meng Hsü was, and was only dimly aware of the frantic activity all around him. Word had spread like lightning. Servants, gardeners and other guards *Ke Tou'd* to him as he walked the one-hundred paces long pathway towards the inner courtyard to where the fountain was making its water music.

Hsü ignored them all. He was savoring his garden, his villa, *his* world. He would have a very long hot bath, alone, but with a very attentive servant to pour piping hot water over his shoulders on request; and then perhaps a light massage. Then he would dress in real clothes. The rags he was wearing would disappear forever into the flames of a fire. There would be a meal of some real food, which he could eat at his leisure with a pair of ivory chopsticks instead of his fingers, enjoying the taste of every morsel. He clasped his hands tightly behind his back, with the box safely under his left arm, and savored the moment. He could deal with his wife a little later.

As he walked, he thought about what his arrival would mean to many people, not least the governor and his simpering intellectual minions, as well as that drain rat Hua Rong, the Chief of Police.

His concerns with the consortium were less worrying by comparison. The contents of the box he carried under his arm would more than compensate for the loss of the ship, with a small profit to sweeten the bitterness of the disaster and leave him with more wealth to add to that which he already possessed. It was Joss that he lived at all, and that would mean the placing of burning incense at the altar of his ancestors this very evening.

His private thoughts were interrupted by a high-pitched yelp of excitement, and the small figure of Lun came rushing out to greet him. The boy literally ran into his arms in a display of appalling bad manners, but Hsü seized him and swung him into the air with delight.

"Papa, you came! You are safe!" the boy exclaimed. "Did you come on the Arab ship?" he demanded when he had been placed back on his feet.

Hsü tried to mask his surprise. "Yes, yes I did, how did you know? Ah, I know, your brother told you."

Lun looked uncomfortable. "No, Papa. I, I just knew."

Hsü frowned. "You have not yet met your brother then?" he demanded.

"I saw him with Mama. He didn't talk to me," Lun said, looking up at him.

Hsü patted him on the head. "I must prepare myself. Walk with me, and later you can tell me all about your studies."

"Yes, Papa," the boy said reluctantly, and accompanied him to the inner courtyard. Soon he was babbling happily and holding on tightly to his father's hand. Hsü didn't mind at all, despite the breach of protocol.

Later, much refreshed and wearing clean clothes, layers of silk which had the faint scent of camphor and were appropriate to his station and surroundings, Hsü and the family met at the hour of the Rabbit, just as the sun was dipping below the western rooftops of the city.

Hsü took the head of the table, as he had always done when home, while his mother sat at the other end, and his wife to his right hand. Fuling sat on his left side and Lun was placed in the middle next to Fuling.

Everyone, including his wife, seemed pleased and relieved to see him, although he sensed a certain coolness about her when he arrived at the table. Nevertheless, she greeted him with the usual polite terms, and when he was seated she made sure that he was served first with the wine and the first of every delicacy that came to the table, even to offering him a tidbit with her own chopsticks, making the point that she was his wife in every way.

The conversation was slow at first, but very soon his mother was demanding a full description of his travels from the day he had left. Her main concern was how he had arrived on an Arab ship.

"Your Lun here knew about it even before you arrived, Hsü," she stated, which drew a frown from her daughter-in-law.

"So he told me himself," said Hsü. "How did you know, Lun?"

But Lun squirmed and looked embarrassed. "I dreamed it, Papa," he muttered into his rice bowl.

"Hmm." Hsü decided to leave it at that for the time being and turned to face his wife.

The woman who looked back at him, but then dropped her eyes in the usual coy deference, was still very beautiful, but a mask of hardness had turned her features to stone.

"We have all been very concerned, my Husband. Every member of the family Hong has worried. There were reports of very bad Typhoons this year. Was it one of those that caused your ship to sink?" she asked him.

The news of the disaster had shaken her badly. He knew why. Her brother had been one of the chief investors, along with several other rich merchants of the Hong or merchant group. She had no idea how they might recoup their investments after such a disaster. He intended to reassure her.

"No, it was in the seas of India, not very far west of the long peninsular at the place they call Kalah Bar. A great storm came up from the Southwest and swamped our boat. We also caught fire." There were gasps of horror at this. Hsü could see that Fuling was dying to tell the story, so he waved his hand at his son, indicating permission to continue.

Fuling told a fairly factual account of the voyage and the catastrophic storm, adding only a few embellishments, as his father was present. His audience listened with rapt attention. When he finished there was a long silence as the family digested the tale, and even the servants, who had been silently bustling about, were still.

His wife, Lady Wong Meilin, finally cleared her throat, waved to a servant to replenish his wine, and spoke. "I shall burn incense at the temple tomorrow and thank our ancestors for their protection," she said, then asked, "The ship went down with its entire cargo, my husband? All was lost?" Her tone was full of apprehension.

Hsü had been expecting this. She had been more worried about the riches lost than anything else!

"Hum, yes. The only survivors were myself, Fuling, Jiaya our secretary, and of course Lihua," he added with just a trace of mischief.

He noted her eyes flash just before she looked down. "We are all very happy this is so," she murmured, but her tone was cool.

"So, apart from your business as an ambassador, of which we should talk soon, my son, the venture was a, a terrible set back? The Emperor will require a full report," his mother said from the other end of the table. Her eyes held his, but there was sympathy in them.

"Not entirely, Mother," Hsü said with a smile. "I salvaged enough of our own possessions to pay back the investors, with perhaps a little profit; but alas, nothing like what we could have made had we come home in our own ship."

The relief in the room was tangible. Meilin glanced up with visible happiness in her eyes. "I am so happy, my husband. A year not wasted in barbarian lands after all!" she said.

The women plied the two men with questions for the next hour until finally it was time for Lun to be sent off to his room. He left reluctantly, as the tale of their adventures left him too excited to sleep. Fuling also excused himself, and Meilin dismissed the servants to allow for more privacy.

After pouring some more warm wine for Hsü, she glanced back at her mother-in-law and said, "There will be much speculation, my husband. You spoke of possessions you retained. How so, when the ship was sinking?"

Hsü stood up and shut the door to the dining room, excluding all the servants. He went over to the chest against the wall, retrieved the box from inside where he had placed it earlier, and set it on the table.

"We must keep this a secret for the time being. Fortunately, although we lost the main cargo and much else besides, these small items travel well," he stated as he opened the box.

Meilin could not help herself. She gasped and placed a small, slim hand over her mouth. "Ahmida Buddha!" she exclaimed. "This is a fortune on its own!"

"Yes, it is, but their worth does not match the potential of the lost cargo. However, it is better than coming home with nothing. We could have been robbed by pirates, or even died."

Meilin could not take her eyes off the contents, which gleamed and glittered in the candlelight. Even his mother, who was still seated at the end of the table, could see what was inside the box and was clearly impressed.

"If what I am seeing is not glass, then you have still done well, my son," she stated with approval.

"Not glass, Mother. The rubies and emeralds are very real. It is great Joss that I could bring it and was not robbed by the Arabs," Hsü said. "The Persian named Talon knew full well what was in this box, but he still let me take it from his ship. Somehow he found out, but he said nothing to anyone, even on his own ship."

"He must be very naive to have let you go without demanding some kind of surety," his mother remarked.

"I gave him my assurance, Mother. I think he is putting his trust in me, and I certainly do trust him by now. He could have killed us all and thrown us to the sharks and then gone home a very rich man with this box alone, but he didn't."

He continued. "Your brother is not going to be terribly happy, Meilin, but these Arabs saved us from certain death, so I owe them a great deal. I offered to buy their cargo for a lot more than was being offered in Kalah Bar in order to persuade them to bring me home. Your brother and I, indeed the entire Hong, must now discuss how we can obtain the cargo from them without paying the fines and taxes that would normally be imposed. That would mean that we can sell it for a larger profit, either here in this town or in the capital," he stated. "Of course we cannot avoid all the taxes, as the Emperor's customs duties will have to be paid no matter what. What we can avoid, however, is the bribery that is usually paid to the officials."

"How do you intend to carry out this arrangement?" his mother, ever the practical minded, demanded of him.

"I will need to speak to the right people, of course, but I think that with your brother to help me we can overcome that particular obstacle," Hsü told them.

"I am happy tonight for the first time in months," his mother said. "That little son of yours is a strange one. He dreamed that you were in a storm, and sure enough you were; but what has amazed us further is that he foretold that you would arrive on an Arab ship!"

Hsü looked closely at his mother. "He really foretold that?" he enquired.

Meilin said. "None of us believed him, until today when you arrived the way you did."

"His grandfather used to have dreams of a similar kind. I wonder," he remarked pensively.

Then after a pause he said, "There is something else you need to know."

"What is it?" they both asked at the same time; there was apprehension in their voices. They had heard enough disasters for one night.

"I intend to bring the merchant and his friend, and their wives, to our house for as long as it takes to complete the transfer of the cargo and send them on their way," Hsü told the two women.

He smiled at their appalled expressions. "I know... they are barbarians who eat with their fingers, and there is much else about them that we find revolting, but they did not have to save me. They could have sailed right on by and left us to our fate. In fact, I heard that the captain protested against saving us; but Talon, the merchant, decided to stop and pick us up. I can do no less than take them off that ship and bring them to our house."

"How will we manage? No one likes those people, and their customs are appalling. They are just not civilized!" Meilin's tone was plaintive.

"As we always have," Lanfen, her mother-in-law, said sharply, with a glance at her son, who was smiling sardonically at his wife's discomfort.

Hsü chuckled. "You can teach them our manners and ways while they are here. I think they are willing to learn, although it will be an uphill struggle. They are, after all, barbarians!" He had a half-smile on his face as he said this.

"Now I need to know all the important gossip and what that rat gangster Lu Buwei and his group of thugs have been up to in the drains of the city. No doubt Hua Rong, our illustrious Chief of Police, is scheming right along with them. I am sure it did not escape his notice that I am back."

They talked late into the evening, as the women, who were very well informed, told him of the scandals and gossip going on in the city, and the latest from the court in Lin'an, also known as Chang-zhou.

*****

Later that evening, Meilin took particular care with her appearance and toilet. When the servant girl failed to pay enough attention to her hair, which she was trying to pile high in the latest style that showed off the beautiful planes of her pale, oval face, she rapped the maid on her knuckles with a brush so hard the girl had cried. Impatiently, Meilin told her to leave and to send in the other girl to assist her into her evening silk gown. Eyeing herself in the mirror, Meilin nodded approval. She looked like a fine work of art. Her husband would not be disappointed.

Meilin felt resentment for the 'woman' Lihua, who rivaled her own beauty and had the advantage of being younger and able to move around, not anchored to the chair or the bed by her bound feet. But in the end it didn't matter; she, Meilin, was the wife; she was beautiful and had a right to expect her husband to acknowledge this fact.

It was very late when Hsü finally came to her bed. There was barely a murmur of approval for her beauty, and the lovemaking was perfunctory. It was soon over and her husband made his exit with the excuse that he had work to do. Meilin felt a wave of loneliness come over her, biting back the tears as she watched him leave. Doubtless he was going back to take care of his concubine, she raged.

There was nothing she could do nor say, as it would mean a huge loss of face, and that she would never grant him the satisfaction of witnessing. The tears came in the darkness of the night when no one could witness her shame. How she wished the girl had been drowned. Not only that, her husband now wanted to disrupt the peace of her household with the presence of foreigners! She swore that she would have revenge of some sort on the girl.

*****

The next day at about noon, Talon, who was on deck, noticed Jiaya standing on the quayside with a couple of men. Jiaya was waving his arms to draw attention to himself. Talon pointed this out to the captain, who sent a boat over to collect the Chinese men. Jiaya climbed up the side of the ship and then stood catching his breath in the waist deck before walking in his mincing manner up the steps to stand in front of Talon.

Jiaya was completely transformed from an old man in plain clothes to a sophisticated man dressed in silk robes, albeit a sober dark brown in color, with a small, odd-looking hat perched on his head held in place by a silk cord tied under his chin. After the usual polite greetings and bows Jiaya said, "My master, Lord Meng, sends his best wishes to you and your people, Master Talon, and respectfully begs that you accompany me with your family and that of your companion Master Reza to his house."

Talon breathed a sigh of relief. Ever since the exchange of looks he had had with Hsü he had hoped for something of this nature. Nevertheless, he wanted to know what would happen to his ship and cargo before he abandoned the captain to whatever the officials of this teeming city had in store. His past experience with customs and port taxes in Byzantium made him wary of leaving the ship on its own. In fact, earlier that very day, some official had arrived on a small sampan and demanded to be let on board. After curt introductions, during which he had spoken pidgin Arabic, he had thrust a piece of paper into Talon's hand and left, looking irritated and speaking volubly to himself and the world at large in his own language.

Talon now showed the paper to Jiaya, who frowned as he read it but didn't seem very perturbed as to its contents.

"What does it say?" Talon asked. Reza was now beside him and they looked askance at Jiaya, who replied, "This is a tax for anchorage here in the river, Master Talon. I will deal with it, as Lord Meng has instructed me to handle all the procedures while you are here."

Talon stared at him. "*Lord* Meng, did you say?" he asked.

Jiaya nodded his head and smiled. "I shall deal with the customs, Master Talon," he said.

Talon had a sense of déjà vu. This sounded just like the officialdom of Byzantium. There would be other bureaucratic procedures to endure, entailing bribes, before they could sail away again. Each time, a little more of the profit would be eaten away by some rapacious petty official. He frowned, but nodded. "Thank you, Jiaya. Now where can my crew and the captain live while we are with... your master?"

Jiaya gave a little bow. "Respectfully, first things first, Master Talon. Please to bring your family and some servants with me to Lord Meng's house. All will be arranged for the crew and the ship. These two men," he indicated the two tough-looking, well armed Chinese men who had arrived with him, "will stay on the ship, and some more will come to protect and make sure that no officers come on board without the permission of the Lord Meng. Those are his orders."

Talon remarked to himself that Jiaya seemed to have gained self-confidence and authority now that he was back in familiar surroundings. He drew comfort from this. They would need all the help they could get while here.

Talon looked at Reza, who said, "It seems we are in the hands of our friend Hsü, Talon. How much do you trust him?"

"Our friend is a Lord, it would seem, and I think I trust him, Reza. Do you not?"

Reza shrugged. "He is a very cunning man. I still do not fully trust him. But what alternative is there?" Then he nodded at Jiaya. "This little fellow seems to have found himself since we arrived. Quite a change from the timid little mouse we are used to." They were speaking *Farsi*.

Talon chuckled. "I hope he knows what he is about. I don't want to come this far only to lose the cargo to some thieving customs officials."

A few hours later they were all standing in the outer courtyard of the villa. Hsü was there with his son Fuling, who seemed pleased to see them, and a long line of servants, men and women who were bowing to the newcomers. There was no sign of a wife or any other female members of the actual family.

"Welcome to my poor house, Master Talon and Reza. I welcome you, as does my family," Hsü said in greeting. He beamed at Rostam, who clung to Rav'an's hand. "You too, Rostam. My younger son, Lun, will look after you."

Rav'an wore her veil, as did Jannat and Salem; they were staring around, awed by the beautiful setting. Talon could hardly believe what he was seeing.

"Pedar Sag!" Reza exclaimed under his breath. "This is a real palace! Rav'an and Jannat should be happy now."

"I really think we might finally get a bath in this place!" Talon remarked with a grin.

Cicadas complain of thin mulberry-trees
In the Eighth-month chill at the frontier pass.
Through the gate and back again, all along the road,
There is nothing anywhere but yellow reeds and grasses
And the bones of soldiers from You and from Bing
Who have buried their lives in the dusty sand.
... Let never a cavalier stir you to envy
With boasts of his horse and his horsemanship

—Tang Shi II.

Chapter Nineteen

The Path to the Governor

News of Hsü's arrival quickly spread. Visitors began to arrive within a day, and the first was Meilin's brother, Wong Cheng Kaen, who was a very worried man. He barely noticed the distinctly foreign-looking people in the courtyard. He stepped out of his palanquin and hurried towards the inner sanctum, where he found his sister and brother-in-law awaiting him. Fang had sent a guard at top speed to inform them of his arrival.

He was offered refreshments and tea while Hsü calmed him down and told his story, then showed what he had brought back with him. Neither to his family nor his brother-in-law had Hsü shown the full extent of his treasure, but what he did display was enough to make Kaen's eyes pop.

"Some of this will have to go for bribes to the governor and the customs officers, you understand?" Hsü told Kaen, who nodded, but he breathed a huge sigh of relief at the same time. He was not going to be destitute after all, as he had thought. He expressed amazement at how Hsü could have managed to bring such a treasure home with him despite the loss of the ship. "How did you manage to keep hold of this, this treasure?" he asked with an incredulous stare.

"I have the Persians to thank for that. A long story, which I will tell you one day, but I can pay off the other investors over and above their former costs at least by a little, and then we will all share in the profits of the ship's cargo," Hsü continued. He had already told Kaen of the cargo and its composition.

"I will need you to grease the path with the customs people, Kaen," he said, "as I have not only to report to the governor very soon, but will certainly have to travel to the Palace of the Emperor to report the results of my mission."

Kaen had known about the ambassadorial role that Hsü had played, so he willingly agreed. "Did you know that the governor is seriously ill?" he asked.

Both his brother-in-law and his sister looked surprised. "I knew that he had been ill," Meilin replied, "but not as bad as you imply, Brother."

"The doctors are with him almost every day now, and there are rumors that he will not last out the year," Kaen told them. "The Emperor will have to appoint a new governor, and quite soon." He sipped his wine and watched for a reaction.

There was none from Hsü, who kept his face inscrutable, but Meilin gave a little gasp and turned to Hsü with a smile on her face. "Does my husband stand a chance with the palace officials?" she asked in a very low voice.

"If Lord Hsü can give a very optimistic report, coupled with the right, er, payments, this could be a possibility," her brother informed them.

Hsü thought about this. He had known the governor for many years and respected the man for being well educated and kindly; perhaps too kindly, as the role of the governor was a hard one. The position of governor of the province of Guangdong was very important, not least because the city was a gateway for trade with the outside world. Whoever controlled the province and Guangzhou would be a very powerful person, and eventually very rich.

Kaen broke into his reflections. "You will, of course, find that there will be competition for the position if you declare an interest, Hsü," he said.

Hsü nodded. He was only too aware of that fact. Potential rivals might already be canvassing the eunuchs and the administrators in the Emperor's palace for support. There were administrators and prefects already high on the ladder who could qualify. Then there was the chief of police, who was very ambitious and might want the position for himself. In which case, the others would have to watch out, as that man would resort to every dirty trick in the book. Did he really want the job, he wondered?

"I would have to think carefully before I commit myself," he told them. "I need to see the governor first and make my report, and then see if he wants me to go to the Emperor.

"I think you would make a first-rate governor," Kean told him with an ingratiating smile, while his wife Meilin simpered and nodded her head. "What a gift to your ancestors! I know you would be a perfect choice," she told him.

They left it at that.

For the rest of the week, Meilin played host to all manner of people, from ship's captains to high up officials who wanted to learn what they could about Hsü's experiences. The very fact that Hsü had returned on an Arab ship was the cause of much interest, but for the time being he evaded and deflected questions about that. Instead, he focused on telling anyone who wanted to listen that there was still a lucrative trade to be had on the Indian continent for those who wanted it and promised to write letters for people to the sultan of Gujarat. It was time to reopen the trade routes via the sea.

*****

Several days later, he had himself carried to the palace of the governor in a palanquin. It was taken across the intervening waters of the Pearl River by a boat hired for the purpose, then he was carried the several *li* along the main road that led to the gates of the palace itself. There was a polo game going on in the park that he would have liked to watch, but he had pressing business today. He reminded himself to bring Talon along some time to watch the game.

Leaving Fang to guard the palanquin at the gates, he chose to walk through the main entrance and present his papers to the clerk at the top of the stairs leading up to the interior of the palace. Ornate, red painted pillars on either side supported the curved tile roof and lent an imposing front to the center of governance of the province of Guangdong. He felt that he was very much the outsider; he had not visited the palace often, despite the urgings of the governor Murong himself.

He was ushered into the waiting room and sat on an expensive ebony chair, carved with dragon heads on the ends of the arms, and with claws for feet. The silk paintings on the tall walls were pleasant to observe. While he waited and stared about him, he thought he detected a Zhao Ji painting, on silk, of a flock of cranes. There was also one of a small group of goats gamboling on a knoll.

Little seemed to have changed since his last visit. There were cobwebs in among the carvings above his head that had not been there before, and some of the paintings had succumbed to the ravages of insects. He noted with some sadness that nothing ever lasted, and that included good servants to keep a labyrinthine palace clean.

After waiting for nearly an hour, someone he knew, a tall, thin Administrator by the name of Li Shou-cheh, stepped forward silently and bowed to him. "The Governor will see you now, Lord Meng," he said with a thin smile of welcome.

Hsü got to this feet and adjusted his tunic. It was of rich, heavy silk brocade with intricate patterns on the front, not too ostentatious, just enough to make a statement. It would have been a grave loss of face to ignore the protocols of dressing in this world that judged one on manners and dress. Shou-cheh, who held his hands out of sight in his sleeves, eyed him critically and then said, "You do not look much the worse for your ordeal, Lord Meng."

"I shall take that as a compliment. I was shipwrecked some months ago, so I have recovered since," Hsü said. "It was good Joss that an Arab ship came by just in time."

"Word is all over the town. Gossip is the food and drink of this city, and the word is that your Joss is good. We should have some wine and talk about it, soon," Shou-cheh said, with a meaningful look at Hsü.

Hsü nodded his understanding and acceptance. Shou-cheh wanted to tell him something.

"Why don't you come to my house and visit me?" Hsü suggested, knowing the answer even as he asked.

Shou-cheh gave an imperceptible shake of his head and smiled again, glancing about him from under his plucked brows. "Perhaps a place where we can talk in private?"

Hsü nodded again. "Very well, send a messenger when you are able, and I shall meet you wherever you like."

Shou-cheh bowed and then led the way out of the antechamber.

Hsü had not expected to encounter the Governor lying in bed. They had walked, not to the audience room, but instead up a flight of stairs to a secluded room. Covering his surprise, Hsü bowed deeply to the occupant of the bed, who was supported by cushions in a half-sitting position.

The Governor lifted a hand in acknowledgment of his presence and spoke.

"I have missed you, Lord Meng. I am delighted to hear of the good Joss that has attended you, although it seems to me to have been mixed."

"I am also delighted to see you, my Lord," Hsü said. "I survived with my son, and we were fortunate to be picked up by an Arab ship; good Joss on the whole, I'd say."

The governor dismissed the men hovering about his bed with a gesture. "Get out!" he grated. The men left hurriedly. Hsü assumed they were the doctors.

"They are like vultures, just waiting for me to go so that they can pick over my carcass," the governor said in his reedy voice. Murong was clearly very ill, but there was a strength of will there yet. "I want to talk to you, Hsü," he said, using the familiar. Hsü dipped his head politely.

"Come closer. The walls have ears, and I want what we say to one another to be private."

Hsü stepped closer to the bed and leaned over the wrinkled old man lying in state. There was a smell of death surrounding the bed that was unpleasant.

"I am dying," Murong murmured. "When I am gone there will be a fight for this position. It takes an honest man to do this work and... for the most part I have been honest and firm when it was needed. Do you not think so?" he asked, raising his eyes to those of Hsü, his faded old eyes pleading.

"Without doubt, my Lord. However, you are merely ill and will surely recover very soon," Hsü assured him.

Murong gave a grimace. "Bah! Those doctors will see to it that I do not." He beckoned Hsü to bend over, closer. "I want to have you appointed after I am gone," Murong said, almost in a whisper.

Hsü was startled and instinctively glanced around to see if anyone had heard other than himself.

"I am not sure I am the right person for the role, my Lord," he said quietly.

"Nonsense! Of course you are! Now that you are back from your adventures as an ambassador for the Emperor you are very qualified. Not only that, you are not corrupt, like those sycophants that plague me every waking hour." The old man took hold of Hsü's wrist and held onto it to make his point. His wrist and hand were blue-veined on an almost fleshless limb, but despite that his grip was firm.

"I do not have much time, and even less to debate this with you, Hsü. I will be sending a letter to the Emperor advocating you as the best person for this position. You have all the right credentials. You have Confucius at your fingertips. I have heard you spouting him often enough," he insisted when Hsü made to declaim.

"You must reflect on this carefully and then decide how you are going to win this race," Murong told him, as though the decision was made. "I can only recommend. After that, you know what needs to be done. Remember what Sun Tzu said? 'After having made assessments, the one who first knows the measure of far and near wins'."

Hsü nodded agreement. Both he and the Governor were students of Sun Tzu's philosophy of the Art of War.

"Be very careful, Hsü. The office is a prize that many would give much to have. You will be in danger, and perhaps even your family. That is not my wish but ... this province needs a good leader."

The Governor released his grip and settled into the cushions with a sigh of exhaustion. Hsü bowed low and departed. He waved the doctors over urgently as he went out of the room. He hoped that Shou-cheh might be there, but there were only some agitated-looking servants hovering about in the corridor. As he was on his way down the hallway, he felt that he was being observed. He glanced to his right and noticed one of the senior Administrators standing between two pillars watching him.

Hsü paused and bowed politely. He was familiar with the man, who bowed back and said, "Lord Meng. I am delighted to meet you again after so long. I am Prefect Wu po-ku."

"I am delighted to meet you again, Prefect." Hsü knew perfectly well who the man was. He had a reputation for pedantry and was a very clever administrator. Perhaps too clever, because somehow he had become very rich for a mere administrator. However, Hsü was not going to give any indication of his reservations now.

"How did you find the Governor?" Wu asked politely enough.

"Sadly, I did not find him well. It must be of great concern to yourself and the other members of his staff," Hsü said.

"We must continue to hope for a swift recovery." Wu bowed with a smile that displayed his small, even teeth between thin lips. The discussion was over.

Hsü left the palace to go home.

*****

Several days later, Hua Rong was seated at an expensive eating house some way from his office along the main street that led to the Examination house. With the Chief of Police was a man who was in his own right a very rich and influential man, albeit on the wrong side of the law most of the time. His distinguishing features were his fleshy nose and his very wide mouth, which gave him some resemblance to a toad. No one in his right mind would ever say as much to his face, and even when not in his presence people were wary of making fun of this man. His light brown eyes indicated that he was of mixed blood. Rong strongly suspected that he might even possess some Mongol blood, God forbid!

None of this bothered Rong, however; his purpose for staying close to Lu Buwei was a mutual sense of greed.

"You now know, as does most of Guangzhou, the circumstances of Hsü's arrival and what befell him in the Indian ocean, I dare say?" Rong asked Buwei after they had started the meal.

"Of course. My spies tell me everything," Buwei said through a mouthful of shrimp. His chopsticks were never still when he was eating, and even Rong had to look away when it became too much to watch the full to bulging mouth leaking juices while he ate.

"Did your own spies tell you that despite the loss of his ship he somehow managed to bring back a box full of treasure?" Buwei mumbled though his full mouth.

Rong was startled. "How is that?" he demanded.

"Ah, so you don't know all there is! Hah!" Buwei shook his head and swallowed. He took a swig of hot rice wine and burped.

"A treasure, you say?" Rong asked stupidly while he took a more deliberate sip of the *tsjuw*, a fermented drink made from millet, which he preferred. It didn't cloud his mind quite so quickly.

"Yes indeed. Quite a little fortune, I hear. I'd love to get my hands on it before he dispenses it to such people as the Governor, and perhaps even the Emperor's minions."

"I wouldn't worry about the Governor at this moment," Rong said.

"Whyzat?" Buwei was in his cups already.

"His doctor told me it is unlikely he will last out the year."

"Ah well, that is very interesting. I knew he was ill of course, but not, as you say, terminally?" Buwei mumbled as he stuffed more food into his mouth. "You should try those small pastries over there. They are *delicious*!"

Rong was more interested in discussing the likelihood of a successor to the Governor than stuffing his face or bragging about whose spies were more adept at reporting secrets. Watching Buwei demolish a table loaded with food dampened his appetite.

"You and I could profit from the right man being in the governor's office when the time comes," he said in a low tone, with a glance around the busy eating room. There were faces in this room that he knew well, but he wasn't in the mood to talk to anyone other than Buwei. Not today.

Buwei nodded, and his jowls wobbled. He wasn't as drunk as he seemed. "Who do you have in mind for the job?" he asked.

"Well, apart from you or I," Rong smiled. There wasn't a hope in hell that Buwei could get the post. He hadn't qualified as an administrator and lacked a degree; that was one of the prerequisites of the job. But he, Rong, was qualified.

"I was thinking of Wu po-ku," he said, then continued rapidly before Buwei could respond. "He took his exams around the same time as I did. He is a Prefect, which means he has experience in the process of running a complex government; and furthermore, he is, um, malleable."

Buwei nodded and started in on the sweet Aga Aga jellies and rice biscuits now being laid out in front of them.

"You don't think General Hayan Zhuo would be the right person?"

Rong recoiled. "Heavens, no! He is far too principled and has sworn to clean up this city if he ever gets into a position to do so. I couldn't bear to have to *Ke Tou* to that sanctimonious old fart."

Buwei laughed, a deep belly laugh. "Ha Ha! I agree, just testing you. We can't have that now, can we? Who else is there to worry about then, if we plump for Wu?" he asked, wiping his large, fleshy lips with a napkin.

Rong leaned across the table and murmured, "There is Yen Wei, also a Prefect." He named several other potential candidates, then said, "And there is a rumor that Lord Meng might be in the running. He visited the Governor the other day. I couldn't get a man close enough, and that closed-mouth crisp of a man Li Shou-cheh wouldn't provide any information, using the excuse of confidentiality."

"That can make for a short life, if he behaves like that too often," Buwei stated. His eyes became hard pebbles in the folds of his face. Rong might be the Chief of Police, but Buwei was reputed to be the leader of a Tong. He controlled much of the crime in the city, and all the opium dens.

Rong wasn't focussing. What on earth was all this about a treasure in Hsü's house? Now that bore investigating.

"Hello, Rong? Are you paying attention? I just said that I can probably take care of Yen Wei, but if the rumor is true and Lord Meng is a contestant, things could be difficult. He has a reputation for honesty, but he is also tough and quite well protected. Not something you find often in the merchant community. Anyway, doesn't the appointment have to be approved in the court of the Emperor? It will need his chop."

"Anyone who wants the job will have to have the Emperor's seal of approval, yes," Rong said. "We will have to place some high-level bribes in the palace, and we will have to do it soon."

"We must begin work to ensure that neither Yen nor Meng get any ideas about running for the job," Buwei stated. "It would be amusing to use some of the treasure he brought back with him to bribe people in the palace of the Emperor," he observed.

It was as though he had read Rong's very thoughts.

*****

From the first day of their arrival at his home, Lord Meng Hsü had treated Talon and his family as honored guests. To the foreign visitors, the cluster of ornate, storied pagodas and other buildings, with the four courtyards and and two fountains, resembled a palace.

It was a busy week before Lord Meng could spend some time with them, and for this he laid on a modest feast for his entire family and this guests. The two small boys were included, but they soon began to fidget, and Hsü gave them permission to go into the gardens under the supervision of Lun's nurse.

His wife Meilin maintained an aloof coldness and disdained to converse with any of them, making her disapproval of the visitors very plain. Her poor manners annoyed Hsü and his mother, who made a valiant attempt to put their guests at ease. However, it was not very long before the women of Hsü's family took their leave from the large, lacquered table. Lihua was present in the guise of a translator at Hsü's request, to the fury of his wife, whom he chose to ignore.

The table, with its embroidered cloth cover, was strewn with bowls of rice, saucers of shrimp in chili sauce, and small bowls of fried pork. Hsü refrained from telling them the meat's origin, pointing out instead the fried duck delicacies and the delicious morsels of fish, dumplings in soup, and vegetables, each one worth sampling. The main course had been stir-fried beef cubes surrounded by pickled kale and bean sprouts. Its flavor was rich and varied, with a hint of a sour taste. Rav'an had declared it delicious and asked its name.

"*Kum Ngan Yuk Ngau Sze,*" Lihua had told them with a straight face and then smiled, putting her hand delicately in front of her mouth as she did so. She went on to explain how it was made. None of them could remember its name within minutes of being told.

Talon was eager to try out his newfound skills with the chopsticks and fumbled his way through the meal, more often than not dropping slippery pieces of meat or vegetables onto the table cloth, to his evident chagrin. The others had not practiced, so it was even worse for them. The wine had its intended effect, however, and soon the mortified looks became giggles and laughs, accompanied by titters from Lihua as she instructed them. Hsü and his son watched with amused expressions.

Hsü sat back and enjoyed the scene, but his reason for the meal was to provide a forum for a meeting to discuss the immediate future. When the servants had finally cleared the table and left the fruit: lychee, bananas, cherries, and peaches, with some more warmed wine, he opened the discussion. He spoke slowly and in Arabic, as their Chinese was still virtually nonexistent.

"Talon, now that you are here and my honored guests, my man Jiaya will be working very with you to assist with the complex customs procedures. In normal circumstances, if you had arrived alone without me aboard, you would have been subjected to the usual difficulties imposed upon all foreign traders."

"What do you mean, 'the usual difficulties, Hsü?" Talon asked, and a frown appeared.

"It is, shall we say, the law, as imposed by the local guilds, or Hongs, that your cargo would be impounded by customs and held until other ships had arrived, at which time theirs would also be bonded and held. At a certain time, dictated by the customs, when everyone had arrived who was going to be here this year of trading, they would release all the cargo at once, and you would have to sell what you could in a market where the prices had fallen dramatically because of an glut of the same goods." He raised his hand to forestall Reza, who was about to protest. Talon had a sinking feeling in his gut.

"There is a way around this problem," he stated.

What are you proposing, Hsü?" Talon asked. His expression was grim. Rav'an and Jannat wore dismayed expressions. Had they come all this way out here to be robbed at the last moment?

"Jiaya can arrange it, with bribes, of course, so that you do not have this, er, problem."

"How do you propose to bypass the customs, and how will we deal with it?" Talon asked. A distant ray of hope had started in his head.

Hsü took a sip of his rice wine and then said something to one of the servants. Within a few minutes Jiaya arrived, bowed to the assembly and seated himself at the end of the table. Fuling provided him with a cup of wine.

Hsü continued. "It is time to tell you more about my holdings and what that could mean for you as traders," he said. "I own two silk factories, and land outside of the city where we have mulberry trees, millet, and rice. My fields alone can feed half this city. I also possess, in the mountains to the west of here, a tin mine, and a silver mine that my Grandfather discovered and developed. My wife's family owns two iron foundries and water mills for grinding the rice to flour. Jiaya here is now the chief administrator for these operations and has a small army of clerks and workers who see to it that they operate well." Hsü leaned back against the back of his beautifully worked chair and adjusted his voluminous robes.

Talon was stunned. If Hsü was telling the truth, this represented enormous wealth.

"If you are so well off here in Guangzhou, why did you take the huge risk of going to India? You must have known about the dangers," Reza asked before he could go on.

"Ah, yes, well, I did know, but I was appointed by the Emperor for the purpose of reopening the trade routes. You and I have already discussed the main reason for this, Talon. The old silk route is all but closed to the merchants of the Sung Empire. In other words, I had to do what I was told." He smiled at them disarmingly.

Talon smiled back. He glanced at Rav'an, who had remained silent. She caught his look and lifted her shoulder just a little to indicate that she would listen but not say anything. It was up to him to discuss the cargo and find a solution.

"On the subject of the Emperor, I have received a message from his Chamberlain telling me that I have to report on my voyage within the month, and that means that I must leave quite soon," Hsü told them. "I shall be gone for several weeks."

In response to their dismayed looks, he added, "Do not worry; I have arranged everything, including a visit to my factories that might interest you gentlemen, and there is much for the ladies to see while I am gone. Lihua will be escorting your wives about the town. She can help them with the language and will make sure they do not get lost. It is a big city.

"Fuling will be your guide in all else, including a visit to a special place that I think you will find very interesting. While I am away, Jiaya will be working with you to ensure that the captain and crew are properly housed and the ship is safe."

"What were you proposing regarding the cargo?" Talon asked, his impatience overcoming his good manners.

Hsü glanced at him with mild disapproval, then said, "The way that would ensure you get the best prices for your particular cargo is to allow Jiaya to place all of it in my godowns under my protection."

Reza and Talon looked sharply at one another. "This means that our entire cargo is in trust to you?" Reza asked, with a dangerous look.

Hsü looked him in the eye. "Yes, that is right, Reza. But I will give you a written guarantee that I will pay you for that cargo, either in kind or cash. I cannot think of a better way to protect your cargo. To leave it in the care of the customs would be a serious mistake, I promise you. I can also assure you that the price I will give you will far exceed that of the unpleasant gentleman in Kalah Bar was offering." They all laughed ruefully at this. Sing and his offer were still fresh in their minds. "You will not be disappointed," he paused to allow this to sink in.

Even as Reza's face had darkened with distrust Talon had brightened considerably while listening to Hsü. He began to see some daylight at the end of what had seemed a long, dark tunnel; and if the truth be told, he had not known where to begin with the process of selling his cargo. To his chagrin, he realized that he still had much to learn about the world of trade. Then there was the added imponderable about what he should buy, and where from, to take away with him from China. He didn't want to go home with an empty ship.

Hsü had anticipated him. "I want you to see my factories because I am sure we can come to an arrangement as to what you, in turn, can buy while here in China. You must not forget you have two tasks while here: to sell your cargo, yes, but also to buy what will be well received in your own country. I will also have Jiaya negotiate with some of the other factories that make porcelain, the precious pottery that I hear is so valued in your lands." He tugged lightly on the corner of his mustache with the tips of his fingers.

He turned to Lihua and said, "We have all had good meal, but it would be nice for our guests if you could play some music to relax us for the evening, my dear."

Lihua bowed and went to the side of the room to pick up a stringed instrument that resembled a rounded Tar. She came back to sit on a low bench in front of a silk-patterned wall covering and began to play. Soon the room was filled with the rippling notes from her instrument as her fingers danced over the strings.

*****

Later, Talon, Ra'van, Reza and Jannat gathered in the guest room; they wanted to talk before going to bed. It had started to rain, preventing them from enjoying the evening outside. On the other hand, because of the cool breeze the mosquitoes were not yet a nuisance. They sat on a thick pile of carpet in a semi-circle. All four preferred to sit cross-legged on the floor rather than on the chairs that the Chinese seemed to like.

"We are finding ourselves more and more beholden to Hsü," Rav'an observed.

"That worries me too, Rav'an," Talon agreed. "I don't know what else we can do, other than to trust him at this time. What he and Jiaya have told us, if true, could make a huge difference between us leaving with no profit and leaving with a large one."

"I have seen Jiaya with the customs officials, and he does seem to have them in the palm of his hand," Reza admitted reluctantly.

Talon raised his eyebrows. He knew how effective Reza could be as either a spy or an assassin, but in this city even he might have trouble remaining invisible.

"Is there any protection for us to be had from the Arab community?" Jannat asked the group at large.

"It's a good question, Jannat," Talon replied. "Fuling told me that the foreign community is allowed to run themselves more or less, as long as they stay in the area designated, on the West side of the city docks. They need papers to come and go, like the ones Jiaya obtained for us. There is a court there, called the *Quädi,* where disputes are resolved. But we have gone around the normal processes, and it is far too late to change that now," Talon informed them. "We have to remember, too, that it is highly unusual for foreigners to be the guest of a Chinese host. There is not much in the way of interaction, other than the business of trade."

There was a long silence after this. "Then we have to trust him," Reza said in *Farsi* with a look at the door and window. "However, if he does double cross us, I shall personally take care of the problem."

Talon nodded once in agreement. "Meanwhile, we should all be very happy at what Hsü is telling us. Let's wait and see, but if things do not go the way they should, then Reza is right, there will be a reckoning. We must see this through."

Both the women looked at their men, knowing what they were capable of.

*****

That very night Hsü left the compound, accompanied by Fang. They made their way on foot by a dimmed lantern to the wharf side and were taken across the Pearl River in a small sampan. Between the river and the main city were two walls of some size. Once ashore, they made haste to walk up the gentle slope to the Petition Gate. It was opened when Hsü produced a piece of paper that carried the Governor's chop.

The two men hurried up the hill to another gate, which allowed them to gain passage to the main city. It was late, but the darkened city still hummed with activity. They were just another couple of anonymous pedestrians in wide hats and cloaks walking briskly along the same road that would eventually bring them to the Governor's palace.

However, tonight this was not their destination. They turned right well before the palace and its extensive park, then strode into the dark back streets of the town where torches and lanterns were few and far between. The glow of lamps inside the better off houses did little to illuminate the street as the two men, alert to danger and the possibility of being accosted by robbers, hurried towards the meeting arranged for Hsü.

They came to a doorway with an elaborate lintel composed of a square stone beam with two snake heads on either side. Two lions made of carved limestone posed as guardians on either side of the entrance. Hsü blinked when he entered the room, squinting at the light from lanterns placed all around the room. Several people were eating at tables, and the smells of cooking and alcohol were thick in the air. The unmistakable sweet smell of an opium parlor in the back room drifted into the main room; the fumes permeated the air with an unpleasant mix of odors. In one darkened corner sat the man he had come to see. Hsü placed a hand on Fang's arm.

"Please wait near the entrance, Fang. Be alert for trouble. If there is any disturbance we need to leave in a hurry." Fang nodded and took a station just inside the door, where he could watch the room and keep an eye on people who came and went.

Hsü made his way towards the corner, where he had spotted Li Shou-cheh. Shou-cheh greeted him with a short bow from the waist as he remained seated. Hsü sat down on a stool with his back to the rest of the room and nodded; he didn't take off his hat. A waiter appeared, but Hsü shook his head, and Shou-cheh waved him away, then turned back to Hsü, who had an expectant expression on his face.

"Now this is very secretive," Hsü observed with a wry smile. "I would have preferred to go to the Golden Dragon to drink their good wine," he added.

"I have to be careful, Hsü," Shou-cheh said. He sounded nervous. "Even by sending a messenger to you I may have jeopardized myself."

"All right, I understand, but tell me, what is this all about?"

"The Governor is getting worse by the day. The doctor, who is a quack and a charlatan, gives him about three months. I give him about six weeks. The two doctors I had recommended were disallowed by Wu po-ku. The news has reached the Emperor's palace in the capital, and there has been some correspondence."

"Wu can actually decide these things?" Hsü demanded, his tone incredulous.

"He's the Senior Prefect, so yes, he can. The Governor is too ill to do anything about it," Li Shou-cheh said, shaking his head.

"What is the news?"

Li Shou-cheh scanned the room again before answering. "There are factions in Hangzhou who are interested in you and Yen Wei, and perhaps a couple of others who really don't count. But there are those who are more interested in finding someone more, shall we say, more amenable than you or Prefect Yen."

"That doesn't come as any surprise," Hsü told him. "Is Prefect Yen a serious contender?"

Shou-cheh shrugged. "No, I don't think so; he hasn't much clout with the palace. But your name has come up in a conversation recently between Hua Rong and Lu Buwei."

"Ah, and how do you know that? Do you have spies everywhere?" Hsü asked with some surprise.

Shou-cheh shrugged. "I have spies and others have spies. However, *others* are beginning to suspect that you might be going for the position, and they consider you to be a real threat. Hence they will do anything to stop you."

"Anything?"

"The person who overheard them had that impression."

Hsü felt a cold trickle down his neck. "Then I had better not run for the governorship and make sure that everyone knows my decision," he said with a wry smile. "That should solve that particular problem. Let Prefect Yen run for it."

He noticed the look of utter dismay on Shou's face.

"What did I say to upset you?" Hsü inquired, knowing full well.

Shou-cheh took a deep breath and then said, "Lord Meng, I do not wish to be disrespectful, but you must think carefully about this. Prefect Yen is a good man, on the whole, but...." Shou-cheh looked scornful. "He is not up to the needs of this city. He is weak and will be easily corrupted. The city of Guangzhou needs a strong man to run things. Again with respect, Governor Murong is a nice man, but he was not firm and did not keep the Tongs in check. Consider the corruption and crime that has flared since he became governor. He is an honest man, and that kind of person is very hard to find, but what has been going on under his nose stinks of intrigue."

Hsü sat back. "Are you saying that I should do as Murong asks and try for the position? Surely these other factions would dispute my claim."

"Oh yes, you can be sure of that. There are many who would like nothing better than to have a chance at the job, but there are only a few people who would have the funds and influence to compete for it, and one is not even qualified to begin with," Shou-cheh told him with a sniff.

"I know who they are," Hsü said tiredly. "Hua Rong and Wu po-ku, with Lu Buwei lurking around in the background."

"Correct, but Rong is pretending he would rather have Wu po-ku than himself. It doesn't really matter to him whether he gets in or not, as long as there is someone like Wu he can control who will do as he is told."

"Do I have any friends in this sorry business?" Hsü asked.

"Oh yes. As I mentioned, there are people at the palace who seem to be on your side. You will have to bribe them to ensure their votes, of course. The fact that the Emperor is known to be pleased with you helps. A few well-placed bribes might bring others around, and then you can focus on taking care of your enemies here," Shou-cheh said in all seriousness.

Hsü gave a low bark of laughter. "'When we see men of a contrary character, we should turn inwards and examine ourselves," he quoted.

Shou-cheh blinked. "I could make sure that General Hayan Zhuo was on our side, but I would need some financial help with that."

Hsü sighed. His ally Shou-cheh simply had did not grasp the irony of it at all. Of course he would provide whatever funds were necessary. What Shou-cheh didn't know was that the General was a close friend of Hsü.

The role of governor had some appeal, he mused. It did represent enormous power and prestige. His ancestors would be pleased. More to the point, the challenge of taking the prize away from those two villains, Hua Rong and Lu Buwei, and that pompous Prefect Wu, made the prospect all the more enticing. It began to look increasingly like a game he liked to play called Go.

In his mind's eye, he had just placed one of his white stones on the board, where were already placed several black stones. He would have to take great care, and he was already somewhat behind. The stakes in this game were very high indeed.

When the Emperor sought guidance from wise men,
*   from exiles,*
He found no calmer wisdom than that of young Jia
And assigned him the foremost council-seat at
*   midnight,*
Yet asked him about gods, instead of about people.
—Li Shu

Chapter Twenty
Of Cargo and Goods

Hsü's pending departure for the capital city initiated a flurry of activity in the villa that involved almost everyone.

Talon was informed that a visit to a silk factory was immanent, to which he replied that all of them would like to go. The farm was located to the west of the city, so it involved a boat trip.

They arrived outside a nondescript entrance to a small walled compound with a decorated lintel of writhing dragons with ferocious faces and glaring eyes. The color red was used extensively on wood, Talon noticed. He could not make out what the symbols meant that were painted in gold leaf vertically up the length of the pillars.

They were ushered into the work building by an obsequious man dressed in a dark over robe with long sleeves into which he had tucked his hands. He bowed deeply to Hsü and the others, and then Hsü held a small conference with him. The sing-song tones went back and forth, and then Hsü turned to Talon. "I shall have Fuling go with you and the head man, who will show you everything and explain the process to you. I must go over his reports, so I will see you later, and we shall share a meal." He waved them off.

There followed a fascinating walk through a place that neither Talon nor any of his companions could ever have imagined before. Fuling translated for them while the manager of the factory took them from one end of the extensive building to the other. He was clearly proud to show these foreigners the workshop and rattled off much information in a high voice.

They were first shown the trays full of tiny white grubs. Women were lifting large flat trays lined with green leaves and moving the creatures, placing them in racks. Fuling smiled at their surprise. "Yes, the silk begins with a worm," he told the astonished group. Not even Talon had fully understood this.

"Here they sort them out, the smallest to the largest, and take only those which are the largest. They are placed on the trays with the green leaves. You will have seen the mulberry trees outside, but most of these are brought in from the countryside, where we have many trees. The healthier the tree, the better the silk."

"They like mulberry leaves?" Rav'an asked him.

"They eat *only* mulberry leaves."

They walked to another side of the large room.

"When the worms are ready, they are placed on twigs where they can make their cocoons. Here again, there is a space of time before we go the next stage. The cocoons are weighed and the largest and heaviest are selected. Then over there," he pointed to a steaming vat, "they are soaked in very hot water, which will kill the larvae; after which the process of threading and reeling the silk begins."

They were shown the rotating racks where the silk thread of multiple cocoons was being wound. "The women who work at this end are very skilled at finding the end of a thread and then making sure that the silk is wound without breaking," Fuling explained. "The entire process has to be carried out with great care and at the right temperatures."

When they had finished gawping at the winding process and admiring the deft manner in which the work was done, they were shown into a busier, noisy place where there were many looms at work. They were shown the pots where the silk was dyed a variety of colors, ranging from bright red to dark blue. The clacking of wooden looms almost drowned out any conversation. They moved on to the store room, where great bolts of silk were stored. Their guide showed them an extraordinary array of silk cloth with a great variety of patterns and designs.

"We have to have this fabric with us as part of our cargo," Talon said to Reza as he fingered one bolt of silk. "I cannot believe the skill that they have in the making of these designs!"

"I am beginning to see what all the fuss is about," Reza told him, stroking a particularly heavy fabric.

"They have silk in Byzantium, but only the very wealthy can afford it. Here almost all the merchants wear silk, and the women everywhere seem to be able to afford it," Talon remarked.

"There are various qualities of silk. We take the very best that we have, and these go to the Palace of the Emperor." Fuling had overheard them.

Rav'an and Jannat exclaimed excitedly over the intricate designs. "I have never seen loom work that is so exquisite! If I had not seen it with my own eyes, I could not believe these were woven. I would swear they had been painted on the material!" Rav'an said.

Fuling smiled at their enthusiasm. "My father wanted you to see the working process of the silk. The patterns we make here are among the best you can find in Guangzhou, even perhaps in China. As I said, the palace buys our silk!" he told them. "I will one day inherit this, and so I, too, must understand it well. This industry is a huge part of our economy for trade and... it is also a part of the tribute, too." For a moment his face darkened.

Talon thought he might not have heard correctly. "Tribute, did you say, Fuling?"

But Fuling's expression had changed back to the bland expression he wore most of the time. "I meant nothing by it, Talon," he said hurriedly, and he led the way out of the workshop into the courtyard, where they were served tea in exquisitely delicate porcelain cups. Talon looked after him, wondering what he had meant.

*****

Some days later, Talon and Reza were seated outside in the courtyard, drinking tea with the women, when they were alerted to the arrival of high-level visitors to the villa. It was evening, and Rostam was with them, playing near the small fountain when they heard activity and shouting at the main entrance.

Curious, the two men got up and went to the entrance of their courtyard, which gave them a view of the main gateway. Fang was striding towards the closed gate where two of his soldiers were standing at attention, waiting for his orders. He gave a gruff command, and the gates swung open to admit first two Chinese soldiers, then a single palanquin carried by two stout, sweating men in expensive uniforms, followed by a small retinue of servants.

Fang called out something and bowed very low indeed, waving the palanquin in. Then he shouted something at the men at the gate, and they rushed to close it. He strode after the palanquin, which disappeared into the inner courtyard of the main house.

"I wonder who that was," Reza commented.

"Probably just another visitor," Talon remarked. "There have been many of them in the last couple of days; Nobody of any interest to us."

"Ever since I noticed Fang and Lord Hsü leaving late at night without any escort, I am more curious than ever about our host," Reza said.

Talon glanced sharply at him. Reza had told him about the nocturnal departure of Hsü and his bodyguard, but the mystery of why they had left so quietly remained.

"You don't trust him, do you?" he asked his friend.

"A little distrust is a healthy disease, Brother. We have only his word that he will do all these things for us. Until that happens, then no, I do not trust him, or anyone else here."

Talon sighed and scratched his head; then he threw his arm around his friend's shoulders. "You might be right. I don't suppose it is anything to do with us, but it won't hurt to be watchful," he said.

"I intend to find out where he keeps that box of his," Reza told him while they watched the guards settle down.

Talon took his arm off Reza's shoulder. "You what?" he gasped.

"It won't hurt to know, just in case. You know, if we have to leave in a hurry." Reza grinned at him. "Don't worry. I won't get caught."

"*Don't* be caught, Brother. It will be the end of us all if you are," Talon said. "Just be careful," he admonished as they returned to the women.

"What was going on out there?" Rav'an asked them.

"It's nothing, just some expensive visitors," Reza told them. Talon looked over at the women and liked what he saw. They now dressed in the Chinese manner, in dresses of silk under folds of loose over robes that emphasized their slim figures. His eyes roved over Rav'an, taking it all in with deep appreciation. His eyes came to rest on hers, which were smiling.

Lihua had insisted that they dress as did the Chinese to be less conspicuous while walking around the city. Despite her initial reluctance to be their guide, the request, more of an order, had come from Hsü. Lihua had now become their full-time guide and quite enjoyed showing off the city, of which she was very proud.

She was not above enjoying the admiration her beauty attracted. Her youthful, fine features, her unblemished, almost white skin and delicate form attracted many admiring glances. She soon noticed that because Rav'an and Jannat were beautiful women in their own right when dressed in the long flowing silk robes currently in fashion, they too drew admiring looks. Their hair was now coiled high on their heads and pinned with bejeweled, ivory hairpins, showing off their equally fine features and slim necks.

For Lihua, their presence became a welcome distraction, because otherwise she would have spent her time alone in her room or the garden. Shunned by the Lady Meilin and barely tolerated by Lady Meng, neither a servant nor a member of the family, her position was a lonely one.

She had asked Hsü to bring in a teacher for their guests, and he had readily agreed. It was hard work for all of them, but Talon was insistent. "We should learn what we can. It is a sign of respect, but also I hate not knowing what is being said in front of me."

"I agree," said Reza. "I know they are saying bad things to me while they smile. I want to be able to smack one of them just when they least expect it!"

"Reza! That is *not* the right way to behave!" Jannat scolded him. Talon and Rav'an laughed at their friends. Talon was sure that Reza behaved badly on occasion just to get a rise out of Jannat, who considered good manners to be very important.

So they endured the difficult process of learning Cantonese, which Hsü told Talon was the universal language of China, although there were many dialects.

Every morning while the men were going about the business of seeing to the ship and its cargo, either with Jiaya or Fuling, the women gathered around a low table in the courtyard, enjoying the cool morning air. The two maids who attended to

Lihua's toilet would go to work on her new friends. By the time the maids completed their work, there were exclamations of delight as they scrutinized themselves in the mirrors provided by Lihua. Rav'an had never before seen such quality in a mirror. She could see her face as though looking into the clear, still waters of a pond. Another item for the cargo, she decided. She would laugh and reach for the fan that Lihua had presented to her and fluttered it, pretending to simper. The others would imitate her, amid much laughter.

It amused Lihua to be with the two foreign women and show them what she could of the Chinese culture. She took them across the hazardous river, where they were subjected to ribald compliments from passing boatmen, to land at the main city dockyards. They would disembark and pick their way carefully across the crowded, dirty quayside, up the slope towards the first of several gates. Hsü had insisted that they were accompanied by at least one of Fang's guards at all times, but the guard would keep a discreet distance.

They would stroll over the busy stone bridges that arched elegantly across the lily-bordered canals below. Here they would pause and lean on the carved side of the bridge to admire the swans and the ducks as they swam between the sampans or dived for food that people tossed to them. Then, at the urging of Lihua, they would walk on through the tunnel of the huge open gateway set into the massive stone walls towering over the port. Emerging into the sunlight at the other side, they'd continue along the tree-lined avenue towards the second set of walls, which were even taller than the first. Again they had to negotiate a crowded stone bridge with its stone guardians at both ends: squatting lions with gaping mouths and protruding, wild-looking eyes. Then they would proceed towards a tea house to refresh themselves before visiting several shops, where Rav'an and Jannat could admire the fabrics and pottery on display.

For Rav'an, there was a purpose to this beyond just visiting a grand city in the company of Lihua. Talon and she had discussed at length what they might take back with them to Oman and agreed that she could spend time looking at what was available for things that simply did not exist in their own part of the world.

The first several visits had left her bemused at the sights and sounds of the city, let alone the incredible variety of goods on display. The sheer magnitude of Guangzhou awed them; the smells, the noise, the bright colors of every shade on display as banners or symbols or signs, which Lihua assured them meant something in Chinese, were almost overpowering.

At times she thought she would suffocate with the press of humanity all around, but Lihua was there to guide them into a quiet park, of which there were many, where they could catch their breath. It was the monsoon season, so Lihua gave each of them a parasol made of a bamboo frame covered with oiled paper and painted with figures and trees. Rav'an observed that most ladies carried these as both protection from the sun and to ward off the occasional surprise shower of rain. The working people dressed simply in cotton, and many wore huge wide hats of straw that did service on both counts.

Sometimes, as they walked along the street, they would hear strange sounds emanating from the open front of a shop.

"I cannot believe they call that music!" Rav'an said in a low tone to Jannat, who shook her head vigorously. "It is awful! That person singing sounds as though he is being strangled, slowly."

They walked on, trying not to listen to the wailing of the singer and the ear piercing shriek of the pipes being played by three ragged musicians.

There were armed men to be seen here and there; Rav'an's trained eye observed these things, but they didn't seem very interested in the goings on in the streets.

Extraordinary things were on display everywhere. Neither Rav'an nor Jannat had ever come across such fine art before. They admired the silk and paper paintings, the intricately carved ivory and the worked smooth green stone, which Lihua called Jade and said was very precious, and much else that drew the eye. When they returned, overwhelmed, to their guest quarters, they discussed what they had seen and shared their impressions.

"I shall never become used to their music, nor their singing," Jannat said with a grimace.

"It's too high-pitched for me to consider soothing."

"They are singing about love, blossoms, and the snow on the distant mountains; you should listen more carefully and not be so disrespectful," Rav'an teased her.

"You understood what they were singing about?" Jannat asked in surprise.

"Of course not, but Lihua told me that they sing about those things." Rav'an laughed.

"Well, it sounded to my inexperienced ears as though they were strangling a cat, probably getting ready to cook it too," Jannat said unkindly. "Anyway, that's what Reza said the other day."

Rav'an laughed. "Jannat!" she exclaimed. "I swear that Reza is rubbing off on you! You shouldn't say things like that, and nor should he," she admonished her friend, grinning behind her fan.

Jannat giggled. "I fear that he is.

"And we mustn't tell Lihua how we feel; it will surely hurt her feelings," Rav'an added.

"Did you see that wonderful painting depicting the river and the boats?" Jannat asked, changing the subject. "I have never seen anything so delicate in my life!"

"Yes, but did you also see how the woman paid for it?" Rav'an asked her.

"I noticed that they exchanged pieces of paper for the painting. I wonder why they do that?"

"There was much writing on the paper, as well as symbols, so it might have been a promissory note," Rav'an said. "We should ask Lihua."

They asked her the next day while they were seated in the courtyard. Rav'an was practicing on the musical instrument that Lihua had used the previous day. It was called a *guqin* and had six strings. Rav'an was quite determined to master it, wanting to provide the menfolk with some familiar melodies. Jannat was working on some embroidery in silk that Lihua had provided. On hearing the question, Lihua gave her dainty laugh behind her hand and went away, to return in a few minutes carrying a wad of paper similar to that which they had seen in the street.

"This is money, 'cash,'" she said, and she handed some of it to them to examine.

"You don't use silver and gold?" Rav'an asked in surprise, putting down the instrument as she looked over the thin pieces of paper with symbols and designs all over them. "What do they say?" she asked, holding one up for Lihua's inspection.

"For very large transactions, silver and gold are used," she told them, and went on to explain the value of each of the pieces of paper in their equivalent amount of silver. "It saves having to carry coins, which are heavy," she told them.

"Can you show us these 'coins'?" Jannat asked.

Lihua then produced a wire circle with many of the oddly shaped coins they had seen before threaded onto the wire. "Would you want to carry all this around when you are in the city?" she asked. When they asked about the peculiar shape, Lihua explained, "These paper notes are printed this way to stop people from copying them. It is a crime to do so, as they are only authorized by the governor, and only a limited number are printed."

Neither Jannat nor Rav'an could fully grasp what she was saying.

*****

Talon and Reza were otherwise occupied with Jiaya in the early days. True to his word, Hsü had arranged, through Jiaya, to have their entire cargo stored in his own godown, conveniently close by on his side of the river. The area was known as Honam. His godown was not far from the Honam temple, which Jiaya told them was Taoist and very old.

To unload the ship, they had to go back across the river to the area where the Arab community was located and round up the crew and captain. Jiaya showed a piece of paper to the men on guard at the entrance to the foreigner's area, and they were allowed in. Almost immediately the atmosphere changed from the noisy and bustling dockyards outside the gates to a quieter mood within. Talon thought he could be forgiven for thinking that they were in some Persian area that had been transplanted to Guangzhou. There was even a mosque, in fact, more than one. He noticed other nationalities besides Arabs. Just down the street was a tea house that reminded him of one in Hamadan, while further along were a few shops and places to eat. Most of the side streets were narrow and were sided by large buildings that he took to be warehouses.

They found their men in one of the many inns dotted along the riverside which catered to the Arab and Persian community. The captain was glad to see them, and he had no complaints about the accommodation. He showed them around the inn, which was large, comfortable, and could house more than fifty guests. The entire crew was staying under the same roof, so it was easy to get them all moving towards the dockside.

"We have been wondering where you were, Master Talon," the captain said, speaking for several of them. "We thought they might have robbed you, or worse."

"Or eaten you! These people eat anything!" Waqqas said out loud, ignoring the fact that Jiaya could speak Arabic.

"We are here, and as you can see they have not eaten us, not even a toe or finger," Reza joked, waving his fingers in the air. "And I am not just an 'anything,' Waqqas, remember that."

The banter continued while they were rowed across to the ship to climb aboard. Glancing around, Talon noted that the crew members who had remained on board had kept the ship in good shape. The Chinese guards were excessively polite to Jiaya. After a rapid conversation with the guards, he turned to the captain.

"We are going to sail the ship just up the river to that place you can see on the slope of the hill, Master Captain," Jiaya told him, pointing towards the Honam temple. "We have men waiting there to unload the ship."

"You have permission to do this?" Captain Dandachi asked, looking not at Jiaya but at Talon.

"Yes, Captain, we do; and then you will bring the ship back here."

While the ship was being prepared to sail, Talon took the captain aside and informed him as to the reason for the transfer.

Captain Dandachi shook his head skeptically but said, "It is your cargo, Master Talon. I hope you know what you are doing."

Talon looked at him. "I have to trust Lord Meng, Captain. I don't have much choice. He is providing the only way we can unload, sell our cargo, and leave with another cargo without losing our profits. *Insha'Allah* he will be as good as his word."

The captain shrugged and put the crew to work to set sail. "It is you that I and the crew trust, Master Talon. We'll do as you ask."

After shouting some orders and telling Tarif to take the helm, he turned back to Talon.

"We have heard many stories from the people in the Arab settlement since we arrived. Few of them are good. The Chinese customs are robbers, and many of the foreign merchants,

Persians, Indians, and Arabs too, have been here for a very long time, unable to sell their cargos. In many cases, their cargos of spices and peppers have spoiled, and there are fires in the warehouses that happen without good reason. All this has beggared some of them so that all they want to do is to go home on the next tide, and they can't even do that without paying tax! I was beginning to wonder if the journey was going to be worth it."

"Hsü hinted at this, which is why he is offering me this chance to sell our cargo without the pain that normally goes with trading here," Talon murmured. Jiaya was one deck down and might have heard the captain.

"He has the power to do this, Master Talon?"

"You have not yet seen his palace. We dragged a very wealthy and influential man out of the water, Captain. Good Joss for him, as he would say, and perhaps for us too!"

"What is this 'Joss' thing?" the captain asked.

"It means the same as good fortune, but I am sure that here in Guangzhou bribery has a great deal to do with it too," Talon grinned.

Captain Dandachi barked out a laugh, and then went off to shout at Umayr and Abdullah, who were being too slow to get the main sail up. "You spend a few days on shore, and you forget how to be sailors, you miserable sons of whores. Get those men busy, Umayr, or I'll take care of it myself and leave you ashore next time we sail."

Umayr grinned, and his men set to with a will. Abdullah laughed up at Talon, who was watching, and shrugged his shoulders. "Who'd be a sailor?" he joked. The boom with the sail attached was hauled rapidly into place and bellied in the light breeze.

*****

They sailed across the crowded river way and made it to the quayside without incident, although both Talon and the captain were sweating by the time they arrived. The river traffic never seemed to slow down or become less crowded no matter what time of day it was. The unloading of the ship was soon underway, with a chain of men and pack animals moving between the now docked vessel and the *godown,* situated among many others on the island of Honam.

At one point, Reza looked up from watching the activity in the hold and pointed to the end of the quay. Striding down the slope was Fang, wearing his habitual scowl. Alongside him was an elegant palanquin carried by two stout men, which Talon recognized as being that of Lord Meng Hsü.

The men who were carrying the palanquin came to a halt at a gesture from Fang. They placed the contraption on the ground and out stepped Hsü. He was dressed in dark clothing suitable for the street. He beamed at Reza and Talon, and then walked the short distance to the side of the ship, looking around him at the bustle of activity. After a brief word with Jiaya, who was on deck ticking merchandise off on a list as it was carried down, Hsü beckoned to Talon, who was up on the steering deck, and called up, "Talon, please spare me some of your valuable time. I wish to speak with you alone."

Talon glanced at Reza, who shrugged, then he strode down the gangplank onto the wharf and joined Hsü. Together they walked to a relatively quiet place along the quayside near the after end of the ship.

"I could easily have walked the short distance between the villa and here, but Fang would have had a fit and called it undignified for a man of my stature," he told Talon.

Talon smiled, he enjoyed Hsü's dry comments. "We do not see very much of you these days, Hsü," he observed.

Hsü, who had his hands behind his back in his normal, thoughtful mode, turned slightly and nodded, "No, you have not, and I have to apologize, but I have much work to do that needs my attention. When I get back from my visit, we will spend more time together. I would like to take you all to a polo game at the Governor's Park some time; we talked about the game while on the ship, remember? However, I am here to discuss a, hum, sensitive issue with you."

"I am listening," Talon told him. They were facing one another by now, so he could see that Hsü looked concerned.

Hsü seemed to be deep in thought for a few moments, tugging gently at the ends of his mustache, as was his habit when worried; then he shook his head slightly and said, "You know that I have to go and pay my respects to our Emperor; the Illustrious and Heaven Sent Zhao Shen, whose holy name is Xiaozong, has commanded my presence, and I cannot refuse."

Talon made to open his mouth, but Hsü lifted his hand, signaling for him to wait.

"What you do not know, and this is very recent, is that I am being encouraged by certain factions to become the new governor of this city Guangzhou."

Talon stared at him. "What is wrong with the old governor?" he asked stupidly.

Hsü smiled his enigmatic smile. "He is very ill, and has himself asked me to try for the post."

"Should I be congratulating you?" Talon inquired with a grin. "Does that explain all the visitors?" he guessed out loud.

"Ah, yes, that is nice of you; and yes, it is the reason for the visitors. Most of them are wealthy merchants who are pledging help and cash to my cause. Politics can be an expensive undertaking. If fate smiles upon us, then that is good, but... much can occur, and I have many enemies who would rather I did not succeed."

Talon stared into Hsü's eyes and understood. "Will you be in danger while on the road to the capital? Is that it?" he asked.

"Perhaps, but I shall be taking Fang with me and an escort, so it should not be too dangerous. Besides, few would be stupid enough to interfere with an Envoy to the Emperor, which would be my status while on the road."

"What is the problem then?" Talon asked, puzzled.

"I shall be leaving my family and my guests relatively unprotected at the house, and I am concerned that this could be dangerous for you," Hsü said in a very low voice. "Once the word goes out that I intend to try for the post of governor, several things will occur. Some have already happened." He paused and waved his arm around him. "Those who intend to oppose me will try by whatever means possible to discredit me, in this city and at the palace. Those who want me to succeed will visit me, as they have been, and pledge their loyalty. Some will be lying, trying to ingratiate themselves with me while plotting on behalf of other patrons; some will be sitting on the fence, watching to see who has the best chance to win; and others who will actively try to oppose me."

Talon realized what an effort this confidence had cost Hsü, so he gave a small bow and said, "I understand completely, but you should not worry too much, Hsü. Both Reza and I are capable warriors and we will assume responsibility for your family's safety."

Hsü nodded. "I watched you both practicing on the ship. You are very competent."

"Reza is one of the very best bowmen I have known," Talon told him.

"Ah! He told my son that *you* were the very best bowman, Talon." Hsü smiled properly this time. "I shall put my trust in you and your friend. I knew that I could, but I needed to ask," he said, almost in an undertone.

"You did not need to ask, Hsü. Although now we will pay more attention to who comes and goes, now that we know of your concerns."

"I shall be gone two weeks at most. If I don't take Fang with me this time, he will commit seppuku in the courtyard and make a mess. Even worse, I will never live down the loss of face," Hsü said with an amused glint in his eyes.

"Seppuku?"

"Suicide. He learned of this unfortunate habit while with the Nippon. They cut themselves open to atone for something obscure that they have done which they feel has brought shame on them. I swear he is dying to do it someday, but it shall not be on my time."

Talon snorted with laughter. "Is he mad?"

"Oh, yes. He is quite mad, but he is a skilled and ferocious swordsman and deeply loyal to me so... I keep him."

*****

Later that day, Talon and his friends talked about the situation. The others were surprised to hear the news. Talon felt that he needed to explain things in very clear terms. "Hsü said that it might become dangerous for his family because he has decided to go for the post."

"Isn't that kind of position by appointment? Why should it be dangerous?" Rav'an asked with a frown.

"I would have thought so, but apparently he needs to have the support, not only of people in the Emperor's palace, but here in Guangzhou as well."

"Why is that so necessary, Talon?" Jannat asked, sipping tea out of a tiny porcelain cup. He had noticed that Jannat kept pace with Rav'an on many issues, and that included an interest in their presence in Guangzhou.

"He calls them *factions*, Jannat. I think that means that there are rival leaders of certain groups of people. In his case, it is the majority of the merchants in the city, all those expensive looking visitors we have seen come and go; whereas his opponents represent another group, perhaps not such nice people, who want their own man in the office."

Reza picked up a small almond cake and chewed it, enjoying its sweet taste, and then he said with his mouth half full, "Why do they go about it in this manner? Isn't the governor like our sultans? Doesn't he have any heirs to pass it to?"

"It would seem not," Talon said. He was still working this one out in his head. "They do things very differently here in China. I am familiar with the violence of the world and its hideous cruelty, but this country chills me with its cold calculations."

"One thing does not change, no matter where we are in the world," said Rav'an flatly, as she handed a cake to the eager Rostam.

"What do you mean?" Jannat asked, her eyes wide.

"My sister, it's all about power, no matter how they go about it. The winner gains much power," Rav'an told her. Talon nodded agreement.

"From what Hsü implied, the winner gains it all, while the losers ...." He left the rest unsaid.

There was a long silence after this remark.

Finally Jannat asked, "Are you saying that we might also be in danger, Talon?"

"I wouldn't go that far just yet, Jannat, but... we need to be careful and not stray too far from the compound until we know more. Have you noticed that there are more guards than there were when we first arrived? They are also more like real soldiers."

—Oscar Wilde

Chapter Twenty-One

Intruders

Late one evening, not long after his conversation with Buwei, Rong was seated in a dingy room he sometimes used for meetings with the scum of the harbor when Lin Chong arrived at the doorway. Lin shoved someone else into the room who, upon seeing Rong, bowed respectfully. Rong recognized the man. It was Kee Wen Hua; one of the servants from Hsü's villa that Lin had planted there during Hsü's long absence.

"Ah, Kee, I am pleased to see you. How are things working out at the Meng household?" he asked.

Kee peered at him. He could not make out the speaker's features in the shadows. All he could see were the slightly plump manicured hands resting on the table and the rich clothing; the face was concealed in shadow. "All is well with the household, Master." His voice was more of a whine.

"I have a little task for you, Kee," Rong rumbled.

"Master?"

"It has come to my ears that Lord Meng came home with a box of pretty little stones."

Kee nodded his head doubtfully. "This is true, Master. Of course I have not seen them, but I think it is true. Excuse my impertinence, Master, but do I know you?" Kee asked humbly.

He received a clout on the back of his head from Lin that knocked off his cap.

"You show respect when you are talked to," Lin snapped.

"We know where your family lives, Kee. Do you want me to bring the fingers of your little daughter in a box to remind you?" The man in front of him continued.

"No, Master, please, don't harm my family. I will do anything you say," Kee begged as he scrabbled for his cap on the floor.

"Then you need to find these stones and bring them to me, Kee," Rong told him.

Kee fell to his knees. He clasped his hands together in supplication.

"Master, even if I knew where they were, I could not obtain them. They could be anywhere in the inner house, locked away, and it is very possible they are in Lady Meng's quarters. That is the innermost part of the house, and I know of a room within a room with but one entrance. If they are in the house then they are there, but I could not possibly go anywhere near that place for any excuse!" he cried.

Lin Chong raised his hand to slap Kee again, but Rong forestalled him.

"Where does the entrance lead to?" he asked pleasantly.

"It is the Lady Meng's bedroom, Lord." Kee was still kneeling and clasping his hands.

Rong thought about that. The Lady Meng was most likely unable to get out of bed without help, once in it. She, like so many other women, Rong's wife included, had had her feet bound at an early age. She was effectively crippled.

Kee shuffled over towards Rong. Lin put a hand on his shoulder to stop him, but he looked up at Rong and whined.

"My Lord Meng is going to the Emperor's palace this week, Lord."

Lin looked up sharply at his master and smiled. Rong nodded and smiled too.

"Then we shall have to pay the villa a visit. But first, Kee, you will tell us exactly where the box is that holds the jewels. You will find out, you will not get caught, and then you will pass a message to Lin here, who will do the rest."

"Sir?" Kee said.

"What is it, Kee? I am busy."

"There are foreigners in the guest house who are still there. The Persians who brought Lord Meng home."

"They shouldn't be a problem. Lin can deal with any interference from them if they are foolish enough to get in the way. Find out where the jewels are, and make sure you draw an accurate map. Now go, and remember, your family is safe as long as you do as you are told and say nothing to anyone."

Kee nodded and *Ke Tou'd* right there on the floor. He got to his feet and was pushed roughly out of the room by Lin. Rong sat back on his chair and considered the news. Lin knew just the right people to carry out the kind of work he had in mind. Kee simply had to provide a map, and the men could slip in and out without being noticed. The jewels would simply disappear; and he, Rong, could do a great deal with the wealth they would provide, if they were as valuable as was rumored, including getting rid of Hsü and Buwei when the time was appropriate.

*****

A week later Kee slipped out of the compound through a small entrance at the back wall near the stables. Waiting for him was a man loitering in the shadow of a tree in the narrow street.

Kee handed a folded piece of paper to the man, who didn't say anything; he just pushed Kee back towards the doorway and then disappeared around the corner.

Lin produced the much handled piece of paper in Rong's office that afternoon. Rong pondered the crudely drawn map. "Have you looked at this, Lin?" he asked, knowing his man had looked it over thoroughly."

"Yes, my Lord," Lin replied truthfully. "It will not be hard to go over the wall. Kee could let us in, but I don't want him to be seen, as he could still be useful."

Rong nodded his approval. Lin was thinking this through carefully. "There is no moon in five days time. You will have only one chance, I suspect. Who are you taking with you?"

Lin mentioned two names, and again Rong nodded approval. "Three is enough for this enterprise. Those two will be more than a match for Hsü's guards if there is a problem. With any Joss, you will be in and out and long gone before they even discover the items are missing. Hsü must suspect only his own people, and if Kee is in bed with a maid, that will be his alibi," Rong chortled.

It took a huge effort not to rub his hands together with glee. He could only imagine what it would be like to handle so much treasure. Lin, he knew, would be faithful to the end. Not even the wealth the jewels represented would tempt him to betray Rong. He had been taken off the execution field on the mud flats on the East side of the city by Rong himself, who had intervened one hour before the moment.

*****

The news that they might be asked to act as guardians of the villa was generating mixed feelings.

"Does that mean we have to be guards?" Reza asked without any enthusiasm.

"It means that Yosef and Dar'an will be on guard at the entrance to our guest compound until we know better," Talon said. "They can see the main entrance and most of the rest of the compound from our own gate. They don't have to go around making themselves obvious. Hsü told me that there will also be guards at the entrance to the inner courtyard."

"Where do you think any danger might come from, Talon?" Rav'an asked him.

"I don't know, and Hsü was less than clear about it, my Love," he responded. "He seemed a little worried, but he assured me that nothing was likely to happen. I think we should just go about our business and keep an eye on the guards. They are not the most experienced I have ever met," he added.

Hsü departed without ceremony two days later, taking with him Fang, Fuling, and six men-at-arms. On the evening of the fourth day, Talon and Reza were returning from a walk along the river when were stopped by Lihua. Talon had been somewhat surprised that she had not left with Hsü, but then realized that, had she done so, they would have been left with no one to translate for them.

"Master Talon," she called. He and Reza stopped and waited for her to join them.

"My Lady wants you to come and speak with her," Lihua said, after she had bowed respectfully.

"Which Lady?" Talon asked.

"Lady Meng Lanfen," she told him with a smile. Talon nodded. The Grandmother. It was late, but he glanced at Reza with a raised eyebrow and turned to follow her. Reza shrugged and round about to accompany Talon.

Lihua led the way towards the inner courtyard of the villa.

They found the Lady Meng Lanfen seated on a chair that was too large for her in her private living room. Talon noted the small shrine in one corner of the dimly lit chamber. The shutters were closed, but the air was thick with the smell of incense and the scent of camphor. Lihua bowed politely to the old lady, who gave what might have passed for a smile when Talon bowed low in front of her.

She said something, and Lihua smiled and turned to Talon.

"She says that you look good in Chinese clothes, Master Talon."

He smiled back and said, "We are in China, a great civilization. Besides they are very comfortable."

Grandmother Meng nodded approval. With Lihua translating she went on. "My son, Lord Meng Hsü, has informed me that we are under your protection while he is gone. It would seem that he has a high regard for your prowess as a warrior."

"If Lord Meng has concerns about safety, then it is important for my people to be vigilant for all our sakes, Madam," Talon responded.

The meeting lasted only about fifteen minutes, but during that time Talon was struck by her sharp mind."

At one point she asked him what he thought of what he had seen so far.

"I am constantly awestruck at what we see in this country, Madam," he told her truthfully. "I cannot take it all in. In my own country to the far, far west of Byzantium, we still have to learn how to build ships that don't sink in the first harsh wind that come along."

She laughed at that, encouraging him to talk. He went on to mention how impressed he had been by the artwork, the pottery and the silk industry. "We simply do not have any of these things in our own countries," he told her.

*****

On the fifth night of Hsü' absence, Yosef and Dar'an were on guard. Neither wanted the duty, even if Talon and Reza would be on for the other half. However, Talon had stressed the importance of the work. They were standing together at the small gateway that led from the guest quarters to the main courtyard, listening to the night sounds. The frogs and the crickets were noisy tonight. The muted sound of water cascading down the stone fountain could be clearly heard, and the occasional cry of a night bird. They both jumped when they heard the hoot of an owl on the rooftops behind them, then settled back to relax.

Yosef yawned. "I am going to go and see if I can find some tea," he told Dar'an. "I need something to help me stay awake."

He got up and walked across the courtyard and into the main room of the guest house. Dar'an rubbed his eyes. He was tired. They had been on and off duty for four nights now, and there had been nothing to alarm them. The guards on the gate didn't know about their vigil and would saunter about the yard talking to one another at all hours without paying any attention to their surroundings. Talon had told both Yosef and Dar'an that these guards were lax and that Fang would need to discipline them when he came back. The young men didn't want that label applied to them, so they tried hard to stay awake and alert.

Dar'an heard a horse snort and stamp its foot. He peered to his right, in the direction of the stables. The crickets had stopped sawing and the frogs were quieter for some reason. Nothing unusual about a horse stamping, he thought to himself, but then he noticed a slight movement on the pathway the led to the main house.

He rubbed his eyes again and squinted into the night. His night vision was good. There it was again, not one but two shadows were moving soundlessly across the gardens towards the inner court where the Meng family slept. He stared, motionless, wondering if he might be seeing the guards, but his ears told him that those worthies were squatting at the main gate, talking and paying no attention to the interior of the compound where at least two of them should have been patrolling.

Dar'an moved back deeper into the shadows and continued to watch the two dark forms creep along the walls, moving from one dark shadow to another. It was time to raise the alarm. He pulled back and ran silently across the small courtyard to the guest building, where he found Yosef about to bring a small cup of hot tea to him.

Yosef stopped when he saw the alarm on Dar'an's face.

"What is it?" he asked.

"Talon was right, there are intruders!" Dar'an hissed. "Be quiet, they might hear you!"

"Wake Talon and Reza, be quick!" Yosef whispered. "I'll go and keep watch. Where did you see them last?"

Dar'an hurriedly told him, and then ran up the stairs to call on Talon and Reza.

Yosef cautiously peered in the direction Dar'an had indicated, but saw nothing. He could hear the guards, oblivious of any trouble, still chattering to one another by the gate.

Taking his spear with him, Yosef decided to find out where the intruders might have gone. He believed Dar'an had seen something but wasn't sure if he had really seen intruders. He hurried silently across the intervening space, which brought him to the entrance to the inner compound. Nothing. He moved very carefully around the last post of the balcony.

Talon and Reza were awake in an instant when Dar'an knocked urgently on their doors.

"What is it?" Talon demanded, swiping a hand across his face to try and wake himself up.

Dar'an cracked the bedroom door open. "I, I saw something moving in the direction of the inner courtyard, Talon," he said.

"Where is Yosef?" Reza asked in a sharp tone as he emerged from his room.

He is watching for them until you come. He should be outside now," Dar'an whispered back excitedly.

"Come on, Reza," Talon snapped to his friend. "Dar'an, stay up here on guard. Let no one up the stairs unless it is us." He spun around and snatched up his bow and sword. Rav'an was sitting up in the bed. "What is it, Talon?" she asked sleepily.

"Dar'an thinks he saw someone creeping about the yard. Reza and I are going to investigate," he told her, then slipped quietly from the room.

Reza met him at the top of the stairs, also carrying his bow. They sped down the stairs on bare feet to emerge into the small courtyard, and then ran silently through the doorway. Their vision adjusted quickly and their ears became accustomed to the small noises; they could hear the guards off by the gates. There was, however, no sign of Yosef, and nothing to be seen of the intruders Dar'an thought he had seen.

"Where is Yosef?" Reza whispered into Talon's ear.

He shook his head. "Come, we must go over there," he pointed to the main house, "and find out if Dar'an really saw anything," he whispered back.

Like two wraiths they raced across the short distance towards the entrance of the private quarters. They could now see the darkened opening; just inside they saw a dark bundle on the ground. Both men instantly tensed and crept by way of the shadows until they were very close to the motionless form, but not exposed to anyone who might be inside watching the entrance. Any other noises were muffled by the sound of water pouring down into the pond from the fountain and the burping of a lonely frog nearby.

The bundle groaned and a hand scrabbled in the dust, and then stilled. It was Yosef, but neither Talon nor Reza moved forward. They were too experienced to be caught in a trap, even if it was Yosef. Both knew that there was now great danger about, but they could not see where it was. Talon listened hard while his eyes searched the darkness ahead. He reasoned that Yosef had walked into one of the intruders and been struck down. They had to help him, but unless they knew where the intruders were they were in mortal danger themselves. Why were these people here, and where were they hiding?

Reza, who had the keenest eyes, touched him, making him jerk. Reza leaned towards him.

"Someone, to the left. Deep in the shadows. I think he is watching the entrance. Can you see him?"

"We have to distract him somehow," Talon whispered back, his eyes probing the area Reza had indicated. Yes, there it was: a darker shadow than the rest. He began to make out the form of a man in a half crouch holding a bow at the ready. "Yes, I see him now."

They both pulled back from the corner.

"I'll distract him. You kill him," Reza whispered. It was not a discussion. He very slowly laid down his bow and Talon took out an arrow and knocked it in the string of his bow. He knew what Reza had in mind. It was incredibly risky; if the intruder was a good bowman, Reza was going to get killed.

"Ready?" Reza hissed.

Talon touched him on the arm with his elbow. "Yes!"

Reza took a long step, then threw himself across the opening of the entrance to the courtyard and rolled.

There was an exclamation and the twang of a bowstring. An arrow flew past Reza, who was back up on his feet and on the other side out of sight, while Talon leapt into the opening with a drawn bow. He released his arrow and it sped to strike with an audible thump the dark form twenty feet from him.

The figure dropped his bow with a clatter and fell with a choking cry face down on the verandah.

Reza and Talon ran past the dead man and on toward the house, where they stopped: watching, listening, waiting. The night was still, as though listening with them.

There was no sound from within the building.

"He was good; I felt the wind of the arrow pass me," Reza told him.

"You are just getting slow, my Brother," Talon answered.

The response was a snort.

"I must go in and find out where the other one is, if there is another," Talon whispered.

"One of us must help Yosef, or he is a dead man," Reza whispered back.

"You stay and prevent anyone from leaving. I don't think there is another way in or out," Talon said. "Do what you can for Yosef."

He detached himself from the dark shadow and moved slowly towards the door. It was not locked, so he eased himself into the blackness beyond, and then pressed against the wall to stop again and listen. The quiet of the building, apart from the odd creak, was absolute—or was it?

He thought he heard a slight scuffing sound up the stairs right above his head. The hair on his neck rose as he looked up. He could make out a landing, which led off to several rooms with closed doors. He could barely make them out in the darkness. There was someone up there moving about in a very stealthy manner.

Moving very quietly, he placed his bow on a table and drew his sword. He slipped silently up the stairs until he reached the landing, where he paused. Again he heard a tiny sound, from off to his right in one of the rooms. Moving like a ghost he approached the doorway where he thought he had heard the sound, and touched the door with a finger. The door opened silently on its hinges. There was deeper darkness within and the distinct scent of women's perfume.

This might be a bedroom, he reasoned, as he peered into the darkness. Again there was that tiny shuffling sound, and this time he was certain it came from within. Then he noticed something. There was a light in a corner, but it was very faint. It came from a small taper of incense on a stick that had been placed on a table. The red glow was sufficient to illuminate what might have been a small shrine.

He slipped into the room, noiseless on bare feet, and stepped to the side against the wall to listen again, but the sounds had stopped and there was an ominous silence.

Talon tensed. A black shadow obliterated the view of the glowing stick for an instant and he felt the presence of someone suddenly very close.

Talon could have struck then and probably would have succeeded in killing the man, but he hesitated. One of the intruders was already dead. At the back of his mind he wanted a chance to find out why they were there. He knew in an instant that his hesitation had been a mistake.

The intruder had instincts just as finely tuned by adrenaline and tension as his. Somehow he realized that he was not alone. The figure abruptly made a dash for the door. That was also a mistake.

Talon swung his sword in an arc meant to cut into an arm and disable the intruder. But the man was quick; his own sword was there to block the attack with a shriek of steel edge on steel edge that reverberated around the room. Something on the intruder's back rattled like stones within a box.

Talon disengaged and struck again, but again the other man managed to duck and riposte. Talon felt the steel thrust through his loose jacket and slice the sleeve open. Both men were now so close that Talon could smell the garlic on the other man's breath, which came in short gasps as the surprised intruder now fought for his life.

Neither paid any attention to the hysterical shrieks that now came from the bed as they stumbled out of the living room onto the landing where there was somewhat more light, both of them still lunging and stashing. Abruptly they could see one another, and then the fight really began. Talon recognized that he was up against a good swordsman who threw all he could at him in a flurry of slashing, stabbing strikes. He managed to block and stab back with the same vigor, driving the shorter, dark shape back and back.

The screaming continued from within the bedroom behind them, and now there were shouts from below as servants woke up to rush out with lanterns and stand peering up at the two combatants. No one wanted to become entangled in the savage fight going on above their heads, but they raised their lanterns to see better, providing enough light for Talon to see his opponent with more clarity.

Talon didn't think; he struck and stabbed with a rhythm that he had learned a long time ago. His sword was like a piston and the figure in front of him began to tire. Before very long Talon could see that the intruder was trying desperately to break away and escape: all he was doing now was parrying and blocking while glancing about him for a means of escape.

Without warning his opponent dived into another room, shoving aside someone at the entrance who gave a cry of surprise. The man disappeared into the darkness of the room, Talon in hot pursuit. He brushed past Lihua, who was on her knees, and charged into the room to hear the crash of breaking shutters. The intruder was gone. Talon arrived at the balcony just in time to hear the thump of someone landing like a cat on the ground outside, and then he vanished into the bushes. Talon peered into the darkness and shook his head. There would be no following him in the dark. He would be long gone from the premises by the time Talon made it to the gardens.

He turned back with a weary shrug and walked back to Lihua, who was still on the floor, leaning on one arm and looking shocked. Even in this disheveled condition he noted how beautiful she was as he took her other arm and lifted her to her feet.

"Are you all right?" he asked.

"Yes," she nodded. "I was surprised. I didn't expect to be knocked over in the middle of the night."

He chuckled with approval. She was not too badly shaken.

"I must go to my Lady Meng. She sounds very upset," she told him.

He had to agree. The screams and shouting from that bedroom had not stopped. Servants were streaming up the stairs, yelling and shouting in their strange language, sounding even more high-pitched than usual.

"We need a physician, if there is such a person. It is very urgent," Talon told her.

"Why, are you injured?" she asked with concern. "Is my Lady?"

"No, it is Yosef, one of my people, who is hurt, I think badly," Talon told her.

At that moment the guards burst into the house and began shouting and gesticulating wildly, pushing the servants around and generally increasing the panic.

Talon strode to the edge of the balcony and, imitating Captain Dandachi, roared as loudly as he could at them in his own language to shut up and stop their noise.

They stopped and gaped up at him. All noise ceased as everyone stared at him in surprise.

"Tell the guards to get out into the garden and check for any other intruders, I want to know how they got in without the sentries noticing," Talon told Lihua, who immediately began to translate.

"Tell them also to find a physician and bring him to the guest quarters as soon as possible. We have someone badly wounded."

Lihua translated and the guards left, chastened, while the servants ran about lighting lanterns. Several of the women hurried to the quarters of the family members to attend to them.

"Please tell me, what happened, Talon?" Lihua begged him when order seemed at least somewhat restored.

"Come with me and I can tell you after we have seen to Yosef," Talon told her.

They hurried down the stairs, pushing past the still agitated and frightened servants, to go out into the courtyard, past a prone body with an arrow sticking out of its chest, to where they found Reza supporting Yosef, who was unconscious with a bloody rag tied around his neck.

Reza looked up. "Glad to see you are still alive, Brother. I am not so sure about Yosef; he is in a very bad way."

Lihua dropped to her knees beside Yosef and without preamble opened his sopping, blood-soaked vest to look at the wound. The rag that Reza had tied around his neck was also soaked in blood. His throat had been cut. She gasped, and Talon's heart did a loop as he saw the horror of what had been done, but then Reza said, "If it had been his jugular he would be dead by now. We might still be able to save him." Talon had to agree, although it still didn't look good at all.

"He has lost a lot of blood," Lihua said unnecessarily.

"We will take him to the guest house and do what we can for him there. We *must* have a physician," Talon told her.

"I have told the guards to find one as soon as possible."

"You stay here and take care of the ladies, please, Lihua. We can talk in the morning."

She nodded agreement.

*****

Lihua walked into the bedroom of Lady Meilin to find the woman sitting up on her bed. Meilin glared up at Lihua with hate in her black eyes. She deeply resented the young, slim beauty that Hsü had brought into her house. Her own crippled state prevented her from doing anything useful, even in these outrageous circumstances. Her bound feet inhibited all walking. Any attempt was accompanied by intense pain, forcing her to depend upon servants to carry her anywhere.

Under normal circumstances this established her authority as the lady of the house. Oh, the pain she had endured for this privilege! 'The ten thousand tears of agony' she had been subjected to as a young girl because society demanded it, having her feet bound so that she could not do any work that might be considered beneath the dignity of the lady of the house. Now here she was, crippled and unable to control events, while this wisp of a girl told the servants what to do, probably lied to her and left her here, vulnerable and most likely in danger for her life! A wave of self pity swept over her and she swiped at the tears that began to fall, hating the loss of face.

"I want to know what has been happening!" she shouted, "What has all that appalling noise outside been about?" she demanded, unable to stop the tears of frustration and rage from spilling.

"We were attacked, my Lady," Lihua said calmly enough, in an attempt to ease her fright.

"I am sure it is the foreigners who are responsible for all this!" Meilin shouted. Lihua's very calm only seemed to upset Meilin even more.

"They protected us, my Lady," Lihua said very respectfully. "Intruders came to steal from us."

Meilin continued to glare at her. "What did these intruders want?"

"I think they came to steal the Lord's treasure, my Lady."

Meilin gasped and involuntarily put her hand to her mouth. "Is it... is it safe?" She shivered and plucked at the covers.

"We are safe now, my Lady. One of the foreigners is badly injured; a doctor must be found soon."

Meilin waved her hand at her. "Go! Send in my servants and make sure we are secure. In the morning I want to know what happened in detail."

Lihua bowed and left.

*****

Down in the courtyard, Talon and Reza crouched over Yosef.

"Give me a hand there, Reza," Talon said. They hefted the unconscious boy up and carried him as fast as they could away from the noise and hysteria of the inner courtyard to their own quiet oasis. There they were met by Rav'an and Jannat, with a nervous Dar'an in attendance. "I tried to stop them coming down, Talon but..." he stammered.

"We could hear all the noise from here, Talon," Rav'an said briskly. Then she gasped, as did Jannat.

"What has happened to Yosef!" They both put their hands to their mouths as Talon and Reza placed the boy carefully on the low table in the main room.

Rav'an recovered quickly. "Hot water, Jannat, and many clean rags, as fast as you can. Dar'an, help her!" Jannat and Dar'an dashed off to obey.

"Is there a chance he can survive?" Rav'an asked Talon as she stared down at Yosef.

"Perhaps, as long as there is a good physician available. There is a lot of blood and we have to turn him on his side or he will choke to death. I don't know if they have real physicians in this land. Lihua has sent for one, but I don't think we will see him before dawn. We must try to stop the bleeding and keep him alive until then."

At that moment Rostam came down the stairs. "Mama, what is going on?" he called to Rav'an. With a look of alarm, Rav'an almost ran to him and coaxed him back up the stairs.

"Just a bit of noise, my Love," she said. "Salem, where are you? Please take Rostam back to bed."

*****

The next morning at the villa, residents woke up to a dawn where everything had changed. The guards were wide awake and patrolling everywhere, examining every corner of the compound in the manner of men who don't know what they are doing but feel they have to do something.

Talon rubbed his eyes and face, while in a corner Reza nodded off. The women had gone off to bed once all that could be done for Yosef had been done. They had stripped him and cleaned him of the caked blood, placed him on a mattress under a clean cotton quilt, and watched him as he gurgled and choked the night away. They had to keep him on his side so that he could breathe at all because of the gash in his neck.

There was a disturbance outside that jolted Talon further awake, and Lihua appeared, looking hollow-eyed, accompanied by a tall, thin stranger and followed by a guard carrying a large lacquer painted box that he was told to put down; then he left.

"Good morning, Talon," Lihua said with a wan smile. "I have brought the physician. He is very capable and should be able to help."

The physician wore an elaborately patterned silk robe with wide sleeves from which long bony fingers protruded like claws. He gave Talon a perfunctory nod and then went straight to Yosef. He had sharp features, with a straggly, drooping, gray mustache and beard, above which was a tight mouth and observant, intelligent eyes. His long gray hair was pulled into a bun at the back of his head, upon which was perched a small rimless hat of patterned silk. The man immediately sat down alongside Yosef and took up his wrist to feel his pulse. He shook his head. Then he took out from the box what seemed to be a hollow ivory horn, placed it on Yosef's chest, and began to listen. Only then did he lift the coverings off the wound.

He clucked at what he saw and began to speak to Lihua in a fast, sing-song voice.

"Your friend has lost a lot of blood and his pulse is very low, yet the doctor thinks his life can be saved, as long as the wound stays clean. The doctor says he must stitch up the gash and one ligament because that cannot be left as it is."

Talon blew out a breath of relief, and then sat down to watch the physician at work.

*****

Hua Rong walked into his office to find Lin already there waiting for him, standing patiently at the entrance. After stretching the moment out with a bowl of tea, Rong waved Lin to a seat and asked him, "Well, did you go there last night?"

"Yes, Lord." It struck Rong that Lin was in a somber mood.

"Spit it out. How did it go?"

"Er, well, we, er, obtained the box, my Lord, but..."

Ron felt a surge of pleasure and beamed. The box was his. He barely heard the rest of the comment, but Lin persisted.

"... but we lost one man, dead, and the other is wounded."

Rong stared, aghast. "What did you just say?"

"The plan went well at first, but then somehow one of the foreigners got in the way and they had to kill him. Then another one of the foreigners killed one of our men and caught the other as he was leaving the house," Lin said. "There was a fight and alarms. It woke up the whole household."

Rong stared at him with an appalled expression on his usually tranquil face. His mind was racing.

"You say he was wounded. Did he escape? Is there any way they can trace this to us?" he demanded, his voice sounding like gravel.

"He escaped, my Lord, and he brought the box back with him," Lin said, and produced a lacquered box with images of fruit trees and birds on the lid. It rattled as he handed it over.

"Have you opened it?" Rong demanded suspiciously.

Lin looked hurt. "It is sealed with the chop of Lord Meng, my Lord," he huffed.

Rong examined the box. It was indeed sealed with red wax and carried the singular chop of Hsü imprinted in the wax.

He took out a small knife to open the box and then paused. "Is the man who escaped in a bad way?" he demanded. "Did they have anything on them that could identify them?"

Lin again looked hurt at this disparagement of the professionalism of his men. "Nothing, my Lord, nothing at all."

Rong thought about this for a long moment. "The other one, he knows too much. He needs to go."

Lin bowed. "I shall take care of it, my Lord."

"That man Kee needs to be silenced, too. He will be easy to get to if they decide this was an inside job," Rong told him.

Lin bowed again.

"You may go," Rong told him. Lin vanished.

Rong turned his attention back to the box. He savored the moment. He was rich beyond his wildest dreams, and all thanks to Hsü. Now he could bribe his way into any level of society, and that could include the governorship.

It was one of those beautiful boxes made by a real craftsman, about two hand breadths long by two wide and one deep. For a moment he admired the intricate brush work on the lid. He prided himself on his appreciation of good art. The only thing he had in common with Hsü, he reflected with a sardonic smile to himself. He shrugged and broke the seal of the box with the tip of the knife, then forced the lid open because he had no key.

He finished the work and placed the knife carefully on the table before lifting the lid, then gaped.

Inside the scented wooden box were dozens of small, round stones, the kind that can be found in any stream bed or river. They didn't even glitter in the morning light.

For a very long moment Rong stared at the box as though its contents were a scorpion. He began to tremble,then went into a towering rage. He swept the box off the table to the floor. It fell open and the stones flew everywhere, rolling about on the floor.

"Send Lin in to me!" he screamed.

Her handkerchief all soaked in tears, she cannot dream,
In deepest night before the palace voices sing.
Her rosy cheeks aren't old, but first love has been cut,
Leaning, wreathed in smoke, she sits until the dawn.

—Bai Juyi

Chapter Twenty-Two
Audience with an Emperor

After an uneventful journey to Hangzhou, Hsü sent a message to an old friend named Ts'ao, informing him that he had arrived. It would be at the very least a week or more before Hsü would be presented at the palace. He knew from prior experience that the wheels of administration move glacially in this city within a city. He set about finding accommodation for himself and his small retinue and awaited a reply.

Hangzhou was larger than Guangzhou, with a teeming population. There were enormous projects taking place, the largest of all was the finalization of the huge canal that now reached all the way north to the distant Yangtze River, thus allowing small ships and barges access to the hinterland from the port. Trade was everything in the empire, and the main artery for this trade was this marvel of construction: the canal.

The next day Ts'ao replied via messenger that he would see Hsü later within the week, inside the palace walls, at such and such a pavilion, and gave directions how to get there once he was permitted entry; also a pass was provided for Hsü to use at the gates.

On the appointed day, Hsü arrived at one of the several huge entrances of the palace with his papers, and after what seemed an interminable wait was finally allowed entry. He asked for and received a guide to take him to the right pavilion and was very glad that he had. He knew from a prior visit that this was an enormous space within the palace walls; it would be very easy to get lost and stumble into a forbidden area. He didn't want to lose face to that extent.

His guide walked him across wide and mostly empty courtyards along seemingly endless pathways and past royal gardens, which were a riot of color and indeed awe inspiring. He admired the grand pavilions and pagodas as he was guided past one after the other on his way to a very discreet pavilion, where he met with his old acquaintance, Ts'ao, whose title was Auxiliary Academician. They had studied together and taken their exams at the same time in the prestigious Yuelu Academy near to the Yuelu Mountain in Hunan province. Students of this academy were usually destined for high positions in government. Ts'ao was no exception.

Ts'ao greeted him with a smile of pleasure, and after dismissing the guide they went through the usual deep bows and polite enquiries as to each other's health and that of their families. Then Ts'ao led Hsü aside to one of the smaller anterooms, where they were served tea by a servant who then disappeared.

"There is time before you are required to speak to the Chamberlains, Lord Meng. The Emperor is very busy today, so it might be another day before he will see you, perhaps even longer."

Hsü was not surprised. He counted himself lucky that the Emperor would see him at all, but he knew that there was interest in his mission at the highest levels. What he had not expected was the direction the conversation took after they covered the formalities.

"You are aware that Hua Rong, the Chief of Police in Guangzhou, appears to be spending a lot of money, or rather promissory notes, among the officials here?" Ts'ao asked him carefully.

Despite his efforts Hsü's face must have mirrored his surprise. "I have been made aware that there was someone who was buying influence. I was not aware that it was Rong."

"It took me a little time to find out for myself, but I knew as soon as I was approached by the man who is doing his bidding here in the palace. Rong himself has not yet paid us a visit. In fact I suspect that it is two people buying favor: Hua Rong and another man, who I am sure you know, a much less savory individual, but very wealthy nonetheless," Ts'ao's nose twitched with distaste.

Hsü suppressed a smile. He guessed it might be Buwei. "What do you think they are buying?" he asked bluntly.

"Why, the governorship, of course," Ts'ao said, raising his scanty eyebrows.

"Ah, yes. Well, Buwei is disqualified, no degree; but Rong... perhaps."

"Actually, I don't think it is for either of those two men," Ts'ao mused. "You know a man named Wo po-ku?"

"Yes, he is a Prefect. In fact he is the Senior Prefect at the Governor's palace. Are they backing him?"

"Such appears to be the case. He has risen to a position of influence in the Governor's palace and is well qualified. Some would say very well qualified for the position. He has years of experience in administering the region. Rong is influence-peddling here in the palace with paper, on the promise of payment when there are results."

Hsü nodded. That was prudent, but it opened a tiny door of opportunity for him. He looked across at Ts'ao. Ts'ao was probably going to push for him, but like all the officials in the palace the machinery needed some oiling. It was the way of things."

He fumbled in his voluminous robes for a moment and produced two very small boxes. They were each about the size of a large Chop, but the design on the boxes was beautifully painted on silk. He gave a surreptitious glance about him to make sure that no one was watching. It did no harm to be careful in the palace—walls had both eyes and ears—then he placed both boxes on the tiny table between the two men.

He bowed from the seated position as he did so, to make the point. "Perhaps we can change this state of affairs; but in any case, I brought back a present for you and your illustrious wife." He spoke Cantonese, which few people could follow in this rarefied atmosphere of the palace, Mandarin being the language of royalty in Hangzhou.

Ts'ao touched the boxes with a long fingernail and then slowly opened one. Inside the red-silk-lined box was a large ruby and two sapphires. Ts'ao's eyes widened, but he said nothing, and the boxes vanished into the folds of his robes as though they had never been.

Ts'ao looked up at Hsü. "I know several distinguished people who would prefer to see something, shall we say, more substantial like this, rather than paper promises."

Hsü gave him the thinnest of smiles. He had made his preparations carefully. "Oh, I can assure you of that; no paper, only the real thing; and today, not tomorrow."

Ts'ao nodded. "It might tip the balance our way." Ts'ao was no fool. He knew well that should Hsü gain the position, he would look after his friends when the time came. "I shall introduce you to some interested parties."

*****

Ts'ao was as good as his word and arranged several meetings with high up Academicians and Prefects who were suddenly interested in Hsü's welfare. Hsü's smile was sardonic when he thought about that. Under any other circumstances they would not have given him much thought.

Later Ts'ao informed him that there were to be several firm supporters of his bid for governorship.

His conversations with Ts'ao had revealed some interesting facts which bore careful consideration. It was clear that Rong had exerted a great deal of influence. Administrators who would otherwise have been neutral were now interested.

A week later Hsü received a letter from Ts'ao informing him of the time and place for his interview with the Emperor.

His audience was brief and to the point. He had submitted his written report on arrival, and he knew it would have been read before the audience was granted. Finally he was brought to the Great Chamber, where he shuffled forward on his knees to stop at the base of the platform and *Ke Tou'd* before his great Highness, the Emperor. Placing his hands on the carpet, he put his forehead to the floor and waited until he was told to sit up.

When he did, he was not allowed to look directly at the Emperor; in fact, it would have been difficult, as the Emperor was seated on a dais no less than seven steps above him on a golden throne. Almost everything in the huge chamber was either lacquered black, painted red, or covered with elaborately detailed gold leaf. The idea was to instill awe and humility in the presence of one so august. On either side of the stairs on low plinths were two gilded cranes carved of ebony and ivory that represented good fortune. Above the throne writhed images of fierce dragons, their fangs bared and their huge eyes glaring down at him.

Out of the corner of his eye he glimpse the silk robes of the Emperor, every inch of which was decorated with bright red and deep blue motifs of elaborate designs, including a dragon on the center of the breast. He had a moment to contemplate the sumptuous surroundings of gilded pillars and silk paintings, perhaps hundreds of years old. He knew that priceless treasures had been lost when the Northern Sung regions had succumbed to the Jin barbarians, but much appeared to have been saved.

On both sides of the throne were courtiers in glittering, bejeweled costumes and officials wearing thick silk coats made almost rigid by the amount of gold and silver thread stitched onto them. He felt positively shabby by comparison. He did not fail to notice the kind of people surrounding the throne. They were almost all from the Administrative class; he saw only two uniforms, denoting a general and an admiral, neither of whom he knew.

The Emperor spoke, his voice high and reedy. "We are pleased that you survived your ordeal, Lord Meng. We read your report with great interest. It would seem that your ancestors smiled upon you and preserved you."

Hsü knew this was a high compliment coming directly from the Emperor, so he placed both hands on the carpeted floor again and bowed his head almost to his hands.

"May I have permission to present to your Highness one letter from the Sultan of Gujarat which I managed to keep safe, and a small token of his esteem? I am so sorry that the other gifts could not be saved," he murmured, and then lifted up a rolled length of paper written in elaborate Arabic cartography, tied with a green ribbon. With the other hand he presented a small box of carved jade that was filled with precious stones: sapphires, rubies, and a huge emerald

It was a fabulous gift by any standards, but Hsü didn't make the mistake of trying to take credit for the riches. It would suffice that he had brought these valuable gifts back to his Emperor and discharged his duty.

The gifts were taken from him by an aide, who opened the box to show the Emperor; then the items were passed to the back of the throne."

"We are pleased with the presents. We expect that you will discuss the trade routes and your experiences with my Advisors," the Emperor announced. "We are also pleased to present you with a small gift of appreciation." He raised his hand and an aide walked down the stairs to present Hsü with a painting by Ma Youren, a Cloudy Mountain scene on paper.

Hsü took the painting with great care and admired it for the benefit of the Emperor, who commented, "It is our understanding that you, Lord Meng, value paintings as a product of the cultivated mind, not merely as a skill?"

"Indeed, Your Highness is right. Where would we be if we did not appreciate the arts for their aesthetic value?"

At a nod from the Emperor the audience was over, so Hsü bowed over his hands once again in the ritual *Ke Tou,* shuffled backwards twenty paces along the length of the enormous carpet, then stood and bowed deeply again. He backed out of the chamber, his head bowed and his hands in front of him and out of sight, the painting rolled up very carefully inside his sleeve.

*****

Ts'ao was impressed that the Emperor had presented a painting to Hsü.

"He has provided you with enormous face, my Lord," he said. Hsü agreed; it could not hurt his chances. Now began the real work towards obtaining voters. He spent another four days meeting with ministers and officials to whom Ts'ao guided him. They asked penetrating questions, and all left with a small 'token' of Hsü's appreciation. Ts'ao became more optimistic; he told Hsü that of the seven men who would be responsible for crafting the petition to the Emperor for a new governor, the votes were now three in his favor and two against, while two were wavering. He needed, however, a clear majority if the petition was to reach the Emperor and receive the royal seal of approval, so it could still go against him despite all his efforts.

"You should go home now. Make sure that your friends are still with you and your enemies are not going to do anything to cause problems at the Governor's palace," Ts'ao counseled him.

Hsü needed little persuasion to leave the stifling atmosphere of the royal palace. The armies of servants, eunuchs and notables jostling for space in this cauldron of passions and raw ambition left him reeling. Besides, the protocols were suffocating. His friend Ts'ao described the absurd details to him. "There are a thousand pages of rules for the one room, The Great Hall of Harmony," he told Hsü. "You would have had to spend a year waiting for an audience had the Emperor chosen that one!" He chuckled sardonically.

*****

Hsü returned home a week later to find his household still recovering from the incident with the intruders. His wife had taken to her bed, suffering bouts of weeping from the reaction, and his mother was still much shaken. The servants were almost incoherent with fright after the ordeal, and still unable to provide accurate details. The only person in his entire household who appeared calm enough to explain the situation was Lihua, who told him all she knew, including the battle between Talon and the intruder and the grave situation with Yosef. Hsü concealed his rage at the sheer effrontery and the danger to which his family had been exposed in his absence, and privately swore vengeance. His respect for Talon and his companion had gone up several notches.

"Despite everything that Master Talon did, Lord Meng, alas," here she began to weep with mortification, "they still managed to get away with what they came for."

He patted her on the shoulder. "Do not despair, Lihua. Not everything is always as it seems."

He left her wiping away her tears and made his way to the guest quarters to talk to Talon and his extended family. There he found them drinking tea on the veranda of the building. They greeted him warmly, but there was an underlying tension which was not lost on him.

"I am here to thank you for all you have done, the defense of my family and property from these villainous bandits," Hsü said when the greetings were over. "How is the wounded man?" he enquired.

"Yosef will survive as long as there is no infection," Talon informed him. "Thank you for asking, Lord Meng. The physician is very gifted; he saved Yosef's life, of that there is no doubt."

"It is Hsü to my friends, and I am indebted once again for your help."

"I understand that we were not very successful," Talon said with some regret in his voice. "I did hear that a very important box was stolen despite all our efforts." He was referring to the box of jewels, and both he and Hsü knew it.

"Please come with me for a moment, Talon," Hsü said.

They walked out into the afternoon sun into the orchard where no one could hear them. Hsü turned to Talon and spoke.

"Hmm. I imagine that by now the thieves have discovered that what was in the box was not what they came for," he stated enigmatically.

Talon stared at the man in front of him and decided then and there that he would endeavor never to underestimate him.

"You still owe me a dragon. I have yet to see one," he told Hsü to cover his surprise. Hsü gave a chuckle.

"I shall do my best to find one for you, Talon. It is the least I can do."

Talon gave a wry smile. "What *was* in the box?" he asked.

"Stones for throwing, perhaps. The real treasure is hidden somewhere else. Now we need to find out who told them where to look." The look in Hsü's eyes became very intense.

*****

Hsü was as good as his word. It took him less than two days to find out that it had been Kee who had provided the robbers with the necessary information and had even given them a map. One of the female servants had seen him walking out of Lady Meng's rooms one day and had wondered why he had been there. After the attempted robbery she had passed along her suspicions to Grandmother Lady Meng. It was a simple matter to get him to confess in one of the back rooms of the stables. Fang could be very efficient with thin bamboo sticks pushed under the nails and set on fire. Kee was bound, helpless, covered in sweat, and he stank of his own soil.

When the last bout of screaming behind the gag had stopped because Kee had passed out, Hsü sat back in the chair from which he had watched the proceedings with an impassive face. He was very thoughtful. He motioned Fang to release the gag, as he didn't want Kee to die choking on his own vomit. Kee had not been able to name the man in the darkened room; he had only been able to provide a sketchy description.

The man was obviously wealthy, as Kee had noticed rings on fingers that knew no physical work, and the rich clothes had said something about the man. One detail in particular had struck Kee as significant. He had sweated copiously as he desperately tried to describe the design: a large ruby surrounded by seed pearls in a gold ring. He had gasped out this information while watching his fingers burn.

Kee had also spilled all he knew about a man called Lin. He didn't know his other name, but described a scar that ran from his right ear down the back of his cheek. From what Hsü could deduce, this man Lin was the other person's hatchet man. They had to find him somehow. In the meantime, he needed to keep Kee out of sight and secure from any possibility that the robbers might come back and kill his only lead. There was also the troubling issue of how to protect Kee's family.

Therefore one who is good at Martial arts overcomes others' forces without battle, conquers others' cities without siege, destroys others' nations without taking a long time.

—Master Sun Tzu. The Art of War

Chapter Twenty-Three
Dojo

Not long after the incident with the intruders, they were all gathered about the table, sipping wine and nibbling at some sweet wafer-like biscuits, when Hsü brought up the subject of martial exercises.

"I have watched you and Reza working with one another in the other courtyard. You are very disciplined, and I notice that no more than two days go by without you going through a drill in the mornings. Incidentally, your archery is remarkable," he told them.

"Thank you, Hsü. We were well taught and… our training has proved to be beneficial from time to time," Talon said carefully.

"I wonder…" Hsü stopped, his expression thoughtful.

They were now familiar with these little pauses, so they waited. He looked down at the table and rubbed the balding patch on the top of his head, by now a familiar gesture.

"You have seen Fang and the way he practices, have you not?"

Talon and Reza shook their heads.

"Hmm, we must rectify that. Tomorrow Fuling here will take you to the school that I went to and where Fang still goes from time to time. He has been trained by a man from the islands of Nippon."

Neither Talon nor Reza had ever heard of these islands, so they looked blank.

"These people are great warriors; in fact, I would say they are the best swordsmen in the world," Hsü remarked in an offhand manner.

Talon was intrigued despite himself. He considered himself to be a good swordsman, and he knew that Reza was a match for most men. However, the nagging doubt persisted that he could be better.

"Will we be able to observe their practice?" he asked.

"Indeed you may, in fact I have asked the Sensei there to provide you with lessons, if you so wish," Hsü said with his enigmatic smile. "It will be my gift to you."

*****

Later that evening, Talon and Reza were seated with Rav'an and Jannat on the balcony of their wing of the extensive guesthouse. Salem had taken a protesting Rostam to bed, but the adults were enjoying the night. The muted din of a city that never seemed to sleep came to them on a light night breeze. A nightingale warbled in the mulberry trees, and several streets away an owl gave a low hoot.

"This is so very peaceful here, quite different from life on the ship, my Talon," Rav'an said with a sigh of contentment.

"His house is full of very beautiful things; it is like a treasure house," Jannat, too, sighed. She sounded content.

There were no demands made on them, and they could come and go as they chose, but most of the time if the women ventured out it was with Lihua, who seemed happy to show them her city. The guards, however, been doubled, and they went out less frequently. Talon didn't want to add to Hsü's problems by contributing more victims.

"The food is quite good too," Reza remarked.

"Quite good? If we ever eat like this again anywhere else I shall be surprised, and so will you, Brother," Talon admonished him.

"Hmm. So what do you think of this 'school for swordsmen'?" Reza asked. His tone was skeptical.

"I shall go tomorrow and see what it is all about. It's probably not as good as Hsü makes it sound. Remember, you are to go with Jiaya to the quay to be present when the customs people come," Talon reminded him. "Our goods have now been in Hsü's warehouse for weeks and they have just decided to come. They know how to take their time, those people."

"You are very thoughtful these days, Talon." Rav'an said to him.

"Am I? Yes, well, it is perhaps because of the troubles that appear to be bothering Hsü, but also because I am in a constant state of awe since we have been here. I feel," he paused, "unbalanced."

"I have to agree," Jannat said. "It is in some ways like a fairy land of new things to see, and touch, and taste."

"It's not just that," Talon said with a sigh. "It's more that they are so... so far ahead of anywhere I, we, have been before. They do things here that I could never have conceived of. Even Constantinople, which is the richest city in our world, is nowhere near as rich as just this city. I have never seen such beautiful workmanship of every possible kind. Their mills, their workshops, their carvings, paintings, everything they do is far and way ahead of anything I have ever seen before. It is humbling."

"Then we should be glad that we have come all this way to see this beauty," Rav'an remarked.

Talon shook his head. "You are right, of course, but sometimes I wonder if it is not all an illusion. Are we living a dream of some kind?"

"Dream or not, I intend to learn all I can from that physician who comes to look after Yosef. The boy can sit up in bed now and almost speak. I cannot believe how skilled that man is. Doctor Haddad would be awed by what he has done," Rav'an stated. "I have to go up and tuck Rostam into bed." She left with a touch on Talon's shoulder. "Dream on, my Husband. We should learn all we can before we leave."

*****

Talon walked on bare feet along the open corridor that the novice had told him led to the training space. He had given it a name, but Talon could not remember what it was called. He was accompanied by Fuling.

He arrived at an open courtyard surrounded by the loggia walkways the Chinese built everywhere, to find that there were a small number of like-dressed novices seated cross-legged around a square mat of about six paces by six. It had a surface that, while firm, gave just a little under his weight. The novices regarded him impassively and in silence. They, too, were waiting for something to happen.

He carried his own sword with him and stood at the edge of the mat, waiting for someone to tell him what to do. He looked around at the ornately painted wood architecture of posts and beams. It was quite different from the crude work he remembered seeing in France and elsewhere.

Fang had informed him that the numerous symbols that decorated the walls and pillars everywhere in the pavilion were writing, mostly proverbs. He was still contemplating and admiring the red-painted beams when a very old man with a long, wispy, white beard strode onto the mats. He carried a sword in an ornate sheath, but as he walked onto the mat he gave a sharp command and a novice jumped up and took some long, wooden, slightly curved rods from a rack. They were the same kind that Fang had displayed to him and Reza at the villa. There were bindings set at regular spaces along the shaft.

The old man took one and handed the novice his sword, then the novice walked over to Talon and presented the other stick with both hands open and a low bow.

The old man stepped onto the mat and motioned for Talon to do the same. Fuling, who had been hovering next to one of the ornate pillars, muttered to Talon.

"Please to go onto the mat, Master Talon. The lesson is about to begin."

Talon nodded, took the proffered rod and handed over his own sword to the novice, then hefted the stick. It was very slightly weighted at the tip but otherwise well balanced. The handle was wrapped in cloth gray with old sweat, with a round guard set between the handle and the 'blade'. He thought of all the stick work he had performed in the past and felt confident that this was going to be a simple lesson to start with.

The old man by now was at the center of the mat, where he stood with his feet slightly apart and the tip of his stick resting on the floor. As Talon approached, he bowed. Talon responded politely but clumsily with one of his own.

Then the old man shouted something and attacked. It was so fast that Talon was almost caught off guard. The old man's stick, held in both hands, came whistling down with ferocious speed for the top of his head. He only just managed to lift his own to block it, deflecting the other's weapon with a sharp crack, but it numbed his wrists. Talon had to leap out of the way as the man followed this move with a flurry of stabs and slashes; Talon was driven back onto the edge of the matting and then stumbled off altogether.

The old man immediately stopped, withdrew to the center of the mat and waited for Talon to come to him.

It rapidly became very clear to Talon that he had no defense against this Djinn with a stick that hit him in all the exposed places. On the second round, within a few seconds he was slapped hard on the ribs and arm. The old man's small black eyes never left Talon's face, but neither his eyes nor his expression ever gave Talon a clue as to what his next move would be. It was unnerving to be fighting such an expressionless machine.

Talon was unable to get in even one strike. The entire session was spent in frantic defensive moves. Soon enough he was stopped cold, as the old man with a shout that almost paralyzed him slipped inside his guard and placed his stick alongside Talon's neck. Talon froze where he stood and waited. The old man muttered something and then stood back, bowed, and left the mat. Talon stood alone, wondering what had just happened.

He turned towards Fuling with a question in his eyes.

"The master says that you did reasonably well... for a beginner," Fuling told him as he handed Talon back his sword. His expression was impassive. "Do you wish to come back here and learn more?"

Talon wiped the sweat away from his forehead with his sleeve and thought about it for a long moment. "Yes. Would it be possible?" It had been a humbling experience, and he was still remembering the bewildering speed and the manner of the attacks. He shook his head in amazement. The speed of this old man who barely came up to his shoulder had been astonishing. "Yes, I would like to be taught more," he said again.

Some of the other students paired off on the mat and began to practice. Talon watched them for a few minutes, observing the style of fighting. It was very fast, with one person attacking furiously, seeking an opening of any kind to complete the finishing strike, while the other defended with equal speed and fury; the clack of sticks echoed in the confined space of the training area. Talon had never encountered this method of fighting before but he could see that it was highly effective compared to the normal engagement of hack and stab that was used in his world. Before his bout with the Sensei he had been very sure of himself as a swordsman; it shook him to discover otherwise. He rubbed the welts on his arm ruefully and decided that he should come back as soon as possible, with Reza. They had some learning to do.

*****

Later that day he sat with Reza and Fuling at a small tea house, absently observing the pedestrians, and much further along the crowded dockyards where their ship was moored. They talked about the school.

"Do all the warriors of this nation go to schools like this?" he asked Fuling, rubbing his arm, which was still sore.

"No Master Talon, we do not value warriors the way you seem to, and certainly not as the Nippon do. They worship war in a manner we find distasteful. We Chinese prefer to win by trade and diplomacy, so warriors are not considered to be of an honorable class. My father, however, disagrees with this attitude, as do many military officers, pointing out that the Mongols pose a deadly threat to our entire nation. The Mongols believe only in the warrior class; they have nothing else to offer. Their cavalry is unstoppable in battle, yet they are ignorant barbarians; but my father says that our nation is in peril from them. The advisors to the Emperor, however, think that they can negotiate a peace rather than go to war."

"I think your father is a very wise man," Talon told him, the memories of the beleaguered Kingdom of Jerusalem still fresh in his mind.

"With so many people in this country, you must possess vast armies with which to fight the Mongols," Reza remarked as he fumbled with his chop sticks, trying to fish a morsel of meat out of a bowl of soup. "I wish I had a spoon," he complained.

Fuling smiled at his efforts, and then said. "We do have big armies, but we do not have a warrior class who study war with dedication and determination. There was a time, my father told me, when we did have great generals; but today the jealousies of the palace undermine the military."

"The school you took me too today, that was very impressive. The teacher must surely be a highly respected man among the society here."

Fuling shook his head. "Remember, my father told you that this school is not well known, and in fact does not want to be well known. Few go there. You might recall, Talon, we did not see many students."

"I cannot imagine why not. He is truly a master of the art of swordsmanship, Fuling."

Fuling nodded with a small smile. "He is one of those who come from over the sea from a land to the North and East of China. Fang worships him. My father sailed there some time ago and met the people. They have fierce and deadly fighters. The man who fought you today is one of them. He calls himself a Samurai. Fang was trained by them, which is why my father keeps him on as a family bodyguard."

Talon and Reza looked at one another. "We should go to this man and learn all we can from him," Talon said. Reza nodded, but Talon laughed at his skeptical expression.

"You wait, Brother. You will be as embarrassed as I was when you meet him. Let's see if you want to stay when he is done with you."

"I think you are just getting old, Brother. Once you were fast but now... well," Reza waggled his hand, pretending to shake. "Old age has crept up on you. It happens to all of us, you know?" he finished wisely, with a grin.

"You wait!" was all Talon said, pretending to take a swipe at him. He was savoring the moment when Reza, too, would find his own considerable skills inadequate."

They returned to the school later in the week, again with Fuling in tow. This time it was Reza who stood on the mat waiting. When the old man walked onto the mat, Reza directed a comical look back at Talon as though to say, "Are you sure this is the right man?"

Talon smiled, shrugged, and gave Reza a bland look. The inscrutable faces of the students sitting cross-legged around the mats told Reza nothing; hence he was not prepared when the old man, his long beard flying, leapt at him. This time it was Reza who was humiliated, although Talon had to admit Reza did somewhat better than he had. It still took about the same time for the old man to have Reza off the mats. Later, when the Sensei had left, Reza joined the grinning Talon and shook his head in disbelief.

"I have never met anyone like him before! 'Pedar Sag', but that was embarrassing!" he muttered. Talon laughed out loud at his friend's chagrinned expression. "I said we should learn all we can from him, Brother. We have other skills, but this is a golden opportunity to learn much more of our craft. It is as though we have struck gold. Thereafter, they both went to the school as often as they could. The lead student would take them through a grueling set of exercises before taking them onto the mat in another area of the compound. They could hear the shouts of the other students in cadence over the rapid clack of staves as they battled one another.

The unsmiling student, called Liu, who was training them would use Fuling to translate for him. He showed them the rigorous stance that was needed to unleash the devastating rain of blows upon an adversary. The emphasis was upon keeping the center of the body's gravity so low that nothing could displace it, thus providing the fighter with as strong a base as possible from which to deal out punishment to his opponent.

They would arrive back at the compound tired and bruised to tell the women of their latest humiliation.

"Just as we manage to get of his silly exercises right and can barely move he punishes us for working so hard." Reza complained.

"How does he punish you?" asked Rav'an, who could barely contain her laughter at the disconsolate pair.

"He challenges one of us to a fight and thrashes us soundly," Reza said with a scowl on his normally cheerful face.

Jannat laughed, then put her hand on his arm. "I'm sorry, Reza, but I thought you two were the best there were!" she said, sounding sympathetic.

Talon didn't think he heard enough sympathy in her tone.

"On one occasion he challenged both of us come to him and then finished us off in a minute!" Talon heard himself whining. He couldn't forget the speed and precision of those blows.

"Do you think Hsü sent you there for a purpose, Talon?" Rav'an asked, trying to be serious for a moment.

"Probably just to humiliate us and see the back of us sooner rather than later," Reza grumbled. Talon knew he didn't mean it. Reza didn't dislike Hsü as he first had. The man was providing them with a gift, and they both knew it.

"It feels like we have been sent back to school and found wanting," he said.

"What has Hsü said since you started going?" Jannat asked. She had trouble controlling her laughter.

"You've see him. He looks us up and down from across the table, to see if we still have both our arms and legs, and asks us how we feel; but then he doesn't wait for an answer and quickly changes the subject," Reza told her.

"I'm going to go and practice on Rostam. At least I have some chance of winning," Talon told his laughing companions with a rueful grin.

Talon and Reza knew well enough that they were receiving lessons they could not hope to learn anywhere else, so they took the beatings and the bruises without too much complaint. Although both men were lean, very strong, and had lost none of their speed, they still came back to the house of Hsü bruised and exhausted at the end of each lesson.

On several occasions, when bathing Talon's back and shoulders, Rav'an would exclaim over his welts. "Are they doing this to you, my Talon? It is terrible to see!"

Talon winced as she applied a hot cloth to one particularly painful welt and mumbled that it was in a good cause.

He and Reza would sit over tea with Fang and discuss the lessons. Their communication was halting but improving slowly.

"You are learning from one of the best the highest art of swordsmanship, Master Talon and Reza," Fang assured them. It was bleak encouragement.

It was hard sometimes to know if they were making any progress, but over tea one day Fang said, "I have heard from the student Liu that you make progress and that it will not be long before you will be given practice swords and taught how to use them. You must understand that it is only because of the influence of Hsü that you are being taken through this training so quickly. Normally it is years before a student is allowed to move up in this manner."

The punishment from their teacher Liu continued, with very occasional visits from the old man, who watched how they were doing in silence and then was gone again without a word.

Before long, however, they began to see results. Liu was fond of beating the two of them together in one battle, but one day Reza and Talon managed to drive him off the mat with a very aggressive attack from both sides. Thereafter he would only take on one of them at a time; but now they made him work for every pace he tried to take away from them. Other times they were pitted against one another and, just as in the days when they were in the castle of Samiran learning how to use knives in their training as *Fid'ai*, they found they were very evenly matched; Reza was slight and wickedly fast, while Talon brought more cunning and strength to the bouts.

Then Liu brought in other students and they began to apply the difficult lessons to good effect. Both Talon and Reza could bring to bear their experience with real battles and fights. They began to defeat the other students regularly. Only the top two teachers were impossible to get past, and they meted out punishment vigorously.

One day Liu came back with another man, who carried three wooden swords that had been carved to the length and shape of a normal sword. This was a slightly older man, and Liu, who obviously respected him, made them understand that he would now be their instructor. Liu smirked and said, "If you think I have been harsh, then you are in for a surprise. Your new instructor is ruthless. This is Qian, who is the best swordsman next to our Master. Do as you are told, and learn."

Both Talon and Reza, by now familiar with the etiquette, bowed to Liu's departing back.

"I'm glad he is going away. I was just about ready to smack him on the head and take his pigtail away from him," muttered Reza.

Talon stifled a laugh. "Now we have to start all over again, Brother," he said, and then bowed very low to the new man, who bowed back, but not so low. He tossed a wooden sword at each of them and walked onto the mats. He began to speak as he showed them how to hold the new swords. He explained to them that each movement was defense, attack or preparation for either, and he showed them the moves: at first slowly, but then he demonstrated how it should be done.

They didn't even see the motion of unsheathing his real sword. One moment he was still, the next his blade was in both hands and he was on guard. His body and the unsheathed sword were a blur of action and gleaming metal that ended with him back in the middle of the mat with the sword held in both hands, point up in the on guard position.

One day he barked a command at a student, who had been respectfully sitting on his heels on the edge of the mats next to a pot where a single stave of bamboo was sticking out of the middle to a height of four feet. The student leapt to his feet and placed it in front of Qian in the middle of the dojo. Qian touched the hilt of his sword and stood staring at the two inch thick pole in front of him. He shook his shoulders.

Then there was a blur of motion, the sword flashed, there was a tiny sound like a 'snick' and he was back on guard. For the space of almost two heartbeats the bamboo stayed upright, then a piece of the pole fell off onto the mat. Talon and Reza gasped. Qian's sword was back in its sheath

"Now *this*, I must master," Talon whispered to Reza, who nodded agreement in awed silence.

*****

Hsü was in fact very interested in their progress. He was keenly aware that he owed them his life and had wanted to find a way that was more than monetary to repay them. He had suspected all along that these two men were very good fighters. The reports Fuling brought back confirmed it. The instructors were impressed, and the Sensei Saiki was prepared, for a handsome sum, to spend time with the two foreigners and teach them.

Having witnessed their practices with bow and stick on board, Hsü knew that he was bestowing a gift upon them for which they might thank him one day. "Ask the Sensei to teach them the arts of fighting without weapons as well as the sword. I shall be happy to pay for the lessons," he instructed Fuling.

*****

Weeks passed and the pain continued, but as time went by both men began to master and feel the new skills they were being bludgeoned into learning. When they came back to the house and joined Fang for tea in the garden, they discussed these things with him, and he would nod his head and offer small encouraging comments. "I, too, went to that school, even after I had been to the monastery up north, because my master Hsü insisted. You will not regret it, although it is hard." He smiled and slurped his tea nosily from one of the eggshell-like cups he possessed. "We have a game which I will teach you to play when you feel ready," he told them.

After a few weeks Reza did remind him.

Fang nodded, then gave each a wooden sword, well balanced and exactly as long as their steel weapons in the dojo.

"You will stand in front of each other. The first to draw and touch the other on either the head or the neck is the winner," he told them. "I will demonstrate."

He had Talon stand in front of him, just within range of a sword blow. Reza was instructed to drop a silk cloth. As he did so, there was a blur as Fang drew his 'sword' and tapped Talon on the side of the head, sheathed his weapon and stood back. Talon had drawn his own weapon, but it was a long way from touching Fang, anywhere. He rubbed his head where Fang had tapped him, none too gently.

"This is how arguments can be settled on the street... very quickly," Fang rumbled. Reza and Talon looked at one another and then began to laugh. They found this very amusing, its value not lost on either of them.

Fang was pleased with the speed with which they learned the game. They could even, on occasion, tap him on either the neck or the temple when he joined in.

"You are making good progress," he told them one day. "To do this to an enemy is to demoralize his companions. One moment they have a live friend, the next his head is rolling on the ground."

"You honor us with your tea, Fang. I am glad we are friends," Reza told him.

Fang shifted. "It is because you brought my master and his son home, Reza. We owe you for saving their lives. Had it been otherwise I doubt if we would have met. The Chinese and the Arabs trade, but there is not much friendship there, and your religion is difficult for us to understand."

Talon had become aware of the tension between the two peoples. It was not that evident on the surface, but there were dark undercurrents. He had not been able to pin it down before, but Fang had opened a tiny window. They had found that this man, reticent and older than either of them by a number of years, possessed a keen insight, and he closely followed the street news and currents. Talon had always found that the information gathered from the street was of great use.

"You as a people follow the teaching of this wise man called Confucius, is that not so?" he asked.

"Yes, but many of us are Buddhists, and that has conflicts with the Confucius way of thinking. To us Chinese the approval of our ancestors is above and beyond anything else. It provides us with a deep sense of continuity.

"The differences between our religion and yours are profound, so when people from the Arab trading station try to impose Islam upon the local people, it does not go down well," Fang told them.

"Was there trouble in the past?" Reza asked.

Fang looked uncomfortable. "Yes," he said after some hesitation and a reflective sip of tea. "There was much trouble. But now there are laws, which are enforced, and the Arab traders are confined, as you know, and have to have a pass to go elsewhere in the city. It prevents aggravation. Each to his own customs, and still we can trade," he finished.

Their training continued, and finally they were allowed to bare the blades in practice.

Qian made them work very hard, especially at drawing the blade and striking, all in one flash of movement, with the inevitable result that on more than one occasion there were cuts inflicted and some blood flowed. Rav'an and Jannat complained that they were patching up their menfolk more than they should be.

"How is it that today it is Reza who has cut you, Talon? The other day Jannat complained that you had cut Reza!" Rav'an exclaimed as she cleaned the light cut on his arm. "Are you not supposed to be expert warriors and capable of avoiding this kind of silliness?" she asked him, her voice dripping with sarcasm. "What if there is a real accident and Rostam loses a father? Have you thought of that?" she demanded.

Talon winced yet again as she administered to his wound. "It is all to the good, my Love. Reza and I are very closely matched, and a cut or two is going to happen. You should see the kind of swords they use! They are magnificent! The steel is unlike any other steel I have ever seen; even the Verangians do not have this kind of metal for their swords!"

Rav'an rolled her eyes. "You men! You are never so happy as when you are fighting! Or talking about weapons! Who are these Verangians you are talking about, Talon?"

"Er... they are a people who live up in Byzantium, my Love. I'll tell you about them some day," Talon said. "At least we both still have all our fingers. There is one student there who lost two of them when he made a mistake."

"Your fingers! Talon, stop making jokes like that. I don't want to hear them!"

He sighed inwardly. "No more jokes, my Rav'an. I apologize. How is Rostam doing with that young boy Lun?"

"They have become friends, I think," she told him. "That is more than I can say for the wife of Hsü. She is as cold as a fish and will not speak to us. The older lady, however, is curious about us and uses Lihua to help translate. She asks many questions about our home land. It is difficult to explain to her where we three come from."

Talon nodded sympathetically.

Chapter Twenty-Four
A Visit to the Police

Hsü spent some time pondering who might have ordered the break in to his house; certainly someone who had influence enough to threaten Kee convincingly enough to suborn him. Not just anyone could do that. He decided that it might be worthwhile to go see the Chief of Police and let him know what had happened. It was his duty to report such things, especially if there were dead men involved.

He decided to take Talon with him on this particular visit, to show him yet more of the well-established administration of Guangzhou. Fang was ordered to stay at the villa and not to set foot outside it as long as they were under the threat of attack. His duty was to the Lady Meng and the household. He was also ordered to knock the guards into shape. Hsü had been unimpressed with their performance during the emergency. It should not have been up to the foreigners to defend the property. Even Lun was told that he should stay close to home for a while. He did not seem to mind missing school, Hsü noted.

Fuling was studying for his final exams, so he had to go to college, but he was ordered to keep his wits about him and not tarry on the way home. A guard was ordered to attend Fuling while he was outside the compound.

Hsü and Talon arrived at the offices of the Chief of Police just before noon, a time when Hsü was fairly certain that Hua Rong would be at his desk. They found themselves on the ground floor of a multi-storied building where people were in constant motion. Armed men, whom Talon took to be enforcers of the law, were coming and going. Some hauled along men in chains and dragged them, crying and weeping, out of sight; others, Hsü told him, were there seeking redress.

"This is where people come if there has been a robbery. Not everyone will, but many will report a crime, just as we are now," Hsü informed Talon.

Talon stared about him and wondered at the busy offices where dozens of people sat at desks and wrote down statements from others, who appeared to be telling their woes in detail and at length. He had never witnessed anything like it before.

Hsü was known, so it was not long before a harassed official came shuffling down the wide stairs at the back of the lobby, bowed low, and asked them very politely to follow him.

"If we had known you were coming, Lord Meng, I would have personally been here to greet you," he said as they walked up the stairs. The second floor was much quieter, although there seemed to Talon to be just as many people working at desks.

"Please wait here, Lord Meng," the man said politely, and disappeared into another room towards the front of the building.

They were served tea by a pretty girl who crouched almost at their feet as she poured. She examined Talon carefully as she got up and left.

"You are creating a bit of a stir here, Talon. Not many foreigners are seen dressed as you are," Hsü remarked in a dry tone. Talon had adopted the Chinese form of dress.

He had noticed the curious looks he received but by now was used to it, so he shrugged the comment off.

Within half an hour Hua Rong himself came bustling out of his office to greet them. "Lord Meng! It has been so very long since I last saw you! Welcome to my humble offices. Come, please, come in."

He bowed respectfully, as did Hsü, but not quite as low as Rong, and Talon followed suit, then they were ushered into Rong's offices. After polite greetings, Rong showed them to chairs and returned to his own chair on the other side of a large table that served as a desk. It was piled high with papers.

"We all heard with great relief that you had survived your arduous journey," Rong gushed. His glance flicked to Talon. "Would this be one of the people who helped you?" This time his eyes roved over Talon with mild disdain.

"It is a great pleasure to see you again too, Chief Hua," Hsü said, with as little sincerity as Rong. "Yes, this is Master Talon, who is the owner of the ship that brought me home safely." He waved his hand at Talon casually and smiled.

Rong steepled his fingers. "You have not been to this office before, Lord Meng. Might I ask what brings you here today?"

"I wish to report an attempted robbery," Hsü said, watching Rong carefully. Out of the corner of his eye he could see Talon, who could not understand very much of the conversation, so was looking around at the expensive furnishings. He was clearly impressed. Hsü knew that Talon was looking for anything unusual that might point to Rong being involved, although that was unlikely. Hsü's money was on Buwei.

Rong leaned forward, looking surprised. "What is that you say?" he demanded.

Hsü went on to tell him about the break in, making no mention of the fact that there had been one robber killed.

"I am here to do my duty and report the incident, although I do not expect much to come of it," he told Rong.

"Of course, of course!" Rong said. He was sweating a little; the day was very humid and it looked as thought it might rain later. He dabbed at his forehead with a small cloth.

"It is very hot today. I hope it will rain and clear the air," he said, and smiled crookedly. "Guangzhou is full of thieves and murderers. I have too few men at arms to police the entire city. It is a tragedy, and many innocents suffer."

"Was anything taken?" he asked, almost as an afterthought.

"A little box, a family heirloom," Hsü said carelessly, waving his hand dismissively. "It was full of small stones from one of my wife's ancestral graves in the northern regions before the Sung lost the territory," he informed Rong with relish. Did he detect a flash of something in those shifty eyes?

"Do you want my people to come and carry out an investigation?" Rong asked, looking hopeful.

Hsü smiled and said, "That will not be necessary, Chief. We have carried out our own investigation, but... it led nowhere. I feel that I have performed my civic duty by informing you."

Rong asked a few more questions, but he seemed so preoccupied that finally Hsü shifted, ready to leave. Rong hurriedly stood up from his table and saw them out of the office, talking all the time. "You must have lunch with me some time now that you are back, Lord Meng. I would love to hear all about your adventures." He gave Talon a perfunctory bow as they parted.

Hsü left the building with a strange look on his face. Talon, who could by now read him better, waited until they were well away from the building and walking slowly up the crowded street before he asked Hsü how the meeting had gone.

"Oh, I think it went very well, although I confess I am a little surprised."

"What do you mean?" Talon asked, as they dodged a rickshaw that came barreling down the main street.

"I think that the Chief of Police was involved! I would have thought it would be Buwei instead," Hsü mused.

"Tell me, what did you notice, about him, the man himself?" he asked Talon, who obligingly told him what he had observed.

When he came to mention the way Rong pitched his hands, Hsü stopped him.

"What was he wearing on his fingers? Do you remember, Talon?"

'There were two or three rings on each hand. On his right hand there was a big gold ring with a ruby in the middle. I can't remember what the others looked like, he had many rings on his fingers, but that one was distinctive."

"Ah ha!" Hsü exclaimed. "I saw that too. With little pearls around it?"

"I think so, yes," agreed Talon. "Hsü, what is going on here?" he asked, curious now.

"You would not have noticed, but when I mentioned a few things he looked nervous. There was... just that something, that isn't right. You know what I mean?"

Talon nodded. "It doesn't explain why you think he is involved," he said.

"I shall tell you when we get back to the villa. In the meantime, I want to take you to see a game of polo. You and Reza have talked about that game. You should see we also play the game here in China." He strode off up the hill towards the large park that surrounded the governor's palace.

*****

While they watched the game, which enthralled Talon, Hsü's mind was elsewhere; he listened with half an ear to the crowd and watched the polo with detachment while he continued to ponder the issue nagging him.

Then an idea occurred to him. What if the robbery had been about just a little more than the treasure? What if Rong, or perhaps Buwei, had assumed that while he was away they could easily obtain the treasure by whatever means, to take care of the paper promissory notes? Surely he could exploit that, he reasoned. He thought hard.

The last chucker came to an end and Talon turned to him, looking pleased.

"Do we play as you do in your country?' Hsü asked him.

"The game is universal; it is a tiny replica of war," Talon said, his eyes still reflecting the enthusiasm with which he had watched the way the players battled. "Do you think there is any substance to that legend you talked about while we were on the ship, Hsü?" he asked.

"There is often a smattering of truth behind legends. Come, we will go home. I want to talk to you on the way about something."

They fell into step and walked all the way down the slope to the main entrance to the city. Under normal circumstances, Hsü would have had to take a palanquin to prevent Fang's blood pressure from popping, but with Talon it was a simple thing to walk through the crowds without ostentation and talk at the same time.

Hsü explained the situation to Talon, who listened attentively. By the time they had reached the city gates Talon had been brought up to date on events.

"I have to admire the way you have manipulated the situation in your favor, Hsü," he said with a chuckle at one point. "You appear to have some nasty opponents for this race for the governorship. What will happen if you lose?"

Hsü stopped in mid stride to turn and face him. "My enemies will see to it that I and my family will perish. It will be as though we had never existed. The stakes are very high."

Talon stared hard at Hsü, who looked straight back at him. Talon was sobered by this information, the precious excitement of the game forgotten.

"You have to prove your suspicions. How do you propose to do that?" he asked.

They were standing on one of the several decorative stone bridges between the two great walls, looking down at the lilies and swans drifting on the still waters of the canal. It was relatively quiet here; the midday traffic had slowed in the sleepy early afternoon. No one paid them any attention. Hsü glanced up at the sky. It looked like it might rain.

"The box that they stole might still be around somewhere. There is the faintest possibility that it could still be in Rong's office. If it is not there, then I must discover where another man, whose name is Buwei, has his office, and see if it is there. I will have to ask Fang to find someone who can get into Rong's office and perhaps find some evidence. There is always the risk that it has been destroyed, of course, in which case I have a big problem."

Talon turned to face him. "Are you saying that you need someone to break into the office we were in today and find a box?"

Hsü nodded, looking unhappy. "Yes, but those kind of people are hard to find and do not come cheaply."

Talon stared out at the canal below, watching a sampan negotiate the narrow passage between two banks. The swans made way for the boat with ill grace, and then it was moving right underneath them. Suddenly Talon pushed Hsü sideways and pulled back sharply. A small knife flew by to rise into the air and then drop onto the stones with a metallic clatter.

Hsü had fallen to the stones and was about to say something indignant when he realized what had happened. Talon ran to the other side of the bridge just in time to see a man in blue cotton pants and jacket jump off the boat onto the bank and disappear into the labyrinth of streets. There was no way he could follow. Passersby who had seen him push Hsü out of the way and had not noticed the knife began to collect around him, gesticulating and shouting at him. The foreigner had struck one of their own! Talon was surrounded by indignant people all talking at once.

Surreptitiously picking up the knife by its handle and tucking it carefully into his sash, Hsü pushed his way through the small crowd and called for order. "He is with me and didn't mean to push me. All is well," he explained calmly. He took Talon's arm and hurried him away from the muttering people down the slope towards the other gate.

"Thank you for what you did, Talon. Your alertness may have saved my life," Hsü said, as he drew the knife out of his robes to show it to Talon. "Handle it carefully, as I think there might be poison on its blade."

Talon nodded and said, "I saw a man running away. He jumped off the sampan and disappeared into the streets alongside the canal. No way of catching him."

"That doesn't surprise me," Hsü said. "Well, now we know that they want me dead, so we must move quickly."

"What do you have in mind?" Talon asked.

"I need to go ahead and find that box and prove that at least one of my enemies has committed a crime. For that, they can go to jail, or worse."

"About that visit to the office," Talon said.

Hsü cocked an ear. He had been waiting for this. Not very long ago a message had come to him from the Dojo. The Sensei Saiki had written a very polite note saying that he wanted to talk.

They had met at the Dojo, and there Hsü had learned some interesting news.

"These men you have sent to me, they are not what they seem," Sensei Saiki had said in an aggrieved tone. Hsü had lifted an eyebrow.

"They might have had much to learn of the finer points of swordsmanship, but when we came to knives no one can touch them. I have also had my instructors teach them hand-to-hand, and they learned that faster than anyone could have guessed. Then you told me to teach them stealth. They make fools of my people!"

Hsü had blinked but he had nodded with agreement. These two men were indeed not what they seemed. "What do you want to do?" he'd asked.

"I will continue with the sword training and the hand-to-hand work, but it will be a waste of my time to continue with the other skills They can teach my people a thing or two," the Sensei had grumped. Hsü had smiled and sipped his tea.

Now Hsü waited.

"If you need someone to simply go to his office and retrieve the box, Reza and I could help with that," Talon volunteered.

Hsü pretended to be skeptical. "This is a very dangerous thing you are suggesting. Are you sure you know what you are doing?"

"Hmm, yes, I am sure. Reza and I can go tonight. It looks like it might be raining by then."

A nerve twitched at the side of Hsü's neck. The confidence that Talon displayed chilled him. He feared for anyone who tried to get between these two and their objective.

*****

Later that night, while it was still raining, Hsü had Fang escort Talon and Reza across the river and guide them to the offices of the Chief of Police. Because of the rain, the streets were almost deserted. The building was closed; the police in Guangzhou didn't work around the clock. It was a simple matter for them to evade the sleepy guards, who were sheltering from the weather, and then gain entry while Fang stayed out of sight in the shadows of the street to keep watch.

Once inside, Talon and Reza hastened past the deserted tables and chairs of the many clerks. They glided up the stairs to the second floor, which they also found empty and silent. They even heard a mouse scuttling away along the polished floor, it was so quiet. Talon led the way to where he remembered the office of Rong to be. They found it in darkness, only faintly illuminated through the windows by the lanterns in the street below. They began their search, their eyes accustomed to the dimness by now. Talon had explained in detail what they were looking for to Reza, who was eager for some excitement. He had come along willingly. They had not told Rav'an or Jannat about this particular foray.

While Reza kept watch at the door, Talon went from shelf to shelf, but he found nothing remotely like the box described. He was about to open a low level cabinet door when they heard a sound outside at the top of the stairs. Someone was moving stealthily towards them. Reza gave a small "psst" to warn Talon and slipped into the deeper shadows of the room. Talon vanished into an alcove, and they waited.

Someone arrived at the entrance to the doorway of the office and paused. The intruder was carrying a lantern that shed very little light, more of a thin beam, but sufficient for the intruder to see enough to move into the room. It quickly became apparent that this person was also searching for something. He lifted the lamp up to inspect the shelves, and then the dark figure began to concentrate on the cabinets very close to where Talon was hiding.

He opened a small door of the second cabinet and shone his beam into its interior. There was a soft exclamation, and an arm reached in and took out a small box. The person held it up for examination in the light and hissed with what sounded like satisfaction. Talon deemed it to be the right time to strike. He reached across the short gap and hammered the pommel of his knife onto the top of the intruder's head.

There was a muffled cry and the figure fell forward, unconscious, dropping the box and the light with a clatter. Talon snatched up the box and pushed it into his coat pocket. He set the lantern upright and waved to Reza that it was time to leave. He contemplated picking up the intruder and taking him with them, but decided that this might make evading the guards difficult. It was one thing for the two of them to move past the sleepy individuals; it would be tempting fate to have a body hanging over his shoulder as they left, especially if the man woke up and made a fuss.

It took a few minutes to get past the sentries, who had not moved since they entered the offices, and to make their way down the dark street to where Fang waited for them. He emerged from the shadows, seeming relieved to see them.

Later, after they had arrived back at the villa and were telling Hsü about the incident, he looked the box over while he listened.

"Yes, this is without doubt the box that was stolen," he told them thoughtfully. He showed them the broken seal and the damaged lid. It was empty of the stones he had placed inside.

"I wonder who it was who sent a Ninja to steal it from Rong," he mused.

"What is a Ninja?" Reza asked him.

"They are people from Nippon who are skilled at gaining entrance to secure places. Rather like you two." Hsü laughed quietly at their surprise.

Oh when will autumn moon and spring flowers end?
How many past events I've known?
The east wind buffeted my room again last night,
I cannot bear to remember the bright moon of the old
country.
The marble steps and carved balustrades must still be
there,
The people's rosy cheeks are all that's changed.
How much sorrow can one man have to bear?
As much as a river of spring water flowing east.

—Li Yu

Chapter Twenty-Five

Factions

Now that he was back from his visit to the palace, Hsü was kept very busy with the almost constant flow of visitors to his house. The news of his possible appointment had spread far and wide throughout Guangzhou. Some of the visitors pledged cash and produced it to prove their sincerity, while others promised cash but failed to show up with any. All of them kept him informed as to the state of the city. Since his departure his enemies had been busy. Now that he was back, his supporters looked to him for help. Recently the news had been disturbing.

Some of the merchants who were known to be friendly to him had been harassed in the streets, their palanquins pushed over and the bearers beaten up. In one case there were more serious injuries. To a man they were sure the threats and attacks came from Buwei and his gangs of thugs. The gangs were going to do his bidding and side with whomsoever he told them to, but no one was quite sure who Buwei was supporting; as he did not qualify it had to be someone else.

The rumor was going around that it was Hua Rong, the Chief of Police, which everyone considered to be an absurd idea. Hsü suspected that they didn't want to face the nightmarish prospect of a thoroughly corrupt police chief becoming the governor of Guangzhou. Rong was a very ambitious man, but he was also cunning and would pretend to be disinterested in the office while doing all he could to further his aims.

One blustery wet day Hsü's brother-in-law, Wong Cheng Kean, came to visit and told of an incident that had occurred in the streets while Hsü had been away.

"I was in my palanquin when there was a disturbance ahead up the road, and before I knew it I found myself on hands and knees in the dirt with a ruffian standing over me brandishing a cudgel and threatening me!" he whined. "Right in the middle of the city! People only came to my aid when the hoodlums had left!"

"What did he say?" Hsü asked, his mind's eye seeing his brother-in-law scrabbling around on the ground in an undignified manner. If it had not been so serious he might have been amused: the man was obsessed with his dignity.

"He told me that I should not support you, Hsü, that my *family* would be next." Kean was wringing his hands. His sister Meilin passed him a cotton cloth with an expression of distaste on her normally impassive face. He wiped his eyes and then looked appealingly to Hsü. "What am I to do?" he all but wailed.

"You should reconsider what you are doing, Hsü," he continued. "Things are getting very ugly. Before long there might be loss of life, and then what will we all do?"

"Did he say anything else?" Hsü asked, barely controlling his disgust. There had already been lives lost.

"He told me that my family would suffer if anyone found out that I had paid you money towards the position," Kean bleated.

"But it's too late! I have already done that! You should pull out of the race; it's too dangerous for us all."

Meilin looked startled and then sent a frightened look at Hsü.

Hsü's face tightened as he leaned over the table towards his brother-in-law and almost snarled, "You are beginning to disappoint me, Bother-in-law," He paused to let the insult sink in. "If I do not try for this post, then who will?" He raised his voice an octave. "Tell me that! Who? Any one of your gaggle of fat, opium-smoking merchant friends? I don't think so! Firstly you come to me all smiles and simper that the post of governor is right for me, and now it's 'Oh dear me, it's much too dangerous, now we have to get out'!" He paused to glare at their white faces.

"Now let me tell *you* something. Its too late for that! Rong and his friends, both at the palace and in the gutters of this city, Buwei among them, will control the city even more than they do now! You will all be crawling around on your knees trying to lick the shit off his boots in order not to loose your fortunes and your heads, and your families will be hostages to his whims. It will be a disaster all round," he continued in a more controlled manner.

"Did you see the smoke yesterday? Yet another godown has gone up in flames in the dockyard. I suspect it was Rong's doing, because the Arabs will now be desperate to sell off their cargoes at a loss, and they will be eager to get out of Guangzhou as soon as they can. It is short-sighted and stupid to treat them so, for the word will go out and they will cease to come here. Then what will we do?" He raised his voice. "I am resolved to change that if I am made governor. Rong is leaving his mark on everything he touches, and it stinks of shit!"

Kean drank down his rice wine in one gulp. "There's no need to be vulgar," he objected feebly. "How can we protect ourselves in the meantime?" he asked. "The gangs on the streets are harassing anyone they think might be associated with you."

His tone becoming just a shade truculent; he had drunk too much wine.

Hsü sighed and sipped his own drink to allow himself a few moments to calm down. "I can talk to some friends of mine who will provide you with an escort. Give me a day, and they will come to your house. They will bear a letter from me. Don't let anyone in unless they produce this letter. They are expert swords men and will be able to deal with any of the thugs out there harassing you and the other merchants. You can't trust many people these days, but these you can."

He continued with words of encouragement and promised that he would remember favors done and support offered, should he gain the position. Kean left not long afterwards in his palanquin, too drunk to think.

Meilin watched her brother go out the door, then asked Hsü, "Do you really think you can win against these odds, Husband? You know what they will do to us if you fail?" She was ashen with fear.

Hsü shook his head. "I do not know if I can win, and don't remind me of the penalty of failure, Meilin. The stones are now on the board. There is no going back." He felt a mild disgust at his wife and her brother. They had been eager enough before when their greed drove them, not taking into account the high stakes of the game. Now that they were being intimidated, their thin veneer of courage had deserted them. Suddenly he felt very tired and longed to be in Lihua's arms.

*****

Hua Rong and Buwei were seated upstairs in a private room, away from the clamor and noise of the clientele on the ground floor. They had started with fish, *Hero's Three in One:* fried sea bass with finely shredded ham, white radishes, and a mixture of soy and garlic, with hot bean paste on top, which was a favorite of Buwei's. They were drinking wine while they waited for Prefect Wu po-ku to join them. Rong had been drinking heavily. Buwei tucked into the food to the point where it precluded any kind of conversation until he had finished.

Rong gulped another bowlful of the fierce *Moa-T'ai*, a flavored rice wine with a kick to it. It was a favorite of the upper classes. He poured himself yet another as he watched Buwei slobbering over the food on the low table. Buwei's big nose seemed to be sniffing the food before he snapped it up with his busy chop sticks. The spectacle, coupled with the leaden ache in his gut, took Rong's appetite away.

Buwei spoke with his mouth full of fish. "So, your attempt to get the treasure, if that is what it was, failed. Is that what you are telling me?" he grumped, then opened his mouth to take in yet more food. Rong thought he was going to be sick.

"Well, yes. They did get in and out with a box." He wasn't going to mention the man who died and had subsequently shown up in the Pearl River. "However, they got hold of the wrong item, which is embarrassing," he muttered. Rong hated having to lose face like this, but he now desperately needed Buwei's help. He knew Buwei would make him pay for it.

Buwei gave Rong a speculative look. He knew all about the 'box' that had rattled, presumably with the gems inside. He had sent his man to Rong's office on the assumption that the treasure would be in the box. The man had reported back with a big gash on his head, and the box he had found in a cupboard had vanished by the time he woke up and escaped. Buwei had not been pleased. At this moment, he was as frustrated as Rong. He took a long swig of his wine.

"Are you saying that your people did not obtain the right container?" His look was incredulous and withering at the same time.

Rong looked as though he was going to choke with embarrassment. "It was a box with some ancestral stones inside."

"I hope you got rid of those incompetents," Buwei grunted through a mouth full of boiled clams with soy sauce, some of which dribbled down his chin.

Rong nodded, averting his eyes. Lin had taken care of the second man. He, too, would show up in the river, but further down stream, well away from the port itself. No one would be the wiser.

"That's a great pity," Buwei mused. "We needed it to finance our little endeavor. Your paper money won't be any use if Hsü gets in with his gems. His merchant friends will help him with silver, and bribes will talk, if they are real and not paper. This will set the slimy administrators thinking badly of you. What exactly is this 'treasure' of Hsü's, anyway?" he demanded as he took a swig of *Moa-T'ai*. "It is gems and things like that, isn't it?"

"The servant who told me about it said that one of the maids had caught a glimpse of it: a box full of sapphires and rubies. Maybe even some diamonds," Rong told him. Where was that man, Kee? He had disappeared off the face of the earth. Lin could tell Rong nothing.

Buwei was very thoughtful after that. Then he said, "You know that Hsü has been to the palace in Hangzhou, but did you know that he was a very busy man while there?"

Rong nodded. "I know. Curse his ancestors, he was buying votes."

"Not all," Buwei said. "In fact, I have spent quite a bit of silver on one of the Administrators, who is wavering. He told me he would reconsider, but also suggested that one way to get Hsü out of the picture is to have him sent on another mission."

Rong stared at him with slightly bleary eyes. "A mission?" he enquired.

"Yes! Will you stop biting your nails? Is the food so bad that you have to eat yourself?" Buwei snapped, with his mouth so full a spray of food flew onto the table cloth.

Rong hurriedly put his hand out of sight and reached for the cup instead. Buwei shook his head in disgust and continued. "The annual payment of Tribute? Remember that? It is due, and it is Guangzhou's turn this year to provide the bulk of the cargo."

Rong knew all about the tribute. It was something that he as Chief of Police was expected to organize, with the assistance of the senior officer in charge of the convoy that would go up to the border to meet with the dreaded Mongols.

"Who is the officer in charge of the convoy this year?" Buwei probed.

"General Yang Hsün is the man who will lead the military contingent. He is not someone we can bribe. General Hayan Zhuo can't go, because he is the resident officer in charge of the province. I wish we could get rid of both of them; Zhuo in particular is going to be a nuisance." Rong considered Buwie's suggestion.

"Hsü might never return from the journey, should we be able to get someone into the group who can arrange for an accident," Rong mused. He wondered if he could possibly find some form of leverage to persuade the general enough to take care of that problem. His spies might be able to find something but it had to be soon. Hsü was leading a charmed life. Lin had confessed that the attempt on the bridge had been thwarted by the damned foreigner. Rong had been ready to strangle his henchman. Lin was now adamant that the foreigner was a danger. The speed of his reactions had surprised him.

Buwei nodded approval, and then thought for a moment. "In order for us to secure those votes in the palace, we have to have something to back up the paper money. You have made promises with those checks, but we don't have enough to support them when they are called in, unless we go on a robbing , and the barracudas in the palace would be sure to follow up on that. We have to gain access to Hsü's gems. Those palace people are insatiable; I'm appalled at how corrupt they are."

Rong glanced up. It was difficult to tell when Buwei was making a joke; either way, he was acutely aware of the problem. It was one reason his stomach was aching. He thought he might be coming down with an ulcer, it was so painful. If he could not back the paper with substance it would be considered a crime; he could be charged, and his future would become very precarious. He dabbed his forehead with a fine cotton cloth. "What are you suggesting?"

"We have to obtain the treasure by whatever means possible. This time I shall send my own men. You should have come to me before, and then perhaps we wouldn't have had this debacle," Buwei sneered.

Rong bit back an angry retort. He needed Buwei more than ever now, and it wouldn't do to annoy him. Losing face, while grave, was nothing when placed against the big picture, and that did not include Buwei in the final analysis.

"Word has come to my attention that your men are busy on the streets," he said to change the subject. Buwei nodded and shoveled more food into his mouth.

"Yes, you don't object do you? They are, after all, working for us towards our mutual objective," Buwei smirked. "A few palanquins tipped over here and there can be very helpful at deterring would-be supporters of Hsü. It is just as important to make sure he has no financial help as it is something those morons in the Palace will watch for. They will be sensitive to the lack of support here in the city once they are made aware of it, and that could sway the Emperor. They don't like having unpopular officials in high places, nor do they like the idea of unrest. Anything for the sake of tranquility," he chuckled.

Rong had been informed that more than just a few palanquins had been tipped over, but he had to agree, Buwei's methods might prove to be effective. As long as he was not seen to be involved in this overt intimidation, it really didn't matter.

They were interrupted by the arrival of Wu po-ku. The Academic Prefect was dressed in the height of official fashion, full, flowing dark silk robes and a small hat of office tied to his greying hair. He minced into the room and bowed just low enough to show respect, but in such a way as to make it plain that he was the chief functionary here.

They greeted him, and then the discussion came around to the health of the governor.

"The physicians don't think he will last for another month," Wu po-ku informed them. "What have you two been discussing?" he enquired with a look of distain at the mess on the table. He accepted a cup of warm wine from the obsequious servant who had been hovering about.

"We are discussing Lord Meng, who is endangering us with his bid for the governor's office," Buwei said through a mouthful of shrimp.

Rong went on to outline their new scheme to get Hsü taken out of the city. He deliberately left out the plan to obtain the elusive box of jewels. Wu po-ku didn't need to know about that. Rong noticed that Buwei was watching him with his beady black eyes.

Wu gave no indication that he knew anything about the treasure and seemed to approve of the plan to get Hsü removed from the city. He sipped his *Moa-T'ai* and averted his eyes from the battle with the food going on in front of him.

"We wondered if there might be a chance that the General in charge of the convoy could be bribed to take care of... things," Rong finished.

"I don't think so. General Yang Hsün is from the old school, too locked into the military world with nothing much else in between his ears." Wu spoke contemptuously. "We will have to find another way. However, I can certainly influence the people in charge of the mission and get them to have Lord Meng assigned."

Rong breathed a small sigh of relief. Wu was going to get involved. That meant that Rong might be able to gain some kind of leverage over him, which would be useful in the future. Wu was so much more refined than Buwei, who Rong considered to be somewhat of a loose elephant in a small compound.

"How do you propose to ensure that he doesn't come back?" Buwei demanded.

Wu looked over at Buwei with barely disguised disgust. The man lived like a pig, and his operations were crude and heavy-handed.

"I'll take care of this little problem myself," he assured them. "First I think it is time to look into the loyalties of the other administrators in the palace and the Examination house. I know several of the administrators would like to see a man like Hsü running the province."

"With the kind of experience you can offer that would be absurd." Rong flattered him.

Wu glanced over at Rong. He knew full well that Rong was dangerous but would support him if he turned a blind eye to the nefarious goings on with the incoming trade goods. He was quite sure that Rong had made himself rich by bullying the Arab merchants. He would tolerate that, as long as he was given a share. "I agree I have the experience, but I also know the Governor sent a letter of commendation to the most senior Prefect at the Emperor's Palace. It is not good news for our cause."

"Why is that?" Buwei mumbled through a mouthful. He sucked on a prawn.

"He recommended Hsü for the position after he dies," Wu said bluntly.

"Did you intercept it?" Rong asked nervously.

Wu flicked a piece of dirt off his immaculately clean robe. "Of course I did," he murmured. "The letter will never arrive." He suddenly noticed the waiter hovering nearby.

"Bring me a warm cup of wine, and hurry up about it. Then leave us," he told the nervous looking boy. He looked up at the other two. "Should he be allowed to stay in the room when we are talking about these things?" he demanded.

Rong looked guilty. "I hadn't thought of that," he said with a slight slur to his voice. 'He is always here when we come to eat."

"Then you need to be more careful," Wu admonished him.

*****

Shou-cheh sent word to Hsü that he needed to see him as soon as possible. The same meeting place would do.

Hsü left that evening on foot, accompanied by Fang. Talon and Reza observed the departure, and on impulse both decided to follow them.

"Its not that I don't trust him but well... I don't trust him." Reza said.

Talon went along for entirely different reasons. He did trust Hsü, but didn't think that Fang on his own might be enough with the number of enemies that their host appeared to have accumulated.

The two men had to be very careful, as they knew that Fang had eyes in the back of his head and would not hesitate to turn on them and attack should he become aware of their presence. In the dark he might not realize that they were his friends: his overriding rule was the protection of his master.

Hsü and Fang arrived at the inn without incident and went into the smoke-laden room alert to any danger. They located Shou-cheh in a dark corner with a hood covering his face and a small jar of wine in front of him.

As before, Hsü left Fang at the doorway and crossed the room to seat himself opposite Shou-cheh, who glanced up at him warily. It was clear that he had had a couple of cups while waiting. His normally pale features were flushed.

"Ah, there you are, Lord Meng."

"What is it that required me to be abroad in the dark of the night? You know it is dangerous for me to be out at this late hour," Hsü remarked.

"My spies tell me that there is a little group of men who want to get rid of you, Lord Meng," Shou-cheh said without preamble. Gone was the usual impassive administrator's face which he wore habitually in the palace.

"You seem worried my friend," Hsü said, peering at him.

"I am, Lord Meng. You should be very careful." He named Rong and Buwei, and then Wu po-ku as being suspect.

Hsü sat back and stared at Shou-cheh. "Well, I had guessed that. What else is new?'

"I don't know the where and the when they will attempt to do this, Lord Meng, but you must be very careful. Also..." he hesitated.

"What is it?" Hsü demanded.

"Wu po ku has stirred a witch hunt in the palace. The word is, he is so sure of himself that he is looking for your supporters within the ranks of the administrators, and he will dismiss them from their position in the palace."

"Ah."

"It will not take him long to find me if I am not very careful from now on," Shou-cheh said. He sounded frightened.

"Do you need protection?"

"Not yet, but it might come to that. If I am dismissed then it will be very dangerous for me. I saw Wu come into the palace, and as he walked past me he looked my way. It was not a friendly look. I think I will be on his list of people to be dismissed, or worse, should he become governor."

"I understand," Hsü sighed. It was going to be a rough road from here on. Shou-cheh was committed to him but could not be asked to sacrifice his own life, nor the well being of his family.

"You need to lie low. I can manage for the time being. Just send a messenger when it becomes necessary to inform me of any developments, but take care."

Shou-cheh nodded then ducked his head lower as Hsü got up and headed towards the door.

Hsü and Fang made their way warily down the darkened and nearly deserted streets, then walked through the two gates of the inner city without mishap. They reached the quayside where the boats were waiting. Most of the oarsmen were asleep on their sampans, but a few were awake.

Fang had just waved one over and they were watching him sculling towards them when they both heard the patter of several pairs of running feet behind them. Both men whirled and saw dark figures that had detached themselves from the darkness of one of the narrow streets and were racing towards them. The attackers brandished spears and long swords, which gleamed in the starlight. Without a word both Hsü and Fang whipped out their swords and went on guard. They were badly outnumbered and the river behind them offered no retreat. The silence of the attackers would have unnerved less experienced men than Hsü and Fang.

The assassins apparently planned to drive them into the water, where they could be easily picked off by spears or arrows, but Fang gave a ferocious yell and rushed straight at them instead. His sword flashed this way and that, rasping against other swords and parrying stabbing spears. But he also made contact with flesh, because the eerie silence kept by the assailants was now broken by yelps of pain. The attackers drew back, surprised at the vigor of their would-be victims.

Hsü realized that a counter attack was all they had left; he, too, gave a great shout and rushed into the fray. His sword flashed and struck at the bristling array of weapons, and alongside Fang he parried and struck, stabbing and yelling at the dark figures in front of him. He counted six men, but one was already down, writhing in agony from a stab inflicted by Fang, who whirled and struck like a devil gone mad.

It could only have been a few seconds before another force appeared from behind the attackers. Two men emerged from the darkened street and threw themselves into the battle with yells of their own, but this time Talon was shouting at Fang and Hsü that he and Reza were there to help and not to mistake them for the enemy.

It was not long before two more figures lay on the stones of the quayside. The remainder hesitated, whereupon another died from a blow delivered by the thoroughly berserk Fang. The other two scampered off as fast as their legs would carry them.

In the sudden quiet broken only by a groan from one of the wounded and the distant patter of running feet, the four men peered at one another in the darkness.

"Talon? What are you doing here?" Hsü gasped.

"Keeping an eye on your back," Talon responded. He wiped his blade with a cloth and said, "We should leave, quickly."

Hsü agreed; time for questions later. He beckoned to one of the boats and waved it over to them. "We should take that boat. Get aboard."

He turned to Fang and said something. Fang kicked over the man who was had been wounded, then shook his head. Hsü muttered what sounded like a curse.

"That man is dead. We won't be able to find out who is responsible for this tonight."

They crowded hastily onto the boat, and at a sharp command from Hsü the fearful boatman pushed them off and sculled them rapidly out into the darkness of the river. Just in time; soon there were lights showing and shouts from the quayside.

"That was close," Hsü said to Talon and Reza. Fang stayed with the boatman at back of the sampan, watching the lights to make sure no one followed them.

"You looked as though you were able to deal with those offal," Reza replied with a grin; he appeared to have relaxed his opinion of Hsü somewhat. He wiped his blade carefully with a cloth, then sheathed it with a snap.

"I think it would have been a very near thing, despite the energetic efforts of Fang. I owe you my thanks for arriving when you did. Incidentally, how did you happen to be there? "

Talon hesitated. "We saw you leave and were concerned; it was late, and you only had Fang. It has been clear for some time that you are in danger, and at night it is doubly so, as we just found out. Fang is a formidable warrior and a worthy guardian, but we also have a vested interest in your safety, Hsü. Thus we followed you, just to make sure."

It was Hsü's turn to chuckle. "Well, your instincts were right, and we certainly would have been in trouble had you not been there. This has raised the stakes even more, it would seem."

"What have you learned?" Talon asked.

"That I have many undeclared enemies in the city and in the palace who want me dead, and that they will stop at nothing to see that done."

'Then we must thwart them at every turn," Reza said, as their boat arrived at the other side of the river.

*****

The next day Hsü sought Talon out and invited him for a walk. This was not the first time they had gone for private walks in Hsü's gardens. Since he came back from the Palace, Talon's host had seemingly decided to trust Talon with his innermost thoughts.

Today, while they listened with half an ear to the sounds from the stables and the chatter of the servants, they discussed the previous night's events.

Talon explained, "We are now quite concerned about the safety of everyone in the compound. Even before the foiled intrusion, we had posted our own guards because we don't fully trust the soldiers at the gates. I hope you understand; we have to protect our own."

Hsü nodded. "I agree with your sense of caution, Talon, and neither I nor Fang can find fault with your being where you were when those thugs came at us. I am just glad that they didn't try inside the City, as we would have been on our own then. It might have turned out very differently."

Talon agreed. "We didn't know where you had gone, but we were sure that you would come back to the passing boats. As it turned out, it was a good idea to wait."

"My brother-in-law is so afraid, and so is my wife!" Hsü said. He sounded exasperated.

Talon's expression bore a question.

"He came yesterday and had the gall to beg me to withdraw from the governor's race." Hsü explained. He looked up at the sky, which was beginning to cloud over. "It's much too late for that! To withdraw would be tantamount to cowardice and a death sentence. Besides, it wouldn't stop these people. I told him so."

"What did he have to say to that?" Talon had already grasped the risk to all of them, but now Hsü was clarifying the danger.

"He looked like a centipede that had just had a pin thrust into his back! He wriggled so hard he nearly fell off his chair. I didn't give him any room for more excuses and sent him home loaded with wine!" Hsü grinned at the memory

Chapter Twenty-Six
The Dragon's Breath

The next week a courier arrived from the palace of Hangzhou with a letter for Hsü.

When he read the message he became livid with rage. He turned away from the messenger to hide his expression, thinking furiously. The missive, which was from Ts'ao, was very apologetic. There was, however, nothing Ts'ao could do but to counsel Hsü to make the best of it. He emphasized that been commanded by the Emperor himself to go on a perilous mission was an honor; he would be rewarded appropriately, should he complete it successfully. The papers with the Emperor's orders would be forthcoming. Hsü decided that he should inform Talon, as the news would affect them all.

He barely noticed Fuling walk by with his arms full of books and a haggard look on his face from all the nighttime study. The exams were only a few weeks away. He waved encouragement to his son but was too distracted to do more.

When Talon arrived with Reza, he explained the situation.

"I am ordered to go north. This is an expedition that happens once a year," he told them. Both men remarked that the normally imperturbable Hsü was unusually upset.

"The palace, in its infinite wisdom, has decided that in view of my successful return to China after my ambassadorial duties in India and my great *service* to the Emperor, I should be *honored* with the task of escorting the annual tribute to the Mongols!" His voice dripped sarcasm.

They stared at him, uncomprehending.

"Please do not repeat this to anyone, but I must tell you that this empire is weak. Every year we pay off the Mongols with a huge tribute of silk and silver ingots. It is a thankless task, and very often costs the Chinese delegation a life or two, because the Mongol barbarians cause trouble. No one volunteers for the task, and so they appoint a different leader each time. He has to endure not only a long journey but the scorn of our enemies when they arrive to take delivery of the goods."

"Why you?" Talon asked. "Are there not many others at the palace who could do this work?"

Hsü shook his head. "While I am convinced that my enemies are behind this, most of the tribute will be coming from Guangzhou this year. It is done by rotation, and, alas, it is our turn to provide the bulk of the tribute. All year long it is accumulated in warehouses in various cities, including Guangzhou, until the command from the palace arrives. Then it is transported to the border and handed over."

He shook the piece of paper violently. "They have turned the tables on me, Talon," he grated. "I cannot refuse a command from the Emperor!"

"How long will it take to deliver the tribute, as you called it," Reza asked.

"A month there and back, perhaps even longer. In the meantime, my enemies will foment much mischief while I am away." Hsü stamped his foot.

"Why do your people pay this tribute?" Talon asked him, puzzled.

"Because our illustrious leaders in the palace, who advise our great Emperor, are weak and afraid," Hsü said with contempt in his voice.

"Why not deny the Mongols, whom you say are barbarians, and fight them with your greater armies?" Talon persisted.

Hsü shook his head with a rueful grimace. "This dynasty, and indeed the Tang dynasty before the Sung, has been afraid of military officers of any talent reaching high positions. They fear they will go from there to threatening the throne. Why, they have even executed generals who were successful in battle, can you imagine that?"

Talon shook his head in disbelief. "If you do not have a strong military, how can you defend yourselves from outside enemies?" he asked. He had Byzantium in mind as he spoke.

Hsü nearly spat. "You are, of course, quite right, but they are more afraid of a palace coup than of those barbaric tribesmen in the North! It is utterly astonishing to me, but these highly educated imbeciles in the palace would rather try to pay them off than make a determined effort to destroy them."

"I would like to go with you to the North," Talon said abruptly.

Hsü stared at him. "What about your family?" he asked.

Reza now interjected. "I know what Talon wants. He wants to see a dragon. That is fine, but I shall stay. One of us has to, Brother," he said turning to Talon with a grin.

Hsü nodded slowly as he considered this offer. "Very well, but I shall also leave Fang with you, Reza. He knows where to get help should you need it. It is me they are after, not my family, so and I do not anticipate trouble here. Besides," he smiled for the first time, "I will have Talon here, who has already demonstrated his abilities to me. I shall be safe."

*****

That evening the two families sat down to supper together. By now the visitors could hold halting conversations, assisted by Lihua. Lady Meng Lanfen was cordial and enjoyed talking to Rav'an; she asked many questions, but also shared gossip, which Rav'an took as a compliment.

Rav'an or Jannat would ask her what they were eating, and it would amuse her to tell them of the food.

"Today we are eating rice and duck meat in lotus leaves. Over there by the boys is a bowl of *Sha He* noodles with leeks. Here is pork with cashew nuts," she pointed. "Perhaps you should not eat that?"

"Delicious!" exclaimed Jannat, who didn't give a fig for the rules any more. She loved the Chinese food.

"What is that, Lady Meng?" Rostam piped up in Cantonese, pointing at a bowl.

"Those are dragon's eyes." She smiled at him.

Rostam was awed. "Are they *real* dragon's eyes?" he asked, his own eyes nearly starting from his head.

"Well... no." Then she happened to glance at Hsü. She smiled. "Not these ones, but it is possible sometimes to find the real ones in the market, I believe." Fuling rolled his eyes at his grandmother. The entire family knew about Talon's great desire to see a dragon.

"And those are stuffed pears. Lun, you should help Rostam to have some and not only eat pastries. I have been watching you."

Lun grinned sheepishly and did as he was told.

The list of foods went on in bewildering detail. Talon never ceased to be amazed by what the cook produced, and indeed by the entire Chinese diet, which seemed to include anything that moved or crawled. He could not fault the taste and variety, however, remembering food they had had to eat while sailing.

Hsü conducted an intense conversation with his wife and elder son during the meal. Talon presumed that he was talking about the impending trip.

He and his own family had discussed the matter at the guest house before supper that evening. Rav'an was not happy about it, but she knew that Talon was becoming restless, so she knew better than to prevent his leaving. She just told him sternly to not get into trouble and come back to them. She and Jannat were happy enough to go on visiting temples and parks with Lihua. Rav'an never forgot that one day they would have to leave, and she was preparing. She had her eyes on many works of art, carvings and silk patterns that she knew would sell well in Oman. Lihua had also taken her on numerous occasions to the medicine shop, where Rav'an had asked the owner so many questions he looked exhausted by the time they left with the items they had purchased.

Talon and Reza had another discussion later that night.

"There is something going on that I don't like, Brother," Talon said quietly.

Reza knew what he meant. "If Fang is being left behind, then I need to be vigilant, Talon. He is Hsü's bodyguard; to leave him here means that our host is very worried, no matter what he says. I don't like that they are trying to kill him, either. You might need to be on your guard while traveling with him. Be careful."

"Should I stay then?" Talon asked him.

Reza thought about it, and then shook his head. "One of us needs to protect Hsü while he is on his journey. It doesn't matter who, and I think that with Fang here with me, we will be fine, Talon. Go and find that dragon."

*****

Two weeks later, Talon was looking back at a baggage train that wound its way along the side of the mountain. Many hundreds of feet below them raged a torrent as the river poured through a gap in the hills, while above them the pointed mountain wore a top knot of stunted trees. There were fifty horses and ten camels, all of them laden with either bales of silk or boxes of silver ingots with the chop of the Emperor stamped into them. The remainder of the pack animals carried the baggage of the escort. Hsü had told him that the Mongols stipulated stamped silver, as it represented the treasury of the Emperor, hence was pure. There were several carts that carried some interesting devices that Hsü told him were Erupters. He used the Chinese name, *'bai zu lian zhu pao'*, and Talon had had to work hard to try and understand what that meant.

"They hurl flames and stones or iron balls great distances," Hsü had told him.

"What is the purpose of bringing them with us now?" Talon had asked.

"This is part of the 'flame powder' that we possess in China. It has acted as a deterrent to the Mongols. The reason we bring them is that they fear these devices. We also make hollow balls of iron, which we fill with the powder and fire at the enemy. They explode and cause panic and death to all nearby," Hsü boasted. Talon couldn't wait to see one being used.

Talon was on a bay gelding that he was still getting to know. Ahead of him were one hundred men at arms, while the rear guard consisted of the camp followers and fifty more guards. All the soldiers were magnificently accoutered, decked out in elaborate plates of armor that covered them from their feet to the outrageously elaborate helmets on their heads.

Each soldier carried a bow, a quiver, two spears, long swords, numerous knives around their persons, and wore cloaks with the emblem of their leader embossed on the fabric. Their horses were of the very best. The General and his officers wore even more gaudy outfits of picturesque armor, incredibly shaped helmets, and gleaming weaponry. The entire company of armed men seemed overdressed to Talon.

Talon had chosen to wear his chain mail, which had drawn some attention, and had taken a cloak with him to protect him from the weather, which was still occasionally wet. He now sported a sword of the kind that he'd first encountered at the

Dojo. He also had his bow and arrows in a holder under his left thigh. His helmet of steel hung from the pommel of the saddle. His skill with a bow had drawn much attention and admiration from these men. While the Chinese had some very skilled archers, who provided the small army with meat from the hunt, none could bring down a flying pigeon at thirty paces while seated on a horse; and the General happened to like roasted pigeon whenever he could get it.

Hsü rode next to him, wearing a simpler form of armor than the General, and he carried only his sword, the one he had brought aboard those long months ago. Talon, now that he knew what he was looking for, saw that the scabbard was beautifully inlaid with gold filigree and the blade was of the finest. He wanted to have one like that and had asked Hsü as to where he could buy one. Hsü had told him to be patient, and that he would help locate one when they returned to Guangzhou.

The journey thus far had been an experience that Talon could not have imagined in his wildest dreams. He had never been through such a varied and strange countryside. They passed through flat valleys where rice was grown in abundance and buffaloes pulled plows in the knee deep water; they came to terraces that climbed in serried ranks up the sides of the low hills; then they left the emerald green of the terraces and climbed narrow tracks that led into mountains that seemed to go straight up, steeper than any mountain he remembered in Persia, but not as high; they were of crumbled stone that gleamed white where they were bare, but their sides were most often clad in stunted trees, now tinged with yellow and red to mark the change of the season to autumn.

Just when he thought he had seen the strangest and most beautiful sights that nature could provide, they crested the passes, and before them in the distance were mountains whose peaks wore a mantle of vapor which the wind tore into white tendrils, and valleys shrouded in mist from rain and waterfalls.

As they rode along high plateaux overlooking impossibly deep gorges, Hsü would point out immense openings in the cliffs far below and suggest, with a perfectly straight face, that these might once have been the lairs of dragons. It only served to whet Talon's appetite for a glimpse of one of these elusive creatures.

Villages and small towns clung to the sides of these strange mountains, built on earthen terraces that appeared ready to tumble into the fast moving waters of the numerous rivers. The locals either travelled by boat or crossed over by stone bridges, or less substantial constructions of vegetable fiber. The people who lived in these areas were mostly peasants who seemed wary of strangers and gave the travelers a wide berth as they marched by. Those who could not hide would crouch, nose down in the dirt, while the entourage rode by.

The boat trips, of which there had been several because of the vast number of lakes and rivers, had proved to be an organizational nightmare. Hsü was nominally in charge, so if fell upon him to negotiate with the Prefects of towns and village headsmen for accommodation and supplies, and to dicker with boat men to get his small army from one place to another with the minimum of delay.

They had been very much at the mercy of the winds and weather while traveling along the rivers; if a river was in spate because of a storm further upstream, or if the wind was blowing against them, it caused further delays. However, when the winds and elements were with them, they could make far better progress than on land.

Eventually they arrived at the banks of an enormous lake called Dongting. There Hsü pointed out fishing boats where cormorants sat right next to the men. "They train the birds to catch fish," he told a skeptical Talon.

"How do they stop them from eating the fish?" he asked.

"Watch, see how they tie a string around their necks? It is to prevent them from swallowing what they catch."

As he spoke, a cormorant rose out of the water and quite comfortably squatted on the side of the boat. The fisherman took hold of the bird and relieved it of the fish half stuck in its gullet, then released the bird, which joined three others as though waiting its turn. The man gave it a tidbit, which it gulped down, and then it tried to steal one of the fish in the open basket, receiving a slap on its head for its pains. Talon grinned at the sight. Was there no end to the ingenuity of these people?

Finally Hsü told him with evident relief that they were about seven days from their destination. Siang Jang was a town located just inside the Sung territory on a huge river called the Yangzi. The small army embarked in a flotilla of boats and, taking their animals with them, sailed across the lake.

Talon regarded the dark depths of the calm lake with some trepidation.

"Do dragons live in these waters?" he asked Hsü in a very low voice, so as not to be heard by the other men.

"I think we are safe enough, Talon. They prefer deep caves," was the cool response. Talon looked at the poker-faced man sitting next to him. A tiny flicker of doubt crossed his mind.

Hsü noticed his look and said, "We believe that our rivers were made by a dragon and that wherever there is turbulence the dragon has stirred it up. If the water is calm, as with this lake, it reflects the dragon's true nature."

"Why, is it not fierce? It seems to be in all those images."

"True, but in fact it is a benevolent creature, and we Chinese try hard to keep it so with offerings and incense."

"In our lore, it is a deadly and dangerous creature," Talon remarked.

"Oh yes, it has the power to be, but rarely uses that power to punish men," Hsü told him. This left Talon to ponder if the fabled 'dragon' was more of a god than a creature of flesh and blood.

They sailed for a whole two days across the lake to join the river Yangzi , then sailed up stream for several days before disembarking and taking a road across a small range of mountains.

General Yang Hsün turned out to be a man who mirrored Hsü's outlook on life. He was a bluff, heavy man who wore the scars of previous battles with pride. Since the beginning of the journey he had entertained Hsü, and by default Talon, at dinner as often as circumstances permitted. In spite of his rather obvious penchant for elaborate dress, he was a very cordial host who enjoyed talking about himself.

Hsü confided in Talon that it was a good thing he was conversant with the writings of *The Art of War* by Sun Tzu.

"The old buzzard likes me to quote that writing," he said. "He himself can only remember a few passages, so he is happy when I chatter about it too."

Talon grinned, but then asked, "Do you have anything on that subject which I can read, Hsü? '

Hsü shook his head and tapped his temple. "It's all up here, but I shall share what I can while we are traveling, and then we can discuss it together."

Talon enjoyed those discussions and began to write the gist of the sayings down for his own benefit. This was when Hsü began to teach Talon the game of Go.

"Life is very like a game of Go, particularly when dealing with politics and power," he informed Talon. "You have to outwit your opponents, even as they observe your actions and try to outwit you. Keeping them off balance is the most effective way to win at Go."

One evening, when they were camped on the side of the Yangzi river, Hsü told Talon they were only ten *li* from Siang Jan, and within a day or so would be handing off the Tribute to the Mongols.

"They are rough, ugly people, Talon. They have none of the refinements we Chinese possess."

Talon was reminded of the tribal Turks he had encountered; rough people, but superb riders and great fighters. "I dare say that they are great horsemen," he commented.

"Of that you can be sure. Better than this bunch of peacocks we have as an escort," Hsü told him in a dry undertone.

"There is a quote that the famous general Sun Tsu mentioned that is relevant to our situation today. *'When the civil leadership is ignorant of military maneuvers but shares equally in the command of armies, the soldiers hesitate. Once armies are confused and hesitant, trouble comes from competitors. This is called taking away victory by deranging the military.'*

"The Mongols come and rifle the cargo and steal some, then tell us that we have not filled the quota," he told Talon. 'The General and I want to try to make sure that the guards have it all under control. You might see the Erupters being used!" He gave a small bark of laughter. Talon had no idea what he meant.

*****

That night Talon went to bed early. He had fallen asleep listening to the General and Hsü discussing in rapid Chinese the arrangements that would have to be made within the next few days for the transfer of the Tribute. Both men were tense because historically the transfer had never gone well.

Talon awoke suddenly in the semi-light to see a figure with a sword charging into the tent towards him. He gave a startled cry and rolled frantically off his bed out of the way, scrabbling for his own weapon. He was even more shocked to see that it was not some stranger but Hsü. His sword swept down and landed on the grass near to where Talon had been sleeping.

By this time Talon was on his feet, his own sword in his hand, its point leveled at Hsü. Then his blood went cold. Hsü had just cut a writhing snake in two. He cut again and the head of the serpent separated from the rest of the body, which continued to writhe for a few moments before it lay still.

"That was close!" Hsü said as he wiped the blade of his sword and sheathed it, and then calmly nudged the body of the snake with his boot. It was just a small serpent, about eighteen inches long and light brown, but Hsü said, "It is a very poisonous snake. You would have died within a minute and none of us the wiser, Talon. I saw someone slipping away from the side of the tent and was instantly suspicious."

Talon wiped the sweat from his brow with the back of his hand. "Who would want to kill me?" he asked.

Hsü's face was grim. "We might never know. I am sure of one thing, however; there is an assassin with us. I'm surprised they didn't try to kill me before this."

"Kill you?" Talon asked stupidly. "Of course! They missed in Guangzhou, but if you don't come home the way is free and clear for your enemies. Who do you think might have arranged it?"

"I am sure it was either Buwei or that scorpion Rong," Hsü said. Talon had sheathed his weapon by now and they were standing together at the entrance of the tent, looking down towards the river.

Hsü grunted with surprise and pointed. Not one hundred paces away, there was a dark figure trying to push one of the smaller boats out into the river.

"That must be him! Quickly, Talon, we must stop him!" He began to run towards the bank of the river, shouting for the guards and drawing his sword as he ran.

Talon, seeing what he meant, ducked back into the tent and seized his bow and quiver. Although he was dressed only in his pants he pelted bare foot down the bank after Hsü. Hsü was shouting and pointing at the man, who was now energetically sculling the boat away from them down stream.

The men who had been sleeping on the boats had been roused by the commotion and were lighting lamps. Their shouts only added to the bedlam that started up all around. Soldiers came running towards Hsü with spears. He shouted at them, presumably ordering them to stop the boat. Some of them had bows and sent arrows after the man, but he was by now sixty paces away and moving rapidly. All of them fell far short and were lost in dark water.

"Hsü!" Talon bellowed over the shouting. "That boat there!" He pointed to another small boat among the cluster of larger cargo boats.

He ran to the craft and began to push it out. Willing hands helped him, and Hsü slapped him on the shoulder. "Jump in, Talon, we have some men who can row."

All four men tumbled into the boat as they were shoved off into the swirling waters of the river with a mighty push by others on the bank. The two guards who had joined them scrambled for the oars and began to row with all their strength. Talon strung his bow and went to stand in the prow. "If they can get us a little closer I can hit him," he glanced up a the star-filled night sky. "In this light, I would prefer to be about forty paces away."

Hsü gave him a look, then nodded and exhorted the straining rowers to do better. The gap began to close. Their quarry was sculling furiously, using one oar at the back of his boat. He looked back over his shoulder, saw his pursuers and applied himself even harder to his oar, but they were gaining.

Talon steadied himself and carefully notched an arrow, then drew back the string till it was level with his cheek, allowing the rod of the bow to settle into the cup between his left hand, thumb and forefinger, which he closed slowly on the wood to grip it lightly. He stood like that for a long moment, taking in the motions of the two boats and the frantic movements of his target, then loosed the arrow. The bowstring twanged and the arrow sped away into the night. They all heard a light thump, a choking cry and a clatter. The dark figure tumbled into the well of the boat, which began to drift sideways in the current.

There were delighted exclamations from Hsü and the rowers when they realized what had happened. They caught up with the drifting boat and Hsü jumped aboard with his sword drawn. The man lying in a puddle of blood on the bottom of the boat groaned. The arrow had struck him in the small of his back, wounding him grievously. Hsü breathed a sigh of relief; they had a live prisoner. He looked up at Talon. "That was a very good shot," he said.

They bound up the prisoner's wound as best they could and were rowed back to the bank, towing the fugitive's boat behind them. The rowers directed respectful glances at Talon while they covered the distance. They arrived back at the camp to find the General and his aides waiting for them on the bank.

"What was all that about, Lord Meng?" Yang Hsün demanded gruffly when they stepped ashore.

Hsü gestured behind him at the two guards, who supported the limp prisoner. "I suggest that we ask this man, General. He almost succeeded in killing my companion, Master Talon here. However, I think he may have been after me."

"Why would someone want to kill you, Hsü?" the General demanded.

"Perhaps we should go to your tent, General?" Hsü invited him. "It will be more private."

The General agreed and gave orders to the guards to bring the prisoner along while he stamped off to his tent. Hsü went to his and Talon's tent to collect the snake, then came and tossed the body and head onto the floor in front of the officers. The General's eyes widened when he saw it. "That is a Krait!" he exclaimed, picking up a lantern to peer at it in the light.

"It nearly bit Talon, here. I was walking to our tent when I noticed someone creeping around nearby and looked in. This thing was slipping under the tent wall and making for him while he slept. They like warm places." Hsü's smile was wry. "Then this fellow tried to escape down the river. Had it not been for Talon's skill with a bow, we might have lost him."

"You said that you would explain the reason for the attempted assassination, Hsü," the General prompted him.

"Ah, yes. I am running for governor, General. Didn't you know?"

The General's face registered genuine surprise, and then he smiled. "I had no idea, Hsü!" he exclaimed. "I am delighted. You are a dark one; you never said anything until now! I hope you win. We have need of a good man for that office, as Guangzhou has become notorious for its crime. I shall certainly support you in that endeavor. You only have to ask me for help."

"I thank you sincerely for your support. I might just do that, General. Now we should see what we have here before our prisoner expires. He is badly wounded."

"Hmm, it would seem that you have some enemies who would rather you did not return to contest the position. Bring in the prisoner!" the General bellowed to his aide, who winced; he was standing right next to him. The aide hastened to lift the flap of the tent and called to the guards. They had to carry the bedraggled man in, and he hung limply in their grip. His tunic was covered in blood and he was as pale as a ghost.

"We don't have much time. He is going fast!" Hsü said urgently when he saw the condition of the man.

"Who sent you, and for what purpose?" the General said to the prisoner, whose eyes were closed. He slapped him none to gently on the face. The man opened his eyes and grimaced with pain. The General slapped him again harder and gripped his lower jaw, forcing the prisoner to lift his head. "You tell me now, or my people will dismember you piece by piece. If you confess I will allow you to die intact!" he told the man, who grimaced again but nodded.

"I was sent from Guangzhou. Wu...." He gasped with pain. They all leaned closer. "Who sent you?" The General demanded loudly."

The man half opened his eyes and stared at the General. Then slowly his eyes glazed over and his head lolled back. The guards still held him upright, but one of them peered at him and said, "I think he is dead, my Lord."

"What do you make of that, Hsü?" The General asked, with an annoyed expression on his florid face.

"I heard the name Wu, but not the rest. I know of only one person by that name, but I wouldn't be too surprised," Hsü said with a thoughtful expression. "I still find it hard to believe that an administrator would attempt this kind of thing."

The General shook his head. "Ambition can make men do ugly things. See if he is carrying anything on him," he ordered.

The soldiers went through the pockets of the dead man carefully. One of them gave low exclamation of surprise and dragged out something from the breast of the man's shirt. It was an oil cloth pouch. He passed it to the General.

"What have we here?" the General muttered and opened it.

His expression changed at least twice while he read the short note. Then he handed it to Hsü. "You had better read it," he said. His expression was bleak.

Hsü took the letter and read it carefully by the light of the lanterns. He finally looked up. "I think we have enough evidence now, General," he said.

"Indeed you do. I shall be reporting back to the palace as soon as I arrive. I will have a copy made tonight, and I shall make absolutely sure that this information is handed over to the Chamberlain... and certain others of interest. An attempt upon the life of anyone on official duty is treason. You should take the original with you and present it to the Governor."

He brightened up and said, "We should toast the good Joss of your friend here. You saved his life, and now you know who your enemies are."

Wine came, and the two men sat down to play a game of Go, with Talon watching and trying to learn.

*****

They breasted a rise that overlooked the town of Sian-Jang two days later and were confronted with an astonishing spectacle. Before the walled city were hundreds, perhaps even a thousand black and brown tents. Talon had seen a sight like this when he had been on the ill-fated expedition to Myriokephalon with the Emperor of Byzantium. Then it had been Seljuks, but this scene was all too familiar.

Hsü rode next to Talon and glanced at him as they stopped to stare. "You do not seem to be surprised to see this, Talon."

"I have seen this kind of thing before. I'll tell you about it some time," Talon said. "So these are the famous Mongols."

"Infamous is the word I would prefer to use," Hsü told him. "These people are barbaric and have nothing to offer a civilized people such as we. But our elitist advisors buy them off when they should instead be making a concerted effort to drive them off our land."

The General heard him. "I agree with you, Hsü." His voice was grim. "Until we have leaders in positions of influence who fully understand what kind of people these are and the threat they represent to our empire, we are doomed to submit to their whims and wills."

The General gave orders for the caravan to camp on the gentle slopes of the hills facing the river. "That way," Hsü told Talon, "we can defend ourselves if there should be trouble."

"Will there be trouble?" Talon asked him.

"There should not be, but historically there always has been. Those people are led by chiefs who owe allegiance to no one but their supreme leader. Until recently that was Khan of Khamag, but rumor has it that he has died, or been deposed, and now there is another called Genghis. He will not be here today. One of the lesser chiefs is always designated for the task of collecting the tribute. That means that it will be up to the chief whether there is trouble or not."

There was a strategy to the positioning of the encampment. General Yang Hsün wanted to have the maximum advantage over the people in the tented city below. The Mongols knew the Chinese had arrived because there had been outriders watching their progress for a couple of days now, but no one had tried to interfere with them. This was, after all, Chinese territory; although to see the scouts lurking on the hilltops one might have thought otherwise.

This was when Talon finally had a chance to see the Erupters, as Hsü laughingly called them. These cumbersome bronze tubes on heavy frames were among the first pieces to be unloaded and placed on a level space that faced the tents on the plain. The men who labored to mount these curious things appeared to know what they were doing and moved at a steady pace to set them on the ground and anchor them. The muzzles of the tubes pointed into the air in the general direction of the Mongol camp, while the back was propped against some sold pegs hammered into the ground. They piled stones alongside both Erupters, along with some iron balls. They also placed some small kegs nearby, which Hsü told Talon were full of the 'flame powder'.

"Today we will not be firing stones or iron, just making the powder explode," he told Talon. "Hold your mount close, as it will be frightened by the noise, and cover your ears; that is, if you can do both things at once," he said with a smile. "The General intends to announce himself to the barbarians."

They were about thirty paces away from the four Erupters. The men were standing around waiting for an order; the General arrived on horseback dressed in all his finery, his face half obscured by the huge horned helmet on his head. He looked very fierce and was accompanied by numerous aides in armor; drawn up behind him were fifty of his mounted troops. They, too, were dressed in their finest uniforms and could be seen clearly by anyone down in the tent city, which was less than half a league away.

The General raised his hand and men stooped over the devices, each with a smoking stick in his hands. As soon as the General dropped his arm, they pushed the smoking sticks into a small hole in the back of each tube. There were small jets of flame from the holes and the men jumped back. All four Erupters went off simultaneously. The serried clap of thunder that followed felt like a sledge hammer to Talon's ears. The long jets of flame that came out of the muzzles of the tubes blinded him and made him gasp with shock. His horse reared and would have fled had he not been deep in the saddle and partly ready. Hsü had been expecting the crash of noise, but even his horse shied with fright. The horses of the Chinese troops shifted nervously, but for the most part they were held in check. A cloud of smoke swirled about the Erupters and the men who commanded them.

The sound of the enormous explosion reverberated around the hills, repeating itself a hundred times, becoming fainter until it finally died away. Talon stared wide-eyed at the devices, awed that they could make such an awful, head-splitting noise. His ears rang and his eyes were burning from the drifting smoke that carried with it an evil stink.

The General barked something and laughed. His men roared with laughter.

"What did he say?" Talon asked Hsü.

"He said, 'That will show the bastards,'" Hsü told him with one of his rare smiles. "He calls his weapons 'The Dragon's breath.' They certainly stink like it."

Talon gave a shaken grin. He was beginning to like General Yang Hsün. His men clearly worshipped him. Indeed, these weapons were just how he imagined a dragon might breathe.

The reaction below them in the tent city was immediate. The distant figures down in the camp ran about in all directions. Horses had broken free and were running loose across the short plain. A herd of goats and sheep took to the hills, with their herdsmen chasing after them. Men dashed out of their tents to seize their horses and leap upon them, and then they formed up in loose packs to ride pell mell for the base of the hill to a point where the General was now leading his troops.

Hsü motioned Talon to join them. "This you must see, Talon," he said. "We will leave a guard to stop the bastards from looting the Tribute before we can hand it over."

The General and his grim-faced honor guard had formed up at the base of the hill well before the Mongols arrived: more of a mob of hairy, shouting horsemen on shaggy ponies than an organized company of troops. They stopped twenty paces from the thin straight line of the Chinese cavalry and slowly the shouting and excited gesticulating died down.

From out of the mob of milling horsemen rode three men. They were clearly leaders, as the other riders showed them respect, making way for them.

Talon examined each of these men with care. All three were large men compared to the others, although they rode the ubiquitous shaggy pony like everyone else. Their hair was black, except in one case where it was graying, and tied back in a knot: they wore fur caps that must have been hot in this climate. They also carried animal skins rolled up behind their saddles. It was as though they could care less about the heat of the day and were prepared to live on their horses no matter where they found themselves. Talon's nose picked up the smell of mutton grease that wafted towards them as the Mongols jostled in front of the impassive Chinese.

All three wore stained silk jackets, over which they wore ringed armor that had known better days, but they carried their weapons as though they knew how to use them. The bows, Talon noticed with interest, were similar to those of the Seljuks, and just as the Seljuks did, they carried the scalps of their enemies hanging off their belts. Their faces were covered with sparse, unkempt beards and their expressions were hostile.

"So these are the Mongols?" He murmured to Hsü. "I have met their like before."

Hsü gave him a keen look.

Chapter Twenty-Seven
The Duel

One of the Chinese delegation rode his mount forward and spoke to the Mongols in their own tongue. The greetings began on a sour note. The three leaders were angry at the way the General had announced his presence, but they were also awed by the voice of the Erupters.

Hsü translated for Talon as they sat listening to the introductions and the conversation that followed. The leader of the Mongols was a man called Prince Badzar, and he was at pains to tell the translator the meaning of his name: The Thunderbolt. He was the one with the greying hair and the long scar down his left cheek.

He in turn introduced the man on his right as Muunokhoi, or Vicious Dog, another scarred warrior who grinned wolfishly when being presented, displaying pointed teeth. The third man was introduced as Khoonbish, or Not a Human Being. He was the largest of the three. Talon took an instant dislike to the man. He sat his horse and spat contemptuously on the ground in front of the Chinese soldiers.

The Mongols demanded to be entertained, and the General knew that he had little choice but to invite them to his tent, which he did; but he asked politely enough that the rest of the Mongols kept clear of the caravan while the discussions were ongoing. They sullenly agreed, and with some sharp commands Badzar sent the bulk of the mounted rabble away. They trailed off down the slopes, leaving the three men and a couple of retainers behind.

Further introductions were made and Hsü was pulled into the discussion, which left Talon to drift off and spend some time with the men who had fired the Erupters. His Cantonese was barely good enough to speak to them, but they knew a little about him and his prowess with a bow, so they were friendly.

They showed him everything, from the barrels to the frames that supported them, and explained with much laughter the process whereby this equipment could be fired. He asked many questions; one of these on a ship could make it as dangerous as one of the Byzantine galleys with Greek Fire, he reasoned. He would have to talk to Hsü about the possibility of purchasing one for his ship, maybe two.

Evidently the entertainment went well, because the Mongols left late that night, full of expensive rice wine and food.

"Fortunately not fighting drunk," Hsü remarked to Talon.

The next day would be the day when the fortune in silk bales and silver was handed over. The caravan would move down to the plain, where the animals and the goods would be transferred to the Mongols.

The Chinese were looking forward to this eagerly. It meant that they would have discharged their duty to the Emperor and could leave these dirty, hairy people to their own devices and go home to their families.

The next day the camp rose early, and soon the pack-animals were ready to move. The General made it clear that half his contingent would escort the baggage animals, while the remainder would stay at the camp and guard it while they were away. Some men on horseback had been spotted on the hill behind the camp. Sure enough, it wasn't long before some scruffy-looking Mongols rode up and, ignoring the guards, dismounted and began to strut about the camp as though they owned it, staring at everything. Finally the Aide to the General had to ask them to leave, threatening to talk to their chief if they did not. They left with ugly looks. The camp was tense by the time the caravan began to wend its way down to the plain.

Talon elected to stay. It was none of his concern what happened down at the tent city. The tribute was being paid, and they were going to leave soon after. He went away from the camp to practice with his bow.

He arrived back at the camp to find it in an uproar. The Mongols had returned and there had been an incident. Talon pushed his way through the crowd to find a group of Mongols threatening the officer in charge, whose men were pointing spears at them.

"They are like animals!" muttered one man. "They think they can take what they want whenever they want."

So much for the policy of appeasement, Talon thought to himself. These people didn't care how far they went, they only respected force.

It looked very tense and Talon could not understand what was being said in either language, although he caught some of the Chinese. The Mongols had come back and had begun to steal what they could, blatantly ignoring the Chinese soldiers who demanded that they leave. Finally one man had had enough and had pushed a burly Mongol away, only to receive a knife in the belly. He was in one of the tents dying as the uproar continued.

The Mongols shouted what seemed like insults and then decided as a group to leave. They pushed through the guards, contemptuously shoving their spears aside, and mounted up. One of them sneered down at the glowering men and waved his bow threateningly, then they galloped off, laughing.

When they were about forty yards away, one of them sent an arrow back into the crowd. It struck one of the guards in the chest, killing him instantly. Without thinking, Talon raised his own bow and sent an arrow back directly to strike the man who had fired. He tumbled off his horse to lie dead on the ground.

The silence which greeted this act was deafening. The Mongols turned as one and rode back to the body of their man, and their looks at the Chinese were full of menace. The guards, however, were now fully alert to the danger and the Mongols faced a hedge of spears, and several bowmen had come to join Talon. There was no doubt that the men around Talon approved of what he had done, but he was also painfully aware that he had helped make the situation far worse than before.

*****

Hsü and the General had heard the Mongol's version of the story by the time they returned. Talon was sent for, as was the officer in charge, who was very nervous.

While the officer was talking to the grim-faced General in a nervous stutter, Hsü turned to Talon. "Their camp is up in arms. According to them, you killed one of their people who was just visiting and trying to be friendly," he said with a wry twist to his lips.

Talon snorted, but then said, "They had already killed two of our men who tried to stop them from stealing." He told Hsü the rest of the story as he knew it.

Hsü nodded somberly. "They are talking about revenge, or certainly redress. Apparently you killed a cousin of that big ape, Khoonbish. He wants blood for blood."

The General had finished with the officer and dismissed him. Hsü explained Talon's version to him and he nodded.

"It allies exactly with that of my officer. He was very complimentary of your action, Talon, but also very sorry indeed for the problem that has been created."

"Will we be going home soon?" Talon asked. "Did the transfer go well?"

"Um, yes it did; and no, unfortunately, we will not be going home until this is resolved," Hsü told him.

Talon bowed very low to both men. "I had no business creating this situation. I am deeply sorry and wish to make amends however I can."

The General smiled and slapped him on the back. "I might well have done the same, Talon," he said. "We need people who will stand up to these barbarians. Unfortunately, we have to navigate this particular situation and hope for the best," he paused. "It matters not at all to them that they murdered our people. They think they are inviolate and always take the stance of the aggressor."

*****

In the middle of the huge, untidy city of tents and horse lines was the field where the duel was to take place.

The Chinese contingent was clustered at one end, a colorful group of nervous administrators and soldiers. Among them was the General with his entire entourage of officers and Hsü. At the other end were the milling horsemen of the Mongol contingent. The negotiations for redress had gone on until late the night before, and Hsü had finally informed Talon that the Mongols would not accept their side of the blame and had insisted on a duel to settle the matter.

Hsü walked over to where Talon sat on his horse watching the activity at the other end of the field. Hsü was clearly nervous, something that Talon had not witnessed very often in this man who was usually self-contained.

"How are you feeling, Talon?" Hsü asked him in Arabic.

"As well as I can expect to be, given that Khoonbish, or whatever his name is, will be trying to kill me in a short while," Talon responded.

"You seem calm; that is very good. I know you to be a warrior and so do they, but they have not seen you with a sword... not yet."

Talon looked down at Hsü. "What do you mean, Hsü?"

Hsü handed up his own sword to Talon. "Take it," he said. "It is far superior to the one you have and twice as sharp. You will need it."

"I can't thank you enough," Talon said as he took the sword, drew it from the sheath and felt its superb balance.

"Just make sure you bring it back to me when this is over." Hsü's smile was lopsided as Talon passed the sheath back to him.

"Listen, Talon," Hsü said, his tone urgent. "You must get him off his horse, then you will have the absolute superiority. Remember all your training at the Dojo from Sensei Saiki? It will stand you in good stead, but I fear that he has the advantage while on the horse."

Although it rankled to have to admit it, Talon had to agree with Hsü. The Mongols were phenomenal warriors while mounted, but bandy-legged and awkward when on the ground. His own skill on a horse was beyond dispute, but in this instance he required an edge. He resolved to be very careful.

A horseman galloped over towards them and halted his animal in a small cloud of dust in front of Talon. It was Muunokhoi, and he had an unpleasant grin on his flat, round face.

"We are ready, *Wàiguó rén*! Or are you too frightened to come and face our man?" he taunted.

Talon glanced at Hsü and spun his horse around to join Muunokhoi. "Your men didn't do so well earlier, Mongol," he said. "Perhaps you are next?" It was bravado and he knew it, but he was not going to let this greasy man from the steppes intimidate him. They cantered to the middle of the field, where several riders were waiting, among them Khoonbish, who glowered at Talon, and Prince Badzar, who smiled cheerfully upon their arrival.

"Are you ready?" he inquired, baring his bad teeth.

Talon nodded, as did Khoonbish.

"The rules are... that there are no rules!" Badzar stated with a laugh. The Mongols within earshot found this very amusing and roared with laughter.

"The victor is the man still on his feet and the loser is the one dead," Badzar belabored the obvious, to more amusement. "The payment for losing will be made by the loser's followers and family at once, or they too will be put to death. Is that understood?"

Again the nods of acceptance.

"You will both ride away from me in opposite directions for fifty paces at a walk and stop, then turn your mounts and face me. When I drop the silk you will begin. There will be no stopping until it is finished. Now ride away."

Both men wheeled their horses and rode away at a walk for the prescribed fifty paces. Talon felt the familiar flow of adrenalin and took several deep breaths to calm his senses. His heart was beating hard, but he knew he must focus or die. The Mongol was quite determined to kill him.

He turned his horse and collected the animal, just enough to sharpen its attention and get it onto the bit where it would respond immediately to the slightest command. His life depended upon it. He felt the balance of the sword he now held and knew it to be a superb weapon.

He saw the silk drop and closed his legs hard. His horse jumped away from a standing position and was into a full gallop within a moment. Talon's vision, sharpened by the adrenaline, saw that Khoonbish had done almost the same, but one tiny detail caught Talon's attention even as he closed on his enemy. Khoonbish's horse was not as responsive as Talon's. He settled deeper into the saddle and felt the smooth gallop begin whereby he, the rider, could focus all his attention on the danger approaching and not concern himself with controlling the animal beneath him. They were as one.

Within seconds the two riders were upon one another. Khoonbish had his sword raised for a downward strike that would kill in one blow and was yelling. His fur and braids were flying wild, his black eyes glaring at Talon, his mouth in a ferocious grin, and his heels were pumping the sides of his galloping animal.

Talon was waiting for the right moment. Just as they were about to pass each other, he drove his left heel into his animal and swerved it right into Khoonbish's pony. The horses crashed into one another's shoulders. Khoonbish's animal staggered and nearly threw its rider, who had been ready to strike. Now of a sudden the Mongol had to keep his seat and his blow went wide. Talon had anticipated the shock of the collision and stayed well seated. He blocked Khoonbish's weakened blow and rode past, trying to strike with a back hand as he went. It sliced the cloth of his opponent but did little else. He rode on and then whirled his animal to begin the next attack while Khoonbish was off balance.

But the Mongol was nothing if not a superb rider and within a split second had his pony back under control. He also spun his animal around to leap forward and charge towards the oncoming Talon. Talon knew that he had to do better this time. Khoonbish let out a bloodcurdling yell as they approached and brandished his sword high.

Just as it seemed they would pass one another, right hand to right hand, the onlookers were astonished to see Talon's animal swerve, and before the Mongol could react, Talon was hurtling by on his other side. Khoonbish had already committed to the death strike: a wide, sweeping blow that, had it connected, would have cut Talon in half; he was standing on his stirrups leaning out over the right side of his animal when Talon switched sides.

With a yell of surprise he swung over to confront Talon, but as fast as he was he was not fast enough. Talon leaned well out to his left, the handle of the sword held firmly in his right hand, the center of the blade supported by the palm of his left hand. The force of the horse's gallop was sufficient for the blade to penetrate the exposed side of the Mongol in a horizontal sweep. The steel cut through the small shield as though it had not been there and sliced deeply into the lower rib cage of the man. Then Talon was past and spinning his animal on its heels. Once again the horse moved as though a part of him. Talon, looking over his shoulder, was about to race back to take advantage of his strike, but then he closed his hand on the reins and the very hot and excited animal responded to the light touch and pranced in place. He murmured gently to his mount and it calmed down.

There was a spray of blood from Khoonbish's side and he was flung over the back of his pony to crash face down in the grass. The animal galloped off to stop a couple of dozen paces away, its head down, looking back at its fallen rider.

There was an audible murmur of shock from the watching crowd of both groups of people. No one had expected this. The entire Mongol army was watching, along with the chiefs who were in the center of the field.

Talon sat on his horse, waiting. He hoped it was over. His own breath came in short gasps as the exhilaration of the encounter began to drain from him. However, Khoonbish was not done for yet. He lifted his head from the grass, shook it groggily, then got to his knees and sat back on his haunches. He stared down at his gaping wound and the pulsing blood. He shook his head again, his braids flying, and then with an effort, lumbered to his feet. He looked around for his sword and staggered over to pick it up, then he whirled, spraying blood as he did so, to find Talon seated on his horse twenty paces away watching him.

"You can surrender and honor would be satisfied," Talon prompted him in bad Cantonese.

Khoonbish shook his head, barely understanding, and hurriedly tore his sash off to wind it around his chest and bind it in a tight knot at his side. It stopped the stream of blood, but very soon the yellow silk sash was bright red. He wiped his brow and snarled back in his own tongue.

"You had some luck there, Foreigner. Try it on your feet, or do you want to kill me from up there? I shall kill you one way or the other." He laughed and brandished his sword.

Talon sighed. He had no wish to kill the man, no matter how obnoxious he had been or still was. The cut was fatal, and all he had to do was to wait. If they continued to fight, the wound would hamper Khoonbish badly. He could hear the yells and calls of the Mongols on the sidelines, who were demanding a fight on foot. So be it. Hsü would have his way; and now he, Talon, would find out just how good he was with this sword.

He dismounted, murmured a word to his horse, and then spanked it on the rump with the flat of his hand. It trotted off a few paces and then stopped, just as had the other mount, and waited, watching him over its shoulder, the reins trailing.

Talon held the sword in both hands, as he had practiced in the dojo. He didn't have a shield, but the sword was designed for this, and he didn't think he would need one. Khoonbish grunted and tossed the split remains of his shield away with a grimace of pain. Then he squared his shoulders, tossed back his braids and advanced on Talon, who waited for him.

Talon had no intention of exerting himself more than he had to; it was up to his enemy to do all the work until he was exhausted from loss of blood. However, he realized that he should not underestimate Khoonbish, even in this condition. He placed his feet apart on the grass in the pyramid form where all his strength would come from his lower body and let his mind think of nothing.

Khoonbish seemed to think that charging would take care of his enemy, so he began to run at Talon, bellowing and swinging his sword from the right to left in a killing arc. The trouble was that, apart from a screech of steel on steel as Talon's blade deflected the other, Talon was no longer where he should have been. Khoonbish stumbled past and the crowd sighed.

Talon whirled about and again stood facing Khoonbish, his sword held in both hands, the blade pointing just above his opponent's head, his knees slightly bent, waiting. He could have dealt a killing blow but had not. There was a sheen of sweat on Khoonbish's face and the silk bandage was soaked with blood, which now trickled down his belly and leg, soaking his pants.

He nodded in salute to Talon. "You are good, *Wàiguó rén*. I'll admit it," he grunted grudgingly. Then he ran in again. This time their blades clashed several times before it was Khoonbish who had to step back, because Talon had driven the Mongol's sword off to his side with a sharp tap on his sword hilt. Again Talon could have either cut off his hand or killed him with one blow, but he was biding his time and his enemy was weakening before his very eyes.

Khoonbish had begun to realize this too, as his own eyes had a new look in them. He was contemplating his own death, something he had never had to do before. Here in front of him was a wraith with implacable green eyes and a sword that could keep him, Khoonbish, at bay no matter what.

He tried several more times to get past Talon's guard, and once came close in a desperate series of thrusts and slashes, but each time Talon was able to deflect the increasingly clumsy swipes or simply to evade them by side-stepping out of the way. Hsü had been right, Talon reflected, as he watched the Mongol sway with fatigue. He lacked the balance of a true swordsman when on his own two feet.

The bandage had slipped down and blood was once again pumping out of the wound in Khoonbish's side. The man's face was gray with pain and loss of blood, and he was panting with the exertion. Talon waited and watched in silence as his opponent staggered back one last time, stared at Talon with eyes that were clouding over, and then fell, first to his knees, then forward onto his face, his sword falling at Talon's feet. Talon bent to pick it up and tossed it away, still not trusting the man, and then waited for a full minute. By then other men had arrived on the field, shouting and gesticulating as they reached Khoonbish lying prone on the ground in a pool of his own blood.

A man knelt by his side and turned him over. Khoonbish was dead.

Talon turned his back and retrieved his horse, which had been calmly grazing while his master fought to the death. He mounted and was about to leave when Prince Badzar rode in front of him. Talon tensed, his grip on his sword tightening, but Badzar gave him a lop-sided smile and said, "Khoonbish has killed many men. I watch you; you are very good warrior."

Talon nodded and walked his horse by the prince, then cantered towards the Chinese without looking back. Hsü and the General strode over to him with looks of profound relief on their normally hard to read faces.

Talon dismounted and handed the still bloody sword to Hsü, but made sure he did not present it blade first. "This is the finest blade I have ever used," he said. "I want one!"

Hsü stared at him for a long moment, and then he bent over, slapped his thigh and laughed, shaking his head. "Is that all you can say?" he demanded, still shaking his head.

The General looked at them both with astonishment, and then he too began to chuckle. Before very long, all the men who were close were laughing too; Talon suspected that they didn't hear the General, laugh often, but when they did it was a very amusing sight.

"It is high time this happened," the General said finally, wiping his eyes. "We need to leave soon before they invent another dangerous game for us to play."

Hsü said, "The General is right. We need to get you away as soon as we can, Talon. Who knows what excuse they will invent to start another quarrel?"

Talon had to agree. He had seen a speculative look in the eyes of the Mongol named Muunokhoi as he rode past.

*****

A small train of horses and baggage straggled into the Chinese camp that evening. Prince Badzar possessed some honor it seemed, for these had been the possessions of Khoonbish, who had accumulated some wealth in his time. The train was accompanied by several women, some slaves, and many children, whom the translator said were now Talon's possessions. Talon was aghast.

Hsü was amused. "Take what you want from it, and then send the rest back. They can fight over the stuff, and the women, as I am sure they will," he remarked dryly as they stood looking at the pile of clothes, weapons and some small chests of silver lying on the ground, next to which were seated cross-legged Khoonbish's erstwhile women.

"Please tell the General that I want the goods of any value to go to the families of our men who were killed. The rest can go back to where they came from," Talon said, and walked away. He listened with half an ear to the wails of the womenfolk and children when they were driven out of the Chinese camp and sent back to the Mongol tent city.

*****

Hsü and Talon rode out with a guard of four men the next day at dawn, while the General and his men and retainers broke camp in a more leisurely manner. The small group retraced their path along the river and over the spectacular mountains. Talon never tired of looking at their shapes and contours, and at the raging torrents that they either rode alongside or crossed on fragile-looking bridges. Hsü pointed out that this was not an area where construction of any real substance was carried out because of the ever present threat of the Mongols. "We need to be able to destroy easily what we leave behind, should it be necessary to retreat," Hsü told him.

Before long they were in the hills again, and townships were beginning to show up, perched on the sides. Evidently Hsü had something in mind, because although he was in a hurry to get back, rather than taking the direct route back to the great lake they made a short detour. One day he pointed up to a three-storied pagoda perched high above them on top of a wooded mountain.

"That is a monastery, Talon. I would like to show you one of these places before we go home."

"I understand the meaning of monastery to be where men of like mind go to pray and live apart from the rest of the world."

"That is correct. It is the same here in China. There are many such places run by Taoist priests, who are very pious people."

Leaving their men to take care of all the horses and rest at an isolated inn, they set out for the monastery the next morning. It took the better part of the day to reach the building, the trail being very steep and narrow, winding its way between short pine trees and scrub all the way up to the summit, which today was shrouded in a smoke-like mist.

They arrived near the top out of breath. The trees here were more dense, and the path widened into a paved path with stone walls on either side. It was quiet up here where the wind soughed through the pines, and tendrils of mist clung to the trees. They could hear the sharp hollow sound of a woodpecker tapping rapidly in the distance. Hsü had said nothing on the way up. Talon simply assumed that he was catching his breath.

Then they rounded a corner and the building was directly in front of them. It was quite substantial, with a wall all around a red-painted three storied construction with the usual elaborately tiled roof that Talon had grown quite fond of seeing. In front of the monastery there was a very beautiful rounded bridge of carved stone that crossed a small ravine. It wasn't the bridge that took Talon's attention.

At the front of the bridge, standing right in the path of anyone who wanted to cross over, stood a dragon. He gasped and stared. It was of white marble, but was so lifelike and its appearance was so abrupt that he instinctively put his hand on the hilt of his sword. They both stopped, but for different reasons. Talon was admiring the stone dragon, and Hsü was watching Talon's expression. The animal was a combination of scales and short legs with formidable claws, a tail that appeared to be lashing with anger, and a huge head that was fearsome to behold. The bulging eyes and the thick mane above a wide open mouth full of long fangs were an impressive sight.

Finally, after a very long pause, Hsü said, "I humbly ask for your forgiveness, Talon. I have not lied to you, but I have misled you. This is the only good-looking dragon that I know of in China. Dragons are part of our culture, but they are long gone into legend. All you will see in this land are images of them. I had to show this one to you. It is very special."

Talon sent him a grim look. "You have deceived me! I came all this way to China to see a dragon, and you show me a stone one? Did someone turn it into stone by magic?" he demanded, his tone heavy with sarcasm and his expression forbidding. He looked and sounded very upset.

Hsü was sincere in his contrition, but had he detected a gleam in Talon's eye? He shook his head. "No, Talon. I am so very sorry. I had to get home somehow, and you did have a cargo that you needed to sell." He smiled disarmingly, searching Talon's bearded face for any sign of amusement. His friend continued to look grim.

"If anyone asks, I have *seen a dragon*," Talon stated firmly. He glared at Hsü, and then at the dragon, as though either of them might argue with him.

Hsü nodded, his face solemn. "You have indeed *seen the dragon*." His tone was equally firm.

Talon turned to grin at him, relishing his friend's former discomfort. Hsü was not an easy man to unbalance. "Hah! I was beginning to think this might be the case, that you were leading me on. But as I have seen for myself, China is a very large place, sooo... you can never tell. Perhaps they live somewhere else!"

Hsü chuckled and reached forward to embrace him. Then they walked past the stone creature that guarded the bridge. Talon stroked a shiny patch on the top of its shaggy head as he went by.

"I have never brought anyone else to this place before," Hsü said. "One day I shall bring my sons. I want very much to introduce you to an old friend of mine. The Abbot of this monastery and I have known each other since I was a boy. His name is Hu Ssu-ch'i. We will spend a pleasant evening with him, and then we must hurry back to Guangzhou."

Chapter Twenty-Eight
Fang

With Hsü and Talon gone, the villa settled back into its tranquil routine. The ladies would rise at mid-morning and perform their toilette. Rav'an and Jannat would wander over to meet with Lihua when the bath house had been prepared; they would bathe and chat and plan for the day. Several times, Lihua arranged for a masseuse to come and work them over. Neither Rav'an nor Jannat had ever been pampered like this before, so they reveled in it.

"I didn't get this well treated even when we were in the harem!" Jannat exclaimed.

If they were planning on going into the city, they would meet again at about noon and take the sampan across the river. Now they had an escort, however, as Fang had insisted upon this. Rav'an understood the need for security, but found it irksome nonetheless. The guards accompanying them were rough men who, while very polite to the women, were a little too eager to protect them and on occasion were unpleasant to unwary passers-by whom they thought might be about to bother their wards.

If they were not going into the city, they might meet up with Lady Meng Lanfen and sip tea or some *guoqi jiu,* a very tasty lychee wine that was Lady Lanfen's favorite. On the days when the sun was warm, they would sit by the fountain in the garden, which Rav'an had come to love, as it reminded her of the Persian garden in Isfahan where she had lived with the doctor and his wife Fariba.

Once she had overcome her initial reserve, the old woman appeared to enjoy the company of the foreigners. Lihua, who more or less ran the household, ensured that they enjoyed sweet cakes and tiny mint sweets while being entertained The need for translation lessened, although Lihua's help was still needed for the more intense conversations. By now both women could speak halting Cantonese, which pleased Lanfen. She was very curious and asked about their countries and was especially interested in the Persian way of life as described by Rav'an.

She introduced them to the game of *Shi pai,* telling them that once it was fashionable to use poetry cards, but that was now less popular. The present game consisted of thirty-two pieces of carved ivory, with pips carved onto the bone. Lihua called the game *xuan he pai.*

It was a form of dominos that required four people to play, as there were tricks to be taken. Many afternoons were spent outside, if the late September weather permitted. They would be seated on low stools around a lacquered table, playing the game to the sound of clicking tiles, laughter, and the ever present sound of water flowing from the fountain.

Lun and Rostam had taken to the game called Buda. It was a ball game which was very popular with the maids and servants of the household. In the late afternoons, they would all come out into the main yard in front of the stables and play. Each player had a stick with a curved end, which they would use to drive a small wooden ball over a distance into a hole in the ground. There was always much banter from the servants, and the boys ran about shrieking with excitement as they played.

When not playing Buda, the boys would rush out of the gates to watch the ships moving by on the river. Lun no longer had to fear the gang of boys, Fang had seen to that. They also watched the kites flying on the other side of the river.

"Why can't we fly those kites ourselves?" Rostam asked Lun one day.

"I don't know, Rostam. I shall ask my brother."

Later that day he cornered his harassed-looking older brother and asked him if he could have a kite to play with.

Fuling had dark rings around his eyes. He was exhausted from his studying; his exams were only three weeks away now, so he replied, "Leave me alone, little brother. Can't you see I'm busy? I don't have time for this. Why don't you go to go to Low yen Bong the gardener and ask him? Tell him I sent you."

Lun yelped his thanks and ran off with Rostam to confront the old gardener and ask him.

The old man was on his knees cleaning up a flower patch. He sat back on his haunches and looked at the two eager boys. He stood up, handed off the work to a young assistant, looked down on them for a moment, then nodded his head. "I can make you a kite, Master Lun. You must tell me what kind of animal you wish to have painted on the wings."

Lun thought about it, and then conferred with Rostam. "He says we can have an animal painted on the wings of the kite. What should we have?"

"A horse?" Rostam ventured.

"No! Not fierce enough. It has to be a fierce creature to fight the wind! I know! We should have a dragon!" Lun exclaimed.

Bong, who had been listening with some amusement, raised his hand for permission to speak. Lun nodded imperiously. 'Would you not consider a crane, young master?"

Lun thought about this and then nodded. "You are right, Bong. We shall have a crane."

He set about explaining this icon of good luck to Rostam, who agreed with him. Good luck, or Joss, as Bong called it, was a good thing to have.

Within two days Bong called them over and presented them with a large contraption that resembled the ones they could see flying on the other side of the river. Its frame was of fine strips of split bamboo, over which thin paper had been glued to form a shape with an impressive tail. Rostam could hardly believe how life-like the huge bird was. The boys were delighted and chased one another around the compound, screaming with glee as they tried to haul the kite into the sky. They couldn't succeed, so eventually Bolin, one of the servants, took pity on them and helped them get it airborne.

Before long the delighted boys were able to hold the kite, the huge white bird with a long neck and black markings on its wings, in the sky at about one fifty feet and to play it in the changing currents. Rostam was in heaven. He delighted his mother by showing off his newfound skill to her and Jannat one day.

*****

Reza spent much of his time with Jiaya making sure that all was well with the cargo, as he didn't fully trust the merchants and wanted to make sure that Talon's investment was secure. He also paid frequent visits to the Arab settlement to make sure the crew and the captain were comfortable and not too restless. It was an opportunity for him to sit and have tea with the men and catch up on the gossip and rumors. He made sure that Yosef and Dar'an accompanied him, as they were both becoming restless with little to do in the compound except to keep an eye on Rostam. Yosef's wounds were healing, although he still could not talk.

Captain Dandachi enjoyed these visits. While he was content to loaf about with his men, there was not much to be done while they waited for the cargos to be sold. He busied himself with repairs to the ship, and whenever he needed something Jiaya was quick to provide it. The other inhabitants of the Arab quarter, while polite, didn't go out of their way to seek Reza's company. He attributed that to his being Persian and not Arabic, but the captain told him one day that it was because he and Talon appeared to have the run of the city, which they did not, and this engendered some envy.

"They can obtain passes, just like the one I hold, and Yosef and Dar'an here. Why don't they go out and look around?" Reza asked, somewhat annoyed.

Captain Dandachi looked embarrassed. "We don't speak the language, Master Reza, and the Chinese don't like us. They will trade, it is true, but there is always a distance. Even the Chinese agents who come here to negotiate with us make it clear that they dislike us."

Reza, who now dressed very much like a Chinese man of means, had insisted that Yosef and Dar'an did the same. He had told the two young men once when they were raising feeble protests that the great rule was to 'hide in plain sight'. This is what they were doing in the city. They might not be Chinese, but few people looked directly at another in the street, hence they were almost invisible while walking about dressed like the natives, as long as they didn't talk.

Dandachi went on. "You also speak the language, Master Reza. I am astonished at how quickly you have accomplished that."

Reza laughed. "Captain, I am being taught, but I know very little. What I do know is barely enough to order food!"

"Ah yes, the food! It's good food, but what would I not give for a *Barbari* or some good Nan and goat meat!" the captain said wistfully.

Reza sighed to himself. Just as Talon had said, some people would not change, no matter what.

There was one piece of interesting news that the captain passed along. "Remember the stop we made at Kalah Bar, Master Reza?"

How could he forget? That was where he had suffered the indignity of having to eat that awful fruit, and there had been that interesting man called Sing. He nodded. "Yes, I remember."

"A ship came in yesterday that had been attacked by pirates very soon after they left the area for the South, along the Salaht straits. They barely escaped with their lives and lost much of their cargo, as they had to jettison it to enable them to flee."

Reza looked at him sharply. This boded ill for their return journey, as return they must someday. "Have you any other news?" he asked.

"Another ship was lost completely. Only two men survived. They were picked up on an island right at the tip of the Malay peninsula. They said their ship had been attacked by pirates, who stripped it of everything, killed most of the crew, and burned it to the water. He said that the pirate ship possessed a terrible fire-throwing device that destroyed their ship and killed many men."

"This sounds worse than the pirates on the Bahr Al Hind!" Reza exclaimed. He resolved to talk to Talon about this new threat.

"We were all thinking about this," the captain confessed. "Ah, here come the others. Salam, Salam!" he greeted Waqqas, Tarif, Abdullah and Umayr as they arrived with smiles of pleasure on their weathered faces. After the greetings and the kiss on both cheeks, they all settled down to drink tea and to talk.

"We have not seen Master Talon for some time now, Master Reza. Is he well?" Waqqas asked politely.

"I believe he is well. I hope so, anyway. He has gone north to have a look at the people called Mongols with the Lord Meng. He said he wanted to hunt a dragon while on the way, and Lord Meng assured him that he would do so. Nothing could stop him after that; he had to go."

"I have seen images and paintings of these fearsome serpent things they call dragons," said Abdullah, "but I have never seen a live one. They look like very fierce. I hope he is successful in his endeavor. We could stuff it with straw and take it home with us."

"I hear they live in caves in the remote mountains," Waqqas informed them.

"I have heard that they live at the bottom of huge lakes and eat unwary fishermen," Umayr said with great authority.

The conversation continued in this vein to a point where everyone became thoroughly concerned for Talon's safety.

"We must all pray for his deliverance." Reza told them all, sounding pious. He'd had a difficult time holding in his laughter at some of the more absurd statements.

*****

Early one evening Fuling went to visit Fang. The bodyguard had been sulking in his room most evenings, as he was not invited to the family meals, and he felt that he should have been allowed to accompany Lord Meng on his northern journey. He stood up and bowed to Fuling when he entered the room. His breath smelled of rice wine.

"There was a fight between some Tongs and the guards of a rich merchant on the other side of the river," Fuling told Fang, who nodded. He had heard the same thing. The guards had been from the dojo and they had defended the elder son of Wong Cheng Kean from thugs, who had lost the fight, leaving some dead and wounded behind.

"We had oral exams today at the university, but as I was coming back I am sure I was followed."

"Did you see who it was, how many were following you?" Fang prompted him.

"No, but I think it was more than one man, and they followed me all the way home. I made sure they could see my sword, so that might have deterred them if they were thinking of attacking me."

Fang nodded thoughtfully. Fuling could defend himself in a tight spot but would not do well against a skilled swordsman, not yet. And if he was set upon by many....

"I shall personally escort you to the examination hall tomorrow," he told Fuling.

Then he sought out the foreigner, Reza. He found him with the foreign women, seated outside enjoying the evening air. The sun had just set.

He bowed deeply to the group, his hand on his sword and the other rigidly at his side.

"I wish to talk to you, Master Reza," he barked without preamble.

Reza got up and joined him just outside the guesthouse entrance.

They were able to converse in halting Chinese. Fang explained to him briefly what Fuling had told him. "I must escort the young Lord Meng to the school tomorrow and bring him back in the afternoon. It is becoming increasingly dangerous for the relatives and friends of Lord Meng in the city. Please, will you be in charge and make sure all is well during the day?" Fang asked him.

"Of course, Master Fang. I shall be on my guard and make sure nothing happens while you are away," Reza assured him.

"I shall inform the guards, Master Reza. Remember, the quick draw," Fang told him with a friendly glower. He grimaced fiercely and pretended to start drawing his sword. Reza laughed and nodded. "Yes, the quick draw. I shall remember."

Fang nodded, gave a short bow and left.

That night he sent a message to the Sensei at the Dojo.

*****

The next day started off uneventfully, just like any other.

Meilin's brother came to visit and went straight to the inner sanctum of Lady Meilin Meng, where he stayed for several hours. Rav'an and Jannat contemplated going out on the town, as Rav'an wanted to buy some fans and dominos to take home, but Reza tactfully suggested that it might not be a good idea that day. She understood immediately but said nothing, not wanting to alarm Jannat.

However, she went to see Lihua to warn her of Fang's concern. Lihua in turn went to see the old lady.

"I am told that Fang is worried, my Lady," she told Lanfen.

"What can possibly be worrying Fang, I wonder? My son tells me that he is always on the edge of going mad. Meanwhile, my daughter-in-law is conferring with her brother. Ai ya! but I can hear his whining even from here."

Lady Lanfen had gradually come to like Lihua, having found her not only very polite but a very capable house manager. Her former reservations had been dispelled by recent events. The fact that she shared her son's bed was a matter of indifference to her.

"Who told you of this... this problem?" Lanfen asked Lihua.

"It was Rav'an, my Lady," she responded.

"Hmm, those people seem to have a nose for trouble," Lady Lanfen said. "Perhaps it is because they face danger all the time in their world. I am glad we do not have such problems here."

That afternoon, while they were all seated on the balcony of the guest house playing dominoes, Rav'an stretched and sighed.

"I wish Talon were here. It is so peaceful and pleasant; I could almost stay in China forever. What is it that has made me fall in love with China?" she asked the world at large. "The colors are so intense. The life is so intense. They say that whatever it is that you seek, you shall find it here in Guangzhou!" She laughed happily.

Jannat smiled and placed a domino block on the table with a snap. Reza groaned. "You have taken my place!" he grumped. "I was going to do that."

"Lihua taught me well. I shall take the set in a minute!" she chortled happily.

Reza, who was eating some small pieces of squid with his chop sticks, suddenly jabbed at something in the air. A morsel of squid flew off and landed in Jannat's lap.

"Reza, what are you doing?" she demanded. "Look, you have spoiled my dress!" she complained.

"Uncle Reza is trying to catch flies, Auntie Jannat," Rostam told her. Reza glowered at him, looking sheepish, which made the boy giggle.

"What is this about?" Rav'an asked from where she was seated with some embroidery work in her lap.

"Uncle Reza and Papa are trying to be like the warriors of the Nippon and catch flies with their chopsticks. It means that they are very, very fast if they can do it. Papa is faster than Uncle Reza, he nearly got one," Rostam volunteered.

Reza leveled a threatening chopstick at Rostam, who sent him a cheeky grin.

"Fang told us a story about a Samurai from the Nippon who was so fast with his chop sticks that he could catch flies in midair. No one dared to fight him because he was so fast," he explained, sounding embarrassed.

"You men! You think of the silliest things to do," Jannat scolded him, wiping her dress. "No more of that at this table," she ordered. "Concentrate your speed on this game, where I am beating you."

*****

It was almost dusk when they the heard a shout at the gates. In a flash Reza was up and had seized his bow. Yosef and Dar'an jumped to their feet and joined him to move swiftly towards the main gates. Reza looked back at the women, but Rav'an was already moving towards the stairs that would take her and Jannat out of the way, and to where her own bow was waiting.

"Rostam!" she called as they went.

"Rostam, where are you?" she called again, more urgently this time, becoming alarmed. Rostam had wandered off with Lun.

"Reza, Rostam is not here!" she called out to the departing men. "Please find him!"

"We will look for him immediately," Reza called back, as he ran towards the gates and the agitated guards, who had just opened the gates.

Fuling stagger inside, supporting Fang, who appeared to be wounded. There was blood all down one side, and his left arm hung loose.

"What happened?" Reza demanded, as they eased Fang off the exhausted Fuling.

"They waited until we were on this side of the river where there are fewer people, and then attacked us. We fought them off. But one got behind us and struck Fang in the arm. Then they ran off because he killed two of them."

"How many were there?" Reza asked him, as they half-carried Fang towards the guest rooms where Reza knew Rav'an would be able to dress the wound. It didn't look mortal, but Fang appeared to have lost much blood. The guards hastily shut the gates behind them. Reza wondered how useful they would be in an emergency; they looked frightened.

"There were six of them. I have never seen any of them before. They were certainly after me, perhaps for a ransom?"

Reza nodded. Under the present circumstances he thought that it might well be the case. Fuling told Reza that he was going to the main house to warn the servants of trouble, and ran off. It was now dusk, and darker shadows were beginning to form. The last of the red streaks in the clouds above had faded, leaving everything in tones of gray.

Reza turned to look for Rostam. It was not unusual for him to be playing with Lun, too preoccupied to notice the passing of time. Reza made for the stables.

It was very quiet, except for the horses themselves. The placid sound of them munching hay and the occasional stamp of a hoof to ward off flies was the only sound he could hear. He walked closer and heard the low sound of the boy's voices, which stopped abruptly.

"Uncle Reza! Look out!" Rostam screamed.

Reza instinctively ducked and spun on his heel at the same time. The man who had run towards him had made almost no noise at all and was about to strike downward with a sword. Reza drew and struck without thinking. His blade sliced into the side of the unarmored man and stopped him in his tracks. In a split second Reza was up and his sword lashed out like a striking snake. He barely felt the shock of the blow as the man's head tumbled to the ground, closely followed by the trunk. There had been scarcely a sound throughout the engagement. He felt a cold sweat come over him with the reaction. He should have heard the man! Were they that good?

The two boys stood rooted to the ground with shock at what they had just witnessed. Reza realized there was no time to waste. With a hasty look around for more intruders, Reza seized Rostam by the hand. "Come on, Lun!" he whispered urgently, giving the frozen boy a nudge with his elbow. The three of them raced across the compound to the guest house, where Yosef stood at the entrance.

"Keep them close, Yosef, we are having visitors. You and Dar'an defend this place. I must go to the main house." He turned away, but then saw two dark figures coming towards him. Both held swords in the ready to strike position.

Reza went on guard immediately. "Stay back, Yosef. Guard those inside!" he called back in *Farsi*.

The two shadowy figures advanced on Reza, silent and purposeful.

Reza heard rather than saw what happened next. He heard the twang of a bow string behind him; an arrow hissed past and landed with a thump in the chest of one of the shapes, who collapsed to his knees with a gasp before tumbling forward to lie on the pathway. Reza didn't look back, but he knew who had shot it. Rav'an was standing on the balcony overlooking the entrance, holding a bow; she had a perfect view.

The other figure glanced down at his companion and was just about to flee when Reza leapt forward and skewered him with his sword. The man screamed with agony and fell forward to lie twitching alongside his companion. Only then did Reza look back and raise his sword. "My Lady," he saluted her. She lifted her hand in acknowledgement as he raced off towards the main house. "Go with God, my Reza," she murmured, and turned back to help Jannat with Fang, who was struggling to sit up.

"You must rest, Master Fang," she told him sharply as they pushed him back down onto the mattress.

He began to babble in fast Chinese which the girls didn't understand, so Rav'an said to him, "Speak slowly, Fang. We cannot understand you."

He looked at her feverishly. "They are coming. Just as Lord Meng said they would. I, I have called the dojo for help...." He finished with a sigh and closed his eyes. Beads of sweat had appeared on his forehead with the exertion, but then his eyes snapped open. "You must bind up this arm!" He waved his bleeding arm at them, scattering drops of blood all over the bed. "I go now to fight!"

Rav'an knew when she was dealing with a man who could not be deterred, so she and Jannat bound up his upper left arm and helped him to his feet. "Where is my sword!" he almost shouted. She handed it to him and he seemed to calm down when he hefted it and nodded.

"You stay here, and I shall go and kill them all!" he growled. He stamped off down the stairs with new energy, his still bloody sword held high in his right hand.

"He is quite mad!" Rav'an told Jannat as they watched him stride across the short distance to the main house where Reza had already disappeared.

"I'm glad he is on our side. I do hope Reza is going to be safe," she fretted.

"Come, those two boys are looking shocked for some reason," Rav'an said, and led the way to find Rostam and Lun.

*****

Fang met Reza at the entrance to the main house. It took a moment for Fang to register that it was Reza, but then he grated a word of welcome.

"I have come to fulfill my obligations. Where is the young Lord Meng?"

"I am here, Fang," Fuling said. He held up a Nippon style sword for Fang to see.

"Good, then there are three of us to fight whoever comes," Fang muttered.

"Who is it that is coming?" Reza asked.

"The enemies of Lord Meng. They are coming," Lihua called from the doorway to the main house.

Reza whirled. "Are they still after that box of gems?" he asked, staring at her. "You should be inside with the doors shut, Lihua."

"I will do what I can, Reza, thank you. Yes, they are still after them, I am sure of it."

"Are they here?" he asked in Arabic, referring to the jewels.

"They are safe... somewhere else," she told him in the same language. "I don't think anyone told them, which is why they are back," she finished dryly.

Reza snorted with amusement. Lihua was a plucky girl.

The three men edged back into the shadows by the entrance to wait for anything that might happen. Reza hoped that the enemy, whomsoever they were, would have had enough. They had lost three men already.

He tensed. There was the sound of many running feet in the growing darkness.

"Reza! We are here, let us in!" Rav'an called in a low tone as she rushed towards them.

He realized what she had done, the rest of the family and the servants from the guest house were with her. Better to have them all in the same place than vulnerable in separate houses. He wished that he could have been able to send a message to his boat crew to come and help. The prospect of a full scale assault on the compound was not appetizing. He wondered what the guards were doing at the front gate. He had not heard a thing from the ones who were supposed to be patrolling the wall at the back. They were probably dead by now, he reasoned.

"Come inside, quickly!" he called out to Rav'an. They all rushed past him into the courtyard.

"I didn't think it wise to stay separated, Reza," Rav'an explained with a nervous edge to her voice.

"You did the right thing, Rav'an. I should have thought of it myself. Go to Lihua upstairs; she will look after the boys."

"I brought my bow, and so did Yosef and Dar'an," she told him.

"Good! Go upstairs to the balcony where you will have a better view and prepare yourselves. We might need you, again."

*****

Lady Meng Meilin was aware that something was going on but could not get out of bed. Lihua sent one of the maids up to keep her company. The servants who would normally help her were downstairs in the living rooms, where Lihua had told them to stay for the night for their own safety. After comforting Meilin, who had temporarily forgotten that Lihua was her competitor in the matrimonial bed and taken from her a small dose of a powder that would help her sleep, Lihua went to see the old lady.

She found her calm and unruffled and aware of the danger; her maid had told her in hysterical bursts. "Are you all right?" the old lady inquired from her chair in the room.

Lihua smiled, she had been about to ask the same question. Lady Lanfen refused to go to bed in the present circumstances. Lihua admired her for her courage.

"It is about time Hsü came home," Lanfen remarked to Lihua, who nodded. "Yes, my lady, it has now been almost six weeks."

They both heard a noise outside on the balcony of something heavy landing on it, a sound of scraping, and a light clink of metal.

They exchanged looks with wide eyes, then Lady Lanfen signaled Lihua to get the attention of the others.

Lihua rushed silently to the balcony on the other side of the building and tapped Rav'an on the shoulder. Rav'an whirled in alarm.

'Oh, it's you, Lihua. You gave me such a fright!" she whispered.

"There is someone coming up from the other side of the house!" Lihua whispered urgently, then she whirled around and disappeared. Lihua was not going to leave Lady Lanfen to face danger alone. She left the door to the corridor open so others could follow, then went to back to the old lady. With all her strength, she lifted her out of her chair and carried her to a small stool in a dark corner near to a wardrobe, where she put her down and whispered, "Forgive my impertinence, my Lady, but I must protect you!" She pulled out a long knife she carried. She snuffed out the candle, plunging them into darkness. They held their breath and waited.

There was a small scraping sound at the doorway that led to the balcony, and they could see the door open very slowly. A dark figure crept into the room. It was so dark they could not see the color of the clothing nor the face, just the pitch black shape that moved.

Lihua heard a small sound outside the door to the corridor at the same time as the intruder, who froze. A figure stepped into the opening, and before the intruder could react a bow twanged and an arrow struck flesh with a loud thump.

The figure jerked, then hissed with pain, indicating that the arrow had at least struck; but he then leapt towards the doorway where Rav'an still stood. Evidently he could see her silhouette and wanted to grapple with her before another arrow found its mark. Lihua moved quickly, throwing herself at the dark figure and dragging him down to the floor. Another hiss, this time of surprise and anger. Lihua tried to hold onto the kicking and slashing intruder. One kick landed on her shoulder, nearly breaking her collarbone. It knocked her backwards to land on her rump with a yelp of pain. Rav'an had meanwhile stepped into the room where she could only just perceive the two on the floor. She proceeded to poke hard with the end of the bow at where she thought his face might be. It struck something soft and she was rewarded with a roar of pain. Her chest tight with fear she decided that the best thing to do was to keep attacking so she lifted the bow and beat down at the black figure nearest to her with the bow.

"Take that!" she shouted with pent up fear. Whack! went the bow on the figure's back. "Ouy!" shouted the figure.

Whack! Whack! Whack! "Ouch! Ouch!" snarled the intruder giving up all pretense of stealth. "Take that! And that!" yelled Rav'an, desperately hammering at him on the head with the bow, wishing that she had a spear instead.

The blows raining down on the intruder and the recent wound he had received convinced him to abandon his mission and to try for an avenue of escape. He whirled around, trying to find the open balcony.

By this time Jannat had arrived at the doorway, holding a lantern on high. She gasped at the sight of the thrashing figures on the floor and of Rav'an belaboring the back of a man on hands and knees in front of her. Jannat instinctively drew her own knife with a cry of warning to Lihua, who was right in the path of the intruder as he scrambled to his feet and headed her way. An arrow was still embedded in his shoulder but he was still very much alive, and now he was enraged. He roared with pain and frustration as he ducked and dodged the blows from Rav'an, who followed him, yelling abuse at him all the while. Lihua stuck her foot out as the man stumbled past, bringing him back down on all fours.

He lashed out with his blade and caught her forearm in a painful slashing stroke, forcing a cry of pain from her. Then Rav'an threw herself onto his back, which caused him to fall on his side. He stabbed backwards at Rav'an but she wriggled out of the way just in time and the blade thumped into the wooden floor.

"Pedar Sag!" she yelled, by now thoroughly angry and clawed at his face from behind, going for his eyes and trying to bite his ear at the same time.

"Arrgg!" He roared and dropped his knife to protect himself. Lihua was on hands and knees, crawling towards him. She reached for the abandoned knife which she now clutched with a murderous look in her eyes. He struggled even harder as he realized what she was about to do.

"Do it Lihua!" Rav'an screamed from behind the struggling man. With another cry, this time of rage and fear, Lihua reached forward and stabbed down at his chest. He shouted something at her and knocked her arm aside, but then Rav'an, still yelling and struggling half under him, caught and held onto his arm just long enough for Lihua to raise her knife high and with a yell of her own stab downwards with all her strength. This time the knife went home between his ribs and into his heart.

There was a huge jerk from their adversary as he gave a strangled shout; then he relaxed and was still, his body now draped backwards over the supine Rav'an. There was a heavy silence in the room, other than the labored breathing of the women as they realized what had happened. Rav'an was the first to recover. She pushed hard at the deadweight of the body lying across her. "Jannat help me! He's bleeding all over me, houuf!" she gasped, as she struggled to get the body off.

Jannat rushed forward to help her, and between them they managed to shove the body out of the way. Then the three women, still kneeling, disheveled and frightened, stared at one another.

"Do you think he is dead?" Lihua asked. Her voice trembled.

"Oh yes! He's dead!" Rav'an gasped, still breathing heavily and prodded the body with its own knife. "Are you all right?" she asked Lihua, who was clutching her arm. Blood was seeping down her arm and dripping off her elbow onto the already bloody floor.

Jannat gave out a choked off laugh that bordered on hysteria. She was shaking and reached out to hold onto Rav'an who gave a deep sigh of relief and clutched her back.

"I didn't know you could swear just like Reza!" Jannat giggled, as she held onto her friend. Both women started to laugh, but then looked over at Lihua, who, wide-eyed, was staring at the dead man. She was beginning to shake. Jannat slid across the floor and embraced her. "It's all right, Lihua; the danger is past." Lihua slumped into her arms, trying not to weep.

Rav'an was not so sure they were safe yet and was about to get to her feet when there was the sound of rapid footsteps outside. Yosef charged into the room.

He took in the situation at a glance: the women on the floor and the body lying nearby with blood everywhere. "My Lady," he croaked, "are you all right?"

Rav'an gave him a shaky smile and tried to tuck her fallen hair back over her ears. "Yes, Yosef, I think so, but Lihua here is wounded. There might be others," she waved a hand at the dead man and then at the balcony. "You should make sure."

*****

While they waited, Reza thought about the people who were behind all this. From what he could deduce from conversations with Talon and Hsü, the man called Hua Rong was deeply involved. They had recovered the box from his office, and now people were either trying to recover the evidence or making another attempt to steal the gems. They were not particular how they obtained what they were seeking, either. Reza mentally tipped his hat to Hsü; the man seemed to be able to anticipate his enemies and friends alike.

He was interrupted by loud female yells and screams from above and behind him. Dar'an was desperately trying to get his attention. "Reza! They are trying to get in from the other side, come quickly!" he called.

Reza told Fuling to stay with Fang and rushed silently up the stairs to where Dar'an was standing. He pointed urgently to the entrance to a bedroom, from which came a dim light.

"Keep watch on Fang and the gate," he ordered Dar'an, and rushed into the room. He saw Rav'an kneeling on the floor, and Jannat holding Lihua around her shoulders. Lihua was choking back tears and supporting her arm, which was covered in blood. A dark, motionless figure lay sprawled on the floor nearby and seemed to be quite dead.

Checking quickly to see that Rav'an and Jannat were all right, he hastened to the open doorway and the balcony beyond. Yosef was already there, peering down at the garden below in the darkness. There was no sign of anyone else lurking in the bushes, so Yosef hauled up the rope that was still attached to the rail and dropped it on the floor of the room.

"I have not seen anyone, Reza but this is how he got in." He showed Reza the rope.

Reza nodded. "Stay here and keep watch," he told Yosef, and turned back into the room.

"I think you dealt with the problem, Rav'an," he complimented her.

"We need to help Lihua, she is hurt," Rav'an said. She sounded shaken.

"Take care of her. I'll look around," he said, and patted her reassuringly on the arm. "I want to hear all about it later." He grinned and left the room to check on other areas of the house.

Jannat joined Rav'an, who bound up Lihua's wound and said, "You are so very brave, Lihua. I'm glad he didn't do worse to you."

Lihua bit back some tears and said, "I was terrified! Can you help me move my Lady Meng?"

Turning, they found the old lady, still sitting quietly in the darkness of the corner by the wardrobe. She had witnessed all that had happened. The three of them lifted Lady Lanfen up and carried her to her chair. When they had made sure she was comfortable, Lihua left the room to find some servants to help dispose of the body.

While she was away, Lady Lanfen said to Rav'an, pointing at the body, "That took great courage. Are all the women warriors like you where you come from?"

Rav'an gave a small laugh. "No, my lady, but when you have been around Talon and Reza you soon learn to be. Don't forget that it was Lihua here who finished him. She is very brave."

"Yes, I would agree with you there," the old lady said with a smile.

*****

After inspecting the rest of the upper story of the house, moving as silently as a ghost, Reza arrived back at the entrance to join Fang and Fuling at the gate.

"Nothing yet, Reza," Fuling said quietly. He had no sooner said this than they heard a shout from the stables and the clear sound of swords clashing. Men were fighting; but who?

All of a sudden, men in dark clothes and masked faces appeared out of the dark in front of them. Reza estimated that they outnumbered his group three to one. This was not just an attempt to steal something, these people had come to harm the family Meng. Fang, who at last had a clear target, gave a great shout and charged recklessly to meet the men running towards them. Fang, screaming madly, his sword a whirlwind of flashing steel, cut and parried and struck with amazing speed.

Reza put a restraining hand on Fuling's shoulder. "Don't move. You will be cut to pieces by Fang if you do. Wait a moment."

Then he said, "Now!" Both of them hurled themselves forward, swords readied. Above them on the balcony Dar'an snarled with frustration; he could not see clearly enough to shoot his arrows from there.

Reza took one man down immediately, while Fang slew his third. Their enemies suddenly found themselves fighting for their lives; then another group appeared out of nowhere and rushed to join the mêlée, the leader shouting at Fang in Chinese, and they joined in the ferocious battle. For a few mad seconds there was the ring of blade on blade, the sickening sound of blades cutting through flesh, and the screams and groans of the men struck.

Then, as suddenly as it had begun, the fight was over; enemy men lay dead or dying all around them. Only two men were left standing.

Reza looked around for Fang. Someone held up a lantern for them to see, and Fuling found him lying face down, draped over two men whom he had just slain, still clutching his sword. When Reza turned him over he lay limp and without motion, nor was he breathing.

"This is the doing of that man Hua Rong!" Fuling ground out as he squatted next to Fang's body. "I'd like to kill him with my bare hands!" he raged, swiping tears from his eyes with his sleeve.

"Are you sure?' Reza asked him. He looked down at the body of the man he had come to respect and placed a light hand on Fuling's shoulder. "He was a great warrior, Fuling."

Fuling nodded with his head down. "Yes, I am sure," he mumbled, then nodded. "Yes, Fang was a great warrior."

Someone came and stood near them. "He died as he would have wanted to doe, fighting for his Lord and dying with honor," a new voice said.

Reza looked up. The man standing over them was dressed in dark clothes like the enemy, and his face was covered to the eyes, but even as Reza tensed he recognized his instructor from the dojo, Qian.

"Thank you for coming, Qian. Who did you bring with you?" Fuling asked him.

Speaking slowly for Reza's benefit Qian said, "Our teaching seems to have paid off for you, Master Reza. I brought Hedé, Liu, and four students who need the practice. Fang sent us a message. I am sorry we did not get here earlier."

"Ah, now I understand." Fuling shook his head tiredly. "At least now he will know peace," he said, looking down at his bodyguard.

"We must secure the house and the yard, Fuling," Reza reminded him. For the rest of the night they kept vigil, and with the dawn began the hard work of cleaning up after the battle and laying Fang out.

*****

Several days later, the morning at the office of Hua Rong the Chief of Police began much as it always did. He arrived in a palanquin and walked up to his office, where his secretary presented him with a pile of papers, while a pretty young woman prepared tea for him to sip while contemplating the sins of the city. He enjoyed watching her as she carried out the task. He prided himself in his taste of women and decided he might very well take her this evening if he was in the mood. He had to attend an execution that day. The Governor couldn't, because he was still bed-bound, so it fell to him to appear and witness the final moments of the sentenced prisoners. He always found that distasteful; the girl would be a good antidote to the unpleasantness of the execution.

He did not anticipate with any relish the endless stream of supplicants who continued to come, day in day out, to ask for favors: asking for money or, heaven forbid, for redress for crimes committed against them by the numerous villains in the city.

He sent for his secretary, ordering him not to disturb him and giving him the task of bringing the Arab contingent to his office the next day for a conference. They were still whining about the taxes imposed upon their vessels for anchorage in the roads of the river. They would doubtless say that if they could sell their goods and leave they should be allowed to. He shook his head and smiled to himself. It simply didn't work like that.

Then Lin appeared, and he knew from his henchman's expression that his day was ruined.

"What happened this time?" he asked, his stomach lurching painfully.

"So sorry, my Lord, but as you know, Buwei sent his men in last night," Lin said in a low voice.

"And what?" Rong almost shouted. "Do *not* tell me they also failed!" He gripped the side of the table with white knuckles.

Lin looked frightened. "They were nearly all killed, Lord. Only two got away, and they were wounded."

"Get out! Get out of my sight!" Rong snarled, thumping his fist onto the table, which shuddered. Lin vanished.

He had to think. This was an utter disaster. He mopped his sweating forehead with a cloth as he frantically searched for answers in his mind. He had to find Buwei as soon as he could, but he needed to think first.

Rong didn't hear the door open, but he felt a presence. He looked up. Someone strange was standing over him. "What do you want?" he demanded.

A few minutes later a man dressed the same as any of the secretaries made his way through the crowded offices and out onto the street. No one had noticed the man going into Rong's office, nor leaving it.

A few minutes later, Reza and Fuling were being rowed back across the river and Reza was casually watching the river traffic and tugging at his new, extra-long mustache. Fuling was consumed with curiosity. "What happened? What did he say?" he demanded.

Reza shrugged. "Well, we didn't really talk. My Chinese isn't very good. But... I think Fang would have been pleased."

*****

About a half hour later, the girl walked into the office with another pot of tea and found Rong. Her reverberating screams were heard all the way down to the first floor entrance. Guards came sprinting up the stairs two at a time, and secretaries hurried to the doorway of Rong's office. The crowd at the door gasped with horror at the sight, and one eunuch even fainted.

Rong's body was slumped back in his chair with his head thrown back; a trickle of blood had flowed out of the corner of his mouth and dribbled down the exquisite stitching of his tunic collar. His sightless eyes were staring up at the ceiling and there were two bloody chop sticks protruding from the front of his exposed throat.

"Never give a sword to a man who cannot dance."

—Confucius

Chapter Twenty-Nine
The Spirit of The Dragon

Talon and Hsü walked down the mountain early the next morning after bidding the abbot and his monks farewell. Talon was looking forward to the ride home, and so was Hsü, but he was preoccupied with his coming battle for the position of governor.

Neither was paying much attention to their surroundings as they came down the final slope to the inn, until Talon looked up and noticed there were many more horses near the inn than before, but no signs of life. He checked and was about to point this out to Hsü, who had stopped because Talon had done so, when an arrow thudded into a tree very close to his head.

Both men immediately dropped onto one knee and scanned the bushes ahead. They stared at one another in surprise, but they were left in no doubt that they were under attack when another arrow landed in the dirt right between them.

"We are ambushed!" exclaimed Hsü, and rolled off to his right. Talon dived after him and then they both scrambled for denser cover in some bushes, just below the pathway down the steep slope. More arrows were thudding into the trees and the ground around them. Talon was not impressed with the archery but didn't want to test it too far.

There was a shout from the bushes nearby which didn't sound like Chinese. "They are Mongols!" Hsü gasped in a bewildered tone. "What by heaven are they doing here?"

Talon shook his head. He had no idea, but one thing was certain: they mustn't be captured; they had to flee. They scuttled into the bushes as more shouts rose, followed by the sounds of pursuit.

Without warning, the ground in front of them fell away in a dizzying drop to the river below. They both teetered on the very edge, staring down at the pools and raging rapids far below, as the sounds of pursuit drew closer.

"Dear God!" Talon exclaimed, looking around him desperately for another avenue of escape. Hsü was doing the same, and then he pointed. There were several Mongols on foot climbing the only route they might have taken down the other side of the hill away from their ambushers. The Mongols hadn't yet seen them and were shouting up to their companions, who were still hidden by the dense undergrowth above them and beyond the two fugitives.

Talon glanced again at the the fast flowing river below and had a moment of vertigo. It seemed a very long way down. Hsü clutched at his arm. "We are dead if we stay," he said; there was a frantic note to his voice. "They don't seem to want to negotiate. We have to jump. Ahmida Buddha protect us!"

Talon agreed, although it took every ounce of will power for him to stand and contemplate what they were about to do. "Then we jump! I will see you in the water, There is a pool just below; try and land in that, and then perhaps God will protect us," he said. Dear God, but it seemed such a long way down!

They launched themselves from the cliff. Talon just heard a shout from behind them as they did so, and another arrow sailed over their heads, but he wasn't paying it any attention. His stomach lurched into his throat and he couldn't breathe. His mouth was wide open in a silent scream and his legs and arms were flailing as he tried desperately to stay upright while he fell what seemed an impossible distance. He knew instinctively that should he land any other way than feet first he was dead. This was his only hope.

He forgot about the flailing, roaring man next to him as the long drop ended abruptly with a numbing splash into the raging waters of the river. He plunged deep into the icy torrent, and then felt himself being swept along the bottom across sharp stones and being turned over by the fierce current. He didn't have a moment to congratulate himself for surviving the fall; it was taking all his strength not to drown in the fierce torrent. He felt himself being hammered against rocks, and whatever breath he might have had when he fell in was pounded out of his lungs. Just before he was about to pass out, he surfaced. He gulped in one huge, agonized breath, and then went under again; then he resurfaced and managed with a great effort to keep his head above water. He shook his head to clear the water and his hair from his eyes.

The water was shallower here and narrower, although the current was still dragging at him with a strong, irresistible pull towards some rapids. He failed to get his legs under him and gave up, allowing the river to take him feet first down stream. Now he was able to cast a desperate look around him for Hsü. Where was he? Had he died in the fall? He turned his head to look behind him and thought he saw something surface, but then it took all his attention to prevent himself from being beaten unconscious on the rocks of the rapids that sent the water foaming and spraying. He thought he heard a cry from up stream, but the roar of the water drowned out all other sounds.

He was astounded that he had survived what he estimated must have been a sixty foot drop. Then he realized that the river had widened and was taking him past the inn, which was set some way back from the bank on a slope among trees. Had he been in the water that long? He suddenly panicked and grabbed at his sword in his waist-band, breathing a huge mental gasp of relief. It was still there, but now he worried that it might come loose and fall out.

It seemed prudent to allow the current to take him a little way past the inn, after which he made a desperate effort to swim to a small pebbly beach, overhung by some dense undergrowth and weeping willows. Reaching one tree, he seized the branches which brushed the water and hung on, almost too exhausted and chilled to do more. He got his legs under him and tried for the bottom, and found that he could just touch it with his feet; the water here was neck deep. He managed to keep his balance, and then began to haul himself towards the bank. It looked as though it would provide good cover if he could just reach it.

Then he heard a low cry and turned his head to see Hsü being swept towards him. Talon barely had time to put out his arms when Hsü slammed into him and they both went under. Talon grabbed onto Hsü's tunic and hung on until Hsü was able to right himself in the rushing water. Talon reached up for the branches of the weeping willow again and hung on. Hsü gasped and choked, then clutched at Talon.

"We have to get out of sight," Talon wheezed. The effort of getting to the bank had taken much of his strength. "I don't think they know we are here, yet," he croaked.

They dragged themselves onto the narrow pebbled beach, gasping for breath and moaning with relief. "I didn't think we would survive that," Hsü muttered with a weak grin at Talon, who grimaced. "We still have the Mongols to deal with," he replied. He crawled up the bank and peered over the edge; all was quiet ahead of him. "I wonder if they saw us jump?" he said.

"They must have, but with some Joss they might not know we are here," Hsü said as he joined Talon. His teeth were chattering with the cold. "I hope they think we died in the fall and were swept downstream."

"At first I thought it might be yet another attempt to assassinate me by my friends in Guangzhou," he continued. "Now I know that isn't so. They are after you, I suspect."

"These people seem just as determined as everyone else to see us off," Talon muttered, and lifted his head to peer over the edge of the bank again. "That's the last time I follow you over a cliff," he added.

"I lead by example." Hsü took a deep breath and added, "I was sure we would be dashed to pieces on the rocks." He looked drawn and exhausted.

"At least we still have our swords," Talon huffed.

"'Never give a sword to a man who cannot dance,'" Hsü quoted. "We two certainly did a fine dance on the way down through the air!"

In spite of his soaking wet condition, the cold, and his aches, Talon had to laugh. His friend was not giving up just yet.

"There only appear to be two men over there. I don't see any other signs of life," Talon whispered. "Perhaps there is a chance we can get to our horses and get out of here."

"The Mongols most certainly killed our escort, and then set up this ambush. If they had waited for just a few more minutes we would have been well within range of their archers, but someone was too eager," Hsü commented. Talon agreed with him.

Just then, some men ran into view and Talon sighed; he knew that the opportunity to reach their horses had just passed. "The others have arrived," he said.

Somehow they had to survive until nightfall, which might present them with another chance. He recognized the man called Muunokhoi who ran up to the sentries and began to gesticulate urgently, pointing to the river. The rest of the Mongols clustered about their chief, apparently having a small conference. Abruptly they split up and began to hurry towards the river, some headed down stream, while one came straight towards where they were hiding. Talon couldn't see where Muunokhoi had gone, but hoped that he would not come their way. He dropped back to Hsü, who was lying on his back, still recovering. Talon noted with approval that he still had his sword with him.

"It's Muunokhoi! Perhaps you were right, he's after revenge. Hurry, we have to get out of sight. They know we went into the river, and it looks like they are going to search for us along the bank to make sure we didn't live; those reeds over there!" Talon whispered urgently, pointing.

Hsü roused from his torpor, struggled to his knees, and followed. If they could hide in the water among the dense clumps of reeds, they might yet go unnoticed. Talon made sure that evidence of their arrival on the beach was cleared and eased himself back into the water under the overhanging branches of the willows and among the reeds. His feet could only just touch bottom. They pulled some detritus of old dead branches and reeds over their heads and settled deeper into the water. The water was icy cold and they were both shivering, but their lives depended upon staying quiet for hours, until they could look for an escape.

They had only just managed to settle in when Talon became aware of motion on the bank. Someone was walking above them. They both crouched even lower with only their noses above the waterline. The river swirled past their clump of reeds, leaving them in a form of backwater. When the man passed by without pausing, Talon thanked God that he had not made a determined effort to search for them. Perhaps he didn't believe they could have survived? Talon himself was still amazed that they had managed to fall into a pool rather than a shallow part of the river; broken legs and worse would have been their reward for that.

They remained shivering in the water for many hours. It was a test to the full of their endurance. Talon worried about Hsü, but a glance in his direction met with a responding tense grin that reassured him. He doubted if he could grin back, his teeth were chattering so hard, and his legs felt numb, but they dared not emerge until dusk at the earliest. Talon guessed that the search might have moved further downstream; he hoped it had. Before long the frustrated Mongols would have another factor to consider. Word of their foray into China would soon get out, and the Chinese General Yang Hsün would hear of it quickly enough. He might be riding along this same route before very long looking or the Mongols, and he had several hundred men at his disposal.

Muunokhoi had only a limited time to complete his vengeful mission and then leave without being noticed. Should the Chinese find him here, this far into Sung China, it constituted a clear declaration of war. Talon wondered if that was what they wanted, but discounted it at this time. Muunokhoi just wanted revenge, and it would not have surprised Talon if Badzar had put him up to it. He would never know for certain.

The sun crept overhead and then moved across the western quadrant of the sky. Talon could only judge the position of the sun by some shadows that moved with agonizingly slow progress. No sounds came from the bank to alarm them. At one time, however, there was movement, and they both shrunk deeper into their cold, watery hideout, wondering if they had been discovered. It proved to be a young deer that had come under cover to drink. Its huge ears were flicking back and forth and it sniffed the air continuously, but otherwise it seemed unaware of the two men. Talon watched it carefully to see if it sensed the presence of others, but other than once looking over its shoulder at something, it seemed calm enough. Eventually it leapt up the bank and disappeared, and they were left alone to shiver in the cold water.

Dusk drew in, and finally it was dark enough for Talon to feel safe enough to emerge. He reached over and gripped Hsü's arm. Hsü took a moment to respond, but then he nodded and they both moved slowly out of the reeds towards the bank. They were very careful not to make any unnecessary sounds as they crawled onto the beach on hands and knees, to lie shaking with cold. Talon struggled to take his boots off and empty them of water. It was a huge effort.

Both men knew the urgency of recovering and preparing for whatever might come next, but it took an enormous effort to stir themselves. Talon pulled his sodden boots back on, and leaving Hsü to finish emptying his own boots, he crawled on hands and knees to the bank. He peered over its grassy edge towards the inn and could just see in the gloom that many horses were still there. The dark figures of their guards moved slowly back and forth in front of the buildings. He noted the glimmer of lamplight came from the windows, and thought he heard loud voices, but otherwise there was nothing to alarm him. He tapped Hsü on the shoulder and motioned him over. Hsü joined him and they both examined the distant buildings with care.

"How many would you say are there?" Hsü asked him.

"It is hard to tell in this light, and there are also our horses and our guard's horses, but I would say this was a small party of about sixteen or eighteen men. Three of them are outside. I can deal with those," Talon responded.

Hsü sighed. "Far too many for us to deal with, on our own."

He had to say it slowly, as his teeth were chattering hard; it reminded Talon of how cold he was in his soaking clothes. He had lost his cloak in the river, as had Hsü, so the light wind that had sprung up with the night was chilling them to the bone. His jaw ached from clenching his teeth.

"If I could only get to my bow I could even the odds, even in this light," he murmured.

"They would charge you, and then we would have to get back into the river. I've had enough of that river for a lifetime," Hsü whispered back. Talon smiled. Then Hsü slapped him gently on the shoulder. "I know what to do!" he exclaimed in a whisper.

Talon turned to face his friend. "Tell me," he demanded. "Do you have some of that flame powder on you?"

Hsü snorted. "One thing you have to understand about flame powder, Talon, is that it dislikes water as much as I do right now. Bear that in mind for the future, if we have one. No, I am going to get help.”

“From up at the temple?” Talon anticipated him. “Are you strong enough to get up there in the night?”

Hsü nodded. “I have no choice. The Abbot and his men will help us for sure.”

“But they are monks, Hsü! Warfare is not their trade. The Mongols will cut them to pieces!” Talon objected in a strong whisper.

“You have a lot to learn about monks in this country, Talon. If I can get to them, they will help us.” Hsü sounded very sure of himself.

Talon was skeptical. “Then you should go up there and bring them down. I am sure they don’t want a bunch of smelly Mongols hanging around pillaging this area. They might be next. I shall stay here and keep an eye on our friends over there.”

“What do you intend to do, Talon?”

“I shall provide a fitting reception for the holy men when you bring them down the mountain.”

“What does that mean?” Hsü asked him.

“You will see plainly enough when you get back. However, if I am not seated on the back of a horse, then know that I have lost and that they are waiting for you.”

Hsü nodded in the dark and said, “Be safe. I think you are almost as mad as Fang. Wish me safe journey.”

“Be vigilant, my friend. God protect you. There might be one or two of them on the trail. Muunokhoi knows what he is about.” They gripped hands, and then Hsü eased himself along the bank and disappeared into the night in the direction of the trail. Fortunately he did not have to cross the river again. Talon could hear tiny sounds for some time after he had departed, but didn’t think the Mongol sentries would notice. He continued to observe the dark patch of the buildings. The horses were tied in a line, and the three guards appeared to be watchful, so he bided his time. Hsü would take the better part of three hours to make it to the top, he estimated, and then another two to come down, so it would be almost dawn by the time he made it back to the inn. Talon intended to do something about the numbers while he was gone.

A thin crescent moon had risen low in the East, shedding some light on the ground, for which Talon was thankful. He was feeling somewhat better an hour later, having rested and moved his arms around to get the circulation going.

Now he moved slowly towards the inn, keeping to every patch of cover available. He arrived within thirty paces of the buildings and stopped in a dense patch of shrubbery to take stock; the noise from within had if anything increased. The Mongols were taking advantage of the Innkeeper's stock. At one time a door was thrown open and a man, clearly a Mongol by his dress, staggered out and relieved himself against a wall not ten paces from where Talon was hidden.

The man was obviously drunk and the temptation to take him out was strong, but Talon knew it would be stupid to do so, as this would set off all manner of alarms long before he wanted the Mongols to know he was there. The man disappeared back inside, slamming the door behind him, but not before Talon got a glimpse of the crowd of Mongols inside. He wished that he had one of those pots of Greek Fire to throw into the room.

When the Mongol had walked out of the building he had stepped over a dark shape. It had to be the body of one of Hsü's guards, Talon thought. They had all been cut down and left where they fell. There was nothing he could do for them now, so he waited and watched. He noticed a dilapidated looking shed at the back of the inn yard. It was more of a lean-to with one back wall, but there appeared to be some good cover where he could wait. Within a few seconds he was in the darkness of the shed without disturbing the horses on the line. He knew that they were aware of him, as a couple of heads had gone up, but that hadn't set off any alarms with the sentries. One of the

Mongol guards walked around the building on a cursory check, but then rejoined his companions. It was easy for Talon to avoid him, but he noted the scout pattern for future reference.

A thin shaft of moonlight illuminated a patch on the ground outside and part of the floor of the shed, which he stayed away from. His eyes roamed around the shed; it was full of hay and straw at the back for winter fodder, while at the front were a plough and other metal objects, several of which hung from a beam. He looked them over carefully, and one item that looked like a metal trap of some size gave him an idea. He burrowed into the hay at the back and lay down to rest. He allowed himself to relax to gather his strength. His shivering abated as he warmed up, and then he dozed off.

Four hours later Talon woke up and listened to the night. Apart from the chomping sound of horses still eating along the lines, all was quiet. The noise from inside the inn had stopped. He reasoned that the Mongols had finally drunk themselves to sleep. He eased out of the hole in the hay and slipped along the shadows to see where the sentries were positioned.

One was ambling around the building on one of the sporadic checks; he stretched and yawned as he went. Another was standing at the far end of the horse lines, while the third was squatting with his back against the inn wall at the corner nearest to where Talon was hiding. He glanced up. Clouds were now scudding across the sky plunging the surrounding area into deep blackness. Talon liked that and began to move.

The first sentry didn't hear Talon come up behind him, nor could he react to the dagger that went into his heart from behind. He gave a small gasp, but a hand was placed over his mouth, and he went down with a convulsive twitch and no other sound. Talon dragged him out of sight into the bushes.

The second sentry was still squatting comfortably against the wall when a knife came around from behind and cut his throat from ear to ear. He toppled over on his right side and was dragged, still twitching, around the corner by his killer.

That left the man at the far end of the horse lines. The horses were now aware that something unusual had happened. Their noses told them so with the smell of fresh blood in the air, and several became restless. Talon knew he had only a couple of minute's grace. He pulled off the dead man's cap and hauled on the smelly jacket, took up the fallen spear, then stood up and began to walk towards the far end of the horse lines. He had the good luck to pass his own horse, which whickered to him in recognition, but he patted it on the cheek and whispered it to silence. Then he reached for his bow and two arrows. Cautiously he began to walk towards the sentry, who now became aware that someone was coming.

The man called out something in a low voice. Talon did not understand but assumed it might be a greeting. Noise carried in this quiet night, so he grunted a reply and kept moving with his head down, his bow ready. The other sentry must have sensed that something was not quite right because he spoke more sharply. They were now only ten paces apart. In one swift motion Talon brought up his bow, pulled hard and released an arrow. Almost as soon as the first arrow thumped into the upper chest of his victim he had another arrow set, and this too he released straight into the throat of the Mongol, who had begun to fall to his knees, his mouth open in the beginnings of a scream. Talon raced up and clamped his hand over the convulsing sentry, who tried desperately to pull his hand away. The Mongol's attempts became more feeble by the moment, and then the body went slack. Talon finished the man with a knife to make sure. He then remained absolutely still, listening to the night. All was quiet except for the distant cry of some animal in the deep valley behind him.

It was time to take the horses out of sight. Talon worked for the rest of the night, and by the first light of morning all was ready. He glanced back at the woods, which covered the temple mountain, wondering if Hsü had been lucky with his venture. He hoped so, otherwise he was going to have to face a large number of Mongols on his own who would be as angry as a nest of hornets. He was mounted and about sixty paces from the main entrance of the building, waiting.

As he had expected, when dawn arrived a man threw open the wooden doors of the inn with a crash and stamped outside. The Mongol made for the grass down two steps from the raised porch floor, fumbling with his pants as he went. He was so preoccupied with wanting to relieve himself that he didn't notice anything else. Suddenly he stumbled, and there was a sharp metallic snap. The Mongol fell over screaming with a large metal trap gripping his shin. The trap was intended for wolves or bears and it was a substantial contraption, easily strong enough for a man. The Mongol rolled over screaming in agony, clutching at the iron jaws which had shredded his shin, breaking the bone in the process.

It was only moments before the noise brought the rest of the Mongols boiling out of the door onto the porch to gape at the sight before them. The first thing they noticed was their man rolling about in agony, clutching his leg and screaming with pain. The next thing they noticed were the three sentries standing a few dozen paces away, facing them. There was something wrong about that picture, however. The three limp forms were held upright by spears planted at their backs, but clearly they were quite dead. Any Mongols who looked around might have noticed that their horses were gone.

The dazed men didn't have time to do more than stare stupidly at their comrades when yet another unwelcome event occurred. An arrow flew towards them from behind their dead companions and thumped into one of their number, who tumbled off the porch to fall next to his screaming companion. More arrows flew, and more men fell wounded or dead, before the rest stampeded back into the doubtful safety of the inn.

Within a minute, however, three Mongols reemerged with bows held ready. They spread out and loosed arrows at Talon, who danced his animal out of the way of the running archers.

He allowed his horse to canter away from the nearest one and twisted right around to send an arrow plunging into the Mongol's midriff. The man tumbled over with a cry to roll about in agony clutching his stomach. His comrades, undeterred, continued to race towards Talon, who cantered away from them and, despite the arrows now coming very close to him, sent another of his enemies falling with a well aimed shot.

The last man, seeing how easily his friends had been struck down, hesitated. He sent a last arrow Talon's way, which made him duck, and then the Mongol turned and began to run back to the cover of the buildings. At sixty paces he fell with an arrow in his back. None of the Mongols moved as Talon took up his former place behind the dead sentries, a good sixty paces from the inn, and no one else appeared, so he waited.

He knew the Mongols could escape out the back, but there was nothing to be done about that. Their horses were safely hidden, so they couldn't ride off anywhere. If they tried to come for him on foot he could keep his distance and pick them off, as he had just demonstrated. No one seemed to want to test his accuracy any more. He glanced back at the trail to the monastery. Where was Hsü?

Then he noticed a movement at the head of the trail. Men with shaved heads in dark, voluminous tunics were running in a group, brandishing an assortment of spears, halberds and other long devices with a wide range of ugly looking hooks and points. He could see Hsü at the head of the group and waved, while at the same time keeping an eye on the inn.

The monks raced the last few hundred paces to gather around Talon, and Hsü greeted him. "You appear to have been busy," he said in his usual understated manner, glancing around at the corpses dotted around the field.

Talon was glad to see him. "I didn't like the idea of them leaving before you had a chance to meet them, my friend." Talon grinned, recognizing the abbot and a couple of the other monks.

"We came for a fight!" The abbot told him in slow Cantonese, and waved his spear.

Talon looked doubtful. Hsü grinned. "If we can get those Mongols to come out and fight, you will see something interesting," he said.

At a command from the abbot, the monks spread out in a line and faced the inn. Talon remained mounted and watched. It was not long before the door opened again, but this time it was only Muunokhoi and one other man who walked cautiously onto the wooden walkway; the man who accompanied Muunokhoi called out something in Chinese.

"They want to parley," Hsü said to Talon, who shrugged. "About what?" he asked.

Hsü grinned at him. "I'll try to find out," he said.

He began a shouted exchange of words with the two men, which finished with him shaking his head and calling out one last time. Clearly he was annoyed.

"What was that all about?" Talon asked.

"He told us that he has experienced warriors with him and that they will cut us to pieces if we do not give them back their horses and allow them to leave in peace. They do not want to hurt some innocent monks," Hsü reported with a sardonic smile.

"What did you tell him?" Talon asked, as he watched more Mongols come out and spread out in front of the building. He counted thirteen men. His own group numbered ten, himself included.

"Perhaps we should let them go?" he said doubtfully.

"You know as well as I that once they are mounted they will break their word and kill us all," Hsü snorted in disgust.

"Yes, yes I do, but I don't like the idea of monks getting involved with these barbarians, Hsü. It isn't their fight," Talon said.

Hsü said something to the monks nearby. They began to laugh and some cheerfully brandished their odd looking spears at the Mongols. The abbot indicated Talon and spoke rapidly to Hsü, who turned back to Talon. "The Abbot respectfully declines your invitation to leave, but begs that you remain on your horse with your bow to make sure the Mongols cannot use theirs. We will deal with the rest."

Talon shrugged and said, "So be it. God protect you, my friend, because here they come!"

Muunokhoi had drawn his sword and now shouted at his men. They began to run towards the monks in a clumsy rush. For the second time he realized that these people, born to the saddle, were not well suited to fighting on foot.

Well, he would see now if the monks were justified in their confidence. He drew and shot an arrow at one Mongol who had remained behind and was preparing to use his bow. The arrow struck the man in the shoulder and he fell spinning, dropping his weapon. The other Mongols screamed savage battle cries as they rushed towards the monks, who at a shouted command from the abbot adopted stances that looked suspiciously like those Talon had learned in the Dojo. He shook his head. Hsü had known exactly of what he spoke.

Then the Mongol line arrived and it became a free for all. Talon took down two more men who were contemplating using their bows, and then watched. The monks were adept with their weapons and incredibly fast. They would scream almost in the face of their opponents as they struck, and within seconds Mongol warriors were thrown, tripped or disabled and ruthlessly finished off by the monks.

Two Mongols charged up to the abbot, who calmly waited until they were almost upon him. Before Talon's astonished gaze there was a blur of movement and one warrior fell back clutching his leg, having dropped his sword, while the other found himself staggering back under the onslaught of the abbot's attack. The Mongol whirled his sword and shouted angrily at the abbot but could not penetrate his defenses. Talon noticed that the other opponent had regained his sword and was creeping up behind the preoccupied abbot. Talon sent an arrow his way which took him down, and seconds later the other fell to a well struck blow to the chest from the abbot. All around Talon the monks were dealing with the Mongols as though they were simply practicing. It was a no contest from the start.

Talon stared in utter astonishment at the bodies lying on the ground, some groaning, while others were still. He then noticed Hsü facing off against Muunokhoi. Hsü was using his skills developed at the dojo, so Talon merely had to wait and watch with interest. When Muunokhoi rushed in, hoping to finish Hsü, he found his blade struck aside, and then his head was separated from his body in one savage swipe from Hsü's sword. The body stood upright for a long moment, and then toppled over to join the other Mongols on the bloody ground. Talon was impressed.

The monks began to cheer, waving their bloody weapons in the air and dancing about in unrestrained joy. Talon just shook his head and laughed at Hsü. He dismounted and they embraced. "You are a warrior merchant, it seems to me, Hsü," Talon said with a laugh.

"As are you; and now do you believe me about these kind and gentle people?" Hsü asked.

"I am in awe of these people," Talon stated firmly. "I would never have believed it had I not seen it with my own two eyes!"

"Perhaps they have the spirit of the dragon within them?" Hsü grinned back at him.

"Of that I am in no doubt whatsoever," Talon laughed.

"You too, Talon; there is a dragon within you now; its spirit is with you, along with that of the lion you slew when you were a boy." Talon had told him of that fight while at sea.

*****

It took most of the morning to dispose of the dead and attend to their own wounded, of which there were few. The people in the inn had been slaughtered to a man, the women with them. There was anger among the monks. The abbot ordered his men to dispatch any of the wounded Mongols, saying that there was no purpose in sending any of them back to their own land and he wouldn't keep prisoners. He and his men seemed very impressed at the manner in which Talon had disposed of the sentries, as well as setting the trap and hiding the horses.

"He calls you a *Renzhe*, Talon," Hsü said with a smile. When Talon looked puzzled he explained, "I told you about Nippon Ninja once, remember?" Talon nodded.

"That is what the abbot means."

By now Hsü was concerned about the delay to his journey and explained this to the abbot, who understood. "He told me to depart immediately. They will deal with all of this before the General arrives, if indeed he even hears of the Mongol incursion. I will not tell him of the incident today, as it would complicate things," Hsü told Talon. "That man Muunokhoi is going to disappear completely, and his chief Badzar is never going to know what happened. It will be as though he was devoured by China!"

Talon liked the sound of that. "Hmm, by a Chinese dragon?"

Hsü clearly thought that was very amusing and told the abbot, who roared with laughter and passed it along to the other monks, who fell about laughing.

"We must get to the horses, take some provisions and leave right away. I, too, am concerned," Talon told Hsü when the laughter had subsided.

They left with the monks waving to them, and with the blessings of the abbot.

The Game of Go.
A stone or solidly connected group of stones of one
color is captured
And removed from the board when all the intersections
Directly adjacent to it are occupied by the enemy.
(Capture of the enemy takes precedence over self
capture)

Chapter Thirty
A Game of Go

Talon and Hsü returned Guangzhou three weeks after the ambush to find everything back to some semblance of normal, with one notable exception: the man who greeted them at the gate was not Fang. Instead it was Qian, who, after he had bowed deeply, said, "Greetings, Lord Meng. I wish to report with deep sorrow the death of Master Fang. I am assisting with his former duties at the request of Lord Meng Fuling and my Sensei."

The activity at the gate alerted Fuling, who had been expecting them. He hurried over and bowed respectfully, then said, "Welcome home, Father. We were hoping you could be here before now, but no matter. I shall explain everything, if you will come with me?"

Hsü said, "I shall be glad to come with you, Fuling, but first I must speak with Talon."

He took Talon by the arm and said quietly, "I suspect that shall be very busy the next few days, Talon. You should go and be with your friends and work with Jiaya; I shall send him over as soon as he is free. There is much you have to do to prepare to leave. We will meet up soon, I promise. Give me a couple of days to sort things out." Talon nodded and they clasped hands.

"I would not have missed the trip for anything, Hsü. Thank you," he said. They both smiled and parted.

Talon handed off his horse to a servant and then made his way towards the guest house. He had barely made it across the courtyard when there was an excited cry and Rav'an came flying out of the entrance to throw herself into his arms.

"You are back! How wonderful!" she exclaimed, giving him a heartfelt kiss. "I am so glad to see you, my Talon!" He held her very tight and almost carried her as they walked back to the guest house. He grinned happily down at her upturned face and kissed her again.

"Oh, we have kept busy," she laughed. "Reza is down at the docks with the men. Jiaya is with him helping to prepare the ship. The monsoon is changing, you know."

He glanced up at the sky, which was today clear and almost cloud free. "I suppose it is," he said; there was reluctance in his tone. She squeezed his arm in understanding.

The next person to rush out and greet him was Rostam, who charged out of the house screaming with glee and threw himself into Talon's arms. He tossed his son up into the air and spun around, holding the happy boy at arm's length, hugely enjoying the moment. "You have grown at least two hands since I left," Talon laughed.

Rav'an stood by and smiled at their antics. She was very happy to see father and son in this manner and wanted it to last. Eventually Talon put the boy down and asked him what he had been doing since he left. Whereupon the boy began to chatter excitedly about his adventures with Lun, the kite, the ball games, and so forth. The three of them entered the guest living room holding hands. He looked around the main room with pleasure. It was good to be back in this sparse but very elegantly furnished building with his family again.

He looked at Rav'an, once again admiring the perfect oval of her face, and the huge gray eyes that returned his gaze with an expression of great love and a smile that made his heart melt.

He reached for her and impulsively kissed her again, right in front of Rostam, who squeaked with surprise and became very embarrassed.

Then it was greetings from Salem, who wept when she saw him and whom he embraced, to her acute embarrassment. Jannat came running and embraced him with enthusiasm. Talon laughed and raised his eyebrows at Rav'an over Jannat's shoulder. She cocked her head at him and pretended to glower. "My, what a welcome I am receiving!" he exclaimed with a laugh, as he pushed Jannat to arm's length to take a look at her. "You look well, Jannat," he said.

"We are all so happy you have returned. There is so much to tell you, Talon," she said excitedly. "Rav'an is such a warrior! I have seen it!"

Talon blinked and stared at Rav'an. "What's been going on?" he asked.

Rav'an frowned and waved her hand dismissively. "Jannat is right; we do have a lot to tell, but it can wait until Reza and the boys are back. Now Talon, you look tired and dusty. You should have a good bath, and then we can all sit down and tell each other what we have been doing," Rav'an replied, signaling Jannat with her eyes not to say more at this time. Jannat understood and came to stand next to her.

Talon liked that idea of a bath very much. He handed his bow and his sword to Rostam, who had been hanging around, and told him to take them up to the room. The delighted boy carried the two weapons proudly up the stairs.

The last part of their journey had been hard. Hsü had set the pace, and he had been determined to get back to Guangzhou as quickly as possible to counter whatever mischief his enemies might have concocted. He had discussed the situation with Talon, who understood from the brief outline that Hsü had a fight on his hands and very few friends in high places to help him.

However, he had cheerfully told Talon, he had a few tricks up his sleeve that might still confound them. There had been no news on the road of the Governor, whether he had recovered or not, or if he was even still alive. If he was, it was crucial for Hsü to present the evidence as soon as he could to forestall Wu's attempt at seizing power.

After a refreshing bath, Talon and Rav'an retired to their private room, where he almost tore her clothes off and they made passionate love, ending with a long, low, drawn out wail from Rav'an as she peaked with him. They lay quietly in each other's arms after their lovemaking was over. "I hope no one comes in to find out if you are all right," Talon said with a grin.

"It's your fault, my Talon. It has been much too long, in any case." She grinned back at him with mischief is those expressive eyes of hers. Then she raised her head and supported her chin on her elbow. "We are all very keen to know if you saw your dragon."

"Er, yes, I did. Yes, I did see a dragon," he said. He sounded too vague to Rav'an's ears.

"Well, did you or did you not see a dragon? I want to hear all about it, the dragon I mean, before we go down and you tell everyone about your journey," she said.

"Well... it's like this. It's white all over..." Talon tried to describe the dragon he had seen at the temple, implying without quite saying it was a living dragon he had seen, but he couldn't keep up the pretense for long. Rav'an had been looking at him with a dawning suspicion in her eyes as he spoke. Finally she interrupted him. "I know you, Talon. Better than anyone else in the world, and I *know* you are hiding something. You'd better tell me, and now!" She thumped him on the chest with her fist.

"All right, all right, I'll tell you! Stop beating me to death!" he protested.

"It wasn't a real dragon." His eyes couldn't meet hers.

"Not real?" she gasped, her mouth opened in an O of astonishment, and her eyes went wide with amusement. "We all thought that for sure Hsü would at least show you a live dragon."

"It's all Hsü's fault. He said he would show me a dragon when we got to China. But he didn't actually say he would show me a *live* dragon. There are no dragons in China, at least no one has ever seen one. Sooo, he showed me a huge stone one at the entrance to a monastery. It was a beautiful image. They might have looked like that once upon a time. I nearly killed him, I was so annoyed; but, well, it seemed rather funny after I had calmed down. He apologized and I made him keep it secret," Talon concluded on a sheepish note.

"Hah! Well your secret is also safe with me." Rav'an didn't sound sincere enough to Talon.

"Do you promise?"

"I do, but that Hsü is a bad man. He manipulated us to bring him here."

"I've noticed Hsü is quite skilled at that. He once told me that diplomacy is the ability to allow others to do it your way. He seems to have succeeded in this case! Have you any regrets, my Love?"

"None whatsoever! In fact, I could almost stay here forever, and so could Jannat. It is so, so full of life and beauty," she said, biting his neck gently. "You aren't too tired are you?" she murmured.

He leaned down and nuzzled her belly button and then kissed his way down to her mound. "I have missed doing this to you," he murmured as he began to explore her. She could not help shuddering, and then she groaned and arched her back, snatching at the cushions. "Ah, but so have I, my Lover!" she gasped.

*****

There was a joyful reunion that evening when Reza and his 'boys', Yosef and Dar'an, returned from the harbor. They ate the evening meal in the guest house that night. Rav'an, having talked to Lihua, had said that the family of Lord Meng would be better off left to themselves that evening, as Hsü had a lot of catching up to do.

Talon wanted to know from the beginning what had happened and how Fang had died. First one and then the other gave their version of the story, and slowly he built up a picture of that desperate evening. He beamed with pride at the others' unstinting praise for Rav'an as the bow woman of the moment. Jannat gazed at Rav'an with adoring eyes. She was just a little tipsy from the wine when she said, "I want to be like my sister Rav'an someday, a mother and a warrior too."

"If you stay with Reza much longer that shouldn't be a problem," Rav'an laughed to hide her embarrassment.

Talon was startled at the ruthlessness displayed by Hsü's enemies. It seemed somehow out of place in this extraordinary and sophisticated country. His enemies had displayed a willingness to destroy everything Hsü possessed in order to keep him out of this Governor's race. He recalled the meeting with Hua Rong. "There are dark tunnels underneath this disarming culture of theirs. That Chief of Police? What about him?" he asked. "Is he the man behind all of this?"

There was silence at that. "What is it?" Talon asked, with a puzzled expression.

"He was found murdered in his office. He was stabbed to death with a chop stick," Yosef croaked. He still couldn't speak properly, but the stitches on this throat were gone, leaving behind red welts . Talon stared around him at the blank faces. "So his enemies had a falling out. That should please Hsü," he said slowly with some satisfaction, but he gave Reza a long, speculative stare as he said it.

*****

In the main building the family of Lord Hsü Meng were gathered around the dining table.

The entire family had greeted his arrival with enormous relief. His wife Meilin had broken down and wept in his arms when he greeted her in her own sanctum. It was unusual to see her so upset, but hardly surprising under the circumstances, he reasoned, as he consoled her.

The meal was exceptional, but the only person eating with a good appetite was Lun. The rest of the family was heavily engaged in recounting the story from each of their perspectives to Hsü, who sat through the whole account, his expression stony with anger. He asked the occasional penetrating question and nodded approval to Fuling for having fought alongside Fang and the foreigner, Reza, for whom Fuling had only high praise, coupled with an element of fearful respect which intrigued Hsü.

Lihua came in for great praise from Lady Lanfen, his mother, who described the incident in her room in minute detail, relishing the retrospective excitement of the time and embellishing her story just a little. Lihua still had her forearm heavily bandaged but tried to keep it out of sight and looked mortified at the unwanted attention. Hsü sent a message of profound approval across the table with his eyes. He had not seen his mother so energized for some time.

Lady Meng Meilin maintained her customary aloof attitude, but even she had to concede that the praise was well deserved. Lun, who had witnessed the fight at the stables, gave a voluble account of that incident and labored the gory details to the point where Hsü raised his hand and indicated that they all understood. It was when Lady Lanfen mentioned that Lun had had another dream that Hsü sat up.

"What do you mean, Mother?" he asked.

"Lun, tell us all what you dreamed while your father was away," his grandmother told him.

"I dreamed that you were in a river, Papa," the boy said, almost in tears.

Hsü was speechless for a few long moments, and then he said slowly, "Yes, my son, Master Talon and I did spend time in a river, but all is well now."

They told him of the funeral of Fang. Every one of the household had attended, along with all the members of the dojo, and the foreigners had also been invited. Reza and Rav'an and Jannat had attended. Fuling had been proud to organize the somber occasion.

"I hope it will please you, Father, but I had his corpse placed in a location as close as possible to our ancestral grave. He gave his life to save us all. I felt it to be appropriate."

Hsü nodded his approval. "You did very well, my Son. I would have done the same. Most of us are not afraid of death itself, just the manner in which we have to die. Fang died well."

Now Hsü would have to find another bodyguard. He would talk to Sensei Saiki about Qian. Saiki would be glad to rent out the services of his man, who was a better swordsman than even Fang had been, and certainly not as mad. All the same, he would miss Fang. He would visit his grave soon.

Later that evening, when the ladies had retired and Lun had been sent off to bed, he sat at a smaller table with his older son, listening with pleasure to the calming sound of the fountain outside while he teased out the finer details of the story. He had been very perturbed and angered to hear of the incident, but had been expecting something of the sort. The worries he had undergone while being away had been confirmed with horrifying consequences.

He made Fuling go over his version of the story one more time in detail, and when his son was finally done he sipped thoughtfully from a cup of warm rice wine.

"Tell me again how Rong died?" he asked.

"They found him dead in his own office with some chop sticks stabbed into his throat! The building was full of people! No one remembers anyone going in or out of the office, but when one of them went in later, there he was: dead. It was all over the city within hours!"

Who do you think might have done this?"

"I know so little, Father, but...." Fuling hesitated and looked uncomfortable.

"But what? Spit it out, my son."

"Well, Reza came to see me and told me he wished to report the crime to the chief of police. I accompanied him across the river, and when we arrived at the bank side he asked me to wait in the boat, which I did, and he went away. He came back later on. When I asked him about it, he told me that not much had been said, but that 'Fang would have been pleased.' I remember that as being strange. There was also something odd about his face, but I can't remember what it was. I was so preoccupied with the death of Fang and making all the arrangements that I didn't pay him much attention."

"What are you saying, that Reza might have had something to do with this?"

"Perhaps, Father, but I do not see how he could have. No one reported seeing anything unusual, and an Arab visiting the chief of police would have been noticed! But I am not sorry about Rong's death. Whoever carried out the killing was doing us a favor; at least, I thought so when I heard about it. Of course, I have told no one about this."

Hsü stared at his son for a very long moment. "You should never talk about it, my son. Not to anyone at all. Suspicion is a dangerous thing, it is like a spark in a field of dry grass that can turn into a wildfire without warning, burning even those who sow its seeds."

Fuling nodded. "I would not want harm to come to that man. He has been a good friend and saved us from much harm."

Hsü nodded agreement and lifted his cup to touch that of his son with a small clink. "To friends and secrets," he said with an enigmatic smile.

"Please tell me of your journey with the Tribute, Father," Fuling asked him. "Did the Mongols appreciate the 'gifts'?" he finished with a trace of sarcasm.

Hsü smiled at his son. He was beginning to feel a sense of pride in his offspring that had not been there before.

"Firstly, I want to hear how you are doing with your exams," he said. "Do you feel confident?"

Fuling sighed and sipped his wine. "Yes, I think so, Father. It is not easy, as I'm sure you remember."

"Oh yes, I do remember; but you are persisting and I approve of that. Pass these exams and you can become an administrator of the seventh level. I can then send you to my old academy to further your rank. Perhaps you might even eventually gain a position in the Governor's palace."

"I'd sooner be a warrior poet, Father," his son grinned.

"When I was your age I, too, had had enough of the academic stuff and only wanted to travel, and I did to some extent—after my exams, of course. But the responsibilities of family and business were ever clamoring for attention; so, alas, I could not wander for long," Hsü told him.

Fuling smiled but then became serious. "How do you think it will change the race for you, now that Rong is gone, Father?" he asked.

"It's not over by a long way. I suspect that Rong or that avaricious swine Buwei was behind the death of Prefect Yen." He was referring to the news of the sudden death of the Prefect three days before Hsü had arrived. He had been on his way to his estates outside the city when he had been felled by unknown persons. Some had said it was robbers, but Hsü was quite sure it had been an assassination; also, perhaps, a not so subtle warning to him?

"Who else in the palace is competing for the post?" Fuling asked.

"At present, now that Prefect Yen is gone, and Rong too, it leaves us with a Prefect called Wu po-ku. I want to go and pay him a visit very soon. You will come with me. It is time for you to meet people and see who they are. Tomorrow we are both going to see the Governor, even though we don't have an appointment. It is too urgent to keep."

*****

The next day Hsü and Fuling, accompanied by a watchful Qian, took a boat across the busy river and marched through the great gates of the city, up the crowded promenade to arrive at the entrance of the palace by mid morning.

Hsü asked for Li Shou-cheh, his friend and confidant within the palace. Not long after, Shou-cheh came shuffling along the polished floor of the audience chamber to greet them. They spoke in low voices.

"I am very glad that you are back with us and were able to come today, Lord Meng," Shou-cheh murmured, after elaborate greetings had been observed.

"I wish to introduce my son, Meng Fuling, to you. It is time for him to meet important people," Hsü said. Shou-cheh looked pleased with the compliment.

Shou-cheh gave Fuling a smile and said, "You are very welcome, Lord Meng. Your father is a most respected person in this city. I am much honored to know him, and now yourself. Come," he waved them towards another room. "We should talk in more privacy."

Tea was served, and then, in the manner of diplomatic people, the main subject was reached by roundabout means.

"General Hayan Zhuo received a letter from his colleague General Yang Hsün which extolled your organizational skills and briefly mentioned an incident that occurred in camp before you delivered the Tribute, Lord Meng," Shou-cheh said.

"That 'incident' nearly cost my friend his life," Hsü remarked dryly, concealing his surprise at the speed with which Shou-cheh had heard. "The snake was meant for me."

Fuling stared at him with wide eyes. He had not been told of this the night before.

"Then you will be glad to know that General Hayan Zhou is moving as fast as he can to talk to the right people in the Emperor's palace. He will certainly paint an excellent picture of you, Lord Hsü. He is very impressed. Did you beat him at Go that often?"

Hsü warmed to the man. Shou-cheh had just demonstrated that he possessed a sense of humor of sorts, nor was it lost on Fuling, who smiled into his bowl of tea.

"I am sure we became friends based upon mutual respect. He is a good officer," Hsü intoned with the flicker of a smile.

Shou-cheh nodded agreement. "That is what I hear."

They talked for a few more minutes. Hsü was interested in any gossip going on in the city. Shou-cheh didn't disappoint him.

"The inexplicable deaths of Prefect Yen and Hua Rong have everyone talking. No one seems to know how these things could have happened. In the case of Rong, it was quite horrible, from what I have heard." Shou-cheh gave a delicate shudder of revulsion.

"Do they know who it was? He had many enemies."

"Indeed he did, but no one knows a thing." Shou-cheh looked directly at Hsü. "It is well known that he and you were competing for the post of governor." He smiled at their surprise. "Yes, indeed, Rong was actually contemplating the post for himself. You could have been implicated, but your absence upon the Emperor's business is irrefutable, so there is no question of anyone pointing any fingers at you."

"Would it be possible to see the Governor soon?" Hsü asked carefully. He had begun to feel they were avoiding the subject.

Shou-cheh looked awkward. "I'm afraid he is exceedingly ill and will see no one at this time, Lord Meng Hsü."

Hsü gave him a sharp look. "Really? No one?"

Shou-cheh looked more uncomfortable. "Only the doctors, I'm afraid. That is the *command* of Prefect Wu po-ku. He is the senior Prefect in the palace and has the final say about who can visit the Governor, unless the Governor asks for someone directly, of course. This has not happened for some time now."

"Of course, I understand," Hsü said, but his mind was swirling. "Perhaps we can arrange something?" He slid across the tea table a tiny box, similar to those which he had taken to the palace in Hangzhou. It disappeared into the silk folds of Shou-cheh's sleeve.

"I shall investigate all possibilities, My Lord." He bowed, and then it was time to leave.

They collected Qian at the gates and walked slowly back down the hill towards river. Fuling remained silent as his father walked deep in thought along the busy promenade.

"Is this a blow, Father?" he finally asked.

"In a game of Go nothing is a 'blow' as such... not until the game is over, my son," Hsü told him.

*****

No news came from the Governor's palace, and Hsü still did not hear from the Palace in Hangzhou either. He was very worried. Prefect Wu po-ku was in the perfect position to bribe the palace Administrators who would recommend the next governor. Furthermore, he could restrict all visits to the Governor, and even the flow of information. Hsü conferred with Qian at length about security around the property.

Then word came that the Governor had died. His relatives put out a notice of his death, but palace officials ensured that the general populace knew by means of huge posters and couriers who shouted it to the rooftops. The Governor had been a highly respected man.

Hsü and his entire family went into mourning, as did the entire city of Guangzhou. He explained the tradition briefly to Talon.

"He was a good man and worked hard in life, Talon. He showed proper respect for his ancestors and has a well-respected name. His ancestors will be pleased to welcome him."

"Did you know him well?" Talon asked him.

"No, not well, but I respected him; however, while he was a good man, there were those who took advantage of his kindness. We have much crime in this city which he could have put a stop to if he had been more firm."

"You mean, with the help of the man who was killed?"

"Ah yes, the man who was killed, Hua Rong." Hsü shot Reza a penetrating glance.

"Do you have to go to the funeral?" Reza asked Hsü, ignoring the look.

"It would be unthinkable not to. The more people the better. We believe there are two parts to death: the *po*, which is to do with the grave, and the *hun*, which is to do with the family tree. From the *po*, which is buried, will come the soul, which has to undergo the judgements of the courts of hell, so the more people who show veneration, and in particular relatives, the less chance of a bad judgement for his soul." Both Talon and Reza looked very thoughtful at this.

Hsü went on.

"There are ceremonies of food at the grave, which must be observed, and he will have a very large gravestone. There will also be a sculpture of some kind next to the grave. You should come to watch."

They were left in no doubt as to the importance of the funeral. Talon and his friends observed the proceedings from the back of the crowd while the procession wound out of the governor's palace down the wide promenade, which was lined with curious people, towards the cemetery on the West side of the city. All the members of the family were dressed entirely in coarse white hemp material, as were the priests. Musicians accompanied the procession, banging cymbals and beating drums as the body was carried to its last resting place, where it was interred in an elaborate coffin. Then the actual burial ceremony took place.

Talon went home in a thoughtful mood. He knew that Hsü would not be able to waste any time henceforth. His enemies would be gathering in the shadows to cut him down.

The compound seemed to reflect this attitude. as the guards were now doubled, and these new men from the dojo looked as though they could handle themselves. Qian was everywhere, patrolling the grounds ceaselessly with several of the men in tow, indicating weak points in the gardens and buildings and assigning guards to patrol them. No one was allowed out without an escort.

Talon resolved to be prepared for the worst. He owed it to his family and crew to leave safely, with a full cargo, no matter what happened in Guangzhou. He and Reza went to see Hsü the following day to talk about cargos.

Hsü was glad to receive them. He looked careworn, but invited them to sit and ordered tea. "You have come to talk about leaving, I presume," he said with a smile.

Talon nodded ruefully. Hsü was always ahead of him. "The monsoon winds are changing, Hsü. It is time for us to go, or we will not be able to leave till next year."

"Do you not like it here in China, Talon?" Hsü teased him.

Talon grinned, as did Reza. "You know perfectly well that we are torn. Our wives are ready to stay indefinitely, but ...."

Hsü raised his hands and laughed. "We will miss you, more than you know; but now let's get down to business. My consortium will offer you eight thousand taels of silver for the whole cargo, and I shall throw in five tons of silk material, which you or your wives can choose personally."

Talon looked at Reza. "This would more than pay for the long journey." The price being offered was very good indeed.

Talon looked back at Hsü and said, "I have to say, it is more than I expected, Hsü. You are being very generous, and I agree to these terms. The goods are already in your warehouse, so my ship is empty and ready to take on our new cargo." Talon paused. What he had to say next was very serious. "With some of the silver, I would like to buy several items to take along," he said carefully.

Hsü looked askance.

"I want to take four Erupters with me on my ship. Reza told me that there are pirates with something like an Erupter who infest the straits in the region of Kalah Bar. I want to be able to protect what is mine. Will you help me install them, and will you have someone teach me and Reza and my men how to use them?"

Hsü laughed and slapped his thigh. "It would not surprise me if those pirates belong to that man Sing. Those weapons impressed you, didn't they?"

Talon grinned. "Yes, they certainly did. I want to take some with me, but I need help to mount them so that they don't sink my ship, nor set it on fire when we use them. And we'll need training, as it does not look like an easy thing to use. I want to buy that special powder and some of those interesting bamboo exploding things that the soldiers showed me."

"This can be arranged," Hsü said with a smile. "Anything else?"

"Yes. Reza and I want to thank you for the training we had at your expense at the dojo. We would never have known about it without your help."

"It seems to me that you have already repaid that debt," Hsü said. "Reza here has protected my house while I was away, and you saved my life." He turned to Reza. "Neither Talon nor I would have made it home at all had Talon not taken down a quarrelsome Mongol. No, Talon, we are even on that score."

Talon smacked his hand to his forehead and said, "I nearly forgot! Hsü, I cannot leave without a cargo of porcelain. My wife will kill me if we do not take a good amount with us. Can you help?"

Hsü laughed again, hugely amused. He couldn't imagine anyone trying to kill Talon but... perhaps his wife. She now had a reputation as a warrior, having killed two men. The servants and guards worshipped her.

"Hmm, yes, I see your point," he said. "Lihua will be your guide in this, and Jiaya will be the man who negotiates the price. We will deduct what it will cost out of the amount stated today. I assure you that Jiaya will be an honest broker."

"He has been the perfect guide to date. I am very happy with that arrangement," Reza stated, sounding satisfied.

"There is one other thing I need to ask, Hsü, if you will permit it." Talon glanced at Reza, who nodded.

"And what is that?"

"The sword you have, the one I used. I told Reza about that. We want to buy one each of the same caliber. Will you please tell me where we can obtain them?"

Hsü shifted uncomfortably on his chair. "I must ask you to be patient, Talon, I will do all I can to find out where you can buy them, but they are not easy to obtain."

The discussion ended there, and the two men went back to the guest house, well pleased, to tell their people of the arrangements.

"He is being evasive about the swords," Talon remarked to Reza.

"He is a canny one, that man. I have a feeling he is up to something."

"Perhaps. But I have learned much from Hsü," Talon said.

*****

They became deeply involved with the preparations and began to buy the agreed upon items, pack them carefully, and have them transported to the ship. Everyone was so involved they barely noticed when Hsü had visitors. One was an important meeting with General Hayan Zhuo, who had sent a message that he wanted to meet with him.

Hsü invited the General to his house, and there treated him with great ceremony and respect. He plied his guest with *Huangjiu,* a yellowish dry rice wine, and fed him on the exemplary food from his kitchen. The General gave him some interesting news in return.

Because the governor was now officially dead, the office was held temporarily by the senior official in the palace, and that was Wu po-ku. He held all the powers of office until the appointment was made official by the Emperor's chop of approval. There was no doubt in either of their minds that Wu would not scruple to use his powers against Hsü and his family, now that he possessed the power to do so. The General said that he considered it to be a very dangerous time for Hsü. However, he also brought some good news, and in return received a nice little present on his way out of the door.

"I will be there the day after tomorrow," Hayan Zhuo said, then he rode away with his escort, leaving Hsü wanting to rub his hands together with glee. He restrained himself; it wouldn't do to let the foreigners nor his own people see him display undue excitement. He walked back to his own building with his hands clasped tightly behind him, his head lowered, looking to all the world pensive and preoccupied.

*****

Two days later, Hsü appeared at the doors of the palace. He had asked his son Fuling and Talon to come with him; Qian was also in attendance. "I cannot go on my own, as it would be an invitation to my enemies; will you attend me? It might be interesting," he had said to Talon, who'd readily agreed to accompany his host.

Once within the palace, Hsü asked for an interview with Prefect Wu po-ku. They were kept waiting for two full hours before an aide finally shuffled up to him, bowed perfunctorily, and told him in Mandarin that the Prefect, Temporary Governing officer Wu po-ku, would see him.

Hsü smiled to himself, Mandarin eh? Wu wanted to make the governor's palace a replica of the Emperor's. Well, they would see about that.

Bringing Talon, Qian and Fuling with him, despite a half-hearted protest from the functionary, he walked slowly into the grand office, which had once belonged to the former governor. He and his men bowed deeply, then stood motionless, Hsü with hands hidden in the wide sleeves of his dark robes. The others remained near the door while Hsü walked further into the room to stand in front of the desk of Wu. Fuling eyed the prefect with mistrust; he didn't know what his father was going to do. Talon and Qian both equally unaware of what Hsü was planning were tense and watchful.

Wu looked up from his papers. "Ah, Lord Meng. Good to see you. What can I do for you today? I am so very busy, as you can see." He didn't invite Hsü to be seated.

The short phrase written by Master Sun Tzu came to Hsü's mind: *"Use humility to make them haughty."*

"I came to deliver something of yours to you, respected Prefect," he said humbly enough, passing over a piece of paper to Wu, who turned it over. There were sweat stains on the creased paper, but the writing was still clear enough to read. Wu's countenance changed from pale to dead white as he read the paper. His hands trembled as he put the piece of paper down on the table. "Where..." he swallowed, "where did you get this?" he whispered.

Hsü had an ear cocked for the sounds coming from outside, and so did Talon, who made ready to draw his sword, but Hsü shook his head minutely to stop him. There was a commotion in the front yard of the palace, the sound of horses and the shouts of men.

"Let us say that I took it off one of your messengers, who failed in his mission as it is outlined in that letter. In some ways he was a careful man, but not careful enough. He died.. That is your chop, is it not?" Hsü said quietly.

Before the ashen-faced Wu could muster a reply, the door to the office was thrown open with a crash, and in strode General Hayan Zhou. He was in full armor, accompanied by two aides and several soldiers carrying spears.

"Ah, there you are, Lord Meng," he called from the door. "Just in time, I see." He waved an official-looking document in his left hand. "Prefect Wu po-ku, you are under arrest for the attempted murder of Lord Meng while he was on a mission for his Highness the Emperor. That constitutes treason. Take him!" he ordered his men, who moved to obey. Talon, Qian and Fuling became mere spectators and stepped well out of the way to allow the General and his men to approach.

Hsü raised his hand. "Just one moment, General, if I may, please?" he asked.

The General harrumphed but nodded reluctantly. "Yes, all right, Lord Meng."

"Why did you do this, Wu?" Hsü demanded of the man who sat quaking with fear, all vestiges of arrogance having vanished.

Wu glared up at him, and Hsü could see the venom in the back of his eyes. "You were the only real obstacle to the post," he hissed. "Those other half-wits demonstrated their incompetence to the world. I could not rely on either of them to take care of the simplest thing!" He spat this out with white-hot hatred. "I was easily the most qualified, but the Governor wanted you, a rich merchant, to succeed him! Not a proper administrator who knew how to run things, like myself. What do you know about governing a whole province?"

Hsü stepped back from the hatred emanating from the man. "Perhaps that is the very reason he chose me, he wanted a leader. There are always administrators to do the paperwork." he murmured. He signaled the men to carry on.

They lifted the limp Prefect up from his chair and frog-marched him out of the room. When the wailing and shouting had faded, General Hayan Zhou handed another package to Hsü.

"We are in the right place for me to inform you," he said gruffly, with a glance at Talon and the other two.

Hsü opened the package and took out a thick sheet of paper written in exquisite calligraphy. He noted the Emperor's huge chop on red wax at the bottom. He read it through twice.

"It appears that I am to be the governor of the province of Guangdong, General."

General Hayan Zhou beamed, then collected himself and bowed very low. "May I be the very first to congratulate you, Governor?" he enquired.

Hsü smiled. "Indeed, General, you may. Now we still have a little unfinished business to attend to."

'What might that be, Governor?" Hayan Zhou asked.

"I want you to arrest Lu Buwei and put him in prison."

The General hesitated. "May I ask why, my Lord, er, Governor?"

"For trying to destroy the property of the Governor and to kill his retainers; in fact, his people did kill one of my retainers. That, I believe, warrants the death penalty. There are also the suspicious deaths of Hua Rong and Prefect Yen Wei to take into account."

The General looked uncomfortable. "If I may point out very respectfully, Governor, didn't that all happen a little while ago?"

"What is time, General?" Hsü queried. "It is but a passing of scenes before the conscious or unconscious mind. I don't think we need to split hairs in this particular issue, do you?"

General Hayan Zhou nodded firmly and even gave the briefest of smiles. "In this instance, I'd be doing the city a great favor, Governor."

"Just so, General."

Hsü smiled at his son and Talon as he watched the General depart; the last of his stones were finally in place on the board. His opponents' stones were completely contained.

"This game of Go is won," he stated.

I am old and you're going away—
You have no choice, I know.
From the carriage I see you off,
brushing away tears I can't hold back.
Who likes to say good-bye?

—Lu Yu

Chapter Thirty-One

Farewell

Talon heaved a sigh of relief. Things could have gone badly for Hsü and his family had Wu po-ku been confirmed as governor, and also for his guests; they would have been in serious trouble because of their association. Now all that had changed.

Nonetheless, despite the change in the political weather, the ocean's weather patterns were not going to alter; the monsoon that would take them home was moving in. They could not delay much longer.

Captain Dandachi was insistent. "If we can catch the monsoon out of here within the month we will have a good chance of making it to Oman in one long run, Master Talon. Otherwise we could be stranded in India."

They were seated at the tea house on the island not far from the Henan temple. Jiaya had made arrangements to put the captain up at a guest house near the docks where he and some of the crew could supervise the loading of the precious cargo they were to take with them.

Talon didn't like the sound of being stopped in India. The muggy climate, the red-hot food, the dust and the noise he remembered from their previous visit were not what he wanted.

All he wanted from India was to pick up a final cargo of spice at Kalah Bar and depart. They would have no need to tarry.

"I shall speak to Lord Meng," he told the captain, who looked pleased.

"Allah has smiled on us while here in this city, Master Talon," the captain said. "You have made a good friend in Lord Meng. Is it true that he is to become the governor of this city?"

"Yes, Captain, he is now the Governor. He has kept his word in everything, except one tiny detail for which I shall forgive him in time."

If Captain Dandachi was curious about that one thing, he kept his curiosity to himself and instead gave Talon a detailed report on the condition of the ship. Talon gave this his full attention.

"Two days ago we received the four large bronze tubes and their mountings that you call Erupters, Master Talon.

Talon smiled. "Their full name is 'Flying Cloud Thunderclap Erupters', Captain; a grand name, but the Chinese like that kind of thing."

"I am waiting for the workmen to come and install them on the waist deck. I understand that Jiaya, bless that man, has been working tirelessly to find the right people to come and finish the work," the captain told him.

"The men who will come are military men, so don't be alarmed if you see soldiers on the dockside. They know what they are doing. I understand that they are saying they will have to cut holes in the side of the ship when they install them?" Talon remarked.

The captain looked alarmed. "I am not very happy to have great holes cut in our ship's sides, Master Talon. Is it really necessary?"

Talon assured him that it was.

"Then we will have to make sure that the hatches are sea-proof when closed," the captain said with a resigned tone.

"Lord Meng told me that it was routine for these things to be assembled on the Chinese ships, Captain. I'm confident they know what they are about."

He and Reza had gone with Qian to the military barracks at the invitation of General Hayan Zhou to test the tubes and have some training under the tutelage of the General's men. The General wanted to demonstrate the destructive power of the Erupters, so he ordered an aide to take them out of the city to a place where his men practiced using the equipment. It had been quite an experience for Reza, who had never heard one of these things being 'fired' before.

Although he had already heard one of these fearsome weapons go off and had clamped his hands over his ears in preparation, Talon still jumped with shock. He had warned Reza to expect a big noise; even so, when the demonstration Erupter was fired, his friend looked shaken and stunned. He shook his head to stop the ringing in his ears.

"That is exactly what happened to me, Brother," Talon laughed, but then he said, "I want to see what they can spit out other than just flame."

The Aide, a lieutenant named Ximen Quing, snapped an order. The men around the Erupter reloaded the tube and placed a round ball of iron down on top of the powder.

"When the tube is fired it will light a fuse on the ball, which will explode in either the air or on the ground," Quing explained to them.

Sure enough, there was the bright flash, an ear-splitting bang, the ground shook and the gunners and Erupter temporarily disappeared in a cloud of acrid smoke. Talon and Reza both saw the ball streak out of the tube, along with the flames, and soar high into the air, leaving a thin trail of smoke behind it. The ball travelled faster than any trebuchet stone Talon had ever seen, and far higher. The smoking ball arced into the sky, then tumbled towards the ground approximately five hundred paces away, a phenomenal distance from Talon's point of view.

Then he and Reza gasped; before it reached the ground the ball simply exploded in a flash and a puff of smoke. The report came to them a split-second later, and the pieces from the disintegrated ball could be seen flying in all directions.

"Pedar Sag!" Reza breathed.

Ximen Quing gave them a sardonic smile. "We have these on our ships, as well as with our armies," he explained slowly in Cantonese for their benefit. "This way we scare off pirates and prevent our enemies from sailing into our harbors."

"Are you going to buy these, these monsters?" Reza asked Talon, his expression full of awe.

"Oh yes, Brother. Hsü has sold me four of them: two for each side."

Ximen Quing had been charged with showing them some other interesting items related to gunpowder and proceeded to do so with great enthusiasm. His men demonstrated rockets that carried arrows for impossible distances, and exploding balls of iron scraps and gunpowder held together by bamboo and resin that could be lit and hurled at close range towards the enemy. These were impressive and made a satisfying bang, hurling pottery shards, metal and bamboo splinters in all directions. Quing admonished them to get under cover whenever they used one, saying that there had been many injuries to the men who had thrown them in the past. Talon and Reza were very excited by these.

"Why, one could even throw one from a horse and get away in time before it exploded!" Reza exclaimed.

"Or toss one on a ship," Talon said, remembering how effective the Greek fire bombs had been.

On their arrival back at the house the women regarded their men with narrowed eyes.

"They are behaving like a pair of boys who have just been playing with something they should not," Jannat remarked in an aside to Rav'an.

"You can be sure of it, my Sister, and I can bet it is to do with those noisy things that go 'bang'."

*****

Later, when Talon and the family were enjoying the cool evening together outside the guesthouse, he and Reza described the demonstration. The men were enthusiastic, while the women were cautious about how effective the weapons might be.

"I remember seeing these things on Hsü's ship just before it went down," Talon said. I wondered what they might be, never having seen them before. He told me that they, too, had encountered pirates in the Bahr Al Hind."

"What happened?" Jannat asked with surprise, looking up from the game of dominos that she and Reza were playing.

"He said that they waited until the two ships came within two hundred paces, and then fired both the Erupters they had on one side of the ship," Talon laughed.

"Why are you laughing, Talon?" Rav'an said.

"Hsü told me that when the smoke began to clear they noticed the pirates were sailing away as fast as they could. There were no more encounters after that."

Reza chuckled. "So when you went north, the General used these things to terrify the Mongols?"

"It certainly startled them, but as to terrifying them, I'm not so sure," Talon said, his tone thoughtful.

"You had some adventures while north. Tell us about the hunt for the dragon, Talon," Jannat begged him.

Talon shot a look at Rav'an, but her face was bland. He sent her a small frown, wondering if she had broken her word and told Jannat.

Rostam, who had been playing with a set of carved wooden soldiers in the grass, looked up and said in a loud voice, "Please, Papa, tell us about the dragon! Lun and I have a Crane kite. It's beautiful."

"I didn't go up there to *hunt* a dragon, just to see one," Talon mumbled.

"Well, did you see one? We all want to know. Even the crew is waiting to hear all about it, Talon," Reza demanded. "They wanted to stuff it and take it home, but you didn't bring one back. I can tell you, they are disappointed!"

"I did see a dragon," Talon said evasively. Rav'an's lips curled into a barely suppressed smile.

"What was it like?" Rostam demanded eagerly.

"Was it huge?" Jannat asked, her eyes wide with curiosity.

"It was big, yes, very big, and white all over."

"White!" exclaimed Reza. "I thought they were all red, like we see here everywhere in Guangzhou."

"That's because the Chinese believe the color red is for good Joss. They paint everything red," Talon said, beginning to sweat. "Anyway, I hope you are all going to wear your best for the dinner that Hsü wants to have in our honor. It will be held in a week, I believe," he told them, desperate to change the subject.

Reza and Jannat continued with their game of dominos. Rostam went back to his toy soldiers, and Talon glared at Rav'an, whose face was going pink with suppressed laughter.

He scowled. Hsü had a lot to answer for, Talon decided.

*****

Talon and Rav'an, accompanied by Jannat, Jiaya and Lihua, made a protracted visit to a porcelain work shop to observe the process of making these exquisite items. Rav'an and Jannat, who had a very good eye for details, picked some of the very best from the pots, jars and plates laid out in front of them. At last they had several bales of pottery, which Jiaya assured them would be very carefully packed to withstand the rough passage of a sea voyage.

Well satisfied with his purchases, Talon suggested a walk for one last lingering look at the city where they had lived for over six months. As they ambled along the road that led out of the walled city, they came to an area where the streets were narrower and the houses less well maintained. Talon glanced around him towards the gates. The crowed street ahead was full of men, women and children all going about their business, avoiding the rickshaws and the palanquins that took up the center of the street.

He caught a glimpse of a man in the crowd who seemed to be watching Talon with an unmistakable look of hatred in his black eyes, but when he realized that Talon had observed him he turned and hurried away. Talon was trying hard to remember where he had seen this man before; seeing the bridge ahead of them jogged his memory.

It was the same man who had tried to kill Hsü while he and Talon had been walking across the bridge all those weeks ago!

"Reza, come with me," Talon said sharply, and he began to run. Reza with a surprised exclamation chased after him. "Stay there with the guards, Rav'an. We will be back very soon!" he called as he ran after Talon.

"What is it, Brother?" he demanded when he caught up with Talon, who was searching a narrow street for his quarry.

"I noticed someone watching us and remembered that he was the one who tried to kill Hsü when we were on the bridge. He ran down here somewhere, I'm sure of it."

Reza glanced down the street, which appeared to be empty of people, except for one old man sitting outside a doorway enjoying the little sun coming over the buildings. Smoke surrounded him, and the by now familiar smell of opium. Otherwise the street was empty; laundry hung on poles outside almost every second floor of the houses, but no one else was to be seen.

"Come on, we'll go down and see if he is somewhere along here," Talon said, and drew his sword. Reza did the same and they cautiously entered the narrow alleyway. The sounds from the main road dimmed as they went further into the alley.

Without warning there was a loud flash and a bang, followed by many more bursts of small explosive crackling, snapping sounds that detonated all around their feet. Flashes and acrid smoke increased the complete surprise of the two men, who jumped back away from these vicious, noisy things erupting all around their legs. Surprise shook Talon, but he gripped his sword and tried to make sense of the commotion and bitter smoke. Just in time, he saw his quarry rushing at him through the smoke with a huge sword raised to strike.

He was so off balance from the many explosions, he only just managed to dodge out of the way of the first downward slash, which might have finished him. He brought up his own weapon and hammered back at the other's with all his strength and then kicked out hard. The edge of his boot struck his attacker's kneecap, eliciting a high-pitched shout of pain.

Before the man could react, Reza pounced and hammered the pommel of his own weapon onto the man's head. He slumped onto the ground among the ashes and debris of his explosive devices, unconscious.

"I thought you might want to keep him alive for Hsü to talk to, Talon," Reza said with a grin. He glanced around them at the mess on the street. "Pedar Sag! Those are terrifying! He very nearly succeeded in his plan! I was completely distracted by those noisy things."

"So was I; something to remember," Talon said with a grimace as he sheathed his sword. He reached down and dragged their would-be assailant to the side of the road, and then he cut a piece of string from a laundry line, letting the clean clothes fall into the road. He rapidly tied the prisoner's arms behind him, then hauled him to his feet.

"We need to get out of here, Reza. The noise is bringing a crowd."

Curious people were emerging from the houses nearby; they were beginning to point and shout. A babble of loud Chinese followed them.

They hustled the still groggy prisoner out of the alleyway back onto the crowded main street. Hsü's guards, who were clustered protectively around Rav'an and Jannat, looked at them with surprise as they walked up with their prize.

Talon quickly explained the situation to them in halting Cantonese, whereupon they nodded and took charge of the prisoner.

"We should go home now," Talon suggested to the others.

*****

When Hsü came home, he had the situation explained to him by both the guards and then by Talon, whom he came to see directly after the guards' report.

"You think this is the same man who tried to kill me, Talon?"

"I am sure of it, and if I had not been sure before he attacked us I certainly am now," Talon remarked. "These things that he threw at us had us so surprised he might have killed us both."

Hsü nodded. "They can be very effective when used in that manner," he murmured, and led the way to the stables where the prisoner was being held. He was bound to a pole and had not been treated gently by his guards, but he was alert. Hsü launched into a long discussion with him. The questioning went back and forth, too rapidly for Talon to follow. However, from the changing expressions on the man's face, he could read something.

Eventually Hsü turned to him and explained.

"His name is Lin Chong. He used to work for the Chief of Police, Hua Rong. He blames you for the death of Rong, but I told him I knew that someone else killed his chief, as you were away when that happened. He has no one to work for now, and is a danger to others. Should I kill him? What do you think?"

Talon gave Hsü a thoughtful look. Then he shrugged. "You could kill him, of course; but he probably knows all there is about what is going on in this city, in the harbor, and the lower ends of society. He might be useful to you."

Hsü smiled and wagged his head. "You have read my mind, Talon. I shall suggest to him that he should work for me in future, and I shall reward him well for his services, better than Rong ever did. I will need some eyes in the streets as time goes by, and who better than this villain here?"

He then launched into a long series of questions to Lin, who registered first alarm, then surprise, and finally nodded his head vigorously with a crooked attempt at a smile. He tried to bow to Hsü, despite his bonds.

Hsü barked a command to the two men guarding Lin; they stepped forward to cut his ropes and then stood back with their hands on the hilts of their swords.

Lin immediately dropped to his knees and banged his head on the sand, saying something Talon could not follow.

Hsü spoke to him again, clearly warning him, then told him to stand. Lin was escorted away between the two suspicious guards.

"Well, you and I seem to be in agreement about how we should obtain information from the streets, Talon," Hsü remarked.

"I have used beggars in the past to my advantage, Hsü. They are hiding in plain sight, but they see everything on the street."

Hsü laughed. "I knew I should not underestimate you, Talon," he said. "Thank you for bringing Lin to me. I shall not be able to let my guard down with him for a while, but we shall see how useful he becomes."

*****

A week later, the ship was laden, the crew members were aboard, and it was docked at the Meng warehouse, ready to sail. That evening was to be the last for Talon and his family and friends at the residence. Hsü had insisted upon a farewell dinner, so everyone was present, including Yosef and Dar'an, who were dressed self-consciously in their new Chinese costumes.

Hsü presided over the meal; next to him was Lady Meilin on his left side, who kept a frozen face throughout the meal. Talon wondered unkindly if it was the powder layered on her face that prevented expression. Then there was Lady Lanfen, who beamed at the visitors as they filed in to be seated. Lihua was also present. At the bottom of the table were the two boys, by now firm friends.

They were served the best that Tem Pau could devise in the way of Chinese food. They started with an appetizer, served on a lacquer tray, that consisted of tit bits that required skill using chop sticks. No one present failed that test. Then there were lotus eggs with barbecued pork slices, preserved cabbage cooked in a meat sauce, followed by what Hsü called Dragon and Phoenix ham. There was a bewildering array of other dishes that everyone was encouraged to sample.

Hsü had a gleam in his eye when he spoke. "Pau wanted to do an all fish meal, but I told him that you would be eating fish for a month or two, so no fish today."

They all laughed; he was speaking Arabic for the benefit of all. "I did ask if there was a chance for some Durian, because I know how much you like it, Reza." His eyes twinkled. Reza's mustache bristled and he made a comical grimace, while Talon snorted with amusement.

After the meal, when the remains of the food had been removed, Hsü raised his hand for silence. The babble of conversation ceased as everyone looked towards him.

"I have two announcements to make. The one is that my office of governorship has the blessings of the Emperor and I will be taking up my duties very soon. In fact, I have done so all ready."

Everyone applauded at that piece of news; they had known of his successful bid, but now it was confirmed.

"I have another announcement to make, and I am very proud to do so." He paused and looked at his older son with affection. "My son Fuling has passed the Seventh grade Exams that will permit him to become an administrator; and should he one day pass the First grade, he can even become a governor of a province in time!" He lifted his wine cup and toasted a beaming Fuling. There were cheers at this from everyone at the table. Fuling gave them a tired but happy smile and toasted his father.

Hsü became serious. "My guests, it is with a heavy heart that I must bid you farewell and wish you a safe journey to the country you call home. We have learned much from you, and I hope that you in turn will remember China with kindness in your hearts, even if your stay has not always been tranquil and safe."

Talon smiled and said, "Of that you should have no doubt, Governor. We will always carry fond memories of this family, Guangzhou and China. We leave with heavy hearts."

Hsü nodded and then said, "There is one more thing."

He motioned to one of the servants, who signaled to someone beyond the door. A small procession of servants came in, carrying some articles that left the visitors openmouthed with surprise.

Hsü stood up and went to the leading servant. He lifted up a sword of the Nippon style that was sheathed in an exquisitely worked lacquer scabbard. He gave a small bow and presented it with both hands to Talon, who jumped to his feet to accept it, also with both hands, too overcome to speak.

"You, my friend, have earned this," Hsü said with a sincere smile. "These have come from Japan. They were made by the sword smiths at Bizen, a region now famous for the very best swords. That is why they took so long to arrive. They arrived just in time. I do not think you will be disappointed in their quality."

Now Talon understood the evasive behavior of his host. He smiled, wanting to embrace Hsü, but knew that would be a breach of manners.

Hsü turned to Reza. "Reza, may I also present you with this gift, because you too have earned it; you defended my family in its darkest hour." Reza bowed very low as he received his new weapon.

The other surprise was that Hsü presented smaller swords to Rav'an and Jannat, saying," You too are warriors, so it is only appropriate."

There were presents for all. Yosef and Dar'an also received swords, all of the Nippon make. All of the recipients were speechless with gratitude.

Lady Meilin presented Rav'an and Jannat with silk robes that took their breath away. They hadn't expected anything from this aloof lady, who was probably relieved that they were finally leaving. Lady Lanfen, not to be outdone, gave them each hair combs of jade and ivory set in gold; while Lihua, with tears in her eyes, gave them a complete set of dominos made of ivory.

Rostam received a brand new kite from Lun, who was very unhappy at his leaving, and a printed poem Lun had managed to negotiate, from the old man on the street, with his own pocket money. He also received from Lady Lanfen, who had taken a liking to him, a small figurine of two leopards, carved out of white jade, standing on a rock of green jade.

It was time to say goodbye. There were tears from the women and wet eyes all round as they left the room and went to their beds that night. The ship had to leave very early in the morning on the tide.

*****

The next day, Hsü, his two sons, and Lihua were there to see them off.

"You will find two small chests that I have delivered to the ship for you to open when you are out to sea, Talon. Please remember that this is home to you. If and whenever you decide to come back and see us, bring a ship full of cargo and we will buy it off you." Hsü's eyes twinkled. "Who knows, I might have found a dragon for you by then." They both laughed.

"I wish you all good fortune with your new post as governor, my friend. One day perhaps we will come back," Talon told him.

"We will miss you," Hsü told him. There were genuine tears in his eyes.

They embraced hard, and then, when Talon had jumped aboard, the vessel was poled away from the dock by workers. The crew let the main sail fill and belly in the light wind from the North, then the ship began to move slowly down river to join the other traffic. They waved until the figures on the quayside were too small to see. As they watched the teeming harbor go by, the boat sailed past the mud flats of the artificial island to the east of the city walls.

Talon didn't wait to reach the sea to find out what was in the small crates. He discovered that one contained a beautiful set of Go. The other was a surprise, and much larger. It contained a small dragon of white jade, about one pace long and five hands high. He laughed. Hsü had had the last word, of course.

*****

No one on the ship noticed the small crowd of curious people standing on the mud flats to the East below the city walls, nor the two prisoners kneeling in the mud, their hands tied behind them, waiting for the executioner's sword. One of the last things Wu po-ku and Lu Buwei ever saw was an elegant, ocean-going Arab ship sailing by.

Chapter Thirty-Two
A Good Captain

Their journey to Kalah Bar across the Chinese seas was uneventful, and once they entered the straits of Salaht the captain relaxed somewhat, saying that they could stay close to the coast of Malaya all the way to Kalah Bar. He kept a weather eye on Al Zabag to the port side of the ship, just in case there were pirates lurking in those mangrove swamps. The winds were benign and they made good time up the straits, only occasionally having to tack to make headway. There was only one nagging concern in Talon's mind.

How would they be received when they arrived in Kalah Bar? They needed to dock there to collect fresh water and supplies for the long leg across the Indian Ocean to Sarandib. He also wanted to take on spices and peppers to carry with them to Muscat. The man Sing might have something to say about that.

He decided that they would not dock on the island as they had on the outward journey but instead go to the mainland harbor of Kalah Bar, located in the state of Kedah. Captain Dandachi agreed with him. They wanted no trouble with the sinister Sing, and Kalah Bar seemed far enough away to avoid any trouble from the island.

They approached the port in the late afternoon. From Kalah Bar they could clearly see the island of Langkawi in the distance to the West. The houses and buildings of the port of Kalah Bar began to show themselves through the humid haze as they dropped anchor late that afternoon to find that there were several Chinese ships in port and even more Arab ships. The weather had been more kind to shipping recently, Talon supposed, as he looked over the ships clustered ahead of them.

Captain Dandachi beamed at Talon and said, "I am looking forward to meeting the captains and finding out how things have fared in Muscat since we departed. You know it is well over a year since we left Muscat, Talon? I pray to God that the *Heyda* did not come to Oman."

He nodded, the captain was right; they had been away for a long time, and news was at a premium. "The first thing we must do, Captain, is to make sure we can leave with fresh water in our casks and plenty of fruit and vegetables. Can you see to that? And don't forget, we must have more rice. You told me we were low on that."

Captain Dandachi nodded, somewhat chastened. "Yes, we must take care of that immediately, Talon. We can socialize later."

Talon chuckled and said, "I will be right there with you when you go to talk to the other captains, my friend. I, too, am starved for news. And I want to find out if any of the China ships will take a letter to Hsü."

There was much to do in preparation for the second long leg of the journey to Kulam Mari on the Southwest coast of Al Hind. The crew needed some time on shore to rest, and Talon was sure that both he and his family could do with some time on land. In spite of the humidity on the mainland, it was a welcome change to be able to walk on solid ground after six weeks at sea.

*****

There were those on shore who observed the arrival of a ship, an Arab-looking ship by its shape and sails; and before long it was known that it had come from China and that there were interesting people on board. The news was passed along from one person to another, then it travelled by boat until it arrived at the island, and after that it came to the table of Sing. The information was delivered in person by Amar, who knew that Sing took a special interest in this particular vessel.

"Those Persians have finally come back to our port," he told his master, who looked up from his meal and smiled. He dismissed the concubine, who was thankful to leave, and the servants who lingered around the walls, attentive to every gesture he made.

"Are we talking about the light-skinned Persian who looks more like a Frank?" he asked.

"The word is that such is the case, Master," Amar said.

"I wonder. They probably have a full hold. Let them collect water and supplies, and then we will see," Sing told him. "Leave them alone to buy what they will. It will all come to us in the end. Prepare your ship."

Amar bowed. He knew what to do.

*****

Captain Dandachi and Talon held a conference the following week while preparations were being made to take on water and supplies.

"We are running out of time, Master Talon," the Captain said with a glance at the sky. "It is now late winter, and I was hoping to be at Kulam Mali by now."

They both knew why they were late. The delays in Guangzhou had been costly in terms of time, but Talon was well pleased with their cargo.

"I understand, but I want to take on as much spice as we are able while here," he replied. "You yourself told me that would pay for the journey on its own, if we can get good terms for it."

The captain nodded his head vigorously. "I agree, we should not lose the opportunity, but then we must sail."

As it happened, the merchants and agents in Kalah Bar were eager to sell. The price was a little higher than Talon would have liked, but the captain assured him there would be little difficulty in selling the spices for a very good profit once they arrived in Muscat.

"The caravans will leave for Baghdad and other places whether we are late or not, and those merchants who missed the first ship to arrive will be glad to have a chance for our cargo," he said, pulling on his beard.

"Then we must make haste to load up and leave. We are all ready to go home," Talon stated.

The crew set to with a will, and before long the ship was loaded to the top of the holds. "This ship smells like a bazaar!" Reza laughed, as the final covers were drawn across the hatchways and the captain shouted to the crew to hoist sail.

"Lets hope we have good weather all the way, as I would hate this cargo to spoil," Talon remarked.

They watched as the port receded into the tropical haze, glad to leave the dense humidity of the mangrove swamps behind for the fresher air of the open sea. The captain took a northerly course to avoid the island of Langkawi to the West.

"We will head westerly tomorrow and arrive at the islands of Langabulos in a week if this wind remains constant," the Captain told Talon that evening. Talon had been carefully working out the route they were to take, using the kabal and the stars. Rostam was with him, enjoying the moment and chattering as he, too, checked their position relative to the stars. They had one other instrument that they had not had on their way out to China.

This was the compass that Hsü had presented to Talon, who had to take a leap of faith with the strange instrument as they sailed. The fact that it pointed unerringly South at all times was a great mystery to him and everyone else. However, it seemed to do just that. Indeed, the captain pointed out that the stars at night agreed with it. When they went southwest to strike the eastern coast of Malaya, it pointed directly south, enabling them to sail without concern when the weather changed to cloudy or there was rain. When they finally began to head north, it remained pointing to the South, enabling them to calculate with some degree of accuracy their direction and position relative to the land on the starboard side. Talon began to gain confidence in the heavy, cumbersome instrument made of brass and iron.

It was Waqqas who brought word of trouble on the second afternoon after their departure from Kalah Bar. He came up to the captain and whispered into his ear, then pointed back over the afterdeck along their wake.

Captain Dandachi turned to look and gave a short exclamation. He stared back along their wake for a long time, and then he told Waqqas to go and get Talon, who was below. Talon came up on deck to find the captain and Waqqas, as well as Reza, standing on the rearmost part of the high afterdeck, staring back along the way they had come.

"We have company," Reza said as he approached.

Talon glanced at the captain and Waqqas, who both nodded.

"The ship behind us has been following us since we passed the island of Langkawi a day ago, Master Talon. They might be just another ship, but we should be careful," Dandachi said. He looked unhappy.

Talon stared at the distant sail. "Have they gained on us?" he asked.

"They are moving very fast and have shortened the distance by half," Reza told him, and Talon knew that his friend was concerned. Their holds were full and the ship was not going to outrun a lightly loaded ship with evil intent. He had to make a decision then and there. He looked off to the West where the sun was about to set. This did not bode well if it should be a pirate: they always had the advantage in the dark.

"Reza, you know how to operate the apparatus on the main deck. Take Tarif and Umayr with you and prepare the Erupters, just in case."

Reza ran off to carry out the order.

Talon noticed the concern on the captain's whiskered face.

"They might just be another ship going the same way as us," he said with a shrug. The captain nodded, but he shouted orders at the crew to bring up the deadly little pots of Greek Fire and prepare them.

"I agree with you, Talon," he said in an unconvinced voice. "But you are right, we should be prepared all the same."

Talon made his way back down the companionway to the passenger deck and let himself into the main room. Rav'an and Jannat were there. Rostam was getting ready for bed, protesting all the way, while Salem scrubbed his face and hands.

"We appear to have company, Rav'an. This time you should all stay below. It might be nothing, but should it prove otherwise then there will be much danger on the deck. I want you safe below."

He smiled to take the worried look off his face, but he was unable to fool Rav'an. She nodded slowly and gave him a nervous smile. Jannat looked worried, but not panicked, he was glad to see. "We shall soon know," Talon told them as he left. He motioned to Yosef to take up a post by the door. "Stay here, my friend. Guard them with your life." Yosef grunted assent and gripped his spear more tightly. He still had difficulty talking, but speech was slowly coming back. Talon clapped him on the back and climbed the stairs to the upper deck.

He watched as Reza supervised the preparations of the equipment. There were two of the deadly bronze Erupters, or Fire Tubes, for either side of the main deck. These weapons had squatted on the middle deck, lashed down and covered with oilcloth, getting in the way of the crew since they left. Talon hoped they would fulfill his expectations today.

Talon had also wanted to buy some Fire Lances, the smaller tubular devices made of bamboo, which could fire a stone, or sand or pebbles a great distance; but Hsü had warned him away from them, saying that they could sometimes explode themselves and kill anyone nearby. On a ship that would be undesirable, he had told Talon, with a small quirk at the corner of his mouth.

They would instead be relying again upon the deadly little pots that the captain had, with great foresight, brought on board in Muscat. They also had some other nasty little devices that Hsü had suggested for the dangerous journey home. "You never know. These can wreak havoc in a crowd, Talon," he had said with that little smile of his. Talon realized how much he missed Hsü at this moment.

He went below to the hold to fetch several 'Thunderbolt Balls' that Hsü had proposed instead. These were a package of scraps of iron and gunpowder in a wrapped core of bamboo and resin. A short fuse could set it off, and it could cause much damage when thrown. He gingerly carried them onto the after deck and stacked them against the side of the ship. Reza joined him soon after and grinned wolfishly when he saw them.

"Where do you wish me to be if there is trouble, Talon?" he asked, as though it was quite natural for him to take orders. Talon smiled at his friend.

"Other than myself, you are the only person trained to use those Erupters properly, Brother. Again, it is surprise that will win this fight, if it should come to fighting."

Reza shrugged agreement. "They are gaining on us, Talon. I suspect something is up."

They walked over to the after railing and stared back at the oncoming ship. It was much closer now, only half a league away. They could make out the white bow wave; it was right on their wake. It seemed intent upon passing them very closely, or else it had some other more sinister intent in mind.

"Captain, change course. Lets see what they are up to," Talon called down to the steering deck.

Captain Dandachi shouted orders and the crew jumped to his command. The ship heeled slightly as they altered course several points further north.

Within a few minutes the other ship altered course as well and continued to follow them, gaining on them every minute.

"Well, now we know. They are after us," Reza said. "I'll go down and make sure the lads are calm. I have put stones in the Erupters. We'll see what effect that has on our friends."

"I don't have any idea as to how effective these weapons are at long range even though we saw some of it in China. The only recourse is to let them come very close and then we can be sure of hitting them every time. Especially in the dark." Talon said.

"Send Dar'an up the mast with some of these," he added. "Make sure he has a flint with him and can light it."

Dandachi nodded his head reluctantly. 'It is as you wish Master Talon."

Dar'an was soon clambering into the lookout perch with two of the thick bamboo tubes and several pots in a bag slung over his shoulder. Talon had spent some time showing him how they worked while they had been at sea.

Talon hoped the boy would keep calm and not throw too soon. It was all about surprise, but this time it would be dark and much more perilous. He cast a look to the West. The sun had gone down, leaving a red glow that reflected off the few clouds, but in the tropics darkness follows sunset very quickly. No one spoke on the decks; the crew were in their positions armed to the teeth, tense and waiting, while Reza was standing ready with a smoking taper next to one of the Erupters.

Talon felt the familiar tightness in his stomach as he watched the other ship drawing ever closer. They would have to let it almost come alongside before he did anything, he decided; it was going to be a test of nerves. He glanced at the captain, who stood with the equally nervous steersmen. He shot Talon a distracted look. "They will be upon us very soon," he said. Talon nodded and tried to smile.

All too soon it seemed the following ship was very close. Talon spent some time watching their approach and trying to gauge what their captain would try to do. The first thing he noticed was the other ship altering course to come alongside their port side, up wind of them. Talon nodded to himself approvingly. Good move: the pirates now had the advantage of the wind. Then he stared. The man on the afterdeck looked very familiar. He strained his eyes in the gathering gloom to see who it might be and then realized with a shock that it was Amar. He was sure of it. He itched to send an arrow into Amar, but he had to wait. "Surprise them and we might win," he told himself.

"We are being attacked by Sing's men! They are pirates for sure," he called out. Someone cursed on the lower deck and there were nervous mutters from nearby. "Stay calm, men. We'll give them a taste of the Dragon's breath!" he called out.

Some of the men gave nervous laughs, but only a few knew what he meant. The other ship now altered course sharply to bring it alongside theirs, almost on collision course. In the gloom of the evening Talon could just make out the men gathered in the waist and the foredeck, the dull gleam of their weapons waving as they prepared to jump aboard his ship.

There was a blinding flash and a deafening report from the other ship. Talon nearly fell over with shock. From the side of the pirate ship a long gout of flame spurted and a missile howled just above the rail of the *Sea Eagle*'s lower deck. Everyone ducked and there was a fearful cry from the men in the waist. They were just as shocked as Talon. This was something they had not expected. The pirates had an Erupter too! The shot had been aimed high to frighten their prey.

"Stay where you are!" Reza roared to the men, and kicked one of them back into place alongside their own Erupter. "Do not be afraid. We will burn them to the water and give them a taste of our own Dragon's Breath, but you must wait!" he called out to the frightened men.

Talon was stunned. He hadn't expected this, but he then realized why the pirates had been so successful. Few ships possessed such weapons. He blessed Reza for holding the men together and then watched as the other ship full of shouting and yelling men began to bring itself alongside. He raised his hand; they were only twenty paces away, well within easy bow shot. He dropped his hand and shouted at the top of his voice, "Now!"

The crewmen leapt up to haul open the hatches in front of the Erupters and pushed on the heavy devices with all their might, grunting and straining to get their barrels pointing out through the hatches. They leaned back on the ropes and waited while Reza ran to the first one and touched a fuse. It spluttered and spat, but then the flame raced into a hole in back of the barrel. There was small jet of flame at the touchhole, then a blinding flash from the muzzle and a huge bang which shook the timbers and made Talon clap his hands over his ears. The device jumped back against the ropes, jerking the men holding them almost off their feet.

Crew men leapt out of the way as Reza danced over to the next Erupter. Again he touched the fuse, and crew nearby made space as it fired off its contents at the other ship with another deafening roar. Both Erupters had been loaded with small stones that were hurled across the water to smash into the crowded ship. At that distance it was devastating. Talon didn't see much after that, as smoke obliterated most of the main deck. The men on the *Sea Eagle* were yelling and cheering as they hauled the Erupters back and began to reload them. In the dark Talon could not see the carnage they had inflicted on the other side, but the screams and wails sounded clear enough.

Talon took one of the Thunderbolt balls and tried to light the fuse. It seemed to take forever to catch as he frantically hammered at the flint. Finally it caught. He waited until the fuse was hissing spitefully, then stood up and hurled the device with all his strength across the space between the ships. He ducked behind the transom—just in time, as he felt the wind of an arrow meant for him as it passed overhead.

He didn't see where his bomb landed because he was frantically trying to light another one, but the explosion on the other ship told him all he needed to know. There were more screams, and he knew they had been hit hard. Men down in the waist of the ship were now hurling smoking Greek Fire bombs at the other ship, their yells of excitement as they saw the flaming results contributing to the general bedlam.

He searched vainly for a glimpse of Amar so that he could send an arrow his way, but the smoke and darkness prevented him from seeing much of anything. Instead he hurled another bamboo bomb at the steering deck of the other ship and had the satisfaction of seeing the flash and hearing it explode. He shook his head. What devilish weapons the Chinese had invented!

However, there was still plenty of fight left in the pirates. Their Erupter roared again and the air all around was filled with the hum of a hundred angry bees. Suddenly his own men were down and screaming. A small missile slapped into the railing, creating a shower of splinters. Talon felt a numbing blow, then a sharp pain under his right eye. He put his hand up to his face and it came away wet with his blood. He hastily tore off a piece of his light cotton tunic and staunched the blood.

"They have only one of these fearsome devices, but they certainly know how to use it!" he muttered to himself as he ducked and then busied himself with another Thunderbolt.

Talon saw another small flash on the pirate ship and looked up. Dar'an must have thrown his bomb down onto the vessel. He nodded approvingly; the boy was growing up. He peered over the top of the transom as shards of wood hummed by, and saw the results of several of the oil bombs that his men had tossed onto the vessel. Flames began to lick at the rigging. Now was the time for Talon to take his bow and to shoot the men down who tried to put out the flames.

"Get us out of here, Captain!" he yelled. There was no answer, so he jerked around to shout again. There was only one steersman standing, and he looked as though he was paralyzed with fright. There was blood on his tunic, the other was down in a welter of blood, and alongside him was the captain. Talon rushed to kneel by the captain's side, but when he turned him over it was clear he was dead. The front of Dandachi's shirt was soaked in blood; there were several black holes in his chest, and his head lolled loosely.

Talon looked up. "Abdullah!" he shouted at the seaman, who was stationed at the ropes with some men. "Get the ship away from them. Now!" he yelled. He smacked the frozen steersman across his face and shouted, "Turn the rudder! Wake up!" the man flinched and did as he was told. They began to pull away to starboard, much too slowly for Talon's liking.

Then there were more flashes and booms from his own deck as Reza fired off the reloaded Erupters. The flames lanced across the water to scorch the side of the other vessel and wreak more havoc among the enemy.

We have to kill the men who are firing at us, or we too will go down in flames! Talon thought desperately. He snatched up his bow and quiver and ran down the steps onto the main deck, pushing past the jostling and yelling loaders. He slipped on the bloody deck and nearly fell; one of the crew seized his arm to steady him. He nodded his thanks and continued until he estimated he was opposite where the other ship's Erupter was located. He could just make out dark figures frantically trying reload their weapon in the flickering light of fires that were now taking hold on the ship. The Greek Fire pots were proving once again to be deadly effective.

"Archers to me!" He roared.

Four of his men heard him and rushed to join him stumbling and colliding their companions who were frantically loading their Erupters with Reza yelling instructions at them.

"Shoot at anyone who is near that Erupter of theirs!" Talon shouted. He stared at the other ship and found that he was looking straight into the black maw of the enemy Erupter. A cold fear swept down his spine. The enemy were about to light the fuse! If they succeeded at this range it would blow him and his men to pieces.

"Shoot them!" Shoot them!' he roared and did just that with his own bow. A cluster of arrows swept across the gap straight into the small crowd gathered near the enemy Erupter.

Men fell but one man still moved forward unscathed with a burning coil to fire the deadly weapon.

His heart pounding as he realized that time was running out, Talon reached for another arrow but found none in his belt, he experienced a moment of sheer panic then glanced at one of his men.

"Here give me one of those!" he called across. He snatched the arrow from the surprised archer and in on swift motion he sent an arrow straight into the chest of the shadowy figure on the other ship, and then another. The man dropped what he was carrying and fell over with a cry. Talon could not see what it was but suddenly everyone nearby was running away from that area of the ship.

A moment later there was a blinding flash and a huge explosion. The pirate ship seemed to jerk to a stop as the fore deck disintegrated in a massive burst, tossing huge flaming pieces of deck into the sky. The side blew outwards and large splinters of wood howled through the air overhead, ripping through the sails of the *Sea Eagle*. One of the *Sea Eagle* crew went down with a choking cry, pierced as though by a huge spear. Talon was temporarily blinded by the flash and had to blink furiously; his eyes had bright red and yellow spots in front of them, making it hard to see.

He turned away from the sight of the raging fires and sensed the shifts in movements that indicated the *Sea Eagle* was finally pulling away from the stricken pirate ship, whose main sail was now ablaze in a terrible curtain of flame that illuminated both ships with a hellish orange glow, casting long shadows that made men look like demons. He stared in awe at the devastation. Without warning another explosion went off deep inside the pirate ship, and it broke the ship in half. He watched as the survivors of the two explosions dived into the water, trying to get away from the conflagration that had once been their home. Within minutes there remained only large pieces of burning timber and the clutter of burnt sails and rigging, around which were men struggling to swim who cried out for help to an indifferent night.

Chapter Thirty-Three

Aftermath

Talon was coldly angry. He wanted one of the survivors.

"Reza, we should get one of them aboard. Only one!" he shouted, not realizing that Reza was quite close and that he too could barely hear. They had all been deafened by the explosions.

Reza nodded. "You will need to get that taken care of," he said pointing to the wound on Talon's cheek. Talon dabbed at the wound in irritation, with the rag he had used before. He had other things to worry about just now.

As they pulled away from the flaming ship, several men managed to swim towards their own, crying for help. Reza picked one of them and had him hauled aboard. The others he dispatched with arrows. It was a kindness, given the shark-infested waters; they screamed and begged for mercy, but he shot them anyway.

The crewmen dragged the one survivor out of the water and threw him on the deck, none to gently. Reza walked over to him and poked him with his sword. The sailor jerked. No one paid any more attention to the burning wreck they were leaving behind.

"Tie his hands," Reza ordered, and when the sodden pirate was sitting up he crouched next to him and said, "You will be hung for what you tried to do. You will have to make your peace with God for what you have done, but if you would rather be killed quickly, instead of very, very slowly, you tell us where you are from and who was the captain."

The man, an Arab, gasped for breath and retched out some seawater. "Have mercy upon me, Lord," he stammered. "I am but a humble sailor who had to do as I was told. We are from the island of Langkawi and my master is Captain Amar, servant of Lord Sing," he babbled.

"What was your intention? To plunder our vessel and rape our women?" Reza shouted at the cowering pirate.

He shook his head, his eyes rolling, and said nothing, too scared to speak.

Talon put his hand on Reza's shoulder. "Captain Dandachi is dead. They killed him," he told his friend.

Reza stared up at him with a shocked expression on his face. "The captain is dead?" he asked loudly. He was still deafened by the thunder of the Erupter.

Others of the crew heard him; word went around like fire itself and some of the crewmen began to wail and scream imprecations at the luckless man at their feet. They were ready to tear him to pieces in their rage.

"Leave him!" Reza roared. Such was their respect for him that they drew back, but they continued to form a menacing circle around the prisoner. Reza turned to Talon and there was anger in his voice as he spoke loudly for all to hear.

"You are now the captain, Talon, as well as the owner. What do you wish to do?"

Talon had been thinking carefully. With Amar gone, Sing might be very vulnerable. He wanted to avenge the captain, and knew full well that his brother and the crew were waiting to hear him say the words.

"Captain Dandachi was a master of the sea and navigator. I have known no one better. He was also a friend. As God is my witness, I wish to avenge his death and clean out the nest of vipers that live on the island," he stated. The crew roared their approval.

"Before then we must clean up our own ship. We have to take care of the wounded and prepare the dead for burial and make repairs. Waqqas and Abdullah, you are to keep the ship on a North-westerly course until I tell you to change; This will take us well out of sight of the island. Umayr, you and your men will assist Reza with the wounded and the dead. Tarif, bring some men and make sure the prisoner is secured. I do not wish him to get away for any reason. But he is not to be harmed until I have decided what to do with him."

He turned back to walk up the stairs to the steering deck, where he paused. The body of the captain had been laid out on his back, staring up at the sky with sightless eyes. The night obscured most of his features, but Talon knelt by his body and closed his eyes, then he rested a hand on his chest. "Goodbye, my friend. I do not know how we will get home without your skill and knowledge." He noticed a drop of blood fall onto the dead man's chest. Only then did he become aware again of the cut on his face. Rav'an would have something to say about that. He fingered it and realized it might need a stitch. She would know what to do.

Talon stood up with a heavy heart and went below to tell her what had happened.

*****

The next day, the *Sea Eagle* was hull down north of the island of Langkawi. It had not been too hard to persuade the prisoner to tell them everything he knew about the bay where the pirate ship used to be kept anchored, waiting for orders to sail out and attack merchant vessels that were on their way home to the Chinese or Arab countries.

Talon held a conference with Reza and the women. He included Yosef and Dar'an in the discussion.

Rav'an was adamantly against the sketchy plan. "I want to sail away as soon as possible and leave this accursed island and its evil owner behind," she stated firmly.

"Why are you and Reza so set on revenge? " she demanded. "Anything could go wrong, and then where will we be?"

It was a reasonable argument and Talon knew it.

"I think that in the heat of the moment I should have thought this through more carefully, but everyone was so full of anger, I made the decision," he told her. "It's too late now to go back on what we promised the crew. They are out for blood!"

"We cannot go back on our word to the crew, Rav'an," Reza added his argument to that of Talon. "They want to avenge a man they admired and depended upon. I for one, want revenge on the man who gave them their orders, Lord Sing. He is murdering merchants and crews and stealing their cargoes. Yesterday he was prepared to take our ship and kill us all. What he had in mind for you does not bear thinking about. I am going to take revenge," he said, with an unusually stubborn expression on his face.

Not even Jannat could dissuade him, so the meeting ended with Rav'an and Jannat declaring their unhappiness but agreeing to stay on the ship with Rostam while the men went onto the island.

Before they parted, Rav'an asked Talon to remain a little longer, and when they were gone she reached up to touch his cheek where the splinter had cut. He wore a crude patch over the cut and his right eye. "You look truly villainous, my Talon," she said softly, her eyes concerned. "I was shocked at the devastation wrought by those dreadful engines of war last night."

"I too, my Love. However, if we had not had them we would all be dead, or worse," he responded. He reached for her and held her very close.

"You will make a fine captain, my Talon," she whispered into his shoulder.

"We shall see, my Love. But ..." he stood back and smiled. "I shall have that scamp Rostam at my side to make sure I take all the readings properly. He will make a fine navigator one day." They both laughed, the tension broken.

"Where is he, anyway?" Talon asked.

"He is on deck, where else? Probably telling the crew men how to clean up the appalling mess," Rav'an said with a wan smile.

*****

Later that day, Reza and Talon had their own small but intense discussion at the after end of the ship.

"You know that you cannot lead this expedition, Talon?" Reza stated.

"Why ever not?" demanded Talon with a fierce look at his friend.

"Because you are the captain now, not just the owner, and it is your responsibility to stay with the ship in case anything goes wrong. If I get killed you can still sail away and make it home, but if you are killed then we will all be at the mercy of the men of this place."

Talon gripped the railings till his knuckles were white and glared in the direction of the island, which could not now be seen from the deck. Reza was quite right, even if he doubted his ability to do all that the captain had done. It rankled, as he wanted very much to see Sing's face just before he killed him. He was very angry over the death of Captain Dandachi, whom he had considered a good and trusted friend, but also over the other members of the crew: four good men lost, and many others wounded.

The captain had guided them without a hitch to China and held the ship together in a ferocious storm, which could have sunk *Sea Eagle* had he not been at the helm. Now he, Talon, was being looked up to by his own brother and the crew to take the Captain's place, and to take them all home. Those were very large boots to fill. For a long moment he said nothing, and Reza waited silently by his side, watching the emotions play across his face. Finally, with a sigh, Talon lowered his head and turned to his friend.

"You are right, Brother. You must go, but I must stay."

Reza embraced him and said, "Thank you, Captain! I wanted to see where your head was, Brother. As always, it is firmly on your shoulders. I shall take good men and we will do the work that is necessary. Have no fear of that."

*****

Talon remained on deck for the rest of the day, supervising the cleanup of the ship and seeing to the wounded as well as preparations for the raid. He had Tarif oversee the shrouds for the dead and their readiness for burial at sea.

If he could not go with the landing party he wanted to make sure there was nothing to go wrong with their equipment. He had the crew bring several of the deadly Greek Fire pots on deck, prime them, and place them in straw in a sack to be carried ashore with the party. He supervised the training in the use of the Thunderbolt bombs. Dar'an, by now confident in their use, explained the operation of the bombs carefully to the men, who regarded them as one might a deadly snake. Observing the apprehension of the men, Talon decided to send Dar'an along with the landing party to make sure the bombs were used properly. The lad was no longer a boy; he had become a man without Talon even realizing it. Dar'an was ecstatic.

The difficulty lay not so much in carrying the dangerous items as in being able to light their fuses at the right time, and in time. The Chinese understood the need for fuses, but even to Talon's uneducated eyes these were crude devices. The Chinese had warned him that they could fizzle out, leaving the wielder with a worthless missile, or flame too fast and blow up before the bomb could be jettisoned.

Talon left Dar'an to figure out how to deal with them. He now he had a ship to sail. Waqqas and Abdullah both interpreted his orders when it came to the actual sailing and when a change of course was needed.

The man they had captured, Hanji, had drawn a rough map of the island of Langkawi. The first thing Talon noted was the numerous smaller islands and outcroppings of rocks dotted along its coastline; the next were the inlets and beach areas, which looked like an enticing anchorage for a ship. He suggested this, but the prisoner told the two men squatting next to him that the island was thick with jungle and the pathways would be impossible to negotiate at night.

"How do we get to the castle by any other way?" Reza demanded; his natural impatience surfacing.

"You must sail to the south of the island and come back up from the Southwest, Master," Hanji told him. Talon had promised not to hang him if he told them everything. He had fallen on his knees in front of Talon, weeping with relief at the reprieve. Now he fell over himself to explain the geography of the complex island archipelago. "You must negotiate the channel to the west of the island of Dayang Bunting and go ashore a league before the town. I can take you along a well worn path that leads up the hill from the beach to the fortress itself, which is overlooking the town," he told them.

"Can this be done at night?" Reza asked. His tone was skeptical.

Hanji looked up at the sky, which was normally cloudy at this time; it was late afternoon. "The rains will not come today, not even tomorrow if you wish to wait. While there may be clouds, there will be a half moon tonight, so we will be able to see enough to march by... and to sail," he said.

"So now I have to sail this ship to an unknown place, in the dark, with pirate as a guide who might give us away at any moment. I must be mad," Talon muttered to Abdullah as they stood on the steering deck, watching the men making preparations down on the main deck.

They raised sail as the sun set, and, with Waqqas assisting him, Talon took the ship several leagues to the west before the lookout told them that the island was out of sight. They then sailed the southern leg, hull down with the lookout keeping them just within sight of the island. They sailed for a good two hours in that direction, during which time night fell and, much to Talon's relief, the half moon came out. They changed course to bring them close enough to make out the dark outline of the island from the deck. Clouds still moved across the moon, plunging them into darkness from time to time, but Hanji seemed confident that they were on the right course.

At one point he asked to go up to the top of the mast, where he studied the land mass. He came down to stand again with Talon next to the steersmen. "We should change course now, Captain," he said.

"Are you sure?" Talon asked him.

"You cannot see it from here, but I could see the entrance of the channel from up in the mast. It will appear within a short while."

Talon issued orders to Waqqas, who called them out to Abdullah and the crew, who jumped to do his bidding. The ship heeled just a little, and the sails flapped, then bellied as they took on their new course.

The ship surged forward, the only sounds being the water hissing past the hull and the creak of stays. Talon had issued orders for strict silence from everyone on deck. It had surprised him that the men were so respectful when he issued orders. He had remarked on it to Reza, who'd laughed.

"Talon, my Bother. You always did underestimate your ability to lead. You have demonstrated on more than one occasion your bravery and leadership. Why would they not respect you?"

"I am not a real captain, nor am I a real navigator. I have always left that to others of more experience," he'd said.

Reza had put his hand on his shoulder and smiled. "I think you will become both in a short space of time, Brother."

Talon drew comfort from his words, and focused on the present. Now he could see the split in the land mass and realized that they were heading into the channel.

"We must stay in the center of the channel, Captain," Hanji whispered. "There are sand banks along either side that could trap us if we do not."

Waqqas heard him and ordered the steersmen to make a small correction. Before long they were deep into the channel, and all the noises of the jungle at night could be heard. The call of the howler monkeys and the grunt of wild pigs in the mangrove swamps came clearly across the water to the men on the silent ship, along with the smell of rotting vegetation and rank, salty water. *The smell of land*, Talon thought to himself, and wrinkled his nose. The open sea always smelled cleaner, just as did the air of the desert.

It seemed only a short while before Hanji touched him on the arm and whispered, "We must take down the main sail and move over to the port side, Captain. There is an inlet over there. Have you noticed the curve to the starboard side of the channel? We will find ourselves in the harbor if we continue much further."

To low-voiced commands the *Sea Eagle's* main sail was taken down, along with the foresail, leaving only the after sail to catch what wind there was. The ship moved very slowly towards the port side coast, and then Hanji touched his arm again. "Here Captain! We must drop anchor here!" His tone was urgent.

The order was called forward and the crewmen at the bows eased the anchor stone into the water. None too soon, as the sand was only ten feet below the keel. Talon looked across at the dark mass of the jungle in front of them. How was the party ever going to find their way through that forbidding forest at night?

Hanji had said he would be glad to guide the party along the pathway that would take them up to the back of the palace. Reza came up to collect him and to warn him.

"Anything at all that makes me suspicious, you will be the first to die," he told the frightened man, who nodded emphatically. "As God is my witness, Master, I shall not betray you," he stammered.

Reza and Talon embraced. Just as he turned away, he saw Rav'an and Jannat come on deck, approaching them in the darkness. Talon could smell their scent in the heavy air as they came closer.

"You would leave without saying goodbye, Reza?" Jannat whispered to him. He seized her in a tight embrace. "Be safe, my warrior," she murmured into his shoulder with a catch in her voice.

He kissed her and embraced Rav'an, then went down to the main deck where the crew were already climbing down the side to the two boats, which had been lowered before they came to the channel.

Talon stood on the steering deck next to Rav'an and Jannat, watching them pull away. Strong men rowed the boats with the oar locks wrapped in sacking to muffle any sounds. Reza was taking ten men with him, which would leave Talon shorthanded if they didn't come back, but less than ten would have handicapped the enterprise. Hanji had told them there were twenty to thirty men at arms in the palace. Once again, the element of surprise was needed for success to be theirs.

Talon, Rav'an, and Jannat stood by the port rail, staring in silence into the darkness long after the boats had vanished. They didn't hear anything of the landing a few hundred paces away.

As though divining his thoughts, Rav'an touched his hand with hers. "It is hard, but you made the right decision, my

Talon," she said. "I shall not sleep until our brother and his men are back with us. God protect them this night."

"The waiting and not knowing are enough to kill me," he muttered, as he gripped her fingers.

"But Reza was right, your responsibilities are far greater than even before. Now you are the captain of the ship and the navigator. Your duty is to this ship!"

Talon nodded in the dark. "You are all right, of course; but I am not good at waiting, my Love. Not like this! I pray to God that he, they, will be safe."

"I pray that they will all be safe," Jannat echoed him, and shivered despite the warm, humid night.

Rav'an hastened to wrap her in her arms. "Jannat, I shall tell you something more about Reza that you do not know. If anyone can take care of this, it will be he, believe me."

Talon remained on deck and kept watch. "God speed my brothers," he murmured.

Till my soul is full of longing
For the secret of the sea,
And the heart of the great ocean
Sends a thrilling pulse through me.

—Henry Wordsworth

Chapter Thirty-Four
Retribution

As the boats pulled away, Reza glanced back at the dark profile of the *Sea Eagle*. He noted the figures standing at the rail, then turned to focus his full attention on the coastline. The rowers pulled hard but silently towards the dim outline of the beach ahead of them. He like all his men was dressed in dark clothing with his face covered up to his eyes.

Within minutes of leaving the ship they eased themselves over the sides of the boats into the water, trying not to make a splash, and then hastily hauled the boats up the beach far enough to prevent them from drifting away. The sea here was very calm; the only danger Hanji had warned them of was water snakes. Reza did not relish that idea very much, but it helped to hasten the men out of the water and to urge them swiftly towards the darkness of the jungle ahead.

Then, in the middle of the sandy beach, they all stopped and stood motionless. The sand all about them had come to life and had begun to move. To their horror, hundreds of large crabs began to scuttle away from them, making a harsh, clacking rattle as they moved. One of the men gave an involuntary yelp of surprise when one ran over his bare feet. Then it was quiet again. They hastened to get off the beach; their nerves, already taut, were now jangling.

Hanji was pushed to the front by Reza, who walked right behind him with his sword drawn in case of any treachery. The man seemed to be willing enough, but Reza was not taking any chances. Hanji had told them that the palace was on the hill almost directly above their position. Its location was west of the town, which was huddled around a large cove on the bend of the channel they had negotiated that night.

Fortunately the rasping of the insects in the jungle hid the clumsiness of the men, who were inexperienced in moving quietly. It was dark and they were carrying heavy loads: Greek Fire pots and Thunderclap bombs, and several small barrels of the flame powder that Talon had discovered was so effective. He had suggested that it might be useful to blow things open, like doors. Reza had agreed, although reluctantly, as his whole being was tied to stealth.

Their path was well used but very narrow, and they constantly brushed past thick bushes and trailing vines which made Reza flinch, thinking they might be snakes or some other jungle denizen that harbored designs upon him; Reza hated snakes. Things he couldn't see in the dark scuttled out of their way as they walked, and he prayed there would be nothing dangerous to dispute their right of way. He began to sweat copiously in the close humidity, straining his eyes to see beyond Hanji's dark form as they climbed the hill through the jungle.

It took them almost an hour to make their way to a point where the jungle thinned, and they found themselves at the edge of an area where the ground had been cleared by men. They emerged from the jungle with relief to see the dark walls of the palace looming over them and the dim lights of the harbor below off to the East. *So far so good*, Reza thought. Their guide had not misled them.

Hanji stopped and allowed Reza to come alongside, then gripped his arm and pointed up at the battlements. Reza looked up and could see the dark silhouette of a guard. The sentry walking slowly along the top of the wall seemed unaware of the visitors huddled at the edge of the jungle below him. The *Sea Eagle* men retreated deeper into the shadows.

"You will stay here," Reza whispered to Hanji. He disappeared, only to reemerge at the base of the walls. Then they witnessed an extraordinary thing. Reza scaled the wall, which was about twenty feet high, as easily as though he were walking up the vertical surface. He reached the top and rolled over the parapet into the shadows, where he waited. The sentry came ambling back, glancing from time to time over the wall in a disinterested manner. He never knew what struck him down, but it was over in a moment. Reza resorted to his usual tactic. He propped the dead man up on his spear as though he were leaning against the wall for a rest.

Then Reza beckoned the others. There was a concerted rush to the base of the wall, where every one waited, listening hard to make sure there were no alarms. Then at a whispered call from Reza, Tarif stepped out and threw a rope up to him. Reza tied it off and signaled to Tarif, who beckoned others of the team to climb the rope. When Reza had four men with him, including Tarif and Dar'an, he gave the rope a sharp tug.

It was a signal for the remainder, with Hanji in tow, to move around the walls to the main gate and wait there. Reza, in the meantime, led the way along the wall towards the area where the main gates were located. There would be sentries posted there who would have to be dealt with silently.

They scuttled along the wall and came onto the pavilion area. The moon came out from behind a cloud, and everyone sank into a darker shadow waiting. While they waited, Reza sniffed the air. The stink of carrion that came out of the darkened compound below was very strong in the humid air. He peered downward and was startled to see a huge shadow moving out of the darker shadows into the middle of the compound to stand near to a tree.

The hairs on the back of his neck rose. "Pedar Sag!" he breathed. He was now somewhat familiar with tigers, having seen paintings of them as the Chinese saw them; he had even handled pottery depicting them. The Tiger was part of the Chinese culture; but Reza had never seen a live one before and it was a terrifying experience, even from the safety of the pavilion. When the clouds parted, the moon illuminated a great beast with stripes over all its body, which he estimated stood at the shoulder as high as his waist. It was looking straight up at him, its tail lashing, and then it growled: a low rumble that was as menacing a sound as he had ever heard.

One of his men had noticed the animal too, and he gave an involuntary whimper of fear. Reza decided it was time to move and get on with what they had come for, before the men lost their nerve. Tearing his eyes away from the pacing beast below, he got up and moved quickly towards the entrance that he remembered led down the stairs towards the main hallway. There was a faint glow of light at the end of the corridor; beckoning the others to follow, he walked very silently and carefully down the stairs toward the opening. They emerged into what Reza recognized as the main foyer of the palace, where he had been once before. Lanterns were still burning in small recesses in the walls, even though it was well after midnight by now. There was a small noise at the other side of the room. Everyone froze and all eyes probed the darkness. Slowly something moved out of the darkness into the dim light of the oil lamps and began to move across the stone floor. Reza went cold with shock. It was a snake, the largest he had ever seen, and it was coming to investigate the intrusion. Without thinking he slipped his sword out of its sheath and held it in front of him.

The men around Reza shrank back in fear and one even made to climb the stairs to get away, making a small sound of panic in his throat. Reza hissed at them to stay where they were and advanced into the room, his sword held in both hands in a strike ready pose. If this was just a python there was nothing to fear, but he would have to dispose of it before it caused more panic among his men. His own heart was pounding furiously in his chest as he watched the huge snake slithering slowly into the center of the room.

The creature noticed him and stopped, then it rose up, and he saw what he had dreaded most. Behind its head was a spreading hood, and he knew he faced a deadly cobra. The head of the snake was not three paces away and level with his chest, its forked tongue testing the air. Reza tried to control his breathing as he had learned in the dojo. He settled his stance and watched the creature intently. His sword point was level with its head. There was not time to lose, he realized; he could feel the fear emanating from his men behind him.

The snake drew back its head to strike. Reza made one stride forward, followed by a lightning fast blow from the side and upwards in a smooth arc. The fine steel of his sword flashed and the next thing the men behind him saw was the head of the snake flying through the air to land on the tiles with a thud and a spray of blood. The rest of the body writhed and convulsed at Reza's feet. Behind him he heard a collective sharp intake of breath from his men. He gave a hiss of relief and lowered his sword, then he took a deep breath and willed himself to stop the tremor in his hands.

Sing's watchdog was dead.

"Come!" he told them, and went to the main door, eased it open a crack then peered out. The men by the gate were asleep. They all slipped through the door and sped across the open yard to the shadows next to the gate. Reza left it to his men to deal with slumbering guards. The two were dispatched with barely a sound and the gates were eased open. Despite the creak of the doors on iron hinges no one woke up, nor did anyone come to investigate. There was no change in the chorus of frogs from the jungle to alert the inhabitants of the palace to trouble.

Reza grabbed Hanji as he slipped inside the door by the collar and whispered fiercely into his ear. "You didn't tell me about a tiger. Nor did you talk about a Cobra."

"The tiger is kept secure, Master. It is used for executions. I... I didn't know about the snake, I swear!" he whined. "There was a rumor of a monster guardian in the palace, but I never came here more than twice, so I don't know!" Reza shook him, unconvinced. There was something here he didn't like.

"Where does Lord Sing have his apartments?" he demanded, while he watched his men place a small barrel against the main gate. They might need it to delay pursuit.

Hanji pointed to a set of buildings attached to the main structures. "When I was here last time I noticed that no one went over there to the other side of the main entrance. We were told to stay away. Those are his private quarters. I've never been inside them. Those over there are for the servants and the guards," he whispered pointing in the other direction, he sounded uncertain.

At Reza's prompting, they hastened back as a group to the main building, leaving two men by the gates. Reza lead the way to the large ornate doors on the other side, which he opened cautiously and peered through. More lanterns; some had gone out, but there were enough to light the corridor and show him arches and doorways leading off from the small foyer. It was very quiet here. He slipped through and then looked at Hanji. "Where?" he asked.

Hanji shrugged and raised his hands. "I do not know, Master. I don't know, as God is my witness."

Reza gave him an angry look and told him to wait with the others. He then spent some time investigating each of the six rooms. Moving like a ghost, he found storerooms and several bedrooms, each with a sleeping woman lying in a luxurious bed. He left them, after making sure they slept alone. One room had a bronze door that was securely locked with a padlock on the hasp that defied his attempts to open it. Then he came to a chamber that was larger than the others, where the scent of a woman lingered and where there was even more opulence.

Even in the dark Reza sensed that this was the master room. His senses were confirmed when he came up to the bed. There were two people sleeping on it, one of whom looked like Sing, while the other was clearly a woman. Both were naked, lying on silk sheets, the humidity being such that they needed no cover. Reza looked down on the bearded face of the sleeping man for a long moment, contemplating how to deal with him. It would have been an easy matter to kill him at that moment, but another idea came into his head.

He pricked Sing awake with the tip of his sword. Sing came awake quickly enough, but stopped breathing when he opened his eyes and saw the menacing shadow standing over him with a sword poised at his throat. He raised a hand in supplication. "Don't," he whispered when he began to breathe again.

Reza gestured to him to get out of bed and not to wake his partner. He nudged the compliant and naked Sing towards the door. Reza pushed him through and closed the door behind them. Sing looked frightened and vulnerable in the dim light of the corridor.

"Who are you? What do you want?" he asked, trying hard to regain his composure. It was hard, given his nakedness and the mysterious visage of the figure before him; Reza's face was covered by a shemagh, leaving only his eyes visible. Something about this man with a sword told Sing that this was not someone he could intimidate or command, and that was the most terrifying aspect of all. Sing was used to commanding by fear all others around him.

"You will know when we are done," Reza told him in a whisper.

"I can pay you!" Sing stammered. " You can be as rich as you like. I have enough treasure to share with you if you will spare my life!"

"Where is this treasure of yours?" Reza demanded.

Sing pointed down the corridor towards the bronze door. "In there. More than you have ever dreamed of! My treasure, and I will willingly share it with you, only spare my life!" he pleaded.

"Open it!" Reza pushed him roughly towards the door.

"I need to have my key," Sing protested. "It is in my bedroom."

With the sword pressed against his naked back, Sing lead the way back into the bedroom where the woman was still asleep. "Get dressed and find the key," Reza ordered him.

Sing moved towards a cabinet while Reza watched him carefully. But in the dark he didn't see the knife that Sing slipped into his clothing, even as he raised the large iron key high and kept it on his forefinger, high enough to distract Reza.

Reza backed off to let Sing pass, but then Sing lunged. The knife was long and could have eviscerated Reza had it cut deeply enough. As it was, Sing underestimated the reaction of his opponent. Reza side-stepped the knife and slashed down onto Sing's arm with his sword. The forearm and the knife fell to the floor and Sing gave a bellow of agony. He snatched at the stump, which was squirting blood, with a look of horror on his face. Reza raised the sword to deliver the final blow, but this last act of treachery made him hesitate.

He knocked Sing to the floor unconscious, and reached for the key, which had fallen to the floor. The woman in the bed woke up to Sing's scream and began to shriek with terror herself. There was no time to lose. Reza leapt over the bed and tapped her on the side of her jaw with the pommel of his sword, then laid her back on the bed and attended to Sing, who was slowly waking up. Reza hurriedly fashioned a bandage over the stump of the wound. He could already hear some sounds of alarm, so he hauled the groaning man to his feet and dragged him out of the room down the corridor towards the bronze door. His men were piling into the corridor, looking anxious. The he felt blood on his leg and looked down. His pants were dark with his own blood, Sing had dealt him a dangerous wound. He didn't feel any real pain yet, but he held the cloth to the area where it was located.

"We have one stop to make!" Reza told the men, and threw Sing into the arms of two of his men. "Hold onto him, do not let him escape. He is our way out." They seized the gasping, groaning man and held him tight while Reza fumbled with the lock and key. He wrenched the padlock off the hasp, slid the iron bars back with a snap, then hauled open the door.

"You are wounded, Reza!" Dar'an cried, pointing to the red stain at his waist.

"'It's nothing. We don't have time to waste," Reza snapped.

The room was in utter darkness, so he seized one of the lamps nearby and raised it on high at the entrance of the doorway. Then he gasped. His men crowded around him at the entrance, and they too gaped at the sight in front of them. There were stacks of silver ingots alongside an open chest of gold and another of pearls. Fine silks were piled high and expensive carpets were draped over boxes. There were other caskets that were closed, but Reza could imagine what might be inside them.

Take what you can carry but we must leave!" he ordered the men as he bound his shemagh tight about his waist. The pain was beginning to bite. One item caught his eye, and he decided that he had to take it. He reached for it and dragged it out from under some silk cloth. He had the strange sensation that he was listening to a game of Chogan as he did so.

"We must leave!" he repeated urgently, with an ear cocked to the noises coming from the other room. He wrapped the item up in a swath of silk and handed it off to one of the men. "Do not drop this, nor leave it behind," he ordered.

The men set to with a will. A couple made threatening gestures with their weapons at the women who were coming out into the corridor, and they screamed and fled back into their rooms. The men laughed. They were sorely tempted to follow, but Reza didn't want their group to disintegrate into a plundering mob of rapists, so he called them sharply to order. They obeyed without question, even as they cast longing looks in the direction of the women. The group now carried six small chests and several sacks of silver, including the bulky item that Reza had given to one man and told to guard well.

"This way!" Reza called as he led the way back towards the main hall and the men reluctantly abandoned the chamber. As they headed for the main hall Reza called out.

"Dar'an, throw one of those thunder ball things into the treasure room when I open the door."

It took only a moment for Dar'an to light the bomb, and as Reza flung open the door he tossed it into the chamber and ducked out of the way, while Reza slammed the door shut and slid home a bolt.

The explosion in the confined space of the treasure room on the other side of the door was like a muffled clap of thunder, and the door sagged. One of the men who had been peering into the main chamber called back urgently.

"There are men in the main chamber, Master Reza! What do we do? They are coming this way!"

That posed a problem. Reza thought rapidly.

"Another one, Dar'an!" He ordered and opened the door to allow Dar'an to toss a hissing and smoking bamboo bomb into the room which now had several guards running across the bloody floor towards them. He slammed the door and waited for the explosion which again deafened them, buckled the door and shook the walls. "These are mighty weapons!" he said to himself with a wolfish grin at the men clustered about them.

Someone laughed and then they were all laughing, baying like predatory hounds who scented a kill. He threw the door open and led his men in a wild charge across the room full of stunned and wounded men. Two men tried to stop them, only to die from two strokes of Reza's sword. The men behind him stabbed at anyone who moved as they ran by. The floor was now covered in human as well as snake blood, upon which the men slipped and slid as they scurried towards the entrance on the other side.

As he went past the main doors to the outside there was a flash of lightning and a deafening explosion from the area of the gates. The very air around them was compressed and hammered at their ears. Earthenware pots shattered and brass lanterns fell to the floor with ringing clangs. Men slipped to their knees, dropping what they were carrying, cursing and holding their hands to their ears. The explosion came from the gates, so Reza figured that the two men he had left there would have heard the noise within and understood that it was time to leave. In doing so they had left a parting gift behind. The gates would be no more.

"Make sure he doesn't get away!" Reza shouted to the two men who held onto Sing, as they all picked themselves up and ran full tilt up the stone stairs towards the pavilion. By now the whole palace was awake. Men spilled out onto the courtyard, but even more now rushed the main entrance, and spears were thrown at the disappearing backs of the men running up the stairs. They lost the last man in line but one; he grunted with pain as a spear found its mark, toppling him back down to the feet of the angry guards who hacked him to death.

The rest emerged onto the top wall near to the pavilion, hampered by their loot. "Throw a Greek Fire ball down at them," Reza called. One of the group knelt and scraped a flint. A stream of sparks fell onto the rag attached to the bomb, it smoldered then caught fire as someone blew gently on the ember. In a moment it was lit and he stood up to toss it into the opening of the stairs.

There was a crash and then a bright flame lit up the stairway followed by screams from below. Two of his group were still holding onto Sing, who was now protesting loudly and calling back to his own men to follow. Despite the pain of his wound he was in a spitting rage.

Who did we lose?" Reza asked the men.

"It was the man Hanji, Master Reza," one of the crew told him. "He was right in front of me when a spear got him."

"Now that is what I call God's justice," Reza murmured. He turned his attention back to Sing

"I will have you thrown to the Tiger, you scum!" Sing screamed. "You are a thieves and a pirates! You will suffer such a fate as I can only imagine for you!" Sing stopped, incoherent with rage, his lips drooling spittle. He spat it out at Reza, who calmly wiped the mess off his shirt and said, "It is you who is the pirate, Master Sing. It was your man Amar who attacked our ship. What harm had we done you? Your servant and his ship are now at the bottom of the sea." His voice was as cold as ice.

Men were trying to get up the stairs to attack the *Sea Eagle* crew, but were being held off with spears and arrows. "Throw a another pot down at them. That will get their attention," Reza suggested. One man gave a fierce chuckle and a flint was produced. Within a moment the oil fuse was burning. Making sure that it was well lit, the man tossed the pot down the dark entrance and pulled back. There was a flare of light and then more screams and yells from below. A Thunder Ball followed to add to the confusion and hopefully to start a good fire.

Sing gaped at him. "You have sunk my ship?" he stammered.

"Your men killed my friend, our captain. That is the reason we are here," Reza stated.

Sing began to shout insults and imprecations. Reza hauled his struggling prisoner to the edge of the wall where Sing stood facing him suddenly aware of what was about to happen to him. "No, No!" he shouted as he pushed back against the sword that was held to his chest, his face grey with terror. It pricked him but he tied to push away from the edge with growing urgency. With a shove of his sword that struck Sing in the ribs Reza pushed back. Sing could not maintain his balance and began to fall.

"No!" he screamed again as he fell over backwards into the compound. They all heard the scream and the thud as Sing hit the ground, and then the shriek of terror, which told Reza what he needed to know. He didn't wait to hear the awful shrieks of agony that were abruptly cut off as the tiger closed with its kill.

The guards, unaware that their leader was now dead, continued to try to gain a foothold on the terrace, but a Thunder Ball kept them at the bottom of the tunnel, its explosion deafening in the narrow confines of he stairway. Fires had started below that were creating even more havoc in the building. Reza led the way to the rope on the wall where his men shimmied down one after the other, still clutching the chests and sacks or tossing them down to others already on the ground then they ran full pelt for the darkness of the jungle path.

Reza waited until the last two, and then he and his men laid another small barrel of powder at the entrance way to that section of the wall, lit the fuse, and then they hurled themselves down the rope and raced for the protection of the jungle. There was a flash that lit up the sky, followed by an explosion that shook the ground and made the air reverberate. Reza glanced up at the walls but couldn't see anything for the dust and smoke that obliterated the scene.

Turning away he stumbled, almost doubled over with the pain of his wound but recovered and hurried after his men down the trail towards the sea. As they ran, the jungle they were running through was showered with stones and large sized rocks which threatened to kill anyone they struck.

Chapter Thirty-Five
The Navigator

Talon stood next to Rav'an who held his hand tightly while Jannat and Rostam stood nearby. Indeed, all the crew who were still on the ship were now clustered at the sides, staring up towards the dark hill where the palace stood. It was well after midnight, and a good hour and a half since the landing party had departed.

Suddenly they all saw a distant flash and heard the flat rumble of an explosion.

"It has begun," Talon said shortly. Rav'an gripped his hand even tighter.

Not long after there was another, larger flash that lit up the entire hilltop followed by a roll of thunder. Then the night went dark and silent. No one spoke on the ship as everyone waited in nervous silence for Reza and his crew to reappear on the beach.

It was a long wait, full of doubts and worries. A full hour later, they all heard the splash of oars, and the two boats came into sight. To the people in the ship it was an enormous relief. Men rushed to the sides to help men aboard who carried chests and sacks, which they dumped on the deck with a clatter. They were greeted with subdued but intense relief.

However, the returning men were not celebrating as they should have; there was something wrong. By the light of the many torches Talon could see the tense and drawn faces of the landing party.

"What happened? Were you successful?" He demanded. His words were greeted with some mumbles. He snatched a torch from one of the crew and searched in vain for Reza. Dar'an came rushing up the ladder to him to tell him what had happened.

"It is Reza, Talon! He is wounded and fainted on the way back."

Jannat gave a small cry and would have fallen had Waqqas not caught her and handed her to Rav'an, who held her while she wept.

Dar'an was all but wringing his hands. "We have staunched the wound, but he must be brought up with great care."

They wasted no time in bringing Reza up from the boat. In the flickering light of the torches the men handled him with all the care they would have given a favorite child, and laid him down gently on the deck. Someone placed a folded sack under his head.

Talon, remembering his role as captain, immediately commanded the boats to be hoisted on board and Abdullah to have men pull up the anchors raise the sails. They needed to back the ship and then turn it in the narrow channel. It would take a seaman to do that and only Waqqas and Abdullah knew how.

Waqqas began shouting orders. As the ship moved back down the channel Talon walked over to where Reza was lying on the deck still surrounded by some crewmen who were babbling and chattering with concern. Abdullah pushed a path through the packed group, shouting over the din, "Make way for the Captain! Give him space to see!" The men pulled back respectfully, some murmuring, "Its the Captain. Make way."

Abdullah wasted no time putting them to work maneuvering the ship out of the channel and towards the open sea.

Talon noticed none of this, he had sick feeling in his stomach. Kneeling, he told the men nearby to raise the torches high to enable him to see better, and lifted away the bloody clothing.

He peering down at the wound and almost wept with relief at what he saw. Due to his fast reaction Reza had saved his own life. The cut was deep and he had lost much blood, which was why he was so weak, but with care he would live. The knife had sliced along his torso below his ribs but had not cut into any vital organs, nor were any exposed. Talon replaced the clothing and said, "Reza will live. He is badly wounded, but God willing, we can take care of that."

The pent up relief from the men exploded in cheers and shouts of joy. Men wept and danced around each other with happiness at the news.

"Take him below and place him on a table where I can take care of him. Be careful with him!" Willing hands lifted Reza up and carried him with great care below.

Talon stared around him at the jumble on the deck. "Tarif, what is all this?" Talon asked, waving his arm at the pile of sacks and small chests all around.

"We discovered a treasure, Captain," Tarif laughed, "and Reza told me to give this to you." He pointed to a silk-wrapped item that was placed next to the chests.

"Take it all below to my cabin, Tarif. I will leave this to you to do. Yosef, help him," Talon ordered. He was too distracted by Reza's wound to think about the treasure. It barely registered that he had been called captain.

"Dar'an go below and see to Reza. Put wads of clean cotton cloth over the wound to stop it bleeding. I shall be down soon," he said next. The men complied willingly.

He told Waqqas and Abdullah to sail the ship out of the channel and to call him when they were clear. He then went up to Rav'an and Jannat and said, "He is wounded and has fainted from loss of blood, but he will be all right as long as we can sew him up and keep the wound clean. Jannat, it will fall upon you to nurse him."

Rav'an gasped with relief; Jannat embraced him, crying into his shoulder.

"We must work fast to stem the bleeding and to sew him up. Come below with me; I will need your help," Talon told them.

****

Two days later they were on a course that Talon had estimated would take them near the Langabalus islands where, should he be accurate enough with his navigation, they would take on fresh water and enough fresh food to see them to Ceylon.

Talon was tired, but reasonably satisfied that they were far enough north to ensure that they made landfall, so he left the steering deck and made his way down below to see if Reza was awake. He found Jannat by his side half asleep, looking wan and exhausted. She had not left his side since he had been settled in a bunk. Reza was awake, and despite his wound he was back to his usual cheerful self.

He greeted Talon with a croak of pleasure, which woke Jannat up. She shook her head and stared owlishly at Talon, who smiled and told her to go to bed. She left reluctantly, with a kiss to Reza, leaving the men alone.

"If the stories I hear from all the crew are to be believed, my Brother, you are quite the hero," Talon said, gripping Reza's hand. "You gave me a fright coming back in that condition. Dar'an was very upset, and so were all the men."

"I was careless, Brother. I didn't kill that Sing when I should have. But then if I had, we would never have discovered his treasure! Besides, he provided a meal for the tiger." He laughed, then winced with the pain of his wound.

Talon grinned. "So he got what he liked to deal out to his victims? It couldn't have been a better fate!"

"Have you had a look at that thing I brought back with me?" Reza demanded. "Didn't Hsü talk about some kind of trophy? I remember one night Chogan came up in the conversation. He told us about this legend of a polo trophy that the Chinese had won in Persia."

Talon nodded as he recalled the discussion, one starlit night when they were all on deck taking advantage of the cool night air. The subject of Chogan had arisen, and Hsü had mentioned the legend of a fantastic trophy that had been lost hundreds of years before.

"Is that what it is? I haven't seen it yet. I wonder how it came into Sing's possession," he mused. "He probably plundered if off a ship. If indeed it is a trophy. I'll take a look at it later. I have been a little preoccupied since you got back from your little jaunt. Its all right for some of us to lie about being pampered by pretty girls, but the rest of us have been busy sailing this ship!"

Reza pretended to try and slap him and fell back with a wince and a grin. "I don't mind the rest, my Brother."

Talon grunted, "Don't do anything to open those stitches. It took Rav'an and me two hours to put them in." He left Reza and went to the storeroom, where he found the object that Reza had talked about. It had been piled in a corner of the room among the other sacks.

He unwound the silk and dropped it about the item that now rested squarely on the flat surface of the low table. He gasped at what he saw.

The object in front of him depicted two fierce looking creatures. On the left was a dragon, while the animal on the right was a lion. They appeared to be locked in mortal combat; the long tail of the dragon was looped around one of the back legs of the lion, the lion's own tail lashing the air high behind it. Both creatures were standing on their back legs grappling with one another on a flat expanse of silver ground, creating a large arch with their bodies. Their fangs were bared in gaping jaws as if they were about to strike at one another with tooth and claw.

The creatures were so finely crafted in every detail, from the lion's mane to the scales on the dragon, that Talon felt he could almost see them breathe. Their claws and their fangs had been carved to perfection from ivory. One of the eyes of the lion was a blank space but the other contained a sapphire set deep in its distorted, rage filled face, while those of the dragon were of pure, deep red ruby and stared malevolently back at its adversary from under the huge bones above its eyes.

Behind the two combatants was a background of the sun formed in gold with the crown of the ancient Shah Han Shah placed on top. The rays of the sun radiated out in an arc reaching the two animals, but that was not all.

Beneath the struggling beasts were two other figures: two men playing the game of Chogan. They rode small, fine ponies and were dressed in noblemen's clothes, cloaks flying, wearing turbans and wielding mallets raised high above their heads with which they were about to strike a ball. The ponies were galloping towards the small ball, which rested in the very center of the piece of ground upon which the two players rode their ponies.

The hand's span high Chogan players were very finely crafted of gold. Clearly they were men of high rank. Their eyes were intent upon the ball in front of them and they seemed oblivious of the mighty conflict taking place just above their heads.

The foundation for this struggle for domination was an oblong plinth of cracked and fissured black marble.

Talon reached forward and his finger stroked the shoulder of the lion. Suddenly he felt dizzy; the cabin darkened for a moment. He shook his head, for he heard the sound of shouting, the thunder of horses' hooves, and the click of mallets striking balls. The hair on the back of his neck and forearms rose at what he was hearing; he gasped and snatched his hand away. The sound stopped instantly.

Talon was shaken. He stared warily at the trophy admiring the magnificent workmanship, detail by detail. After almost an hour he drew the silk up, careful not to touch the trophy for that is what he thought it was, covering the item. He then lifted it to place it in one of the cupboards. There would be time to discuss this with his family later. For now he was almost sure that Hsü had been right. This was the trophy of legend that dated back to a Shah who had lived many hundreds of years ago.

He was still in a state of shock when he came on deck to find Rav'an and Rostam standing on the after deck. "My Talon!" she exclaimed when she saw him examining his wound at the same time. She reached up to touch the area lightly with her fingers. "It is healing well but there will be a scar my Love. Are you well?" she asked with concern. "You look as though you have seen a ghost!"

He was not yet ready to share the experience with anyone, so he said, "I am just tired, my Love. How are you, Rostam?" he asked.

"Well, Papa," the boy said happily. "I like to sail."

"It is true, he does," Rav'an said, looking down fondly at their offspring.

"You will have to assist me with our calculations very soon, my son," Talon told him. "Our first big test is to make the islands of Langabalus. We will need to take on water there to ensure that we can sail all the way to The Island of Rubies."

*****

One week later, the man posted in the basket at the top of the main mast shouted down to them that there was land to their starboard side. Talon was quietly exultant, his first big test was over. He had been consumed with anxiety up to this point, having barely slept, but they had arrived at the islands and could take on water before the long haul. They spent a few days anchored off the largest island, loading up with fresh fruit and vegetables and some goats and chickens. Then on the dawn of the fourth day, with an eye on the weather and still trying to catch up on time, they struck out for Ceylon.

During this stage of the voyage they had time to look over the treasure the men had captured and assess its value. Talon was stunned at what they had brought back with them. He stared at a King's ransom spread across the living room floor, with Rav'an and Jannat in attendance. The work of dividing it up into fair shares would take some time. He did, however, inform the crew that to a man they were rich once they arrived in Muscat. He put aside a good part to pay to Captain Dandachi's family.

He also visited Reza who was still resting. "Now you can marry Jannat, and be quick about it!" he told his friend.

"Should I marry her?" Reza asked seriously.

"If you do not, then you will be disowned by all of us, my Reza!" Rav'an told him as she came into the room, having heard the last part of the conversation.

Reza looked uncomfortable. "Rav'an, I don't have any riches to give her and she is after all, a Princess."

Rav'an stared at him and then at Talon. "I have never heard such nonsense, Reza! Have you forgotten the treasure? You are a rich man. Your share of the treasure alone has made you a very wealthy man. Why, you can even afford your own stable of horses, and much, much more. Besides, don't you realize that she loves you, heart and soul? Although I have no idea why." Rav'an gave him a withering look.

"Reza, you are indeed a rich man in your own right, so that's not a good excuse any more. You can even afford to join Allam in the camel racing business!" Talon laughed at Reza's comical grimace.

"You had better do some serious thinking while we are on the way home, or you will be answering to me!" Rav'an threatened him, wagging her finger.

Reza rolled his eyes, but he was clearly happy; he seized Rav'an's hand and kissed it. "Where would I be without my family?" he asked with a cheeky grin.

*****

Three weeks later, another lookout called down from the basket at the top of the main mast. "I see land! God be praised, I see land! It is the Island of Rubies, I am sure of it!"

The men who were on deck stopped what they were doing and cheered wildly, waving their hands in the air and prancing about, praising God. Others who had been below came running up on deck. All were looking up at Talon with joyful expressions on their sun darkened, bearded faces.

Talon leaned on the steering deck rail, staring down at his villainous looking crew. Inwardly he was bursting with pride. They had made landfall almost to within a few days of his and Rostam's calculations. He blessed his boy. Rostam had a natural talent for navigation, and Talon knew it would stand him in good stead later on in life. The boy had helped to bring them to their most important destination. Those endless days of poring over Captain Dandachi's chronicles and the other navigation texts, along with painstaking observations made with Rostam appeared to have paid off. He had worried himself sick with the thought that even a small mistake could cost all of them their lives. Before the call he had been exhausted from lack of sleep and the constant worry, but not now. This moment was one to savor.

"Why are they cheering, and why are you looking at me like that?" Talon growled at Abdullah and Waqqas, who were standing on the steering deck with him. Both men were hopping from foot to foot and beaming with emotion.

Waqqas finally said, "Why Captain, they are cheering you!" He said this with a wide smile displaying the black gaps in his teeth and waved his hands in the air rather like a praying mantis. Abdullah was also wearing a huge grin on his face. Talon was afraid the two men were going to kiss him. He noticed out of the corner of his eye that Rav'an and Jannat had appeared on deck with an excited Rostam between them. He beckoned them up to join him by the rail.

"We have all been holding our breath for about a week now, Captain," Waqqas said. "None of us are navigators, thus not one of us could help you, so we were in God's hands ... and yours. Had we been too far south there is no land before Africa after Ceylon. We would have perished from lack of water and food.

"Your skill is now established as a Navigator. You are one with our Omani people, a Nabatean, a true navigator of the desert and the sea! God be praised, but now we all know that you will bring us home safely, Captain!"

"You too, Rostam. You are also a navigator," Talon told his son, who was beaming with pride.

Author's Note

When I started on this book I had known something of the nautical skills of the Omani sailors; however, as I progressed with the research I realized just how little I knew. I became more and more interested, and amazed, at what they had accomplished at a time when the European ships could only sail with the wind directly behind them in the relative calm of the Mediterranean Sea. The ships of the Omani and the Chinese could sail much closer to the wind, thereby they could sail almost anywhere, more or less at will. Remember we are talking about the 8th to the 12th Century.

This allowed them to traverse the vast distances of the Indian Ocean and the China sea, survive the deadly Cyclones and Taiphoons and make accurate land fall in remote places. The Omani and Persians were, in their time, navigators without peer. Their navigational books show us how they accomplished these remarkable journeys and, in the very early days, it was without even a compass to assist them! The Chinese invented that instrument.

The Omani and Persian merchants established trade routes that were governed by the Monsoons, "The Trade winds" as they were later known, both to and from India and China, thus establishing a 'Silk Route' via the sea lanes which few Europeans had ever heard about.

It is therefore very plausible that Talon could sail all the way to China, as many Omani did in his time. When he arrived there he would have found a civilization that made even the Byzantium Empire seem backward. I will not list the incredible inventions of the Sung dynasty times, they are too numerous, although I have alluded to some. The Sung dynasty was one of the most remarkable and advanced periods of Chinese history to date, putting them some several hundred years ahead of Byzantium. Byzantium and indeed the Moslem world were themselves at least hundred years ahead of the Europeans, who were still squabbling amongst themselves over patches of arable land.

I invented nothing that was not already recorded and documented about the Sung; they were astonishing enough in their own right.

The great paradox is the fact that even with all their very advanced weapons, highly educated people and manufacturing skills, the Chinese of the Sung were eventually overrun in 1276 by the Mongols. It might lie in the fact that the emphasis across the country, and particularly in the Emperor's palace, was placed upon degreed administrators who, while very learned, did not fully understand the peril their country faced. They were intensely preoccupied with maintaining the status quo. Hence they did not pay enough attention to their military, which was essential, even as it is today, as a bulwark against the barbarians who would destroy the bright light of civilization.

James Boschert

Talon struggled with his tight bonds, trying to feel if there might be any slack which would allow him to move his hands. A hideous ache pounded inside his head. Near him he heard a low groan. It came from Reza, who was lying trussed up within a few feet. Talon lifted his head to look around the darkened room and noticed another body in one corner. It was quite still. He couldn't make out who it might be, but hoped that it wasn't dead.

He nudged Reza, who stirred and lifted his bruised and bloodied face to look at him. "How did this happen?" he asked groggily.

"No time to talk, Brother. They took my boots, so they found my knife. We need to get free at once!" Talon whispered.

"I have a small one on me," Reza croaked.

"Where?" Talon asked eagerly.

"Inside... inside my pants."

"You mean... inside your...?"

"Yes, Brother, inside there."

Talon shook his head. "You are full of surprises. Very well, turn over and I'll try to get it out. You'll have to guide me... if you know what I mean. What does Jannat think of you keeping a knife there?"

"None of your business, now will you get hold of it?"

Reza hunched his way over until he was very close to Talon's back, then even closer to where Talon's bound hands made contact.

"In there?" Talon's tone was incredulous.

"Yes, and be careful... Oooo! Not there!" Reza jerked back. "In the front, above my you-know-whats."

"All right! All right!" Talon grunted testily. "Get closer."

Reza shuffled forward again. Talon's fingers groped and Reza flinched. "Ouch! Do you mind? Not there! Higher up... higher there, inside the belt."

"Sorry, Ah!" Talon's fingers felt the hard handle of a small knife tucked into Reza's under belt.

After much hurried fumbling, they managed to loosen the small weapon so that it dropped onto the tiled floor with a tiny clatter. Reza rolled over and Talon pushed the blade into his fingers, then inched himself towards the knife ,which Reza now gripped.

Within seconds the razor sharp blade had cut his bonds, then it took only a moment to free his brother.

They both scrambled to their feet, rubbing their sore wrists and ankles to get the circulation going again. The bonds had been tight.

"How did we get into this place?" Reza whispered.

"Drugged, and I think I know by whom," Talon ground out, shaking his head gingerly. He still had a monster of a headache. He hurried over to the body lying in the corner, dreading what he was going to find. He gave a hiss of relief when he saw that it was only one of the guards to the gate, evidently tossed in here after they had killed him.

"Wish I had my sword," Reza commented, still rubbing his wrists and looking around him for some way out of this room. It was a storeroom, although there was not much in it. It looked as though it had been abandoned for a long time. Dust was everywhere, and there was little in the way of equipment other than a broken harness lying on the floor.

"We're going to have to get out of here as fast as possible and find out what is going on out there."

"I fear the worst!" Reza said darkly.

Just then they heard the murmur of voices outside and the grate of a key in the lock, then metal bars were slid away with a scrape of iron on wood. Both men rushed over to stand on either side of the door, pressing themselves against the mud brick walls.

The door was thrown open and men, still talking, strode into the darkened room. For a moment they peered into the gloom, looking for their prisoners; it was enough for Talon and Reza to strike. Talon's forehead collided with the nearest man's cheekbone, stunning him; a sinewed hand seized the guard's sleeve and pulled hard, as Talon whirled inside the man's sword arm and then heaved his victim off his feet to toss him, now minus sword, into the arms of the guard who was just behind him.

Reza had slammed his small knife backwards into the throat of the man nearest to him. As the guard fell to his knees, Reza deftly relieved him of his sword and in one fluid motion thrust it into the chest of the man directly behind his first victim. Both Talon and Reza used their new-found weapons with savage intensity, bringing all their training in China to work for them. The guards barely had time to gasp, let alone cry out, before they were lying dead in a heap at the entrance of the storeroom.

Barely breathing hard, the two men paused to look down at their victims. "Just as I thought," said Reza. "I recognize these two. They are from the Master." He looked up at Talon. "He has sent his dogs after us, Talon."

Talon nodded. "Then we must find Rav'an and the others immediately. No one will be safe!"

About The Author

James Boschert

James Boschert grew up in the then colony of Malaya in the early fifties. He learned first hand about terrorism while there as the Communist insurgency was in full swing. His school was burnt down and the family, while traveling, narrowly survived an ambush, saved by a Gurkha patrol, which drove off the insurgents.

He went on to join the British army serving in remote places like Borneo and Oman. Later he spent five years in Iran before the revolution, where he played polo with the Iranian Army, developed a passion for the remote Assassin castles found in the high mountains to the North, and learned to understand and speak the Farsi language.

Escaping Iran during the revolution, he went on to become an engineer and now lives in Arizona on a small ranch with his family and animals.

Force 12 in German Bight

by
James Boschert

Considering that oil and gas have been flowing from under the North Sea for the best part of half a century, it is perhaps surprising that more writers have not taken the uncompromising conditions that are experienced in this area – which extends from the north of Scotland to the coasts of Norway and Germany – for the setting of a novel. James Boschert's latest redresses the balance.

The book takes its title from the name of an area regularly referred to in the legendary BBC Shipping Forecast, one which experiences some of the worst weather conditions around the British Isles. It is a fast-paced story which smacks of authenticity in every line. A world of hard men, hard liquor, hard drugs and cold-blooded murder. The reality of the setting and the characters, ex-military men from both sides of the Atlantic, crooked wheeler-dealers, and Danish detectives, male and female, are all in on the action.

This is not story telling akin to a latter day Bulldog Drummond, nor a James Bond, but simply a snortingly good yarn which will jangle the nerve ends, fill your nose with the smell of salt and diesel oil, your ears with the deafening sound of machinery aboard a monster pipe-dredging ship and, above all, make you remember never to underestimate the power of the sea.

–Roger Paine, former Commander, Royal Navy.

PENMORE PRESS
www.penmorepress.com

When the Jungle Is Silent

by
James Boschert

Set in Borneo during a little known war known as "the Confrontation," this story tells of the British soldiers who fought in one of the densest jungles in the world.

Jason, a young soldier of the Light Infantry who is good with guns, is stationed in Penang, an idyllic island off the coast of Malaysia. He is living aimlessly in paradise until he meets Megan, a bright and intelligent young American from the Peace Corps. Megan challenges his complacent existence and a romance develops, but then the regiment is sent off to Borneo.

After a dismal shipping upriver, the regiment arrives in Kuching, the capital of Sarawak. Jason is moved up to Padawan, close to local populations of Ibans and Dyak headhunters, and right in the path of the Indonesian offensive. Fighting erupts along the border of Sarawak and a small fort is turned into a muddy hell from which Jason is an unlikely survivor.

An SAS Sergeant and his trackers have been drawn to the vicinity by the battle, but who will find Jason first: rescuers or hostiles? Jason is forced to wake up to the cruel harshness of real soldiering while he endeavors stay one step ahead of the Indonesians who are combing the Jungle. And the jungle itself, although neutral, is deadly enough.

PENMORE PRESS
www.penmorepress.com

Fortune's Whelp
by
Benerson Little

Privateer, Swordsman, and Rake:

Set in the 17th century during the heyday of privateering and the decline of buccaneering, *Fortune's Whelp* is a brash, swords-out sea-going adventure. Scotsman Edward MacNaughton, a former privateer captain, twice accused and acquitted of piracy and currently seeking a commission, is ensnared in the intrigue associated with the attempt to assassinate King William III in 1696. Who plots to kill the king, who will rise in rebellion—and which of three women in his life, the dangerous smuggler, the wealthy widow with a dark past, or the former lover seeking independence—might kill to further political ends? Variously wooing and defying Fortune, Captain MacNaughton approaches life in the same way he wields a sword or commands a fighting ship: with the heart of a lion and the craft of a fox.

PENMORE PRESS
www.penmorepress.com

The Chosen Man

by

J. G Harlond

From the bulb of a rare flower bloom ambition and scandal

Rome, 1635: As Flanders braces for another long year of war, a Spanish count presents the Vatican with a means of disrupting the Dutch rebels' booming economy. His plan is brilliant. They just need the right man to implement it.

They choose Ludovico da Portovenere, a charismatic spice and silk merchant. Intrigued by the Vatican's proposal—and hungry for profit—Ludo sets off for Amsterdam to sow greed and venture capitalism for a disastrous harvest, hampered by a timid English priest sent from Rome, accompanied by a quick-witted young admirer he will use as a spy, and bothered by the memory of the beautiful young lady he refused to take with him.

Set in a world of international politics and domestic intrigue, *The Chosen Man* spins an engrossing tale about the Dutch financial scandal known as tulip mania—and how decisions made in high places can have terrible repercussions on innocent lives.

PENMORE PRESS
www.penmorepress.com